THE HOMESTEADS

THE HOMESTEADS

Loletta Clouse

Chicory Books
Knoxville, Tennessee
2003

Sometimes when you have trouble believing,
You have to loan it out, and let others believe for you.
Thank you to all my family and friends, and especially to my
wonderful husband who always believed.

Published by Chicory Books

Second Printing

Order additional books from:
    Chicory Books
    PO Box 31131
    Knoxville TN 37930

Doyle Vaden Prints used by permission of Emma Jean Vaden.

Library of Congress Cataloging-in-Publication Data

Clouse, Loletta,   1948–
    The Homesteads / Loletta Clouse.
        p.   cm.
    ISBN 0-9719417-0-X
    1. Cumberland Homesteads, Tenn. -- Fiction. 2. Community development -- Fiction. 3. Mountain Life -- Fiction. 4. Depressions -- Fiction. 5. Tennessee -- Fiction. 6. New towns -- Fiction. I. Title.
    PS3553.L648 H66 2002
    813'.54 -- dc21

                                                    2002004192
Printed in the United States of America

THE HOMESTEADS

*The future belongs
to those who believe in
the beauty of their dreams*

Eleanor Roosevelt

1

The truck bounced and rocked its way over the ruts in the road until Lacey's teeth ached and she felt bruised from head to toe. That morning they had packed everything they owned onto the back of Oliver Perry's flatbed truck and headed out. Now it was coming on near dusk and she was weary to the bone. Carefully she lifted the canvas and peeked out at the bleak landscape. Fallen tree trunks lay strewn about like dead soldiers on the battlefield. The roads had only recently been bulldozed out of the woods and no gravel had been put on them. She had not been accustomed to a lot of beauty in her life, but the sight of such a raw pathway gouged into the forest left her feeling desolate. Dust swirled around so thick it covered every blackberry bush and Queen Anne's lace by the side of the road until she could hardly tell one from the other. Daniel Lee lay sleeping peacefully in her lap and she pulled the thin blanket up around his face. She searched the horizon for lights from a neighboring house. She could see none. They had left the town of Crossville four miles back.

Lacey could just make out the shape of a barn up ahead. She remembered the day her husband John had come home to say he had found work. They had been living for six months with John's Uncle Felix in Monterey. Lacey knew they had killed nearly all their chickens and used most of their canned goods to feed them. She hated being a burden to them but you couldn't turn family away. It was up to them to move on. That was why she was so relieved when John had found work.

Work was hard to come by for most folks nowadays. John sometimes read the newspaper to her after supper and it told of suffering all over America. Folks were without work and some were homeless and starving. Many of these people were like John and had been in unions but now the factories or mines had

1

closed or worked scabs for a fraction of the wages they had once earned.

John had been a coal miner until the strike came in the summer of 1932. It had been a violent desperate year and they had almost starved to death. In the end, they had lost the struggle to hold on to the union. John had been blacklisted from the mines. They had given up and moved out of Wilder, the coal mining camp where they had both lived their whole lives.

The government had bought 10,000 acres of woodland near Crossville, Tennessee and they needed men to clear it. They were going to divide it up into farms and then let the men buy the farms. John was to get fifty cents an hour. Two-thirds of that was to be credited toward buying one of those farms. John had explained to her that this was a way the government had of putting coal miners and sawmill workers and other folks who were up against hard times to work. Lacey thought it was a dream come true. She had always wanted a piece of land. She loved growing things. She had always been able to scratch out a garden even on the smallest, meanest patch of land in Wilder.

The truck stopped with a jolt and John jumped from the cab to take the baby and help her down. His mother Cora and Lacey's eleven-year-old brother Ben had moved with them and slowly they worked their way from beneath the canvas. They stood looking around blinking their eyes and stretching their stiff limbs.

John and Oliver Perry started immediately to unload the truck. It took only a few minutes before their meager possessions were on the ground and the truck with Oliver Perry driving pulled away leaving them there. Lacey waved until the truck was out of sight. She felt like she had been brought to the ends of the earth and dropped off. Finally she turned to John and smiled bravely. He took her by the hand and led her inside the barn.

John lit a lantern. Lacey looked around at the single open room they were to call home. It had a wood floor and every inch was covered from corner to corner with tarpaper. The barn was small but there was a loft overhead for extra sleeping space. Ben climbed the ladder and claimed his little niche next to two double doors that opened to a set of stairs. "Look here Lacey," he called excitedly. "I bet you can see the stars from up here." Lacey climbed up to join him. There was a screen on the door, a luxury they had never known in Wilder. They walked out onto the small landing and looked up at the sky. It covered them like a blue speckled bowl. She watched Ben's blue eyes stare in wonderment. He had a joy in simple things and life was always amazement to him.

Trees surrounded the barn. Just enough land had been cleared to make room for it. The moon appeared from behind wispy clouds and shone on the treetops and fallen trunks. The light softened the landscape. Lacey looked over the land and marveled at the space. John said that most of the farms would be about twenty-five acres. She pictured where they would set the house and where they would clear the first field for a garden and a chicken house. It would be a lot of work. She didn't dread the work. She was ready to get on with it. They had not just moved to a new place. They were building a new life in a place where people would work together to make something with their own hands that would someday belong to them.

Lacey walked back inside and looked down from the loft at John. "Well, this is fine, John. Real fine," she announced.

"Oh, maybe it ain't much, yet," he said as though he realized how rough it might look to a woman, "but we can get linoleum for the floor and some curtains for the windows. Some folks has done fixed their barns up real nice."

"Lord amercy, John," Cora spoke up. "Lacey said it was fine. Quit your frettin'. I don't know how I give birth to such a solemn youngun," she joshed, giving him a sharp poke in the ribs.

"Ours will be just as nice as any, John," Lacey said reassuringly. "It'll just take a touch here and there to make it seem like home. Don't it smell fresh and new," she said taking in a deep breath of the sawdust still scattered about the floor.

John's green eyes searched her face. Finally convinced she was satisfied, he grinned proudly. "I better start carrying our stuff inside."

As John carried in their few belongings, Cora and Lacey set about making up the beds. A knock on the door surprised them all. Lacey could not imagine how someone had appeared so suddenly out of the blackness of night. When John opened the door a woman thrust a basket at him.

"Howdy, I'm Norma Percy and this here is my husband Jack," the woman said cheerfully bursting through the door as she pointed behind her. Jack stood behind her nodding politely. "We're your neighbors from down the way. We knowed you wouldn't have time to get the stove set up and cook nothing for supper so we brung you some beans and cornbread."

Norma Percy was plump and thick through the middle from frequent childbirth. Her face was plain and open. Lacey liked her right away. "Why thank you," Lacey said stepping up to take the basket. "We are mighty grateful. We're pretty tired after the trip here. I'm Lacey Trotter and this is my husband John."

"I knowed you would be honey," Norma said tenderly. "Jack come around here and meet these folks."

Jack came slowly from behind Norma to shake hands. He took off his hat exposing a sunburned face and slightly receding hairline. "Nice to meet you folks," Jack said shyly nodding to Lacey and Cora. "John and me done met. We cleared the land our barn's built on."

"We been living in a barn down the road a piece for the last two months," Norma explained. "We moved over here from Harriman. Jack used to work in the textile mills until they went under. He was out of work for a long time until this here come along. We was grateful for it."

They were all silent for a moment at the thought. They were indeed grateful but a little nervous at what they might have gotten themselves into by signing on to a government project.

The Percy's seemed like such nice folks to Lacey. They were so warm and caring. Lacey felt less alone. She had worried about not knowing anybody and about not having any close neighbors. In Wilder she had known everyone and the houses had been stacked up around each other like a child's building blocks. She hoped that more of the folks they would be living and working with on the Cumberland Homesteads would turn out to be like Norma and Jack. As they said good night to the Percy's and watched them quickly disappear into the darkness, Lacey took a deep breath of the cool night air and allowed herself a moment of hope.

2

The cry of the train whistle brought Lacey up from a well of darkness. Her limbs were weighted in place. Her eyelids fluttered heavily and refused to open. She could feel the hard ground beneath her and the cold steel of the track on which her head rested. The train called out to her, nearer this time. How long had it been speeding toward her? It seemed like forever. It was a black, angry monster coming for her. Her heart beat so wildly it made her head pulse and the pulsing mixed with the vibrations of the track. Fear was a living thing within her that clawed at her insides and threatened to kill her as surely as the train that raced toward her in the night. It was coming faster now. She could feel the heat from the engine. She willed her body to move with all the strength she could manage. She was weak as though she had fought too long and had nothing left. Her body remained rooted in place. Suddenly, screams began pushing their way up from the deepest part of her like the echo from a well. Finally, they pushed themselves from her throat in an explosion of terror. It was too late. They mingled with the cries of the train whistle as it passed over her.

Lacey sat bolt upright in bed, the moonlight made the shadows in the room a fog of senseless shapes. She struggled to remember that she was now living in a barn on the Cumberland Homesteads. The blood throbbed in her ears until she could hardly think. It was just the dream again. She was amazed each time at the power it had over her.

She became aware of the sounds of the baby. He was not really crying just making baby sounds that grew louder as his patience waned. She wondered for a moment if she had awakened him with her screams. Her husband, John, slept peacefully beside her. His wavy, cinnamon brown hair remained unruffled by tossing and turning. The screams had only been inside her head. A sense of relief worked its way through her body. She had never told anyone about the dream and she did not relish having to explain it. She certainly knew what it meant. It meant that something was coming. It was a sense of foreboding that haunted her that something was coming to steal away the peace and safety she had gathered around her in the past few months.

Gently, she eased herself from the bed. Lifting the baby from the cradle, she carried him to a rocking chair by the window. "Daniel Lee you are a little rascal. Getting your mama up at all hours of the night," she whispered gently. "Why a big boy of six months should be sleeping through the night," she teased him rubbing her finger along his plump cheek as he nursed. He stopped nursing long enough to spread his mouth in a grin that revealed two perfect pearl white teeth. Her heart fluttered in her chest as her emotions swirled together like currents in a mountain stream. "You are a handsome thing, even if I am your mama," she whispered, a sigh of pleasure escaping her lips. His skin was dark, almost red, and since birth he had had a mass of dark hair as black and straight as a raven's feather.

His had been an easy birth and for all her worries about him being puny because there had been so little to eat in those months before his birth, he had been born plump and healthy. She had known when she heard his first mewling cry and looked into his tiny face that she would kill to keep him safe. She had known at first glance that they shared a secret. He was like a gift she did not deserve; a reward she had not earned. He was such a happy baby and rewarded everyone with a huge grin. He's perfect, she thought over and over again every time she looked at him. A sharp pain cut through straight to her heart and made her wince. It was just something in her she could not put to rest, that anyone she loved that much she could not have. Loving someone was like holding your heart in your hands. It tied the two lives together and whatever happened to one, happened to the other.

Daniel Lee's only problem was that he often did not sleep well. Maybe it was as much her fault as his. She had come to enjoy those early morning hours alone with him just holding him and rocking him until the sun came up. It calmed her and soothed her because she too had trouble sleeping through the night. She hummed softly and watched the moonlight through a tear in the tarpaper that covered the walls of the barn where they had been living for the past few weeks.

Lacey still had trouble believing they had been picked for this project. Hundreds of families had applied. The government had sent a woman out to ask them a lot of questions. The woman had made it clear to Lacey that day that not everyone would be picked. They were only interested in honest, hardworking folks who could cooperate she said. Lacey thought the woman was nice enough and just doing her job even if she had asked a lot of personal questions about how she and John got along with each other and their neighbors. At one point Lacey was almost sure the woman was about to check her teeth like a horse to see if she came from good stock. John had to have three people to vouch for his character. The investigation had lasted three months before they finally learned they had been selected.

John had spent the first six months of 1934 living and working on the Cumberland Homesteads while Lacey had stayed behind in Monterey. The men had batched in tents and taken their meals outside on the ground. At the end of a hard week, John would ride home on the back of a flatbed truck. The men had paid the driver twenty-five cents a week for the trip. The work had been hard and there had been a lot of delays because of the weather. They had cleared a little land on several of the farms and built barns for the families to live in until the houses could be built. Finally, John had come home to say the time had come for them to move.

Lacey became aware of the sun beginning to light the ridgeline. The baby slept peacefully in her arms. John had not stirred in the hours she had been sitting there. She watched the rhythm of his breathing so even and unchanging. So like John, she thought. He was a man she could count on; she had always known that. He was a man who would always find a way to give her whatever she asked. He was a good man. There was no other way to describe him. She looked at the headboard of the bed where they both slept. John had carved it himself before they were married and given it to her as a wedding present. It was covered with wildflowers. John had seen the design in a catalog and copied it for her because she loved wildflowers. It was a wonder to her how he loved her. Try as she might, she just couldn't love him back. Not the way a wife should; not the way he deserved. There was no way he would ever know it from her. She would make sure of that.

She eased the baby into his crib and slipped back into bed just as the sun crested the horizon. John stirred and put his hand on her shoulder. She turned and pretended to rub the sleep from her eyes.

"Did you sleep good?"he asked.

"Like an old dog in the shade,"she lied.

He slipped her head into the crook of his arm.

"I didn't have no trouble. Eight or ten hours of wrestling stumps can tucker a man out," he said honestly.

She patted his chest softly like a mother comforting a child. "They're paying good money but they can't say the men don't earn it."

"I have to give it to 'em. They never lied to nobody about the work being hard. It's nothing new to this bunch. Most of 'em is glad to be working again. Me included. It just serves to weed out them that ain't serious about owning a farm. It's exciting, ain't it, Lacey," John said with uncharacteristic glee.

"It's all so new," Lacey agreed. "I don't know how to take it all in some days."

"I tell you, Lacey; we got a chance to really have something here. A man don't mind putting in the work if he can claim it later. Ain't nothing worse than not having a way to make a living and feed your family," John went on once again his serious self.

Lacey touched John gently on the arm, her heart tender with concern. "Things are looking up for us now, John. I think the bad times are behind us."

"You know the first day the men come to work, they hauled us all in on a flatbed truck. We was all standing around wondering what to do. Didn't nobody have a notion as to what was to happen. Some of the men was scared. They thought maybe once you got in you'd never be let out."

John chuckled at how silly a fear it seemed now, but she could tell he had entertained some of the same thoughts that day. John always seemed so steadfast and determined. Lacey had to remind herself that he did not always know the way ahead of time. She was glad she had never mentioned how homesick she had been at times for kinfolk's faces or anything familiar.

"You were right to bring us here, John," Lacey said encouragingly. "We're going to build a fine place to live."

John let out a satisfied sigh and looked at her like she was a cool drink from the bottom of the well. Lacey could feel herself blush.

"Speaking of feeding the family, I better get up from here and start breakfast. It's near light now." It was a joy to her to think about cooking breakfast for her family now that there was food in the house once more. She started to pull away from the crook of his arm.

"Can't it wait?" he asked pulling her closer. He eased his hand under the quilt and rested it lightly on her stomach as shy with her body as a stranger. She put her hand on his face and smiled. He gently eased her gown up around her waist.

_3_

H e was her second choice. He knew he probably always would be. John watched as Lacey sat up on the side of the bed and eased her gown down over her slender hips. She was shy that way, never letting him see her naked. He thought that maybe she was ashamed because she had gotten so thin. Months of hunger had stripped her like a reed and then the baby had taken what was left.

Lacey's long hair tumbled loosely over the back of her gown almost touching the bed. During the day, she wore it braided and knotted at the back of her neck in a bun. He loved seeing it loose, falling down her back in a cascade of confusion. He started to reach out and stroke the dark brown tendrils as rich and glistening as the mahogany furniture he had once seen in the boss's house back in Wilder. Lacey slipped from his grasp to dress behind a screen he had built for her in the corner by the bed. She emerged, pinning her hair into place and padded barefoot to the cookstove. He could hear her breaking kindling and lighting the match to start the fire for breakfast.

John lay back on his pillow, stretching his stiff, sore muscles and pondered his luck. Lacey had married him on a warm spring day in May. It might have been indecent of them with the strike coming to pieces around them, but when Lacey had come to him and said she was ready to set the date he had not hesitated for a second. He had waited a lifetime to marry Lacey Conners and he had almost lost her in the meantime. He did not like to think about that. He did not like to think about her loving another man. It had after all not been her fault. Coy Lynn Wilson had just fooled her. He had fooled them both.

The smell of bacon frying brought him back. It was a smell they had not smelled in all those months of the strike or the desperate months in Monterey when he had spent his time searching for work doing whatever came his way. There had been a time when he had had his life laid out. He was a coal miner as his father had been. His whole life had been rooted to the familiar hills and valleys around Wilder. He had planned to go on living there forever. But then the bottom fell out of the price of coal and the miner was no longer the important worker he had been. He became a burden to the very company he had worked so hard for. The miners had ended up waging a war against the companies. It was a desperate fight to save the only way of life many of them had ever known. In the end they had lost it all. John could hear Lacey humming softly as she moved about the tiny kitchen. It made him smile. As long as he had Lacey he could make a new plan.

"John, breakfast is near ready," Lacey called over her shoulder.

He could hear Cora and Ben stirring in the upstairs loft. His ma had insisted on sleeping in a tiny corner of the loft to give them more privacy in the small open barn. She was a feisty, little thing used to running her own household. John knew she was working hard to give Lacey a chance at her own home. He lifted his overalls from a nail by the bed and slipped into them. He padded across the floor, the tarpaper sticky under his feet. He poured water from the kettle Lacey kept on the back of the stove into the washbowl and sloshed it on his face. He lathered his face and carefully shaved. His face was tender and his pale skin burned over and over by the sun. It was something new to him to be out in the sunshine all day after working in the mines. When work had been good in the mines he had worked many times from before sunup to after sundown just to get the job done. Then when wages had dropped so low that a miner could not survive on the earnings of an eight-hour shift he had worked many a sixteen hour shift and still not made enough to pay for his carbide and powder. It felt odd to him to think about becoming a farmer. He had never pictured himself a farmer. Still he knew it was going to work out. There was no turning back because there was no place to go.

The smell of breakfast was making his stomach gnaw. It was the smell of a new beginning. Excitement shot thought him like a spark from a flint. He was working now, he thought with pride. He couldn't believe his luck. They had gotten over four thousand applications to come to the Cumberland Homesteads.

They were only going to build two hundred and fifty homes. Of course, a lot of the men were not trying for a farm. They had hired some of the men just to give them work.

Cora came down the ladder from the loft and went immediately to the dish cupboard and started to set the table. "Good morning, younguns."

"Morning Mama," John said pulling out a chair to sit down.

Lacey smiled at Cora. She picked up the coffeepot and poured John a steaming cup. Cora took the biscuits, brown and steamy from the oven. John admired the way Lacey and Cora got along. He knew it was not always that way with families.

"Mercy me Lacey, you've cooked enough here for two families," Cora exclaimed spooning the fried apples into a bowl.

Lacey laughed not at all offended by Cora's words. "I reckon I just can't help myself. I swore if we ever got to a place where we could get hold of a little something, we'd eat if we couldn't do nothing else."

John remembered the day he and Lacey had talked about what they wanted most if the strike ever ended. He named work first and felt like a dull sort for not being able to think of anything better. There just didn't seem to be anything better to want. Lacey named off all the good things she would fix to eat. Her ma had never been much of a hand at keeping house and taking care of things and Lacey's pa had come to depend on her awfully early to cook and clean and look after things. He knew how she had scrounged to keep food on the table during the strike. It had rested heavy on her all that responsibility. He reckoned, that was why food meant so much to her. It was her way of taking care of all the folks around her. "Then let's get to it. My stomach thinks my throat's cut now," John said.

"Ben, breakfast is waiting," Lacey called.

Ben was already climbing down the ladder. He went over to the cradle and picked up Daniel Lee. "How are you doing this morning Daniel Lee? Give your Uncle Ben a big hug." Daniel Lee rewarded Ben with a huge grin and a hug around the neck.

"I didn't even know that youngun was awake," Cora remarked. "He hadn't let out a cheep."

Lacey took the baby on her lap and they all fussed and cooed at him until Cora settled them down. "John, you say the blessing so we can eat."

John looked around the table and then bowed his head. He felt full to bursting with the good things that had come his way. It seemed more than a man had a right to. He wasn't much for words. Saying what he felt out in front of folks, even family, was beyond him. So he just said, "Thank you Lord for all the bounty. Amen."

John crumbled the warm biscuits on one side of his plate and spooned the milk gravy over them. On the other side of his plate he piled fried apples sweetened with honey. He saved a place for the side meat, fried crisp and brown. Cora refilled his coffee cup without a word. For some time they ate in silence savoring the goodness.

Lacey fed Daniel Lee from her plate. At first, he leaned back against her and let her feed him, smacking his tiny lips in delight with each bite of gravy soaked biscuit. John grinned as he watched him grow impatient and try to reach for the plate. Lacey looked up and smiled at John. Daniel Lee's tiny hand quick as lightning landed in the middle of Lacey's plate and grabbed a handful of greasy biscuit and gravy. Squeezing it out through his fingers he squealed with delight.

"Daniel Lee," Lacey scolded gently.

They all looked up from their plates and laughed. Daniel Lee clapped his messy hands together, pleased with his trick.

"He's trying to tell you he's old enough to feed hisself." Ben said.

"I reckon he thinks he is," Lacey said trying to take a piece of bacon out of Daniel Lee's fist. He puffed his cheeks out and held on tight to the meat.

"He's old enough to suck on a piece of bacon," Cora commented. "Just tear off some of the lean and let him gum it. When John was a baby he would waller a piece around in his mouth till it didn't have no more color than a corncob."

John could tell that Lacey was not in favor of it but she reluctantly gave in. Daniel Lee clamped his greasy hands around the meat, proud to have his way. Lacey worried too much about the boy, John thought. It was the same way with Ben. There was no curing her of it though. He knew that from watching Lacey the times Ben had had pneumonia. There was no getting between them at a time like that. "What are you up to today, Ben?" John asked turning his attention to Lacey's slender, freckled face brother. They looked a lot alike, Ben and Lacey. They both had a mass of wavy hair with blue eyes and fair skin that tanned in summer and paled in winter.

"I got me a job at the Smith place. They got a farm down Grassy Cove Road. Mrs. Smith lets me shell peas. She says she will give me a gallon for ever three I shell," Ben declared proudly.

"It'll take a lot of work to shell that many peas," Lacey declared.

"I can do it," Ben said defiantly.

"I know you can," John said trying to sound confident. He thought Ben might be beginning to chafe a little under Lacey's skirttail.

"Who are these folks, John?" Lacey asked. "Do you know them?"

"They're real nice. Mrs. Smith likes me," Ben spoke up.

"I'm sure they are nice folks, Ben." Lacey answered. At the same time she looked at John for an answer to her question.

"They've lived around here for years. Own a real nice farm about three miles from here."

"Well, you be careful running around all over the countryside, Ben. I didn't see you from dawn till dark yesterday."

Ben looked down at his plate, but didn't say anything. He searched in his overall pocket and came out with a small rag tied into a bundle. He held it up, a triumphant look on his face. "I brung you these," he said to Lacey.

"What is it?" Lacey asked reaching for the rag and untying it.

"It's gourd seeds. Mrs. Smith says you can grow'em for dippers."

"Well law, yes," Cora spoke up. "We used to always have gourd dippers when I was a girl. I never seen a metal dipper 'till after I was married. I'd love to plant me some of them just to watch'em grow. As a little girl, I always did love to see what kinds of shapes they'd make. Some of them would curl around all crazy like or be real fat with long skinny necks. No matter what they look like, they always put me in a mind of

something. You know like a pig or a chicken or a dog. Mama
would let me mash up polk berries and draw faces on them."

"Here, Cora. You take'em," Lacey said. They all looked at
Cora, taken by her delight. "We'll scratch out a place to plant
them this afternoon. I don't think it's too late to put them out.
I'm thinking about trying to work a place for a few onions and
tomatoes myself."

"I reckon I sounded right foolish going on like that," Cora
said. "It was something meant a lot to me when I was a little
one. Thank you, Lacey. And thank you, Ben. I'm right proud
to get these."

Ben beamed. Suddenly, he jumped up throwing his chair
back behind him. He pointed at Daniel Lee. Horrified, John
realized that Daniel Lee had turned blue, choked on the bacon.
He grabbed the baby from Lacey's arms and held him
suspended by one leg as he pounded his tiny back. A glob of
colorless suet flew across the room. John righted the baby who
was too stunned to cry. Lacey stood pale and wide-eyed at his
side. Without a word, she grabbed Daniel Lee and ran outside
with him. John and Cora watched through the window as
Lacey paced back and forth, tears streaming down her face,
muttering words of comfort to the child.

"He weren't choked all that bad. It come right up," John
said.

"She puts too much stock in that youngun. It ain't good to
put too much stock in one."

"That's Lacey's way," John mused.

"Well, she's set herself a hard row to hoe."

John nodded. He knew what Cora said was true and he
knew, as surely there was nothing he could do to change
Lacey's way. And there was after all, a kind of fierceness and
power in the way Lacey loved Daniel Lee, that just being near
it could make his breath come thick and hoarse in his throat.
The thought came to him the he would give his life to have
Lacey feel that way about him just once. He watched as she
stroked the boy's head and whispered softly to him and he took
what comfort he could from the sight of it.

4

Coy watched the swirling smoke from Bill Cope's cigarette as it joined the thick cloud that surrounded his head. Bill chewed on the end of his cigarette and frowned at the cards he held with both hands. It was easy to see he held a losing poker hand.

Even for a June night, the room was exceptionally warm. Sweat stained the underarms of Bill's shirt and beaded up on his forehead as fast as he could wipe it off with his wadded up handkerchief. No contest here, Coy thought, and sat back letting his mind wander. It was a Saturday night, past midnight and the top floor of the cigar store on Main Street was full of men trying hard to gamble and drink away the money they had worked all week to earn. Some of them had drawn their paychecks only hours before and had not even been home to see their families. They would have some explaining to do when they got home if they were the type that bothered to explain.

Coy's hand was being called. He laid down his cards. It was a full house, aces over tens.

"Blast it, Coy," Bill Cope said. "You need to give me a chance to win." He threw his cards on the table.

The other men around the table grumbled their agreement as Coy raked the chips to his side. "Bill, you get another chance every time the cards are dealt."

"Yeah, but I ain't won a hand all night."

"What about me? I've done lost thirty dollars," another man spoke up.

Coy did not even know his name. This was his first night there and it was obvious he had no talent for cards. He was pale and nervous and Coy was sure he had bet the rent money on the last hand. "That's why they call it a gamble, boys. You just never know when you might get the perfect hand. It could

17

be in this very next deal. Now, if you boys don't want to play, I got men standing over there waiting to get in the game."

"You are just a little too good Coy. Ain't nobody got luck like that," Bill Cope whined.

The other men looked at Coy and waited for him to react. It sounded an awful lot like Bill was accusing him of cheating but he was not about to be baited. "Bill, if you only knew the burden of being this good looking and a good poker player too you wouldn't wish it on yourself."

The other men laughed and slapped Coy on the back. Bill grinned and lit another cigarette. "I reckon I'm in for another hand."

Coy dealt the cards. It was almost too easy. He was three times the poker player any of them were and they seemed so eager to be taken. The fun had worn off of it for him. Wasn't that what Lacey had said about him, that he couldn't stick with anything.

He had licked his wounded pride all the way to his folks' place in Lexington, Kentucky. The hurt had soon driven him to move on to Indiana. Lacey's rejection festered in him like a boil and a deep part of him wanted desperately to prove her judgment wrong.

Coy raked in another round of winnings. "Be daylight in two hours men. I got all night if you do."

"I'm flat busted," Bill Cope said disgustedly.

"Me too," the nervous man agreed.

They all agreed it had been a rough night for poker. The room had cleared out except for the few die-hards left at Coy's table. The men stood up and ambled aimlessly toward the door, reluctant to leave even now. Coy walked the men out and stood on the landing of the stairs. Finally, he was alone. He sat on the railing of the steps and lit a cigarette leaning his back against the wall next to the door. He felt that same feeling he had felt all of his life that he was waiting for something to happen. It was like he had come into this world with something important he was supposed to get done but for the life of him he couldn't remember what it was. He would grab on to a thing and for a while it always seemed like the very thing that he was supposed to be doing. Then the feeling would fade. It never lasted very long. He always felt that he wasn't so much living, as waiting it out, waiting for the thing to happen that would make the feeling go away forever. He had been sure Lacey was what he had been searching for. But despite all he had done to help out with the strike, spying on the mine guards and rounding up food for the starving families, Lacey hadn't seen her way clear to trust him or to believe that he really loved her.

Coy gazed up at the stars. They were harder to make out in the city. He had been in Anderson, Indiana for almost a year and things had gone well for him. He had come into Barrett's Cigar Store to buy a pack of cigarettes and ended up owning the store. Ed Barrett was an easy-going type who had barely made a living for thirty years selling cigars and now was ready to retire. It was going to be tough, he had told Coy, to make it on what he could get from the store, but his wife was sick and he needed to stay home and take care of her. Besides, it was hard to sell a place nowadays with times hard. The whole time the man had talked, Coy had been looking at a tip board he had on the counter. If you paid a quarter, you could pull off a tip and take a chance at winning five dollars. Coy noticed that the men who wandered in seemed as interested in taking a chance on the tip board as they were in buying cigars. He decided to make the man a deal. If he would let him set up a gambling room upstairs, he would give him a split of the profits and he would not have to do a thing. It had turned out to be a gold mine and Coy had soon bought out Barrett and sent him on his merry way.

Coy pulled out a small block of white pine from his shirt pocket and started to work on it with his knife. He was carving a robin. It was to be a fat one, he thought smiling to himself, full of fresh spring worms. He liked carving birds. There was a challenge to carving something so small and putting in more and more detail until every wing feather was perfect. Carving had been a habit for him for most of his life and it never failed to give him a moment or two of peace. He always could do a fair job even when he was a youngun from the first time he picked up a chunk of wood. He wished he had kept some of those early carvings just to see if they had been as good as he remembered. Of course, he was a lot better now. He could carve a robin so real you could almost see its heart beating in its chest. Coy heard a noise and turned just as Chick Holt came out from the back room and handed him a cup of coffee. "Chick, I didn't know you were still up."

"Did I scare you?"

"If you'd set out to kill me, I'd of been too tired to stop you."

"Rough night?"

"About the same as always." Coy wondered why it seemed worse than most. He had won a lot of money. Still the night had left him restless and uneasy.

"Why don't you go on to bed? I can lock up."

Coy just shrugged. They both knew he rarely slept more than a few hours at a time. "You'd better bed down though. It'll be time to open the store in a few hours."

"Don't worry. I won't be late. I haven't let you down yet, have I?"

"I'm not worried," Coy said tossing his cold coffee over the side of the railing. He had dug Chick out of the basement of the cigar store. He had come through the coal chute during a snowstorm in December. Coy could hardly find Chick among the coal soot, he was so filthy. He just followed the sleeping noises to a skinny, tow-headed boy of maybe sixteen. Chick had told him later that when he woke up to find Coy's fierce dark eyes staring down at him, he thought he was about to die. Instead, Coy had told him to stoke the fire and then come upstairs to clean up. He had fed him a good meal and put him to work in the store. Now, with Ed gone, Chick ran the store full time. Coy had tried clerking in his parent's dry goods store in Lexington. He wasn't fool enough to try clerking twice. He and Chick shared two rooms and a hot plate upstairs.

"How'd it go tonight with the cards?" Chick asked.

"I don't know why the fools don't just hand me their money as they come in the door."

"Everybody thinks they'll be a winner sometime I guess, if they just keep playing."

"Hold on Chick. You're getting too deep for me. That sounds too much like life, don't it?"

They both grinned silently, keeping their thoughts to themselves in the early dawn light. In all the time that he and Chick had spent together, he had never asked him where he came from or how he happened to be in a coal chute in Indiana. Chick didn't act like someone who had known hard times and although Coy often wondered about that, he never asked.

"How'd you learn to play poker so well?" Chick asked.

For a moment, Coy thought about telling him about that year in Wilder. Telling him might ease the memory of it. Instead he found himself saying, "The hard way, Chick. The hard way."

Chick nodded. "Good night, Coy."

"Good night, Chick."

Chick turned and left Coy to watch the sun bring another day to life.

Coy didn't really know where he was headed, he just knew that sleep was still hours away. The cigar store he owned was on the west end of a two-block strip of bars, beer joints and cigar stores that fronted for gambling houses in downtown Anderson. It was not the most respectable two blocks in town but a woman could still walk the street without an escort. Coy reached the drugstore on the corner and cut one block over to Meridian. Already he was meeting people coming to work in freshly pressed suits and smelling of soap and aftershave. He became aware of the stubble on his face and the creases in his suit pants. The thought was there in a fleeting-way that he had not been taking very good care of himself. He had been hungry enough in his life to not refuse a meal when it came his way but not to notice much if one didn't. He walked another five blocks and passed a crowd gathered at the bus stop. Men and women who were not as well-dressed with lunchboxes and crumpled brown bags were on their way to Guide Lamp or Delco Remy. He knew better than to envy them their thirty years at a factory even if it meant a steady wage. He had often longed to have his life laid out for him like that but he never lasted long when it was.

He zigzagged his way down Sixteenth Street. He stood at the curb, smoking a cigarette and leaning against a street sign. Clapboard houses stood along side each other down the block. A woman came out on the porch across the street, a broom clutched in her fist. She swept the porch like someone fighting a fire. An angry man's voice yelled at her from inside. She never looked up from her broom. Two houses down, children played in the yard. Coy wondered what he was doing there. He threw down his cigarette, grinding it into the sidewalk with his heel. As he turned to head back up town, a truck pulled up in front of the house. The sign on the side of the truck said

Parker's Auction House. A man got out and went up to the porch steps and stood talking to the woman. There was something familiar about the man. He was thin and wiry with a quick stride. The woman crooked her head toward the back of the house and the man bounded down the steps. In a few minutes he came back carrying a box. He put it in the back of the truck and returned carrying two chairs that looked like they belonged to a dining table. It was when he climbed into the back of the truck to load the chairs that Coy recognized him. It was Will Conners, Lacey's older brother. Coy was across the street and standing behind the truck before he knew what he planned to say or do. "Need a hand there, Will?" he asked.

Will looked up, recognition showing slowly on his face. "Well, I'll be, Coy Lynn Wilson."

He jumped down to shake Coy's hand. Coy took it gratefully. He had not known what to expect. After all, the Conner's family had never held him in much favor.

"If you ain't the last person I ever expected to see in Anderson. What on earth brought you to this town?" Will asked, good-naturedly.

"They was just a train headed this way, I reckon."

"I reckon that was how we come to be here too, come to think of it. We got offered a ride and there sure wasn't nothing holding us in Wilder."

"Did you get out before the strike ended?"

"Yeah," Coy said, uncomfortable with the turn of the conversation.

"You know, John said some right fine things about you. He told near everybody what you done for the union, risking your life and all. Pretty near a hero from what I heard."

"Well, John's a good man to say it but it wasn't nothing like that."

"I'll tell you it changed folk's way of thinking about you,"

"John must of done some talking," Coy said with a wry grin.

They both laughed knowing that Coy had been at odds with Wilder since he was born. "I don't reckon it changed your pa's way of thinking none," Coy asked.

"Pa don't soften none too easy," Will said without apology. "Why he's just now finding something tolerable in me."

Coy grinned thinking of Frank Conners. He must have been a hard man to be a son to. Nobody could have expected more from his children. "Looks like you're doing all right for yourself. Working for an auction company, are you?"

"Ever since we come up here. Got lucky right off. If you don't care I could use a hand loading this table into the truck."

"Be happy to." They went around to the back porch where a mahogany dining table sat looking out of place on the weathered planks.

Will looked at Coy and shrugged as they lifted the table off the porch. "Husband drinks. When he works, they buy up a few things. Sell'em off when he goes on a binge."

Coy noticed the woman wiping her eyes with the corner of her apron as they loaded the table.

"That's how we get most of our stuff. Everybody round here works in a factory. When things is going good, they spend like they was no tomorrow. Thing is, they always is. Next thing you know there's a strike or folks get laid off and they got to sell. It's sad sometimes but mostly I like what I'm doing. Mostly I auctioneer. That's what I love. I feel like sometimes, I was born to do it. You know I always did like to showoff. This way I get paid to do it."

"Sounds like you're a lucky man, Will." Coy said sincerely. Will had always been a bit of a hot-tempered sort, always jumping into the middle of things and getting into more trouble than he could handle. It probably felt good to find a place where he fit.

"Ruby she likes it up north, too," Will went on. "Pa, he helps out when he can. He ain't always up to it. And Ma, she don't miss a night a setting in them bleachers watching. She loves the excitement. I just hope I get to keep it up."

Coy wondered why Frank wasn't always up to helping out but he let it go. "So you got the whole family up here with you, do you?"

"No. Lacey's in Tennessee. Ben stayed with her. You couldn't tear them two apart. You know she married John. Been over a year ago."

Coy didn't know why it hit him so hard just hearing it from Will. It was what she said she was going to do, just like she had promised John. "They're not still in Wilder?"

"No, they had to get outta there after the strike ended. They moved to a place up on the Cumberland Plateau, near Crossville. The government's started a place up there to give farms to people that's willing to work for them. Ain't nothing but woods right now, from what I hear. It sounds like purely hard work to me. You know them two, though. If ever they was two people that didn't mind hard work, they're the ones. They got a fine son, already."

Coy nodded trying not to show his feelings. It hurt him knowing that she had gone on so easily with her life. He could picture Lacey with a baby. She always did try to take care of everybody. It was what he loved about her. It was what had torn them apart. The truck was loaded and he couldn't think of a reason to keep Will. He was reluctant to let go of the only news he had had of Lacey in over a year. Then he thought about what Will had said. "What do you mean you hope you can keep doing what you've been doing?"

"Old man Parker's got plans to sell the place. Says he's getting too old. I offered just to run it for him but he wants out. He wants to move where the winters ain't so hard."

"Why don't you buy it?"

"Don't I wish? He ain't asking but twenty-three hundred dollars. Might as well be a million if you ain't got it. We've lived good since we've been here but you know they's been expenses. We had to have a place to live and, well, I just ain't been able to put much aside."

Coy guessed that Will wasn't much different from the families he bought his goods from. He spent everything he earned and lived well while times were good. Then when the chance had come up to buy the auction house, he had probably kicked himself a thousand times for not having saved a dime. "Well, I might just be interested," Coy said surprising himself.

"You mean it?" Will said excitedly. "You got that kind of money?"

"I might, if it's a good enough deal. I've done all right for myself since I've been in Indiana. And, of course, I'd be looking for somebody to run it for me," Coy said wondering even as he said what he must be thinking. What would Lacey think when she heard about it, he wondered. Could it really be that she had given no thought at all to him.

"Coy, you know I'd do you right," Will said seriously.

"How do I meet this Parker fellow," Coy said, pulling himself back from his thoughts. He was determined now to buy the auction house.

"You just let me handle that. You come around tomorrow around three o'clock and I'll make sure you get a proper introduction."

"Well, thank you, Will. I'll just do that."

"1423 McCleary Ave. You see it right there on the sign," he said pointing to the truck.

"I'll be there," Coy said shaking Will's hand.

Will got in the truck and drove off waving out the window until he turned the corner and disappeared.

Coy tipped his hat to the woman on the porch who looked at him like he was a weed in her petunias. He strolled casually on back up town like he had all the time in the world, wondering all the while where he was going to come up with twenty-three hundred dollars. "Coy, don't you never learn," he said out loud. A man passed giving him a sidelong glance as he hurried by. Coy smiled and tipped his hat to the stranger's back. He didn't need a stranger to give him the answer to that question. Still, he was secretly delighted with himself. Hearing word of Lacey had sent a jolt through him. She hadn't waited long to marry John and get on with her life. If she had any regrets, it didn't show in her actions. Maybe she could be made to regret it, he thought, if he ended up making something out of himself. He was no fool. He knew he had an easy way about him of turning a buck without even putting his mind to it. Maybe if he put his mind to it he could be rich. He could be rich enough to make a dirt farm in Tennessee look like nothing; rich enough to make Lacey regret the day she had sent him away. It was a thought worth savoring. For now, he could hope that when Lacey heard about the auction house, it might throw some doubt into her. Just thinking about buying the auction house made him feel better than he had felt in months. He could not help but laugh to himself. He turned his face to the sun and let a laugh rise up out of him. Lacey always did love his laugh. She said it was like he knew a secret on the world. And now he felt like he did. He slapped his hat against his leg. "Can you hear me now, Lacey? Can you hear me?"

He walked the rest of the way uptown almost at a run. It seemed to him like he had just realized he had wasted a lifetime. Now, every minute seemed precious. Having just a little money did seem to change the way folks thought about him and he might just have a knack for making a lot of money. He had better get busy, he thought. He had a lot to do to become a wealthy man.

5

Susan gave the man fifty dollars. It was her standard arrangement with Joe Wash for finding her brother, Chick.

"He's at a dive on Main Street. A cigar joint. He's been there ever since he ran off. He never left town."

"What is he doing at a cigar store?"

"Working," Joe said rolling his eyes, obviously bewildered by a kid who would turn his back on wealth to work in a cigar store.

Susan continued to stare at the papers in her hands, looking more peeved than concerned. She shook her head to show her impatience with her brother, but secretly she was relieved to learn he was close by and safe. "Well, that's a different twist." Chick had been running away from home since he was twelve, but this was the first time he had managed to find a steady job. It worried Susan because the next time he might just make it out of town and then she could lose him for sure.

"You want me to bring him home?"

"No, just leave the address and I'll go talk to him."

"What about Mr. Holt? I mean, your father might get real mad if I don't haul the boy back here right away."

"Believe me; he would rather see his son come crawling back on his own," Susan said smiling sweetly. She enjoyed shocking the hired help. After all, how could anyone who had not experienced it believe that living in a twenty-room mansion with servants and a father who owned half the town could be anything but enviable?

"Will that be it, ma'am?"

"No, wait a minute," Susan said raking her blond hair back with her fingers. "Who owns this place where Chick works and where is he staying?"

27

"He sleeps above the store. The man who owns it is a guy by the name of Coy Lynn Wilson. He came up from Tennessee last year. He runs a gambling joint above the cigar store."

Susan could feel her lip curl slightly with distaste. She chewed on a polished nail. "Is it legitimate?"

"From what I hear, it's dang close," Joe said with a grin and then caught himself. "Sorry ma'am. I reckon it's fairly on the up and up as them places go. None of them places is exactly respectable."

"What's this Wilson like?"

"From what I hear he didn't have nothing but the shirt on his back when he got here, but he's done right well since."

Just another poor Southerner who had come north to escape the hard times, Susan thought. The town was full of them. It sounded like this one might be doing better than most even if he was just skirting the law to do it. "He must be quite a poker player."

Joe chuckled. "Yes ma'am."

"Does Chick seem happy?"

"He sure does. I seen the two of them laughing and slapping each other on the back."

Susan felt an unexplainable pang of jealousy. Her brother was the only person she loved in the world. And he loved her back. She had come to depend on that. It had gotten her through the rough times. "Well, at least that's good news, Joe."

Joe nodded.

"That will be all for now." She took the slip of paper with the address on it from Joe. She did not get up to walk him to the door but continued to sit until he was gone. She did not like to let someone she had just paid money, see her limp. It always made them feel superior. They might have to take her money but her deformity made them even in their eyes.

Susan called a cab, put on her suit jacket and went down stairs. She knew it was selfish to want to bring her brother back to this place but she knew she would die if she had to stay here alone with her father. She ran her good foot over the polished marble of the foyer. She had been born the crippled daughter of a man who could tolerate nothing less than perfection. He had taken every opportunity to remind her, what a disappointment she had been up until the time of Chick's birth. Charles Samuel Holt II had been born plump and blond and perfect. Susan had nicknamed him Chick because of his fuzzy blond hair at birth. He was the perfect embodiment of a father's dreams. After that, Sam Holt had simply ignored his daughter. She thought for that she should have been grateful but it had somehow hurt more.

Chick was the perfect son except for one thing. He hated his father and everything he stood for. That should have given Susan enough satisfaction to last a lifetime but she wanted more. She wanted everything her father had and Chick was her only way of getting it. So each time he ran away, she went after him.

The cab pulled up in front of a shabby storefront. She thought the building was small and in need of some paint. She asked the cabby to wait no matter how long it took. He shrugged his indifference, but she knew he would be glad for the fare. The sidewalk shone like a mirror from the hot sun and Susan felt suddenly dizzy. What if this was the time Chick refused to come home, she thought and quickly banished her doubts. She straightened her suit, threw back her shoulders and went in. Chick was behind the counter with his back to her. She waited for him to feel her presence. He turned and greeted her with a smile.

"Hi, sis. I knew you'd find me soon."

"Hi, Chick," she laughed surprised as always by her brother's good looks and congenial nature.

"Joe?" he asked.

"Joe," she said with a nod.

"This time is different you know."

"Is that right?"

"Yeah. I got a job. I got a friend. I'm not coming back."

"If you don't come willingly, Sam will send someone after you."

"Let him. Next time I won't stop so close to home."

Susan tried not to let her face show her feelings. "I've tried to tell you, Chick. The best way to beat your father is to play him in his own game"

"Susan, you can live your life like it was a game if you want to, but leave me out of it."

Susan thought it would be great to leave Chick out of the game. She really loved him and wanted to see him happy, but without him her father wouldn't play. He wasn't interested in playing with her. She wanted so very badly to beat him, it made her head ache.

The door opened, startling Susan. She looked toward the door but the glare from the sun outside was too bright and she could only squint at the dark figure approaching. Suddenly, a man emerged from the shadows brushing close to her side. He was the most handsome man she had ever seen. His hair was so black that when it caught the light it reflected a deep blue. His eyes were equally black but they reflected no light. The man looked at her boldly with an amused smile on his face as though he knew a thousand secrets about her. She found herself pushing past him with just a parting look at Chick. She stumbled out onto the street clutching her purse, feeling like a fool for reacting the way she had. She tried to convince herself that her reaction was due to having been caught unaware but she knew without turning around that his black eyes were on her at that moment. She tried to pull herself together, but she was in the cab and on her way home before she finally let out her breath and relaxed against the seat.

6

Cora and Lacey sat in the yard in straight-back chairs from the kitchen table. Their aproned laps were filled with beans they were stringing. Daniel Lee sat on the ground sucking on a raw bean and playing with the discarded strings. Lacey threw another handful into the dishpan next to her chair.

Just before dusk the day before, Kelly Smith had come carrying Ben home in his pickup truck. The bed of the pickup had been loaded down with corn, Irish potatoes and green beans. In the weeks that Ben had worked for the Smiths, they had paid Ben much more from their garden than the gallon of black-eyed peas they had promised. Lacey had never known such bounty. She looked for a way to repay the Smiths and had sent a huckleberry pie by way of Ben. She missed having Ben around during the day but couldn't deny how much the food was worth to them. It was keeping her and Cora busy just putting it by for winter.

"I reckon we can start threading some of these beans for leather britches," Cora said without looking up from her work.

Lacey watched as Cora's hands worked rapid-fire, stringing a whole handful of beans before dropping them into the pan. "I'll get us some thread and needles when I go in to put a pot of these beans on for supper."

"You know I've been putting beans by like this for thirty years. Seems like I couldn't of been no older than Daniel Lee when my mama first handed me a needle and set me to threading beans. Granny Wells that was mama's mother was still alive then. We'd sit for hours at a time till we was stiff as boards. It does seem to fall to the womenfolk to do the tedious work in life. I never blamed no womenfolk for buying their foodstuff at the commissary when they could. 'Course it made it harder on them families when the strike come and they didn't have nothing put by. Some of them women had plumb forgot how to grow a garden and put stuff by for the winter."

"I always did love growing a garden," Lacey said, thinking back on how her garden had kept them from starving that last year in Wilder. "I do believe I can see the bottom of this bushel basket," Lacey said with a chuckle. "Does seem sometimes like there ortta be a better way."

"Goodness gracious, Lacey. That reminds me of something John told me. I clear forgot to mention it. The womenfolk is getting together to start clubs. They'll be one for each road like Highland Lane and Sawmill and Deep Draw and this one will be Grassy Cove Women's Club. Ain't that fine sounding," she said with a wave of her hand.

"What are they meeting for?"

"They're supposed to send folks out, they call them Home Demonstration Agents, to show us how to keep house better and to give us what John called 'culture'. I told John, I keep house better than most folks and I don't know what I'd do with no culture." Cora laughed loudly and slapped her knee.

"How did he take that?"

"He set his jaw and there weren't no joshing him out of it," she said a grin pulling at her lips. "What put me in a mind of it was us stringing these beans. You know they built that little canning house up by the Homestead office where you can take stuff from your garden and can it. Well, canning was one of the things they was going to be teaching at these meetings."

"Do you think John will be expecting me to go?"

"You can count on it. When they said they wanted folks that could cooperate and work together John took it real personal like a pledge. I reckon this is part of some big plan to educate us ignorant folk. Can't have no special planned community and fill it up with ordinary folk. It would be like stocking your pond with carp," Cora said chuckling at her own joke.

"Well, it ain't like they didn't check us out ahead of time," Lacey said going along with Cora.

"We was good enough when they picked us, but I reckon they're planning on smarten us up a tad now that we're here."

"Can't hurt nothing and I would like to meet some of the other women. It gets lonesome sometimes."

"Of course it does with nobody here but an old woman to talk to."

Cora didn't give Lacey time to protest that she didn't mind being with her. She enjoyed Cora's company. She was closer to a mother than her own mother had been.

"You just plan on going. I'll watch Daniel Lee."

"Oh, Cora, I don't have nothing to wear to something like that," Lacey said looking down at her flowered cotton dress, its color washed thin.

"Won't be nobody there dressed any different. If they didn't know hard times, they wouldn't be here now."

"I reckon, you're right," Lacey said tucking the loose strands of hair back into place. She really should have it cut, she thought. Most likely all the other women wore theirs short with a permanent wave.

Cora lifted the last handful of beans from the basket and dumped them into her lap. "That attic will make a perfect place to hang'em to dry."

"It's surely hot enough up there."

"They's times it has near 'bout dried me out. That's why I look so wrinkled, I reckon," Cora said with a grin.

"You know you're welcome to move downstairs."

"Honey, I know that," Cora said reaching over to pat Lacey's arm. "Don't you worry about me. I can sleep outside if I take a notion. Besides it'll start to cool off up here on this mountain in the next month or so. Even for July it ain't all that hot."

"We're lucky to have this big oak so near the barn. It gives up a bit of shade."

"The way they're clearing land around here, we may have to stand guard over it to keep them from cutting it down."

"John says they may start on this place any day now. I wish we knew that this would be our farm for sure. John says that them that signed up first gets first choice over the homes as they get built."

"Well, you two have to be pretty high up on the list."

"He was one of the first ones to sign up. It's just that I already think of this place as our farm. And when they start clearing the land, I know I'll be picturing where the house will be and all."

"I know it has to be done but won't that be a mess and a half while they're a clearing. We may want to pack up Daniel Lee and go visit my kinfolks in Monterey till that's done."

"Why Cora, I think it'll be kinda exciting."

"Oh, it'll be exciting all right. I hear they shot a stump clean through the window of Ethel Norton's barn the other day."

"Was anybody hurt?" Lacey asked trying to imagine it.

"It missed her and the baby by about a foot. Scared the men more than it did Ethel. They thought they'd killed somebody for sure."

"How come it to blow through her window? Surely, they weren't shooting off dynamite that close to the barn."

"Lacey, let me tell you a thing or two. Half the men working here ain't never done nothing like this before in their lives. They's just men who need a job. From what I hear, they packed enough dynamite into that tree stump to shoot it to the moon."

Cora laughed until she had to hold her sides. Lacey couldn't help but laugh with her. She loved the way Cora could see the funny side of any thing that happened in life. She wished that John had gotten just a little of Cora's sense of humor. "You may be right Cora. It sounds like it wouldn't hurt to board up the windows just for the time being."

"Wouldn't John have a fit? I might do it just to get a rise out of him."

"Cora, that's mean," Lacey said picturing how funny it would be.

"I know it." she said throwing back her head and laughing. "We better never let John hear us talk like this."

"I hope it wasn't none of his men that done it. He takes his job as foreman real serious."

"Honey, that's just John. He thinks he's always got to give'em more than they ask. You would of thought he would have learned from working in the mines that folks can ask an awful lot."

"This is different, Cora. This won't be like the mines. John's working so we can own a place of our own someday."

Cora just nodded. Lacey waited for Cora to speak but she went on stringing the beans in her lap. Lacey stood up, the strings in her lap tumbling to the ground, and stretched her back. A flatbed truck was coming up the narrow, rutted road to the barn. The truck had high rails on the sides and twenty men rode standing up. John was on the passenger side. He jumped out before the truck had come to a complete stop and came running over to her.

"We're fixing to start clearing this place," John shouted as excited as a preacher at a revival.

Lacey and Cora couldn't help themselves, after the talk they had just had about boarding up the window. They started to giggle like schoolgirls. Daniel Lee waved his hands, laughing with them like he had caught the joke. John just frowned at them from where he stood. Lacey stifled her laughter and walked over to John, holding on to her aching sides. "I am sorry, John. I guess we was just excited and all," she stammered weakly, barely able to catch her breath. He looked at her like he couldn't even begin to understand but would believe her if she said so.

A young man came up beside John. "Lacey, this here is Thomas Jefferson Morgan. He'll be working on my crew."

Lacey nodded. The young man reached out and took her hand shaking it briskly. "There's five boys in my family, ma'am and my daddy named us all after presidents of the United States."

"Well now, that's real unusual, Thomas Jefferson," Lacey said hesitantly.

"Just call me Thomas. The way I see it, I got off lucky. Daddy was going to name us after state's capitols. I could have been named Boise, Idaho," Thomas said with a chuckle. He then walked over to Cora and introduced himself, picking up Daniel Lee at the same time. He played with Daniel Lee and chatted with Cora like he had known them forever.

"He's got a real friendly way about him," John said.

"It does seem so," Lacey said, shaking her head in amazement.

"Things is moving real fast. I never would've believed it myself. We've got eighty-seven barns built and thirty-four houses underway. If the weather holds out for a while, some folks will most likely move in by the first of next year."

"That's wonderful, John."

"Well, we could move faster but we're taking out ever stump. We're not waiting for them to rot like farmers around here is used to doing."

Lacey looked as serious as she could and nodded solemnly.

"Then we disc up the land and put lime on so it'll be ready for crops. They already got a crop of potatoes out of two hundred acres that was cleared last year."

"Looks to all the world like Cora's going to have a right good gourd harvest herself," Lacey said before she could stop herself. She knew she shouldn't have said it. She didn't know what drove her to say such things when John was being his most serious. It wasn't that she didn't care about what he was saying. It was just that John had taken to the Cumberland Homesteads project the same way he had taken to the Union and the coal miners strike. He acted like he had single-handedly been given the task and been told to make it work.

"Its good soil," he said as though she had made a powerful statement.

She looked at him, batting her eyes in amazement.

"Here, I almost forgot," he said reaching into his overall pocket, "a letter from Ruby."

Lacey grabbed it in excitement. She had not heard from Ruby since she had written to tell her about the move to the Homesteads. Ruby was the closest friend she had ever had. When Ruby had married her brother Will, she had been pleased. Ruby, Will and their baby daughter Rachel had moved away during the strike. Getting a letter from Ruby made Lacey realize how lonely she felt. She looked up to see John watching her. She knew he expected her to open the letter and read it out loud. After all, it was from family. She tucked it into her apron pocket. "I'll read it at supper," she said giving him a smile.

"I need to get back to work, anyway."

Thomas walked over carrying the baby. Lacey took Daniel Lee from him. "He's a cute one for sure, Mrs. Trotter."

"Thank you Thomas. Do you have a wife and family?"

"No ma'am. I'm not married. I'm just working on the relief. My Daddy owns a farm not twenty miles from here, but he got kicked by a mule two years ago and ain't worked since. I send money home as I can."

Lacey just smiled. She didn't begrudge him the job but she had never thought about the men who were just here to earn a wage. And he had called it the relief. Lacey had never seen what they were doing as getting a hand out. Thomas had such an open, friendly way about him that it was hard not to like him right off. "It was nice meeting you Thomas."

"Nice meeting you ma'am."

"We best be getting back to work." John said solemnly.

Lacey watched as John and Thomas walked back toward the truck. Thomas kept up a constant stream of chatter. Lacey wondered how the quiet John took to such endless talk.

"I reckon, I'll go put these beans on for supper," Lacey said to Cora as she sat the baby down and grabbed up the dishpan. She was eager to be alone to read Ruby's letter. "I'll be right back with a needle and thread and get Daniel Lee so I can put him down for a nap."

She carried the beans inside and set them on the kitchen table. With water from a bucket kept by the stove, Lacey washed the beans through three rinses and put them in a heavy iron pot to cook. Into the pot she sliced a thick chunk of fatback and put the pot on the stove to cook.

She went to a shelf that John had built near the kitchen table and took down the sewing basket to search for quilting thread, the only kind strong enough to hold the weight of the beans while they dried. They would be light as feathers strung together after they had hung in the attic over the winter. She took the thread and needle outside and handed it to Cora. "Do you need me to thread that for you?"

"It ain't as easy as it was but I can still hit the eye of that old needle if I try it enough times. And I'd just as soon try it as to admit I need help just yet," Cora said, already squinting at the needle held between her fingers.

Lacey picked up Daniel Lee, brushing the bean strings from his body. She carried him inside to the washbowl and cleaned his tiny hands and face with a damp cloth. He hugged her around the neck pressing his damp cheek to hers. She gave him a drink of warm milk fresh from their own cow John had bought last week when Daniel Lee had shown signs of giving up the breast.

Steam came steadily from the pot on the stove. Lacey let it play on her face a moment, taking in the delicious smell. Lifting the lid, she watched the bubbles working their way up through the beans, the globs of grease like little rafts being pushed around in the water.

Lacey carried Daniel Lee to the rocking chair and rocked him gently until his long dark lashes grew heavy. They opened and closed slowly with each rock until finally he fell asleep. She knew she could put him safely to bed and he would not wake up, but still she held on to him as she slipped the letter from her apron and pried it open with her thumb.

Dear Lacey,
    It was good to hear from you and that things was going so well. I'm glad you like your new home. It sounds real pretty and new. Things is going real good for us here too. Little Rachel is into everything and talking a blue streak. 'Course you can't understand much of it but she sure is feisty with it. She thinks the world of your pa and sits on his lap every evening out on the front porch. I watch them talking away to each other all the time a wondering what they could be saying. You know your pa ain't been well since he caught that cold last year. It just don't seem to get no better even with the warm weather. He won't see a doctor about it and don't like to have nobody fussing over him. I don't think he much likes living up here. He misses Tennessee. Your ma won't even talk to him about going home on a visit. She's took to this place like she was born here. They's always folks stopping by to visit and the bus runs right by here for shopping and such. It's been right good for her. Theys a world of folks here from Tennessee. She don't hardly complain with her heart no more like she used to. She even goes down to the auction house with Will and stays up half the night. Says she likes to watch all the people and see stuff come through. Will has to keep an eye on her to keep her from bidding on stuff. He's told her time and time again that he can get it cheap if she'll just tell him ahead of time. I reckon she just gets caught up in the excitement. Will is doing real good at the auction house. You know we was worried when the owner said he planned to sell out. You can't never tell when somebody new comes in if they're going to like the

way things is or start changing things around. Sometimes they bring in their own folks to run things. Anyway, you won't believe what happened. Will was picking up a load of goods one day and run into Coy Lynn Wilson. I never was so shocked in my life when Will told me he was up here. Will just happened to say something about the auction house being for sale. It seems Coy has done right well for hisself and before we could catch our breaths he'd up and bought the place. He's been real good to Will, letting him have a say over everything. Your pa didn't like it none. Him and Will had a round over it especially after Coy come to the house once to talk business. He never did take to Coy even in Wilder. I know I've wrote too long but I do miss you. We like living here and I reckon we plan to stay. It sure would be good to see you. I don't guess you and John can get away right now with all that's going on down there. We've never even seen Daniel Lee. Does he took like you or John? Looks like me and Will is going to have another baby the first of next year. I ain't hardly that way and I'm showing. 'Course I never was a tiny little thing like you. Write and tell me all about how your farm is coming along. It sure sounds exciting. Write real soon.

Love,
Ruby, Will, Little Rachel
and the folks

P.S. Coy asked after you and John.

Lacey covered her face with the letter letting her head reel in the darkness it created. Coy in Indiana, she couldn't believe it. She read over the letter again searching for the answers to all her questions. Why wasn't Coy in Kentucky with his folks? No need to ask, he hadn't been able to stick it out in the dry goods business. He could never stay with anything once the newness wore off. What was he doing now, she wondered? Ruby said he had done all right for himself in Indiana. How? Did he look well? Was he happy? There was no way to ask the questions and maybe it was best she didn't know. Her pa had been the

only one who had ever guessed about Coy. It was no surprise
to her that her pa didn't want him around again. They had had
their only big fight in all of Lacey's life about Coy. It was the
only time she had ever seen disappointment on her pa's face.
He said he wouldn't try to stop her from seeing Coy, but he
had made it known she would never be welcome back in his
house. It had been the hardest time in her life with so many
folks expecting so much of her. Her pa expected her to always
do as he said and she had until Coy. John expected her to
marry him and settle down to be a miner's wife and she
thought she could. Coy just wanted her to forget all that and be
with him. And how she had loved being with him. They had
laughed over the silliest things. But in the end she hadn't been
able to forget, her family or John. It just wasn't in her to hurt
people even if Coy did think she was being foolish. Oh Coy,
what are you doing, she thought. "Why can't you just leave
things be," she whispered. She felt the locket she wore around
her neck. She put the letter down and took the locket in her
hand. Coy had given it to her on that last day on the mountain.
Inside it held two strands of hair wrapped around each other.
One strand was her hair; the other was as black as a jet button.
She held it against Daniel Lee's head. It was a perfect match.
Lacey's heart pounded. "Leave it be, Coy," she whispered.
Now, the dream would haunt her even in her waking hours.

Lacey became aware of someone in the room. She looked
up to see Cora standing by the stove staring at her.

"Lacey, are you all right? I called and called. When you
didn't come back out, I come to check on you. It's a good thing
I did, these beans was cooked plumb dry."

"Oh my goodness," Lacey said putting Daniel Lee down in
his bed. "I must of dozed off."

Cora cocked her head to one side and looked at Lacey with
a squinty frown but didn't say anything. She turned and added
a few sticks of wood to the stove.

"I guess I better get the bread on. John will be coming in
for supper soon. We really should cook outside on a day like
this," Lacey said fanning herself with her hand. Cora was
slicing potatoes into a skillet of hot grease.

Lacey felt like she had been away on a long trip she
couldn't remember taking. She glanced out the window to see
John and Ben walking up the road together. Ben stood head

high to John's shoulder, so thin his overalls moved around him like a barrel. John nodded listening to Ben as he talked excitedly, gesturing wildly with his hands. She was glad she still had Ben with her. She missed her folks, even her ma. It worried her that her pa wasn't fairing well in Indiana. He had not been a well man for a long time. She thought of Little Rachel sitting on her pa's knee. They had been like that once, she and her pa. Many nights they had sat at the kitchen table talking. She had been his little gal until she'd crossed him on the thing with Coy. It didn't look like he would ever forgive her for it. How could she explain it, why a young girl who had never even kissed a boy before could fall in love with someone like Coy Lynn Wilson. She had never even told her best friend Ruby. She had known that what she was doing with Coy was wrong and she had gone ahead with the lying and the deceiving knowing that in time God would punish her. That was a known fact. Something she had been sure of even at the time. Her greatest fear was that the punishment would fall on Daniel Lee and not on her. That would be more than she could bear. And didn't it say in the Bible that God would never put on a person more than they could bear?

Lacey stepped out into the yard to greet them. "Well, you two seem powerful excited about something."

Ben looked at her like a scolded puppy. "I've been down Deep Draw Road."

"Deep Draw Road?"

"They're building a bridge over Byrd's Creek. I've been carrying lumber for the men."

She nodded, biting back her tongue. She had worried out loud to him more than once about running around the 'whole county' without her knowing his whereabouts. There was just no way to keep him away from all the construction that was going on. Building things was just something he had always loved. With nothing to work with but sticks and string, he had built bridges between the rails of the front porch of their house in Wilder and across little muddy creeks he made in the yard.

"Sounds like you've been busy today."

"I done my work at the Smith's," he said proudly. "I always get my work done first."

"Always?"

"It's not the first time I've helped 'em," he mumbled, losing his boldness.

"Ben's a good hand to help out, the men tell me," John said stepping in to the boy's defense.

Ben beamed.

"We better get in and wash up for supper. Then you can tell me all about it," Lacey said softening.

Ben grinned, obviously thrilled to have escaped Lacey's displeasure. He immediately launched into a description of the bridge, explaining about how they were constructing arches out of wood and then putting field stone over the frame.

He hardly stopped to catch his breath until they sat down for supper. Lacey looked across at his freshly scrubbed face, his hair still damp, and was glad she had kept her worries to herself. Ben was a good boy, gentle and giving. It wasn't right of her to ask him to stay there under her wing just because he had been so sick those times, just because she'd almost lost him. He had a right to grow up. It was what she wanted for him really. It was just hard to let go, to let him out there where she couldn't keep an eye on him. "Ben, will you say the blessing?"

"Thank you, Lord for all this good food. And thank you for not letting Lacey stop me from going to Deep Draw Road."

Lacey looked up to see Ben grinning. She cocked her head and pointed her finger but couldn't carry off her look of anger and burst out laughing. "Ben don't you press me now," she gasped between laughs. Cora and John smiled and waited patiently, watching the two, unsure whether to join in. Lacey thought she should tell them it was all right, but couldn't find the words, "I guess we better eat before the food gets cold," she managed to say at last. They ate in silence for a few minutes, enjoying the food.

"Mrs. Eleanor Roosevelt is coming to the Cumberland Homesteads," John spoke up like he was commenting on the day's weather.

"What'd you say, son?" Cora asked.

"Mrs. Eleanor Roosevelt is coming down here to see what all's been done on this Homestead project."

"Coming to the Homesteads? Mrs. Eleanor Roosevelt is coming here? Can you beat that? We must be right smart important."

"They say she thinks the Homestead's is right special."

"Well, that can't hurt can it, having the President of the United States' wife looking out for us. When's she a-coming?"

"Day after tomorrow."

"Day after tomorrow and you're just now carrying in news about it. Lordy, son you reckon we'll get a chance to see her."

"She's supposed to make a speech up at the Cumberland Homestead's office. I reckon if you're a mind to we could walk up there."

"I know I'm a mind to," Cora spoke up. "How about you Lacey? It'll give you another reason besides them women's clubs to get that new dress you said you was needing."

John looked at Lacey. She felt the heat go up her neck. Never would she have said anything to him about needing a dress and wished for all she was worth that Cora had not. She could see John working it over in his mind. She wanted to tell him it had just been woman talk between her and Cora to pass the time, that she didn't really need a dress or even want one. Before she could say anything, John spoke up surprising her into silence.

"Lacey, why don't you read us that letter you got today from Ruby?"

Cora and Ben chimed in, begging her to read the letter. She pulled it slowly from her apron pocket and unfolded it. She read, keeping her voice steady with effort, to make the words seem more ordinary. When she finished and looked up, John merely nodded.

"Ain't that something," Cora exclaimed. "Coy Wilson a running into Will like that. You know folks always did run Coy down but I couldn't never say a harm word against him after what he done to save John's life. I know John always thought a right smart of him for what he done for the union, didn't you John?"

John didn't answer. He took out the pipe he had started to smoke in recent months and began awkwardly to pack it. Lacey reached over and took the pipe from his hands and expertly packed it as she had so often done for her father. He waited for her to finish, as trusting as a child giving it up entirely to her hands.

"And now it looks like he's gone and done Will a real favor, don't it, John?" Cora said undeterred by John's silence.

John took his pipe and went outside.

"Now, what kinda bee do you think he's got in his cap tonight?" Cora remarked to John's backside.

Lacey got up and started to clear the table. She could feel Ben staring at her from behind. "Ben, Daniel Lee is waking up. Could you get him?"

She could hear Ben reluctantly push his chair back from the table. She knew he wanted to linger and hear any explanation for John's behavior.

"Honey, you just leave them dishes be. I'll wash up and feed the baby. Why don't you go on outside and set a spell with John before dark?"

Lacey didn't want to go outside and she didn't want to stay in either. She strolled out to where John stood under the big oak. "It's a pretty night."

John nodded.

"I like it when it stays light longer," she said pushing a small stone around with the toe of her shoe.

John puffed on his pipe. "Lacey," he said softly, "Why didn't you tell me you needed a dress?"

Lacey looked at the hurt in his eyes and never wanted anything less at that moment than she wanted a new dress. She couldn't answer him. The words stuck in her throat. How could a man feel such a failing in himself over a dress? Part of her wanted to scream that it should have been right obvious to him from looking at her that she needed a new dress but she knew that wasn't always the way with men. She knew that John didn't seem to notice if his socks were mended or if his toes stuck through. He never brought up the patches in his overalls or their threadbare behinds. He just slipped in and out of them as though they would last another fifty years. They had had so little for so long the thought of asking for something was beyond her.

"I'll get Frank Wells to carry us to Crossville tomorrow," John said when she did not answer.

"It only come up today when Cora brought it up about the ladies clubs. It wouldn't have to be store bought. I could get a few yards of cloth and make up a dress. I know we need to be saving. Besides they's plenty of things we need more than I need a dress, John."

John looked off into the distance and she could tell she had said the wrong thing. Why was it that her wanting something always caused somebody pain, even as simple a thing as this? Surely it wasn't like that for other folks.

"No, you're to have a store-bought dress."

She could tell it was a matter of pride to him now. "Thank you, John," she said her voice cracking. She had never had a store-bought dress and she wished desperately that Ruby could go with her to buy it. They would try on every dress in the store, laughing and cutting up like they had as girls.

They looked at the night sky and watched it grow dark. A thousand words remained unspoken. Finally, John knocked out his pipe on the tree and together they walked inside.

Shyly Lacey turned to look at the back of her dress. She stood in front of the mirror in the ladies department of the Hills and Kemmer store on Main Street in Crossville. The sales clerk smiled her approval. She moved about Lacey puffing the sleeves and adjusting the hem of the light blue dress with the rosebud print. Lacey had seen the dress in the window when John had let her off in front of the store but she had let the clerk show her several others before she had finally asked about it. John had given her three dollars and it was more than she had ever held in real money. She had given Ben fifty cents and sent him off to entertain Daniel Lee while she shopped. Cora had set off in search of quilting thread and batting and she was sure that John had found a place on the courthouse lawn with the rest of the men.

She had taken her time trying on each dress but she had known all along that this was the one. She wondered if she could afford it and was unsure how to ask the sales clerk the price. It amazed her that after Wilder she could have any pride left but she didn't want the moment spoiled by someone looking down on her. Inside she felt as fragile as glass. Even before she had entered the store, she had been nervous about appearing ignorant of the way fine folks behaved. She lifted her arm as though she wanted a better look at the dress, hoping a tag could be seen dangling from the sleeve.

"You know this dress brings out the blue in your eyes," the sales clerk remarked. "And for only a dollar and a quarter it's quite a buy."

Lacey knew she had been caught but was relieved to know that she could afford the dress with money to spare.

"Could I interest you in a pair of shoes to go with that? We have a fine line of ladies pumps for under seventy-five cents."

"Thank you, I'd like that," Lacey said trying not to look down at her one run over pair of shoes cleaned up for the occasion.

"You sit right here, honey. I'll be right back with just the thing."

The woman was being so nice to her; Lacey could have hugged her. The thing she missed most was not having Ruby there to share it all with. She looked at herself in the mirror, smoothing her hands over the soft cloth. Her hands went self-consciously to her long hair, braided and twisted into a bun like an old woman.

"You know with beautiful hair like yours," the sales clerk said coming up behind her and startling her, "you really should try one of the new styles."

"Yes," Lacey stammered, "I've been meaning to, I just haven't had the time what with just moving in and having a small baby and all."

"Oh, are you one of the Cumberland Homesteaders?"

Lacey didn't know what to answer. She wondered how the people of Crossville felt about the Cumberland Homesteads. She wondered if they looked down on the people who were settling there because they had all come from such hard times. She nodded.

"Where you from?"

"We come from Wilder after the mines went down."

"Is that right? I had an uncle from Wilder. Paul Beech. Maybe you know him?"

Lacey shook her head.

"Well, he left there in twenty-five. Of course, you were just a baby yourself, then. Here, honey, slip these on."

Lacey let the woman slip the black pumps onto her feet. They felt stiff and tight after her old ones. When she caught sight of herself in the mirror she had to smile.

"Now, doesn't that look nice," the sales clerk said. "If you'd like to wear it, I'll put your other things into a box."

"I'd like that."

Lacey handed the woman two crumpled bills and waited nervously for her to return. She hoped John would like her choice. She felt guilty enough about taking the money for herself when they needed so much but there was no reasoning with John after he had set his mind to her having a new dress. When the woman returned, Lacey accepted the box with a smile. "I want to thank you for being so kind."

The woman patted Lacey on the shoulder. "Now, don't you think another thing about it. A pretty young thing like you deserves a new dress. By the way, I slipped you in a pair of Hummingbird hosiery."

Lacey couldn't help herself; she reached out and hugged the woman. Tears threatened to spill over her eyes.

"Goodness child. I didn't mean to make you cry. There's a beauty shop right up the street. Why don't you go in there and treat yourself."

Lacey could only smile and wave her thanks as she went out the door. She walked up the street wondering whether to squander any more of her precious money on a new hairdo. The women at the store had been so nice. It was embarrassing to have cried. Lacey couldn't explain why it was so hard having folks be nice to her. It just seemed to bring all her feelings to the top. The woman had said she was a pretty, young thing. It had been a long time since she had felt either. Just this once she might spare the money just to see if she could ever feel that way again.

Lacey walked down the street from the beauty shop catching her reflection in every shop window. She looked like other young girls with her hair just touching her shoulders, falling in waves. It all seemed like a dream, buying a new dress, having her hair cut. It didn't seem possible that things could be going so well for them.

She passed an old man sitting on a bench in the courthouse yard. She smiled a friendly smile. The old man nodded to her but did not return her smile.

"I reckon a woman can afford to dress real nice when they're on the dole," the old man said.

Lacey looked at him unable to take in what he had said. She had been in such a good mood that the chill in the old man's voice was like a dipper of cold well water down her spine. She sidled past the old man, afraid he would speak again.

"You know I got me a little farm. I worked it out myself. Took me forty years and I never got no help from the government."

Lacey walked faster and faster down the sidewalk feeling the old man's stare on her back.

"My wife ain't had no new dress in five year," the old man hissed.

Lacey was almost running when she saw John leaning against Frank Wells's truck. She slowed her walk and tried to catch her breath. The old man's words had shaken her to the core. She had not thought of them as being on the dole. She had not thought that they too were working 'on the relief' as Thomas had said. John was working hard for the money he earned and he would someday pay for the farm they were building. Still, she could tell from the anger in the old man's voice that there were folks who resented the people on the Cumberland Homesteads.

She waved to John. He nodded but she wasn't sure he knew her. When she walked up to him, she saw the flash of recognition.

"Lacey, you've had your hair cut."

"Do you like it?"

"If it's what you like Lacey."

"And my dress, do you like it?" She twirled around to show him.

"It's right pretty."

"Oh, John, I just love it. Thank you. Thank you." She kissed him on the cheek. She could see him puff up with pride and she felt bad that she did not thank him enough.

"I want you to have nice things, Lacey. I mean for you to have everything you want," John said seriously.

"I have what I want, John. I have you and Daniel Lee and the farm."

"That's just a start for us Lacey."

"Well, for now, let's just be happy for all we got," she said taking his arm.

"I like seeing you happy like this. You work too hard."

"Oh, hush John. I do no such thing. Now, I'm not going to let you spoil this for me. I've got twenty-five cents leftover and here comes Ben and Daniel Lee up the street. Let's go up to the drugstore and buy us a great big ice cream cone. Would you do that with me John?"

"Lacey, if you wanted me to wrestle a greased pig on the courthouse lawn, I reckon I'd have to give it a try."

Lacey laughed, delighted by John's attempt at humor. She reached out and squeezed his arm. "We'll do that next Saturday, John. Can't use up all our fun in one day."

"Lacey, Lacey," Ben called trying to run and carry Daniel Lee. The baby laughed as he bounced about in Ben's arms.

"What have my two boys been up to?" Lacey asked taking the baby from Ben and planting a big kiss on his cheek.

"Holy cow Lacey, you look real pretty."

"Why thank you, Ben," she said blushing.

"You won't believe what we done," Ben said excitedly. "They got a pool hall down the street. It's got a big sign on it says 'no minors allowed.' Now, what do you think about that. I told Daniel Lee that coal miners was just as good as anybody else so we went in and walked around a while. Didn't nobody say nothing to us. I reckon that learnt 'em."

John and Lacey looked at each other and burst into laughter.

"That sign don't mean coal miners, Ben," John said gently. "A minor is another word for a youngun."

Ben turned red and hung his head.

Lacey wondered if someone had said anything to Ben like the old man had said to her. "Ben, has anybody ever said anything to you about miners being unwelcome here in Crossville?"

"Well, one of them men over there," Ben said pointing to a group gathered at the street corner, "He called me a project youngun. He just said, there goes one of them project younguns. I didn't say nothing to him but the way he said it weren't good."

"That's all right, Ben. We don't want no fights here if we can help it." John said putting his hand on his shoulder. "But you was right in not wanting folks to put down coal miners. We don't have nothing to be ashamed of."

"That's what I told Daniel Lee," Ben said proudly.

"Ben you done the right thing," Lacey said, sincerely. "Now, let's find Cora and get us a big ice cream cone. How does that sound?"

"Great!"

Lacey decided not to bring up what the old man had said. She didn't want to ruin the day for all of them.

7

The crowd gathered at the project offices, the hot July sun already warming the tops of their heads and making them squint to shield themselves from its powerful glare. Most of the men were in overalls, having just put down their tools and come in from their jobs to await Mrs. Eleanor Roosevelt. She was at that moment with William Macy Stanton, the project architect and other dignitaries on a tour of the Cumberland Homesteads.

Lacey stood off a little way from the crowd with Cora and a few of the women who had come to hear Mrs. Roosevelt speak. She had spent the morning ironing and starching her new dress and Daniel Lee's clothes until they were stiff and shiny. She held Daniel Lee in her arms, still fragrant with the smell of soap and starch and his cheeks aglow with a recent scrubbing. She was proud of the way they looked, but she had to admit the insults the old man had hurled at her from the courthouse yard still haunted her. She had been confused from the beginning as to what the Cumberland Homesteads project was really all about. Some folks made it out to be something special where hardworking, honest people could have a chance to build a new life, but the old man had simply said they were on the dole. That made what they were doing seem like nothing more than a handout from the government. Lacey was hurt and confused by the man's words and the resentment she felt in them.

Daniel Lee squirmed to be let down but she distracted him by pointing to a butterfly lighting on a nearby bush. She could not afford to let him down to get himself dirty after all her careful preparations.

Word was that Mrs. Roosevelt had arrived in her automobile accompanied by two friends. She had motored in from Norris, Tennessee where she had been inspecting the work being done on a planned community there. The community was being built to house the workers constructing

Norris Dam, the first in a series of dams planned by the infant Tennessee Valley Authority to control the Tennessee River and its tributaries. Lacey was amazed that the wife of the President of the United States would take it upon herself to drive around the country to look over the work of common folk when there were all kinds of bosses and supervisors hired for just that thing. The thought made tingles go up Lacey's spine and she had the sense that something grand and hopeful was afoot that she could not fully understand.

A hand on her arm startled Lacey from her thoughts. Ruth Alexander, a Homesteader from Sawmill Road stood smiling at her. Lacey smiled back unsure of herself. Ruth was one of the women on the Homestead who was better educated than most and although she did not flaunt it, Lacey was acutely aware of it. With Ruth was an attractive young woman who looked to be about Lacey's age.

"Lacey Trotter, I'd like to present Miss Millicent Meir," Ruth said to Lacey.

The two women smiled shyly at each other.

"Millicent has come all the way from Washington, D. C. with a group of young people to put on an outdoor drama and to teach music to the children of the community."

"How nice of you to come all this way," Lacey said.

"Oh, it is lovely here. I have really been enjoying myself. I'm collecting folk songs from many of the mountain people. Mrs. Alexander has been taking me around to some of the homes."

"Her father is a very important government official in Washington," Ruth whispered to Lacey. "Lacey, I hope you are planning on coming to the first Women's club meeting at the schoolhouse on Tuesday morning," Ruth said more loudly.

Lacey hadn't realized the meetings would start so soon. She had meant it when she told Cora she would like to meet more of the women but in truth she didn't get out much and rarely without John and the thought made her a little nervous.

"We're all to meet as a large group the first time, but we think later each road will have its own club because of the distance between the houses. You know a lot of the women wouldn't have a way to get to the meetings except walk."

Lacey nodded her understanding. Ruth Alexander was just one of those women who always seemed in charge of whatever was happening. Whenever there was anything going on at the school or for church, Ruth's name was always mentioned.

"Now, you'll be there, won't you?" Ruth asked. "We are counting on the womenfolk turning out for this."

"I had planned on coming," Lacey said shyly, hating herself for her backwardness.

Ruth went on talking about the plans they had already made, hardly stopping to draw a breath. A woman was coming from Berea College to teach them how to use the looms in the new Weave House. She had taken classes there and according to Ruth made beautiful rugs. "You know there is a tremendous revival of handicrafts in this country. We don't want to let this opportunity pass us by, do we?"

Lacey thought that sounded interesting and hoped she was nodding in all the right places, but she was alert to the sounds of an automobile engine. The crowd stirred and people craned their necks. She couldn't help herself as she stood on tiptoes and strained to see past Ruth for signs of Mrs. Roosevelt. Ruth watched her strangely for a moment until she seemed to realize that Lacey was looking at a spot behind her. She turned to see what Lacey was staring at just as the people parted and Mrs. Roosevelt appeared. Ruth suddenly grabbed Millicent's arm and rushed to shake the First Lady's hand and introduce the startled young woman. The boldness of it took Lacey's breath away. She felt sick with excitement just being that near to someone so important.

Mrs. Roosevelt spoke to Mr. Stanton, the project architect, who turned and directed one of the men to bring up one of the flatbed trucks. Mrs. Roosevelt wanted to be able to see the crowd as she addressed them. Lacey watched as the First Lady was helped onto the back of the truck. She could see John standing across the way with a group of men and she wished that she had gone to him before but now it was too late. Ben had long ago slipped away with a friend and was nowhere to be seen, after he had begged to come along with them. Cora stood nearby chatting with her own friends and Lacey could not catch her eye. Lacey stood alone holding Daniel Lee looking up at the President's wife wearing a simple cotton dress with a scarf at the neck. Her hair was pulled back and a few tufts had come loose here and there. She seemed unconcerned, as she looked about the crowd her face friendly and open. Suddenly, her eyes met Lacey's and she smiled down at her. She walked to the edge of the truck bed and reached her arms down toward Lacey. Without thinking, Lacey walked toward her instinctively realizing that she meant for her to hand the boy to her. She watched mesmerized as the First Lady took her child holding him in her arms as she spoke.

"I have just come from a tour of some of this wonderful project and I am much impressed by all that has been accomplished here by hard work and the spirit of cooperation," Mrs. Roosevelt said. "We have set ourselves a grave but hopeful mission in this country and the whole world looks on. We are going to create a new way of life. We are building a back-to-the-land cooperative community in which even the poorest who have come here will have a chance to own your own home, to get a good education, to grow your own food and to live under the principles of cooperation where no one exploits another."

"My tour has shown me what is possible when people work together. I have seen some splendid crops already in the ground on such newly cleared land. I have seen fine stone houses completed or near completion. I do have some concerns about these homes and I have spoken to Mr. Stanton about them. It is my feeling that every home should have indoor plumbing and that the houses should be designed to provide this comfort. Also, I have grave concern about how these homes are to be heated in winter with only one fireplace. These are matters that I have instructed Mr. Stanton to look into."

Lacey could hear a murmur pass through the crowd for they had all talked about that very thing and wondered how they would make it through the severe winters on the Cumberland Plateau with just one fireplace and a cook stove.

Lacey watched Daniel Lee's face for signs of discontent and prayed he would not cry in front of everyone. He seemed perfectly happy perched above the crowd oblivious to the importance of the woman holding him. But Lacey was not and hung on every word Mrs. Roosevelt spoke. She had not until that moment really understood what they had involved themselves in. She had never really felt the importance of what they were doing. They were part of a nationwide movement to rebuild a country. They had been given the opportunity and entrusted with the responsibility to right all of the wrongs of the past and make a place where people could live with dignity and hope.

"Only your hard work," Mrs. Roosevelt was saying, "and determination of spirit will make this great experiment in modern living work. We are here to make a world where this boy," she said holding Daniel Lee up to face the people, "will be given a new beginning. The world is watching."

The gathering applauded with enthusiasm as the First Lady walked over and handed the boy back to Lacey. She bent down and reached to shake Lacey's hand. Shyly Lacey stuck out her hand as Mrs. Roosevelt grasped it firmly and smiled. "I am very proud of you young lady. You and your young family are our hope for a brighter future."

"Thank you ma'am," Lacey whispered, overwhelmed to be singled out for such praise.

The crowd waited until Mrs. Roosevelt had been helped from the truck and led to her waiting automobile before they began to break up. People talked excitedly among themselves and she could tell that Mrs. Roosevelt's kind words and sincere nature had favorably impressed them all. Lacey held Daniel Lee in her arms touching his face and rubbing his arms testing for any outward signs that he had been as changed by the experience as she had been. She became aware of John and Ben and Cora gathered around her. "How long have y'all been standing here?" she asked.

"The whole time just about." Ben said grinning. "You just didn't know it 'cause you never took your eyes off Mrs. Roosevelt."

"I worked my way around as soon as I seen her reaching for Daniel Lee," John said.

Lacey gave John a look she hoped expressed her gratitude that he had wanted to be there next to her during such an important moment.

"Hey, Daniel Lee," Ben said patting the boy on the back. "How'd you like it up there? Was you scared?"

Daniel Lee just grinned and played shyly with a button on his mama's dress.

"If he was he sure made out like he was king of the mountain," Cora said chuckling at her own joke.

"I don't think he thought no more about it than the man in the moon," Ben said going along with Cora.

"We'll just have to tell him about it when he gets older," Cora declared. "Won't we Ben. This is the kinda day a feller ort to remember and tell his younguns about someday. Ain't that right John?"

"I reckon, I can't dispute that Mama. I know I'm not likely to forget it myself. It sure makes a man proud to be part of the Cumberland Homesteads."

"She said, the world was watching," Lacey said still amazed.

"Well then we better do'em proud, hadn't we," John teased.

"I reckon, we better," Lacey said laughing, embarrassed to admit she had taken the speech so much to heart.

"I could do'em a lot prouder after I've had me some dinner." Ben quipped.

They all laughed and John ruffled the boy's hair. "It probably would be easier to make history on a full stomach at that."

Lacey gave Daniel Lee a big hug and kissed him on the cheek. "I can tell I'm going to have to get my boys fed if there's to be another thing done around here."

"Now, Lacey," John appealed, "important folks have to eat too. I heard them say that Mrs. Roosevelt was headed straight out to the Hotel Taylor to take her dinner before heading up to Berea College."

"Wonder why she never asked us along," Cora remarked as though seriously pondering the matter.

"She must've knowed I had a pot a beans already warming on the stove," Lacey said, a grin pulling at the corners of her mouth. "Now, let's get along home and eat them. She's done told us we was the hope of the future and we best start acting like it."

They walked off toward home laughing and joking and reliving the morning. Lacey walked along enjoying the morning more with each retelling and becoming more determined with each step to do her part to make the project work. She did not feel like someone who had been given a handout. She felt like someone special. She felt good about what they were doing, made proud and happy by one woman's words.

8

John stood in the office of William Macy Stanton, the architect for the Cumberland Homesteads. He shifted his weight from one dusty boot to the other and peered nervously out the window. Stanton stood talking to the project manager, F. O. Clark. Outside the offices at number one Grassy Cove Road, men moved about in a constant whirl of activity. Empty trucks replaced trucks loaded with lumber from the nearby steam-powered sawmill and dry kiln where the timber taken from the land was being turned into lumber to be used in construction of the houses. Next to the sawmill men made the thousands of shingles needed to roof the homes. A blacksmith was making latches and hinges for the doors and a window sash shop was making windows.

Stanton and the foreman stood where just the day before Eleanor Roosevelt had spoken. Stanton kept glancing toward the building like they might be discussing him. John had been called in the middle of a workday. He had come immediately, sweaty and smelly from clearing land. He hated to leave because they had just started to clear what he hoped would someday be his farm. The man they had sent to bring him couldn't tell him anything. He wondered if it had anything to do with Mrs. Roosevelt's visit. Maybe she had smiled and congratulated with one hand and taken it all back with the other. He wished Stanton would hurry in and tell him what this was all about. He didn't know if he could handle any bad news, especially news like not getting a farm. He and Lacey were just getting on their feet, just beginning to have a few things.

It had almost taken his breath away seeing her in that new dress, hearing her laugh and looking so happy. Of course, it had been a shock seeing her hair cut off like that. She had never said a word to him about wanting her hair cut off. But then she had never said a word to him about needing a dress. Although, after Cora had brought it up about the dress, he

57

could see he was a fool for not noticing it. He would have been happier though, if Lacey had asked him herself. It hurt him knowing there were things she wanted that he couldn't give her, that she would never ask him for. The thought made him impatient to be back at work. John heard the door handle rattle and looked up to see Mr. Stanton coming toward him arm extended.

"John Trotter, isn't it," he said shaking his hand. "I don't think we have ever met but I am told you are one of the best foremen we have working on the Cumberland Homesteads."

"Thank you, sir. I try," John said surprised at the praise. "My pa just taught me to always give an honest day's work."

"It's my understanding that you succeed admirably. I am sorry to keep you waiting. I just had a few problems to iron out about a project we are about to start. In fact, that's the reason I called you in today. We have in mind to start a trading post. It is to be a grocery and general merchandise store. A cooperative effort, of course, as everything is here on the Homesteads. Approval just came in this morning from Washington. It is to be owned and operated by the people of the Cumberland Homesteads. Each person who wishes to join will pay a fee of five dollars a year. That money will entitle them to vote on the election of officers to run the cooperative. If it is successful, which I fully expect it to be; each member will share in the profits. How does that sound to you?"

"Right good, I reckon," John said still wondering why Stanton was telling him about the trading post.

"We hope to sell a variety of food and dry goods and locally produced crafts and homemade items. Also, the cooperative will allow the people to buy seed and fertilizer at a much lower cost. Here, let me show you the plans for the building."

John watched as Stanton spread the large roll of paper over his desk. He studied the lines on the paper admiring their neatness and precision. He waited for Stanton to speak, curious as to why he was being shown all of this.

"As you can see, it is to be a fair sized facility."

John nodded as Stanton flipped through the white sheets with there hundreds of tiny, precise lines.

Stanton turned to look at John. "I want you to build it."

"Sir, I'm a coal miner," John blurted out. "I've never build nothing bigger than a shed."

Stanton laughed. "I'm not worried about your carpentry skills, John. We have a few good carpenters I can assign to work with you and many of the men can be trained to do the work. It will be an opportunity for the men to learn a new trade."

"But why would you want me, sir?"

"You possess a skill that cannot be so easily taught. You are a leader. The men trust you and will follow you. You believe in what we are trying to do here on the Cumberland Homesteads. This is one of the reasons you were chosen from the many people who applied for a home here."

"I appreciate your kind words."

"Then you will do it."

"I'm not as convinced as you seem to be that I'm the man for the job."

He didn't see himself as a leader. He just tried to give a fair day's work no matter what the job.

"Let's go over these drawings and see if that helps convince you. I would like for work to begin immediately. You see this trading post is part of a plan to give the people a way to make a living right here on the Cumberland Homesteads. It had been thought that some outside industry could be induced to build here but it seems that is not as practical a plan as we had hoped."

John looked at him questioningly.

"The distance to market is too great and freight costs have discouraged those who have shown interest in moving plants here," Stanton said as though that explained everything.

John nodded as though he understood, but the words were only beginning to sink in. Their meaning buzzed around his head like a blow fly.

Stanton leaned back in his chair. "The truth is John, farming was never meant to be the sole form of employment for the people here. The farms were meant to provide a home and a way to sustain the people through hard times should another tragedy strike this land as happened in these past years. You see a day will come, and very soon I am afraid, when much of the work that has occupied the men, will be finished.

The land will be cleared and the homes will be finished. And then how are the men to earn a living?"

John didn't know what to say. His head was reeling, not so much from the words but from their meaning. He had never thought ahead to a day when the houses would be completed and most of the work for which they had been so well paid would end. He had never thought past owning his own farm. That had seemed such a dream; he had believed it to be the answer to everything. He knew that most of the other men had not thought ahead either. They were too fresh from the brink of starvation. For most of them, it was enough to have food in their bellies and change in their pockets. He was ashamed of himself for not seeing things more clearly. He had placed his trust in these people and the government to know what they were doing. Like a man laying track for the railroad, he had kept his head down and worked, trusting that someday the track would lead him to his destination. "I have to ask you this, Mr. Stanton. You can take offense if you're a mind to," John stammered.

"Go ahead. Ask me anything."

"Why did the government locate the project here if it's too far from the freight lines? Why didn't they pick some place closer?"

"The need here was so great. So many people without work and hungry," Stanton said sadly looking out the window. He waved his hand as though to bring himself back. "We are presently employing over fourteen hundred men. Obviously, with only two hundred and fifty houses to be built all of these men do not intend to become farmers and homeowners. With so many men out of work, the government felt compelled to give these men work temporarily. We, you and I, must, however, look ahead to the two hundred and fifty families who will make this place their home. How are these men to earn a living to support their families?"

Stanton went on without waiting for an answer from John who clung to every word from his mouth trying to pull as much meaning from it as possible. "We had hoped to attract industry to this area," Stanton went on as though John had given him the answer he needed. "So far we have been unsuccessful, but we still have hope that this will be possible in the future. In the meantime, the next best thing appears to be to build our own industry through cooperative efforts."

"It was to my way of thinking ... well," John hesitated afraid of revealing his ignorance of what the big plan might be and his growing doubt that there was one.

"You thought we had all the answers."

John nodded.

"John, the men in charge of this project are no different than other men. We don't have all the answers, but we do have many of them and believe in what we are doing. This is a time of great experimentation and study in living. You see we have had to build a guest cottage to house all the many visitors who come to witness first hand this great adventure. We want life here to be an example of the best that a community has to offer its people in education, employment, and medical care. We want the world to see what is possible through cooperation. We are committed to bringing a better way of life to the people here. The president of the United States is committed to bringing a better way of life to this country by creating communities just such as this all over America."

"You mean they's other places like this being built?"

"Oh, yes, several for unemployed miners just like you. We have at this time Westmoreland Homesteads in Pennsylvania and Arthurdale and Tygart Valley Homesteads in West Virginia. I'm a member of the Society of Friends. You might know them as Quakers. We have created many communities such as this one. It has long been our belief that people should remain close to the land. Many of the ills we are now experiencing in this land, we believe, have been brought about by the people leaving the land and moving into cities where they have lost touch with their families and their values. When industry failed them they had nothing to fall back on. We believe this is the way to create a whole new life. What President Roosevelt calls 'a more abundant life.' One of the basic principles of that new life is cooperation."

John didn't know what a Quaker was but he was impressed that Stanton's tone of voice and he had caught the statement about industry failing the people. That was something he had never heard a boss say before. He also knew that Stanton was trying to get him to agree to work on the trading post but there was something very honest and straightforward about the man.

He believed in what he was doing. If anyone could understand that, John could. Besides he never wanted to be caught short again. From now on, he intended to find out more about what was going on. He had promised Lacey a new life and he couldn't afford to take any chances.

"So what do you say, John?"

"When do you want me to start?"

Stanton stood up and shook his hand. "Oh, I think tomorrow morning will be soon enough. Be here around six and we will go over the plan. Pick the men you want and have them report around seven. That should give us time. I will send another man out to manage the men who are left."

John nodded and started to leave. Stanton waved him back.

"While you are here let me show you something I've been working on. Much of this was already done of course," Stanton said pointing to a stack of blueprints. He pulled one from the stack and rolled it out for John to see. "Since Mrs. Roosevelt's visit," Stanton said with a wry smile, "it has become necessary to make a few changes. It seems the First Lady feels that every home should have indoor plumbing. So I have been redesigning the plans to allow a bathroom in each home."

"They're beautiful homes, Mr. Stanton."

"Thank you for saying that son. I believe in using the materials available right here in the area where the homes are being built. That's why all the homes are built of stone and pine. The walls are all masonry, twelve inches thick and the insides have tongue and groove paneling and hardwood floors. All the shingles for the roofs and the paneling for the inside walls have been taken from the very trees that stood on this land and the stone from the quarries. We are wiring them for electricity toward the day when the Tennessee Valley Authority will be providing electricity for the whole area."

"They're mighty fine, sir," John replied honestly. He noticed that Stanton had not brought up the problem of heating the homes with one fireplace but he was not about to mention it. "I never thought I'd live in anything like this."

"It's just a matter of time. You know the credit hour system is an old Quaker way. You work and you put some by and soon you have enough to buy a farm. It is a simple way, don't you think?"

"I reckon it makes good sense."

"I have heard that some of the men complain about this. They want their full wages now. They think it is unfair that we hold back some of their wages, especially those who do not hope to buy a farm."

"I hadn't heard that from any of the men."

"Well, perhaps, it is just a few of the men who are not serious about staying, huh?"

"Yes, sir, I reckon there's always a few that can't stick it out nowhere. As for me, I intend to stay," John said turning to go, embarrassed by what he had revealed.

"Well, it does seem a shame. We are paying a better wage than can be had around here anywhere."

"I think most of the men know that."

"I hope so, John. I'll see you bright and early in the morning."

"Yes sir I'll be here."

"Oh, and John, I thank you."

John nodded and went out into the bright sunshine. The light hit his eyes like an explosion and made his head ache. He shielded his eyes with his hand while he massaged his forehead. It was well into the afternoon and he had not eaten his dinner. The thought of eating made his stomach jump and his throat constrict. His clothes had dried on him and they felt scratchy against his skin. He couldn't figure out why he felt so bad unless he had gotten a touch too much sun. He would just go by and tell the men what was up. They were surely wondering what had become of him. It was sure enough strange, Stanton calling him in like that. There had to be half a dozen men on the Homesteads better at carpentry than him. He couldn't figure it. Stanton had said he was a good leader but it didn't seem to take anything special. The men were mostly hard workers, some better than others. Why had he told him all that stuff about credit hours and how some folks didn't like it? It wasn't like a boss to say that much to a worker. Besides it just wasn't his way to take note of other folks complaining and he wouldn't go telling it anyway. It was just the way of some folks to be vexed about one thing or another all the time. He could see now where he had been wrong not to find out more about what was going on. He couldn't believe he had been so ignorant as to not think ahead to how he was to make a living and pay for the farm he dreamed of owning. Now, it seemed he could think of nothing else. It was a sure thing that everybody couldn't work at one trading post. What if they never could get a factory to come in there, he wondered. If there was something astir that could upset the working of things, he was smart to find out about it. And it made sense to stay close to the people running the project for the same reason. He was about half-mad at himself for his own ignorance and it made his head throb. He would just have to try harder to make everything work out. He just didn't know if he had it in him to see one more thing fail.

___ 9 ___

Ataxicab was parked outside the cigar store with its motor running. Coy crossed the street and came up behind it slowly. He shot a sidelong glance into the store and caught sight of the same young blond woman who had been in the store a few weeks before. He had come in and found Chick and the woman talking. The woman had looked up startled. Her eyes were the palest blue without a fleck of another color and they caught his for just a second before she pushed past him without a word. Her expensive, tailored knit blouse and skirt could not hide the one thing that marred her flight. He noticed that she walked with a slight limp, one foot turning inward.

When he had looked to Chick for an explanation of just who she might be, he had simply said, "She was looking for somebody. I couldn't help her." Coy had let it go.

Some time later, Chick had given him three hundred dollars to help pay for the auction house. "Where did you get three hundred dollars?"

"I've been saving it out of my wages. You pay all the rent and food. I don't have any need for money. So I thought I would give it to you for the auction house and to pay you back for all you've done."

"I ain't even paid you three hundred dollars in all the time you've been here. Where'd you get this money?"

"I came by it honestly, if that's what you mean. Now, do you want it or not?"

"I want it. And thanks," Coy said tucking the money into his pants pocket. He hadn't meant to tell Chick about Lacey or any of it, but he had come back from his run in with Will, his nerves like an open sore, frantic to get the money for the auction house. Only he was short a few hundred dollars having enough to buy the place outright. Without warning, he had spilled it all to Chick about why he needed the money so badly. He had told him about Lacey and about his year of spying on the Coal Company. "So you see the way I got so good at poker was from playing with the gun thugs the company hired to guard the mines," Coy had told him with a chuckle.

"Wasn't that dangerous?" Chick had asked his voice a whisper.

Coy admitted he had done it to impress Lacey.

"And did it?" Chick had asked.

"Not enough, I reckon. Lacey ended up marrying the man her folks had picked out for her." It had surprised him when he finished the telling to see Chick staring at him a frown cutting across his forehead. "Hey, buddy, it's not as bad as all that," he had said taking him by the shoulders. "I have to admit it does sound right pitiful in the telling," he had said laughing to break the tension. "I just wasn't respectable enough. If I'd a been killed adoing it, now that might of been another thing. Might of raised me in her sights just enough." Coy had grinned big to let Chick know it was a joke but there had been more than a little truth in what he said.

Coy suddenly realized he was still staring through the window of the store. He watched as Chick turned away from the woman. She continued to talk excitedly to his back. Her gestures were almost pleading. Coy walked around the cab, leaned up against it and began without any great hurry to take out a cigarette. He tapped it twice against the cab roof. "Wouldn't happen to have a match would you, buddy?"

"Sure," the driver said taking a book of matches from his shirt pocket. Instead of handing the matches to Coy, the driver took out a cigarette, and struck the match, lighting first Coy's and then his own.

"Thanks, I was going to go in that cigar store and get a match but there seems to be a woman in there real upset over something."

The cab driver cocked his head toward the store. "Oh, her? Yeah, she's been in there a long time. It's nothing to me as long as she don't mind paying the fare."

"You know her?"

"Nah. I've brought her here before."

"Seems strange don't it, a woman coming to a place like this."

The cab driver shrugged. "You see all kinds of stuff in this business."

"Where'd you pick her up?"

The cab driver looked at him. "Why do you ask?"

Coy took a draw on his cigarette and leaned his head back scanning the sky with a bored expression. He looked down at the cab driver and shrugged, "No reason."

"Corner of Houser and Wingate."

Coy whistled. "Nice neighborhood."

"Ain't no cab drivers living in that neighborhood. I can tell you that," the driver said chuckling at his own joke.

Coy grinned and nodded his head in agreement. He threw his cigarette on the street and ground it out with his heel. And no cigar store owners either, he thought to himself. "Thanks for the light. Think I'll wander in and see what a girl like that finds so interesting about the place."

"Don't tell her I told you nothing. I mean about where I picked her up or nothing."

"Hey, we was just having a friendly smoke," Coy said slapping the roof of the cab with the flat of his hand. He sauntered off toward the store. When he opened the door, Chick and the girl looked up like startled deer caught in a gun sight. Coy advanced on them before they could move and took the young woman by the hand. She was much younger up close than Coy remembered, maybe no more than twenty. With her thick blond curls and pale eyes like lights shining from under her lashes, she should have been beautiful, but she was merely pretty. It was almost as if she had willed it. She held herself with a guarded dignity.

"Afternoon ma'am, I'm Coy Lynn Wilson. I believe I've seen you in here before."

"I... .,"she stammered taken off guard by Coy's boldness. She looked at Chick for help.

Chick gave her a resigned look. "Coy, this is my sister Susan."

The news caught Coy by such surprise that he first looked at Chick and then at Susan unable to take it in.

"Yes, Mr. Wilson," Susan spoke looking Coy in the eye with a knowing grin, "my brother is the better looking one."

"I wasn't thinking that at all, Miss Holt. It is Miss Holt?"

She nodded.

"I was just wondering how Chick could have kept such a beautiful creature as yourself a secret all these months."

She shot him a look that said she was on to him. "Keeping secrets was Chick's idea, Mr. Wilson."

"Call me Coy."

"And you may call me Susan," she said slipping her hand from his. "I appreciate what you have done for Chick. His family has been worried sick about him."

"You are my family, Susan. You have been worried sick," Chick snapped.

"I meant your father and me."

Chick looked at her through narrow slits and turned away from her to busy himself stocking cigars on the shelves behind the counter.

"I am trying to convince Chick to return home."

She had a deep, even voice without a hint of guile. Coy had long been aware of his affect on women and had become accustomed to using his charms on them, sometimes for sport. If she noticed his good looks, Susan gave no sign. "And where might home be?"

"Well, here in Anderson. Westover Heights."

Coy looked at Chick's back. "When I found you in that coal chute, I thought you had been on a freight train for weeks, cold and hungry. I didn't know you took a cab from Westover Heights."

"I didn't take a cab. I walked," he said grinning

Coy started to laugh. Chick joined him. They slapped each other on the back enjoying the joke. Susan stood watching them, hands on hips.

"Your father knows where you are," Susan said.

Chick reacted like he'd been slapped. "It doesn't matter, he can't make me come home. "

"You know that isn't true, Chick. He can do what ever he pleases. Hasn't he proven that enough times to you?"

"Are you on his side now?"

"I'm on your side, Chick. I've always been on your side. It isn't fair of you to say that."

"I know, sis. I'm sorry. It's just that things were going so well here. Coy lets me run the store and well. . . ."

"I know Chick. Father knows all about what you have been doing here and he knows all about Mr. Wilson. Coy."

"Wait a minute, who the hell is this father," Coy spoke up.

"Ever heard of Leib and Holt?" Chick asked as though that explained everything.

And it did. Leib and Holt owned most of Anderson. They probably even owned most of the block on which Coy's store stood. No longer than Coy had been in Anderson he had already learned that Leib and Holt had their financial fingers in every pie in town. Coy whistled a long slow whistle.

"Only there is no Leib. He died years ago. Father owns it all now. And he wants me to take it over and run things when he's gone."

Chick sounded disgusted at the prospect. "That does sound tough, son. Inheriting all that money could put a strain on a man. I wouldn't know cause if any kin of mine ever had two nickels to rub together they managed to piss it away before they made anything out of it. Pardon me, ma'am," he said, bowing to Susan.

She surprised him by laughing a sudden deep laugh. A look crossed her face that he thought he recognized. He reached out impulsively and touched her shoulder. She pulled away slowly allowing his hand to hang in the air a second before he lowered it to his side. "I must be going, now. I'll be back, Chick.," Susan said awkwardly. She turned to face Coy. "It was nice to meet you, Coy. And again, thank you for all you have done for Chick."

"Come back and visit with us anytime, Susan," he said smiling his most winning smile. "We don't get many visits from respectable young ladies. Most of our visitors, it seems, find respectability, at least after hours, an intolerable burden." He took her by the elbow with the intention of walking her to the door.

"That isn't necessary," she said without pity.

He could tell he had hurt her and that she accepted that as just the way things would always be for her. "Just thought I could steal another minute with you," he whispered close to her ear. "You know we don't get this kind of excitement in here every day."

She looked at him her eyes wide and unblinking. They looked him over, checked him out and gave nothing back of what she thought. As he watched her get into the cab and drive away without glancing his way he thought he probably wouldn't be seeing much of Susan Holt.

Susan took up her poker hand and studied it with less than a poker face. She chewed on the inside of her cheek and frowned at her cards. Serious by nature, she took to cards like a general going to battle. Every hand was a life and death matter. And yet she seemed to enjoy it. At first Coy had let her win but she had soon learned enough to catch on to him. She had been furious with him and insisted that he play fair.

He had been wrong about her coming back. She had been back the next week and every week after that for the last month. Even Chick had grown accustomed to her visits and had begun to relax. She had stopped trying to convince him to come home. The three of them mostly spend long afternoons playing poker, drinking whiskey and talking. The talk was most often about Chick, what he had been like as a little boy, the mischievous things he had done. They never mentioned the father again. Nor, did Susan talk much about herself unless it had to do with Chick. It reminded Coy of Lacey and the way she was with Ben.

After a time, Chick grew tired of them and left them to their talk and their cards. It was only when Chick was gone that Susan seemed to relax a little, to let down her guard. Coy wondered if it was the birthright of every older sister to forever watch over baby brothers and for them to never know their good fortune. "Where's your poker face tonight, Susan. You're sitting over there trying to bluff me with a pair of deuces."

Susan looked up. Surprise showed on her face. "Damn you, Coy," she said throwing down her cards.

"You forget, I'm the one who has been teaching you to play."

"So you think I'm a long way from sitting in on your Friday night games?"

"Well, you've picked up the drinking and the swearing right nicely but I'd hold off on any heavy betting for a while."

She laughed her deep throaty laugh. She never sounded happy, just amused. Refilling her drink from the bottle on the table, she wandered over to the window and gazed down at the street. "You know my father probably owns a dozen places like this."

"So I hear."

"You've been asking around about him, haven't you?"

"Turn about, you know."

"And what have you learned?"

Coy had wasted no time in checking out Sam Holt but what he had discovered had surprised even him. "That your father owns property here and in most of the towns around here. That he runs a construction company that pretty much controls what is built in this town. That he's a man who is known for getting his way."

"I think you have it all just about right, especially the last part."

"He wants Chick back. Is that why he sends you here?"

"He doesn't send me, but he doesn't care that I come as long as there is a chance I can convince the prodigal son to come home."

"Why would you want to?" Coy said casually. He couldn't help but think about what it might be like to be begged and cajoled to accept that kind of offer. He couldn't even be in the same room with Susan without thinking about how close he was to real wealth. He might have felt guilty about his occasional thought of marrying Susan for her money except for one thing. Susan seemed to be unaffected by him. She seemed not to notice his good looks or his attempts to be charming.

"Because the best revenge would be to see Chick end up with it all," Susan said her voice rising with emotion. "Then if he wanted to give it all away, he could. I've tried to tell him that."

"He doesn't buy it," Coy said with a wry grin. Coy certainly did not buy the idea that Susan would stand by and let a hotheaded young boy give away a fortune. He had caught the word revenge and heard the edge in Susan's voice. He was beginning to get a glimpse of the force that drove her.

She pressed her lips to her glass but didn't drink. Finally, she spoke almost to herself. "My father has made a great deal of money in the last few years buying up property that others, shall we say, lost during hard times."

"Is that what Chick has against him?"

"That is part of it. Chick feels that our father would sell his children's souls to the devil for a nickel and that we should in turn be willing to do that to our children someday."

"What about your father's soul?"

"That was taken care of some years ago when he allowed our mother to die trying to produce him a son and heir."

"He had you."

"A girl and flawed at that," she said laughing a mirthless laugh. "Like you haven't noticed."

Coy tried not to show that he had noticed. The pain wrapped up in a casual remark stung him. "And you don't hate Chick for all of this."

"Chick is the only person including my mother who has ever loved me."

She said it without pity, without any emotion. The cold reason of it gave Coy a chill. It explained a lot about Susan Holt. He came up behind her and put his hands on her arms. She seemed not to notice. She didn't turn around but continued to stare out the window. "You know there are worse things than selling your soul to the devil. There are plenty of people who'd do it to get what they want."

She turned and looked him in the eye. And he knew he was right. They were that much alike. They both wanted something so badly they would sell their souls to the devil to get it. "The trouble is," he said cupping her chin in his hand, "the devil just ain't buying."

10

Susan sat at the formal dining table opposite her father. She was the perfect hostess, charming and attractive no matter how boring the guest or how late the hour. On her right, sat Horace Fields and his wife. Horace was President of the local bank and an old friend of her father's. Dexter Fields, his son, sat on her left with his recent fiancée, Jenny. Susan had been instructed to invite them all to dinner. It was her father's way of pointing out to her the opportunity she had missed in passing up Dexter Fields as a husband. She and Dexter had been thrown together since childhood as potential mates. Just last year, Susan had turned down a proposal of marriage presented to her like a business contract by the ever anemic and weak willed Dexter. Being practical businessmen, both fathers had seen their children's marriage as a great merger of money and good business sense. Susan had not been surprised by her father's rage upon learning that she had turned down the hapless Dexter.

She had not done it deliberately to enrage her father. Her motives had been more selfish than that. She had always dreamed of marrying someone she loved. She pictured that love lighting up the dark corners of her life and filling up the lonely spaces. It was a dream she was not quite ready to give up.

Unexpectedly, Coy's face flashed in her mind as it did so often of late. She had never known anyone so handsome. She liked to watch him when he wasn't looking. His cheekbones seemed chiseled like the woodcarvings he so loved. His eyes were dark like a starless night. They revealed none of the dangers that lay ahead. He could look so frightening and sullen one minute and then light up the room the next minute with his smile, so like summer lightning. He could be shamelessly charming. Then at times, he seemed genuinely interested in her. Most of all, he could do what very few people had ever done. He could make her laugh.

Since that first time she had run into Coy at the store, she had found every pretense she could think of to go back. At first she pretended she was going to check on her brother, but she knew that was only part of it.

Susan smiled sweetly as Jenny droned on about the lovely china she had received from her grandmother. Dexter looked at Jenny adoringly. Although there had never been anything romantic between Susan and Dexter, she wondered if it might have been more practical if she had given in and married him. Of course, that was the reason her father had made her arrange this little get together. He wanted her to know what she was giving up. He wanted her to know it was not too late to arrange a marriage if she would come to her senses.

She looked down at the other end of the table. Her father was watching her like a cat watches a mouse. He was keeping his paw on her while pretending disinterest. She thought about what her father had said when he learned she had turned Dexter down.

"What kind of man do you expect is going to want you?" he had thundered. "Do you really think you can afford to turn down the only decent offer you've had? And if it weren't for my money you wouldn't have that," he had screamed, his face bulging.

"I don't love him," she had said defiantly.

He had looked her squarely in the face, his eyes full of mean determination to have his way. "Love is a luxury you can't afford."

She had almost cracked at that moment and given in. The thought crossed her mind that if she married Dexter and produced a perfect, healthy grandson, she might still win his love. She shuddered at her own insipid weakness.

"Tell me, Dexter," Sam Holt spoke in his booming voice, "What do you intend to do after your marriage to the lovely Jenny?" Sam took Jenny's hand in his and patted it affectionately.

Susan sipped her wine and watched her father's performance. Sam Holt was not a tall man but he was solid. He had not been born into money, but had gotten his wealth by marrying Susan's mother. He had polished up nicely, but he still retained a few of the hard edges of his poor background. He did not like to be reminded of his background. Although it was true that he had been able to turn the small fortune his wife had brought to their marriage into a much larger fortune, he still preferred that people thought of him as coming from old money.

"I'll be going into the banking business," Dexter said sheepishly.

Susan knew that meant Horace would be taking Dexter into the family business.

"What about that son of yours, Sam?" Horace asked agreeably. "What's he up to these days?"

Susan smiled to herself. Sam had never told anyone about his troubles with Chick. She knew his children were an embarrassment to him. He hated anything he could not control.

"He's staying in New York with some old family friends. I felt he needed to get a wider view of the world. New York is a fine place to get it. And he's in good hands, isn't he Susan?"

Sam looked at her, but he did not wait for an answer. He knew that she was keeping an eye on Chick.

"He'll probably be there the rest the year." Sam lied convincingly.

Susan knew that Sam had not tossed that remark out casually. She knew that by the end of the year, Sam planned on having Chick home. He would have figured out a way to force the boy home.

Sam didn't give Horace time to question him further. He turned quickly to Jenny and asked, "Where will the two of you be living?"

"Mr. and Mrs. Fields have purchased a home for us on the very street where they live," Jenny said proudly, looking at her future in-laws with awe.

"That's to guarantee we will be close to our grandchildren," Horace said.

Sam gave Susan a withering look and drained his wine glass. Susan met his gaze and stopped short of lifting her glass in a toast.

"Susan," Horace said taking her hand in his and patting it gently. "When are we going to get to celebrate your engagement?"

Susan blushed. How she hated that question. It was the favorite question of her father's friends. Horace had been equally upset by her refusal to marry Dexter. Jenny's father was not as rich as Sam was. He owned a small business in Indianapolis.

"I can't see Susan marrying any time soon," her father spoke up, "She's too strong-willed for any sensible man."

I get the message, Susan thought. He hated being defied on anything. The thing he enjoyed most was being treated with respect. She knew he wasn't interested in her happiness and even if she married Dexter it would not change his feelings about her. She suddenly thought of Coy and wondered what her father would think of him. Coy came from the very background Sam had struggled so hard to leave behind. Her father would not like that. Still they had a lot of traits in common. Coy was bold and daring like her father. He seemed to know no fear or to follow any rules. If she married him, she thought, allowing herself to think such a thing for the first time, she would be marrying a rake. But it would show her father she could find someone who wanted to marry her; someone wildly handsome and physically perfect. Coy and her father would have more in common than they might know. They would both have married for money and they would both have the power to destroy her.

11

Trouble had been gathering like a storm cloud almost from the day John had left Macy Stanton's office six months before. When Stanton had asked him if folks were complaining about the credit hour system, it had taken him by surprise, but he had soon learned that it was a bone of contention with a growing number of the Homesteaders.

He was on his way now to the schoolhouse for a meeting to discuss the credit hour system. Thomas Jefferson Morgan followed him like an energetic puppy nipping at his heels.

"John," he argued, "you have to see where folks would want their money now. How do they know they'll ever get it?"

"What makes them think they won't?"

"Years of living, I reckon," Thomas said with a grin.

"You're a fine one to talk. You're still wet behind the ears."

"I'm young, but I know one thing. I don't want no farm. I grew up farming and it's a mean way to make a living."

"Then why did you come here?" John asked impatiently, anger churning in his gut.

"Now, John. Ain't no sense in getting mad. I done told you before that I come here to get what I could get. I come here to learn a trade and move on. If I had wanted to be a dirt farmer, I could of stayed home."

"That's a selfish attitude and the reason we're having the kind of trouble here that we're having," John snapped.

"I reckon you're right," Thomas said agreeably, unruffled by John's remark. "But that don't change nothing. My daddy always wanted to be a teacher. He's got books stacked in every corner of that farmhouse. He never got the chance because he had to take over and help his pa out from the time he was a boy. He ended up marrying and having a passel of younguns. He taught us like we was his classroom, but he never got the chance to do it for real. I don't intend to let that happen to me.

And I'm not the only one. The truth is there's plenty of people here that don't take to this place like it was their religion."

"All they asked of us when we come here was to cooperate."

"I ain't saying that's asking too much of folks, but Jesus couldn't get all the disciples to cooperate and they was just twelve of them."

John had to laugh despite himself. He really should have been mad at Thomas, but the boy had such a way about him. He was just irrepressibly honest and John liked that. "You don't have much faith this place will work out do you, Thomas?"

"I ain't studied philosophy and like you said I'm still wet behind the ears, but these folks ain't used to cooperating with nobody."

He smiled at John when he said it because they both knew that John was the same age as Thomas. John was embarrassed to think that he had been treating Thomas like a boy. At the same time, he felt ages older than his twenty-two years.

"The way I look at it," Thomas went on, "the government is expecting an awful lot of folks. On top of that, they don't have a lot of understanding as to how folks think."

"Why do you say that?" John asked.

"The government has got a lot of big ideas about what the Cumberland Homesteads is supposed to be. Now as I see it, they got them ideas from a vision. Roosevelt and his New Deal men was sitting around a table when the angels come down and showed them what life would be like if everybody had a fine place to live, a good education, a decent job and they all got along. Sounds perfect don't it?"

John nodded, trying to follow where Thomas was leading.

"You know what's wrong with a vision, John?"

John shook his head.

"It's hard for other folks to picture 'cause they never seen it. And no matter how much you describe it to them, they ain't never going to see the whole picture the way you seen it. It's just like Noah building that ark. You might lend him a hand, but it don't mean you really believe it's going to rain. And what's more, by the time it does rain, you done talked yourself out of believing that thing would float anyway."

"Well, it seems you are a philosopher after all, Thomas," John said, although he really did not want to see the wisdom in what Thomas was saying. He needed for the folks on the Cumberland Homesteads to cooperate. He felt that anyone who did not like the way things were going should just leave.

"I guess I get it natural from my daddy."

"But even if folks don't understand all that's going on, and I'll be the first to admit I don't, can't folks just trust that somebody does?"

"Now that's the second mistake the government is making. They're trying to take a bunch of folks that's been bruised and battered and taken advantage of since they was born and ask them to follow some 'ideology' to the promise land. The only ideology these folks trust is the bird in hand."

"You think I'm a fool for putting my trust in this project?"

"I think you're a fine man, John. I wish I could be more like you. But you're a man looking hard for them angels."

"You think I need to lower my sights a bit."

Thomas opened the schoolhouse door and the noise of angry voices was like a beehive. "I don't know, but I don't see no angels in here today, John."

John nodded and went in ahead of Thomas. The room was warm and stuffy from the crowd of sweaty bodies. The discussion was already in full swing as John worked his way along the wall and stood beside where Clyde Reid and Lon Carver were seated. Thomas edged up beside him. Dooley Parsons, from Deep Draw Road, was speaking to the crowd.

"I got me a big family and I can't hardly feed them on a third of my pay."

The crowd roared their approval mumbling among themselves. Some people shouted their agreement. Other people watched in silence. John could not believe Dooley. Before he came to the Homestead he had been out of work for over a year. John wondered how he had fed his family on nothing. At least now he had a paycheck coming in.

Leon Hubert stood up at the front of the room waving a group of papers. "I've got ten letters here written to Washington, D. C. in the last four months telling them how we feel about this credit hour business. I have gotten word back that they are looking into the matter."

"What does that mean, they're looking in to it?" someone yelled from the back.

"It means they're taking your name down and they're going to kick you out for speaking up," Dooley shouted.

John was shocked to hear that Dooley was so suspicious. "Dooley, I don't reckon they'd kick you out for asking questions," John said.

The crowd turned and looked at John with curiosity. Clyde Reid repositioned his fat body on the hard wooden bench never taking his gaze off John. "John, you got some kind of contract with these people the rest of us don't have. I don't remember ever signing no contract that says I'm guaranteed one of these farms."

The room exploded with hooting and shouting. John looked at Clyde and he could not hide his amazement. Clyde was a notorious good-for-nothing who never intended to own a farm and wouldn't work it if he had one. He could tell though that what Clyde had said had struck a nerve with the people there. "The government has kept its promise so far," John reasoned out loud in his straightforward way. "We've been paid for what work we have done and the other money has been credited toward some time in the future when the farms are built."

"You are a trusting sort, ain't you John?" Willie Smith, a wiry little man, yelled from a-top a stool. "The way I hear it, they can't make head or tails of who is to get what. What if they was to come back in two or three years and tell you didn't have no credit-hours due you."

"That ain't going to happen to John," Dooley spoke up. "John's got hisself in tight with them important folks that runs this project. You won't get him to say nothing against them. Ain't that right John?"

John could see some of the people looking around the room as confused by the anger and suspicion in the room as he was. He could almost see the room splitting into sides like the Red Sea parting. "When there's something needs to be said, Dooley, I reckon I'll be the first to say it. And I make a habit of speaking for myself." He looked around the room defiantly, but his heart sank at the hostility he felt in the room. "They are paying us a fair wage. The truth is, if we got our full wage, we would be making better than most folks would around here. I can't see where that would set well with a lot of people, especially with work still hard to get."

"Well, it's easy to see what side you are on John Trotter," Leon said vehemently.

"I didn't come here to take sides, Leon," John said truthfully. "I didn't come to the Cumberland Homesteads to take sides. I come here hoping I would never have to take sides again. I see now, where I might have been hoping against hope."

With that remark, John walked out, leaving the crowd to do what they wanted. He could see now where they would anyway. Thomas was right. He had been straining hard to see the angels, but it was obvious to him now that it was going to take more than a vision to make this project work.

Clyde Reid stood up from his work and stopped him as he headed across the yard to Stanton's office at number one Grassy Cove Road.

"John, I wouldn't go in there, just yet."

"How's that, Clyde," he asked.

Clyde leaned his generous body back into his overalls with an air of self-importance and announced, "There's some right important fellers in there from Washington, D. C."

"When ain't they been? Seems like they pour in here in a constant stream."

"That's the truth for sure." Clyde chuckled and looked at Lon Carver who was still stooped over the flagstone sidewalk they had been working on. Lon did not stop but looked up nodding and smiling. Lon was as wiry as Clyde was stout. His sun-parched face held a perpetual toothless smile. He was what John's pa called 'a worker'. No job seemed too dirty or difficult to force the smile from his face or a complaint from his lips. John could not look at him without hearing his pa's voice saying, "Now, that man's a worker."

"Me and Lon heard 'em talking," Clyde said, Lon nodding in the background.

John knew he was about to hear every move the men had made since they got off the train in Crossville. Clyde was just one of those people who knew everybody's business. Even in a tight little place like the Homesteads where folks were so close they felt obliged to whip other folks children for mischief, Clyde still ranked among the best for nosing out news. He could go into a store to buy a sack of tobacco and come out knowing everybody's credit history and how good the owner was at collecting his debts. John even had to watch himself to keep Clyde from worming stuff out of him. He knew that after the credit-hour meeting Clyde was especially eager for a juicy tidbit. He knew whatever he told would get passed on a hundred times. "Talking were they?" John said casually scuffing the ground with his shoe.

"Yep. Stood in the yard for a while, like me and Lon was trees. So we just listened," he said laughing. "It's all about this credit-hour business."

John's ears picked up but he kept his face a blank. He took out his pipe and made a show of packing it with tobacco. He rarely smoked except after meals but felt the need to keep his hands busy so Clyde wouldn't see how anxious he was to hear his story. "I'm not surprised they sent somebody in here after that meeting last month." John had since heard that the credit-hour system was causing problems in the other projects too. It was amazing to John that it could get people so upset. It just seemed like a practical thing to him.

"That was the beatinest thing. Folks was riled all right. How come it don't seem to bother you none?"

"Folks do seem to have a problem with it," John said trying to sound unconcerned, ignoring Clyde's last remark. John was not about to be goaded into anything. He had made his position known at the meeting.

"Well, John. Now I'm a little short on book-larnin' but when one of them big Washington payroll boys quits 'cause he can't make heads nor tails of it, I'd say it's time to call them dogs in from the hunt."

"Is that what you heard?"

"That's what they was asayin'. They said it was too complicated for anybody to keep up with. From what me and Lon heared, they come down here to see if it made any more sense from down here. One of them fellers is from Labor Relations and the other......" Clyde looked over at Lon. "What was that othern's title?" he asked. Lon smiled but said nothing. "Oh yeah, Comptroller General. With names like that you'd think they could figure out any mess. What we hear is they're about to declare the whole thing against the law."

"Against the law?" John asked surprised.

"Makes sense. Can't nobody say it's right to hold back a man's wages that he done earned. Don't you agree?"

"I've heard it said, often enough," John hedged. He could see where it would not mean much to Clyde one way or another since he never intended to buy a farm. He was just there while the easy money lasted. Farm work would never set well with a man as lazy as Clyde, John thought. Besides, work interfered with Clyde's natural talent for gossip. And as for Lon, he would just do the work and take whatever came his way. John was more concerned with the ill will it had caused in the community. Folks were confused and afraid about what was to become of their money. Having important men down from Washington to look things over was a good sign, he guessed, but it was sure to stir up more worry among the Homesteaders. If they declared the credit-hour system illegal that meant a change would be coming but what was it to be, he wondered. He was anxious to have the whole matter settled, as he knew everyone else was. "How long they been in there?" John inquired.

"Most of the morning. They'll be wanting their dinner before long."

Lon nodded vigorously in agreement, his tongue working over his gums.

"I'm with you Lon," Clyde answered. "I've about worked me up an appetite on this here flagstone. We was up at daybreak fetching this rock from outta the quarry and toting it all the way over here on a flatbed truck. Then we was up near an hour unloading it, weren't we, Lon?"

Lon nodded, his tongue stretched over the corner of his mouth as he strained to lift a huge stone into place.

"Hold on there, Lon and I'll give you a hand," Clyde said, making no effort to move.

John held back a grin as Clyde took out his handkerchief and wiped his bone-dry brow. He had not turned his hand to any work in the last half-hour while John had been standing there.

Just then the door to the house opened and Stanton came out followed by two men dressed in suits. They headed toward an automobile parked some twenty yards from the house.

Stanton looked up and recognized John. He signaled to him
with a wave of his hand.

"John come over here. There's some men here I'd like you
to meet."

John tucked his pipe into his pocket nodded to Clyde and
Lon and headed toward Stanton. He hated that Stanton had
picked that moment to single him out. By not coming out
against the credit-hour system, he knew he had somehow come
out as taking sides with the government and against some of
the people. He hadn't meant for it to be that way. As he looked
back he could see Clyde taking it all in and he knew he would
be fodder for the next story.

12

Lacey stepped out into the bright afternoon sun with Daniel Lee on her hip and the feed bucket in her hand. It was unusually warm for the middle of January. They had had a few chilly days but now it had turned off as pretty as a spring day. It couldn't last. Her granny had called such a day a weather breeder. "They's something fierce a brewing, mark my word," she always prophesied. She believed that bad things often followed on the tail of something good. Lacey had to agree that she was most often right about that. "But not always, huh Daniel Lee? Not so often as to let it spoil our day thinking about it."

Daniel Lee grinned and put his hand on Lacey's mouth.

"I know what you're a wanting. You want mama to make that sound." Daniel Lee patted his hand against Lacey's mouth. "Wa, wa, wa, wa wa. . . You know as much as I want Ben to get the schooling I never got, wa, wa, wa, wa, I do declare, they's times like this, wa, wa, wa, wa, I wish he was here to play with you. He's the one showed you this game. Besides I thought the way it worked was you got to make the wa, wa, wa, wa." She pulled away from his hand and goosed him under the chin with her mouth. Daniel Lee tucked his head into his arm and giggled.

Lacey thought about how much Ben would love to be there too. He had thrown a fit the day she had told him he would be expected to attend school like the rest of the children on the Homesteads. "School is for younguns. Besides I done forgot what I knowed," he declared. Lacey had stifled a laugh then but she had had to stand her ground every morning since then as Ben huffed and stomped about the barn before heading off to school. Finally, she had convinced him if he ever wanted to do more than carry water to the men who built those bridges he loved so much, he would have to get an education. She thought of all the times that she had been kept home to do the wash when she would dearly have loved to go to school. Her ma had needed her at home and her pa had never believed in much schooling even for the boys. Even now she was sorely aware of her lack of schooling. She meant to see to it that Ben and Daniel Lee had the chance she never got. They had built a fine building on Deep Draw Road to hold school in until they could get the regular schoolhouse built. They were sending the high school age children on to Crossville.

They had started a night school for adults and Thomas had already signed up. She had come to like Thomas and she appreciated the way he took advantage of every opportunity offered to him. He was urging her to sign up for night school. She kept the thought in the back of her mind, but she felt too busy with the farm and all her community activities to take on anything else.

The Women's Clubs had really taken off and Lacey attended as often as she could. She felt it was important to do her part. They had all been given study booklets on the meaning of a cooperate community and they picked different chapters for their meetings. They were always having folks in to talk about interesting things like personal grooming and Red Cross safety and even poetry. There was a feeling of excitement among the women that they were making their contribution to the community with each new thing they learned. Lacey was beginning to make friends with many of the women. Mrs. Marie Ervin, the Home Demonstration Agent had quickly become beloved by all. Last month she had shown them how to make bound buttonholes. Lacey thought how proud she had been when she had done as the lady said and her dress had won first place. She had won a Colgate Toilet Set donated by the Homestead Trading Post. She had clipped the article from the Crossville Chronicle where it said her name to send to Ruby. The Cumberland Homesteads had its own section of the paper now. Ruby would think that was fine.

She thought about Ruby as she went about her day. In her mind she was always collecting things to tell her when she got around to writing a letter. She always tried to make it sound especially good so when Ruby read it to her folks they would know she was doing well. She knew too that in the back of her mind, she was thinking that if word ever got back to Coy, she would want him to think things had worked out real well for her.

As they neared the chicken coop, Daniel Lee squirmed in her arms to be let down. He was just learning to walk and insisted on trying his new-found skill whenever he could. His chubby legs still wobbled under him and he had to cling to his mama's finger to steady himself. Lacey opened the gate and fastened it behind them before she put him down. He held on to the side of the feed bucket. The chickens began to cluck in anticipation. Lacey threw out a few handfuls of corn and mash. Daniel Lee held out his hand, squeezing his fingers together in imitation. His tiny legs gave under his weight and he plopped to the ground on his bottom. Two bantam hens scrambled to his side darting their heads back and forth. "Look, Daniel Lee, its Fern and Fannie Mae." Daniel Lee clapped his hands together causing the chickens to flap their wings and scatter. Lacey spread some food nearby and the hens quickly returned. Daniel Lee reached into the bucket and grabbed a handful of the mash. "Throw it, baby. Like this, throw it," Lacey said. Daniel Lee threw out his arm but kept his fist closed. Lacey laughed and opened his fist to release the tiny bit of feed. The hens climbed over his legs to get at the food. She stroked their soft feathers. It was amazing to her how attached she had become to them. John had gotten a dozen Plymouth Rock hens and a rooster when they were only chicks from a man who came by the Trading Post selling them. They had had to keep them in their crates in the barn for two weeks while John built a chicken coop for them. He had built a pole for them to roost on and boxes to line the back wall for the hens to build their nest and lay their eggs. The two bantam hens and a rooster had been a gift from a neighbor. Their runty size and speckled feathers had set them apart early on from the rest of the brood. Lacey thought the two hens acted like nosy, old maid aunts in matching sweaters the way they were forever pecking and squawking around. The two hens flapped about competing with each other for attention. It might be silly of her but she thought she could just naturally have feelings for anything that showed any signs of needing her. Ben had promised to make her a purple martin birdhouse out of the gourds Cora had grown to put near the chicken coop. Purple martins were known to keep

away the hawks that tried to eat the chickens. They would
chase them away and fight them if it came to it.

Fern jumped into her lap and she petted her head just like
a dog. Fannie Mae squawked a loud complaint and strutted
about making her feelings known. Lacey laughed and picked
up a handful of mash from the bucket and fed it to her from her
palm. "Course we don't have to tell nobody that we're keeping
chickens as pets, do we Daniel Lee?" she whispered, sharing
her secret with him. "Some folks might not understand."

Daniel Lee gave her a serious look, his finger stuck in the
corner of his mouth. Lacey bent and kissed the top of his head.
She loved him like the morning sunrise, she thought, but how
could she ever tell him that. "Now, I better get you up off this
cold ground before your Granny Cora has a conniption. Let's
you and me walk down to the mailbox and see if the mail
carrier has been by yet."

She latched the gate behind them and left the bucket by the
fence. As they passed the house, she could hear hammering
from inside. She waved to the men working. She often times
took them coffee and fried apple pies to eat in the afternoons.
John had wanted to be the one to work on the house but ever
since he had started work on the Trading Post he had been too
tied up with that. After the building was finished, he had been
elected to the board of the Cumberland Homesteads
Cooperative. It seemed to take up nearly all of his time and
then when he was home he dwelled on it. Lacey didn't know
why he worried so. Even he had to admit the Trading Post was
doing real well. Most of the Homesteaders were buying their
goods from there and in the spring most likely everybody
would buy their seed and fertilizer through the coop.

Homer Hancock waved to her from a rafter. He was in
charge of the construction crew. "Howdy, little gal. That
youngun sure is a growin'. He's purt nigh to carryin' his
mama," he yelled in his deep voice. It was the same thing he
said every time he saw them even if it was twice a day. He was
a big, dark bear of a man who barked orders at the men and
was quick to catch them in any mistake. It touched her, the
pride he took in what would be her home.

"It won't be long, Mister Hancock. He's a fretting to be let
down to walk now."

Homer laughed his booming laugh. "He's sure 'nough a fine'an."

"Thank ya, Mister Hancock."

In the two months they had been at work, they had completed the stone walls and had begun putting up rafters for the roof. She came up most evenings with John after the men had left to examine each new stone and touch each new board that had been added. At the rate they were going Lacey was sure they would be in by spring. It took her breath away every time that thought came to her. They had gone to the big "Moving in" day celebration for the first ten people to move into their new homes. It had been a big to-do on December first with important people there from Washington, D. C. coming down to speak. Mr. Charles E. Pynchon, the general manager of the Federal Subsistence Homestead program, had been sent personally by the President. He praised the Homesteaders for their hard work and said they had found "acres of diamonds" in the project. One man from out of the State Capitol had said, "You people are on top of the world." Lacey thought that was probably the truth.

Lacey reached the mailbox just as Mr. Jennings the carrier pulled up. "Afternoon, Mr. Jennings. Ain't this pretty weather we're having?"

"Young lady," he said tipping his head. "I reckon we couldn't ask for better. They say the woolly worms was wearing heavy coats this fall. That could mean we're in for a bad winter."

"Sure enough there's worse to come. That's why me and Daniel Lee is out enjoying it while we can."

"That youngun's growing like a weed." He handed her two letters. "Something from your folks in Indiana."

"I appreciate it, Mr. Jennings."

"Looks like one there from Monterey too."

"I reckon that would be for Cora," Lacey said.

"And how is Cora... and the rest of the family?"

Mr. Jennings always asked after Cora. Lacey knew he was a widower. The day Lacey had told Cora she thought he might be interested, her mother-in-law had alternately laughed and pshawed all afternoon. "What in tarnation would he want with an old, dried up thing like me," she had said but Lacey could tell she was pleased. Cora was only forty. Lacey had reminded her that plenty of women her age had remarried. It had been common in a mining camp for a woman to have more than one husband what with mining accidents and all. John's pa had been killed in a mining accident. Cora was lucky she had John to look after her. "We are all just as fine as spring rain, Mr. Jennings," Lacey answered. "Cora's up at the Mattress house working today. I'll tell her you asked after her."

"That woman is a worker for sure."

Lacey nodded as Mr. Jennings drove on waving out the window to her. She had to agree Cora was not one to shy away from hard work. As soon as she had found out the Mattress house had opened she had high-tailed it up there. For every three mattresses she made, she could claim one for her own family. Cora was determined to get one for everyone in the household.

Lacey looked at the letter addressed to Cora and tucked it into her apron pocket. The other letter was from Ruby. She couldn't wait until she got to the barn and got Daniel Lee down for a nap to read the letter. She tore into it and started to read, trying to take in the whole letter at once, she felt so hungry for news. Ben came up behind her and goosed her in the sides before she knew anyone was around. She screamed out loud, causing Daniel Lee and Ben to laugh. "Ben, I swear you scared me. I didn't know there was a soul around." She wadded the letter she had been reading and crammed it into her pocket before Ben could get a look at it. Ben took Daniel Lee from her arms.

"Sorry Lacey, but you ain't hard to scare. Was you daydreaming again?"

"Now, Ben. Don't you turn off like your brother Will. He was forever tormenting me about that."

"Hey Lacey, I didn't mean nothing by it."

"Well, never mind. I never meant to snap at you. How was school today?"

"You know what?" he said chucking the baby under the chin.

"I reckon not."

"Our teacher is from Columbus, Ohio. That's up north. She showed it to us on this big map that hangs on the wall. She says they got places up there called college where a person can go to school right on forever if you're a mind to."

"Well, ain't that something. What did you think of that?"

"I thought it was a good thing we don't live in Ohio or you'd have me a going to school 'til I was a hundred and five years old."

Lacey smiled and kissed his cheek against his will. "I always told you to count your blessings."

"Yeah, but that's usually when you're about to make me do something I don't want to do."

"You know I'd just bet you if I was to check in to it there might be a college right here in Tennessee. Did you ask your teacher about that?"

"No, and you ain't agoing to neither. I got all the schooling I can handle right now."

"Well, I expect it can wait."

"You never even asked me what book I got for you from the bookmobile. That's always the first thing you ask."

"Sorry Ben. I clean forgot the bookmobile was coming today. Here let me see." Ben turned his back to her and Lacey took the book from the waistband of his pants where he had stuck it. She had been thrilled the first time Ben had told her about the bookmobile that brought books around to the school that anyone could take to read. It had opened a whole new world to her and although her reading was still a bit slow, she awaited each new book with excitement. If it had not been for the letter in her pocket, she would have asked about the book first thing. But now, she could only think of the letter and the news it had brought.

They walked on up the road to the barn with the warm afternoon sun on their backs and Ben chattering on about what he had learned in school that day.

Lacey slipped out the front door and eased it to behind her. The full moon made the night look like twilight. She worked her way across the yard careful not to wake the chickens as she passed the henhouse. It had taken everything in her to hold herself together through supper. Cora had been a-buzz with her day, all the folks she had seen and the gossip she had heard. John had been in good spirits because the Trading Post was showing a profit. Their talk had been a drone in her ears growing louder and louder until she was sure her head would explode from it. When everyone had finally gone to bed, she

had lain there for hours unable to believe what she had read in
the letter. As she neared the house, she pulled Ruby's letter
from her pocket, held it against her chest and straightened it
with her hand. The night air was chilly but that meant nothing
to her now. She stumbled over a stack of stone and caught
herself, bruising her hand on a sharp edge. She felt her way
along one wall and slipped down to rest next to it. The cold bit
into her shoulder blades and she relished the release the pain
gave her.

It was too dark to read the letter in the moonlight but there
was no need. Every word was still alive in her head. It had
been since the moment that she had first read the letter. When
Ben had surprised her like that, it had taken all the courage she
could muster to act as though nothing had happened. The letter,
tucked away in her apron pocket, had been like a wild animal
clawing at her clothes working its way into her skin. She was
thankful, at least, that Ben had taken no notice of it. She had
given Cora her letter and made no mention of the other one.

Now, as she sat alone in the dark with the letter pressed
against her the words came back to her like blows.

Dear Lacey:
I reckon you know we are all doing fine so I'll get right
to the big news. You won't believe what has happened as none
of us do neither. Of course, Will always said you could never
go predicting what Coy Lynn Wilson would do and you know
he's knowed him a long time. Well, the thing is he's done gone
and got hisself married. And that ain't the half of it. She's rich
to boot. I cut her picture out of the paper for you to see. Ain't
that the finest dress you ever seen. It weren't even her wedding
dress neither. The way Will tells it they run off and didn't tell
nobody till it was done. Her pa like to died him being rich and
all and probably expecting her to marry somebody had a lot of
money. Ain't that a caution. The whole town ain't talked of
nothing else for a month. I can't see that bothering Coy, can
you?

The letter had gone on for several pages but Lacey couldn't
bring herself to finish it. She had never made it past the part
about Coy. Married, the word made her head reel. Inside the
envelope was the folded piece of newspaper Ruby had sent.

Slowly she opened it. The woman was sitting in a beautiful chair next to a fireplace. She wore a dress with soft folds that went all the way to the floor. It was fine just as Ruby had said. It was the most beautiful thing Lacey had ever seen. The woman was fair and blond and beautiful. She could see why Coy would want to marry her. Her skin would not be chapped and weathered from working outside. Her hands would not be rough and scaly from doing the wash on a rub board. She would be educated. She forced herself to look at Coy. He stood beside his bride, dark and handsome in a suit as fashionable as the woman's dress. They were being honored at a reception given by the bride's father, Mr. Sam Holt, a prominent Anderson businessman the paper said. The bride was the former Susannah Elizabeth Holt known to her friends as Susan. Lacey put the clipping back into the envelope. Her tears made the moonlight a prism of color. She rested the back of her head against a stone and watched as the colors danced.

The truth of all the past months swept over her. She should be happy that Coy was married. It meant that he would not be back for her. In all the months since she had sent Coy away, she had prayed every day that he would not return as he had promised. But it had not been because she did not love him. It had been because she was afraid that she would not be strong enough to face him again. She had never wanted John or Ben or especially Daniel Lee to suffer for her sins and weaknesses. But always in that very private part of her that she had kept the knowledge, quietly where it couldn't hurt anyone, that she still loved Coy. No matter what sacrifices she had made, she would always have that. Now, it seemed a cruel joke. Coy had once called her a fool for the sacrifices she made. It seemed now as she sat alone in the cold, night air, that he had known her only too well. She could almost hear him laughing at her. She must look foolish to him now, a skinny little mountain girl in a cotton dress. From out of her pocket she pulled the clipping of how she had won first prize for the best bound buttonholes at the women's club meeting. How proud she had been. She tore it into a dozen pieces. She clasped the pieces in her fist, crushed them into her eyes, and sobbed great aching sobs. So much of her life had been spent inside herself alone and hurting.

It was for the best, she told herself. Now Coy would never be back. She was free to get on with making a new life for herself and her son. Still, she sat until dawn crying into the night until there was nothing left. If the night creatures took note of her, they made no sign. She dug a hole next to the house and buried the letter and all the little pieces of paper, along with the clipping of Coy and his bride. With it she buried her feelings for Coy a little deeper inside herself. She could bear the pain. Now, at last, she could be free of the fear that Coy might return to destroy her world. She could put to rest her growing fear that Coy might come back and discover the son he didn't know existed.

As she turned to go, a distant sound like a train whistle caught her ear. She knew it was impossible. It must have been a bird. Still, the chill lodged in her spine and she strained to hear it again. Just her mind playing tricks, she thought. Then she walked to the barn to start breakfast for John and the rest of the family, stopping only once to glance back over her shoulder.

13

"Softly and tenderly Jesus is calling, calling for you and for me," John sang, firmly gripping the hymnbook and staring straight ahead. He had never been comfortable about singing in church. Even praying in church seemed too public for him. Lacey had not shown much sympathy for his point of view. She had the tub full of bathwater when he got up that morning. When he had started to complain, she had shamed him into silence with her talk about all they had to be grateful for. The thing about a woman was she could always see to it that a man made it to church.

He glanced over at Ben in his white shirt and suit jacket and they exchanged looks. Prisoners being forced to sing for their noon meal, he thought. Lacey looked at him and smiled. He felt guilty for his thoughts and smiled back knowing she could read his feelings on his face. She had on the prettiest little hat with flowers on one side and a dress she had made herself. She was a good hand to sew and had done herself proud many times at those women's club meetings. He knew it was her nature to be shy and once when it had been her turn to give the devotional at a club meeting she had fretted over it for a week reading it over and over again in front of the mirror. Still she had gone out of her way to get to know folks in the community and become a part of things.

There didn't seem to be much she was not a good hand at, if she put her mind to it. And she had put her mind to most everything with a vengeance since he had first known her. Of course, he could tell she much preferred to be outside to anything else. It was May and her cheeks had burned rosy with the early spring sun. She was a sight to behold out in the garden wearing Ben's overalls, a straw hat and brogan shoes. It sounded crazy but she could just as well take a man's breath away then. They had borrowed a team of mules to plow the garden and she and Ben together had not been big enough to turn them. He had warned her against working so hard especially now with the baby coming but there was no holding her back. She might cut back while he was around, but as soon as he was out the door to work, she was back pulling and tugging to things, down on her hands and knees in the garden. He knew that much about her.

He knew enough to know he was a lucky man to have her. They had had plenty of relatives to come through during the winter. Distant cousins on both sides that had heard they were fairing better than most. There was still many a man out there without work. Lacey had made mats on the floor for them, cooked and cleaned and fed them without complaint. At times he knew it wore her thin. She always said she couldn't stand to see anybody go hungry.

The preacher was giving the final benediction. They were meeting in the temporary schoolhouse on Deep Draw Road for church services. Mostly they had visiting ministers. There had been talk, Lacey had told him, that some folks weren't happy with having just the one church. They were used to going to the Baptist or the Methodist or the Church of Christ and they wanted their own preacher. The government wasn't in favor of folks splitting off to form their own churches. They thought it kept the community together if they went to the same church. They might be meeting in the same place but it seemed to John that stirring them up all together like that wasn't setting well with some folks.

"And let us ask for a special blessing," the preacher prayed, "for the Trotter family who will be moving into their new home on Grassy Cove Road tomorrow. May their home always be blessed with love and happiness, Amen."

As they filed out of the church, almost everyone stopped to shake hands and congratulate them on the completion of their new home. Some of the families stopping by were still waiting for their homes to be started. John tried to offer them words of encouragement. Lacey stood in the yard encircled by women making over Daniel Lee and chatting excitedly. He had to admire the way she had made friends with most everyone on the Homesteads in the short time they had been there.

He'd gotten to know folks mostly through his work at the Trading Post. He was pleased about how well the store had done. The board had even managed to pay a dividend after six months. It worried him that there was still no sign of any industry moving in. There was no way the store could employ all the men that would need jobs when all the construction was finished.

It seemed to him that the government should have been pretty willing at that point to listen to any suggestion they might have as to what could be done. So far the government had told them no to every suggestion. At the idea that they outright pay some industry to come in there, the government had declared it was illegal. When they'd talked about the government owning a factory, Congress had said it was unfair competition. John wondered just who they thought they'd be competing with if there were industry to be found. It was a mystery to him what they could be thinking. And now in the middle of everything, the government had gone and moved them to another department. Somewhere up in Washington D. C. they had been moved from the Subsistence Homestead Program to the Resettlement Administration. He didn't think that most folks on the Homesteads knew the difference one way or the other. A few months back he wouldn't have either if he had not made a point not to be caught short again. He couldn't be sure what it meant to be moved to another department but it worried him just the same. They had sent a man named R. G. Tugwell down from Washington to look the place over and right after that they had been moved to another department. Word was it had been taken away from a man named Harold Ickes who had been critical to the President about the way things were being run because the cost was getting out of hand.

They had been promised that no changes would be made because of the move but already there was talk of increasing the acreage for each farm. Without any available industry, the government was beginning to look at the possibility of selling some of the crops the farmers were growing. It seemed a local Congressman by the name of J. Ridley Mitchell had pushed to have the acreage increased because he had been a farmer for years and he felt that no farmer could make a living on such small amount of land as had been allotted. There was talk that it would be pushed to up to a hundred acres on a farm. John wondered how any of them could afford such a farm.

John had heard rumors that another project up in Arthurdale, West Virginia was also having trouble attracting industry. To make matters worse, they had made a lot of expensive blunders that were showing up in the newspapers and making people angry. Arthurdale was the first of the Homestead projects and it seemed the government had been in a big hurry to get it going. Mrs. Roosevelt had visited the area and had come back to urge the President to bring some relief to the area as quickly as possible. In the fall of 1933 the government had ordered fifty prefabricated cottages for Arthurdale. When the houses were delivered, they had turned out to be designed for summer vacationing on Cape Cod and not for temperatures in the winters of West Virginia that often got below 32 degrees. An architect had been called in to redesign the houses and when he had finished, they had cost two to three times what it would have cost to build them from the foundation up. It was more than any of the Homesteaders could afford to pay. Mrs. Roosevelt had promised the Homesteaders they would not have to pay for the mistakes that had been made. This had made a lot of folks angry and from then on the newspapers had called Arthurdale, "Mrs. Roosevelt's project." John felt like anything bad that happened on one project shed a bad light on the others.

He looked out across the yard to see Jack and Norma Percy waving to him. Jack motioned with his head for John to come over. He eased himself out of the crowd and walked to where they stood. Three of the Percy's five children played noisily nearby with a group of other children. Norma held a baby in her arms. Another child not much older held tightly to her legs. Jack stood nervously clutching his hat. "Jack, how ya doing?" John asked. "Norma."

Norma smiled.

"We're doing real good John," Jack said looking at Norma.

"Good to hear it. Gettin' your fields worked yet?"

"Got the taters in."

"Well, that's a right smart."

"Planted 'em by the full moon. Norma's ma wouldn't hear of nothing but I was to plant by the signs. I never did take no stock in planting by the signs, but you got to keep peace in the family," he said shaking his head.

"If it don't never take more'n that to keep the peace, you're doing all right," John commented.

Jack nodded with a grin. "Yeah, if you go to plant something and it ain't by the right sign, Norma's ma can tell you a dozen stories about how somebody planted taters under a quarter moon when they was suppose to plant'em under a full moon and they didn't grow nothing but little hard rocks with a lot of vine."

John couldn't help but chuckle with a quick look at Norma out of the corner of his eye.

Norma looked at them both like they were naughty children but then she laughed too. "Ma can sure give you a piece of her mind."

"Just wait till we go to hog killing around here. That woman has a world of words to say on that subject."

"Well, you can never tell. Folks that's lived close to the land knows about these things. If it didn't have some truth in it, it wouldn't have been handed down through the years like it has been."

"That's what I told, Jack," Norma spoke up. "It speaks of the signs in the Bible, you know."

"Between the good book and your mama, I reckon a man don't stand a chance," Jack said.

"Good Heavens, Jack. There you go blaspheming," Norma said giving Jack a hard punch on the arm.

Jack just laughed and rubbed his arm. "Say, John," Jack said getting suddenly serious.

John waited for Jack to go on but nothing came. "You got something you need to tell me Jack?"

"It's like this, John," Jack said glancing at Norma who urged him on with her eyes. "Me and Norma was Baptist before we come here. And you and Lacey has been good friends to us."

Jack struggled to find the words. John realized what he was trying to say and wanted to help him but didn't quite know how to go about it. He looked away to give him time to work it out.

"The thing is, they's a bunch of folks that is going to start meeting together," Jack stammered. "You know Baptist."

"Yeah, I heard some folks was thinking about starting their own church," John spoke up. "I couldn't hold that against nobody. I reckon, a man has a right to believe what he wants to."

"That's right," Jack broke in excitedly. "I knowed you'd feel that way. You see me and Norma was going to start meeting with them folks and we didn't want you and Lacey to think bad of us."

"Why would I do that?"

"Like we thought we was too good to go to church with everybody else. It ain't that way, you know."

"I know Jack. I know you and Norma ain't that way."

"Well, we just wanted you to know."

"I appreciate it Jack. Don't you think nothing else of it. A man's got a right to go to church where he wants," he lied, wondering if he did under the circumstances.

"And if you and Lacey ever want to come join us, you're welcome," Norma said warmly.

"Thank ya, Norma. I'll tell Lacey. I reckon, we're right happy where we are for now," John said smiling.

Norma nodded. She called in her flock of children and gathered them around her like a mother hen. They headed off down the road toward home with Jack looking back twice at John to see if he was still smiling.

"What were Jack and Norma saying," Lacey asked coming up beside him, Daniel Lee asleep in her arms.

John slipped the limp body out of her arms and over his shoulder. "They wanted to tell me they were leaving to form their own church. They were afraid we would feel slighted."

"Norma said Jack was afraid you'd think he was working against things here. He knows how much you believe in this project. He just didn't want to do anything that would upset you."

In some ways, that was exactly how John did feel. He thought that if folks couldn't go to church together it was a sign that they couldn't hold together on other things. "You knew about it."

"Of course, Norma told me weeks ago," Lacey said matter-of-factly. "It just took Jack a while to work up his nerve to tell you."

"What do you think about it?"

"That's the way folks are. You can't come between folks and their religion."

"That's what I told Jack."

"Good. I'm proud of you," she said patting his arm. "It ain't worth losing good friends over. We're all in this together."

John nodded in agreement. "That was why I held my tongue with Jack. But, I'm thinking if we was really all in this together, they could have stuck with the church," he said lost in his thoughts. It made him angry that people could so quickly forget their part in the deal in coming to the Cumberland Homesteads.

Lacey looked at him, her brow knotted in worry. "John, you can't expect people to give in on everything."

"Everything," he shouted. "They won't hardly give on nothing. Getting folks to cooperate is worse than teaching a mule to walk in its traces."

"That's because people are not mules." she cautioned.

He could tell he had disturbed her by his reaction. "I reckon, you're right about that," he said to appease her.

"Now, I guess we better be getting home and get some dinner on the table. Mitch Jennings is coming to eat with us."

He frowned at Lacey but she wouldn't look at him. Ever since Jennings had started calling on Cora, he'd been showing up at their Sunday dinner table nearly every week. John liked him well enough, but it was hard watching your own mother court. Sometimes it was downright silly up close. He knew better than to say anything about his feelings to Lacey. She thought the whole thing was sweeter than honey.

The only good he could see had come of it was that Mitch played about the finest fiddle he had ever heard. He had made it himself when he was just a young man from white spruce and curly maple. He had learned it from his pa. After dinner, he'd pull it out and play and it was a soothing sound. It made John envious that a man could have such a way to ease his mind. Mitch had seen him watching and he had offered to teach him to play. The thought had left him flustered. What seemed perfectly all right for some folks seemed like whimsy when he thought of doing it himself. Still, now and again, he was tempted.

"Thomas will be bringing Millicent," Lacey added.

"That little gal that come down from up North to teach music?" John asked surprised. "I thought her pa wouldn't let her come back after he found out she was courting a mountain man."

"Thomas said she told her pa it was over between them."

John could only feel that the way of most folks was beyond him. Most days now, he felt like he was trying to tie up sand with a rope. He just shook his head and they headed home.

"Out of the way, everybody, we're acoming through." Jack shouted as he and John huffed and grunted their way up the steps with the cookstove between them.

"Put that over there." Lacey said like they were carrying a box of feathers.

John tried to look at her like he was mad, but she stood hands on hips, full of self-importance and completely failed to notice his glare. She had been ordering the men around all morning as they moved the bedsteads, mattresses and other household goods over from the barn. He was pretty sure by now that Ben was hiding out in his new room upstairs to avoid Lacey with her broom and dustpan. John grunted as he and Jack eased the stove into place.

"Here, let me sweep under there first, John," Lacey cried.

John leaned on the stove and looked at Jack. They both started to laugh. Lacey looked at them like they were crazy. "Lacey, honey, you've swept ever square inch of this place three times. Why don't you sit down and rest a minute while I hook this flue up."

"If he was to spill a dab of soot, I'll be sure to let you know Lacey," Jack said seriously.

"Jack, now don't you go teasing me. You know I just want things to look nice," Lacey laughed good-naturedly.

"Don't you let them menfolk give you a hard time Lacey," Norma chimed in. "I was the same way when we moved into our house. A woman just has a certain way she wants things to be. Course with five younguns, it ain't easy to keep things that way."

"You know if it was up to the menfolk they would just move the furniture right in on top of the dirt and never know the difference."

John busied himself attaching the pipe to the hole in the chimney and made no reply. He was having trouble fitting it through the opening. "Here Jack, you push on this pipe while

I get under it and see if I can lift it up a little." John got under the flue to get a better look at where it might be sticking. Just as John yelled push, Jack rammed the pipe through the hole with all his might, popping it loose from an elbow joint. Soot shot out all over John covering his face and hands with the black powder. He came up spitting and wiping his eyes. Lacey, Norma and Jack stood staring at him with their mouths open. He was sure Lacey was about to say something about what a mess he had made in her kitchen but he was wrong. Instead she started to laugh and that set the other two off. Cora and Ben came in to see what all the commotion was about.

"What's going on in here?" Cora yelled.

Jack looked at Lacey. "Lacey I reckon we done spilled some soot."

That was enough to send them all into peals of laughter.

"John, you look like a 'possum caught in a lantern light."

"Thank you mama," John replied drolly.

"Come here John and let me wash you off," Lacey said leading him to the sink. "It'll give us a chance to try out this running water." Lacey filled the sink with water and gently washed his face and hands.

"I'll clean this mess up," Norma said. "Jack, you get outta my way. You've helped enough for now."

"I'll slice up some of this bologna and cheese for dinner," Cora said still chuckling to herself. "We don't have time to get this cookstove to working and fix nothing hot."

"Now there, you're as good as new," Lacey said smiling as she scrubbed the last black smudges from John's face. "We might as well rest a while and have some dinner."

"I'm as hungry as a man that's chopped wood all day," John said patting his stomach.

"Me too," Ben said coming from behind the door face where he had been hiding out.

"Well, let's get at it," Cora called.

They sat down to the kitchen table and ate their cold lunch with relish. Daniel Lee sat on the floor crumbling crackers on the new linoleum. Lacey washed out the sink while the others ate. John watched as she lovingly cleaned every inch of it until it sparkled. They had neither one ever had running water or a sink in their lives. It was a pleasure to watch Lacey enjoying it. She looked up to catch him watching and blushed. He grinned knowingly at her. It was worth anything he had to do to be able to give this house and farm to Lacey. "Lacey, you better eat something," was all he could say.

"Who you got watching the younguns today Norma?" Cora asked.

"Ma's there."

"How's she doing?"

"Doing right well. Better since she got used to the place."

"It don't worry you none, leaving them little'uns with her and her near about blind?"

"I figure she's raised a passel of younguns. I always heard folks say they had done something so many times they could do it blindfolded. I reckon it couldn't be much difference than that."

"Her mind still good, is it?"

"Clear as a bell. You'd as well not try to catch her in nothing 'cause if she says something she's more'n likely right about it."

"She speaks her mind about it too," Jack spoke up his mouth full of crackers.

"She's frisky as a new born colt." Norma bragged. "They go after one another," she said tossing her head toward Jack, "but they don't mean nothing by it. It's just their way."

"She's a big help to you, I reckon, with all them younguns," Cora said.

"I couldn't do it without her. She's a fine'un all right."

Cora looked up at Lacey who realized she had been lost in thought listening to Norma talk about her mother. Cora had become to her what she had always longed for her own mother to be. Lacey sat down next to her at the table and patted her hand shyly. Cora smiled back and gave her hand a squeeze.

The men ate in silence as the women talked on about family matters. Lacey had barely sat down and began nibbling on a bite of cheese when she announced it was time to get back to work.

"First you two come in here," Cora said jumping up. "I want to show you something." She led them to the room off the hall that was to be their bedroom. Jack, Norma and Ben with Daniel Lee on his hip tagged along behind. Cora threw open the door. Lacey and John's bed had been made up with the double wedding ring quilt Cora had given them when they married. The pillow cases were new and had tatted lace around the edges. On the windows were freshly starched curtains hand-embroidered with flowers to match the headboard. On the floor was a small braided rug.

Lacey sucked in her breath and tears sprang to her eyes. "Oh Cora! It's the most beautiful room I ever seen. When did you make all of this?"

"Do you really like it?" Cora asked proudly. "I made the curtains and the rug and Norma made the pillow cases."

Lacey hugged them both. "Thank you both so much. It's all so beautiful."

Norma blushed at the praise. "Oh honey, it ain't much."

"Norma, where did you get the pattern for this tatting?" Cora asked.

"Law me. Cora I don't remember. My grandmother used to tat all the time and I just picked it up from her."

The men backed out of the room and left the women to discuss the finer points of needlework. They took straight back chairs from the kitchen and eased their way out onto the front porch for a smoke. The women's voices carried through the open windows. John thought it was a sweet sound on this wonderful day. He packed his pipe and leaned his chair back against the stone wall. They smoked in silence enjoying the warm sun and the fresh spring air. Ben played with Daniel Lee in the front yard.

"Makes a man proud, don't it," Jack spoke up.

John nodded. A year ago he could never have dreamed that he would be living in a stone house on a farm that would someday belong to him. It was all so new to him; he lived in fear of losing it all.

"It ain't been that long since we was near about starving to death. I mean my younguns was hungry," Jack said without further explanation knowing John would understand that that was the worst thing a man could endure.

"Now we're making a good wage and we got a chance to at least grow some food. At least we won't go hungry."

"Speaking of wages, I hear they're going to do away with credit-hours."

"That's what I'm a hearing. It went all the way to Congress. They've decided it ain't legal to hold back a man's wages no how."

"I'm relieved myself."

"What do you mean?" John asked surprised.

"You know they could just as well have decided to keep it as not. We don't have no contract. For all we got to say about it, they could keep the money and the farm. We was told early on that only folks that prove to be satisfactory, could stay on permanently. They've watched might near every move we've made since we got here, telling us when to go and when to come and every step in between and we still don't know if we match up to what they're looking for. Sometimes I don't think they know what they're looking for."

John couldn't disagree with Jack. Sometimes even he felt like the government was trying to melt the folks down and mold them into something completely different. John was just surprised by how deep Jack's suspicions ran and how the credit-hour system had come to represent something so menacing. "I just thought it was a way of making folks more saving. They're paying us a fair wage. This is the first time some of these folks have ever had cash money. I never had nothing but scrip until I come here. I don't think folks will be as saving if they get all cash money."

"Well, that's their choice, or it ought to be. The government shouldn't have a right to tell a man what he ought to spend and what he ought to save. We should be getting a big chunk of money. I want mine now, thank you all the same. I'd of thought you'd felt the same way. You're mighty trusting for a man that went through what you done in Wilder. I didn't see you buddying up to the government then."

"I ain't buddying up now," John said feeling himself grow angry at what Jack was implying. It was one thing to hear Dooley Parsons accuse him of being on the side of the government, but he had expected more from Jack.

"Some of the men think you've gone over to the other side the way you've been hanging around the big bugs."

It was an indication to John of just how bad things were getting when the government was seen as one side and the people as another. "I'm just on the Board," John snapped. "I'm there to represent the people."

"Some of the men think you get the good jobs because of who you know."

"What men?"

"Union men. Men that worked in the mines and the mills."

"You, Jack?"

"I think you're wanting this place so bad has you wearing blinders. You ain't clear to the dangers. I've been in them mills in Harriman. I've had everything took away from me and I don't want that to happen again. We don't even have us a contract on these farms, no guarantee of no kind."

"I know what you're saying Jack. I could be a damn fool. I've been one before." He said it as a joke but he knew the words had more than a little truth in them.

Jack laughed and then quickly turned serious. "You can't never tell with the government. They're like company men. They got the power. They can do what they like. They've never even told us what these farms are going to cost us. You think it ain't cost them a pretty penny to build these fine stone homes and clear every stump and log off of ten thousand acres? Don't you think they'll be wanting something back for that? We ain't got no union to speak for us. Of all the people, I'd a thought you could see that. You was a big union man."

"I still am," John said holding back his anger. "Are there many men feel the way you do?"

"They's aright smart. We've been tossed around a might here. We've been told one thing and then another. Mostly, we're being told and not asked. Folks get tired of that."

John nodded but didn't say anything. There was truth in what Jack was saying. With each passing month, the government had taken more and more decision-making power away from the people. In the beginning, the local board had had almost total freedom to make decisions about the project. Both the government and the people had made a lot of expensive mistakes. The projects were costing too much. The government was demanding tighter controls.

They smoked in silence each one lost in his thoughts. Finally, John knocked out his pipe on the porch post. "I reckon we better get back in there before the womenfolk have any more time to think up chores for us to do." As they stood, he put his hand on Jack's back to show there were no hard feelings but he thought that maybe too many folks wanted a guarantee up front that they wouldn't have to suffer again like they had. It was strange to him how a starving man couldn't think of anything but getting his belly full and then as soon as he did, he could think of a thousand other things he needed before life was worth living.

He could see too where it might look like to some that he had gone over to the other side. He had been so busy trying to hold on to what he had, he hadn't given much thought to how working at the Trading Post and being on the board might look to other folks. Just having something in life could leave a man always working to hold on to it. Still and all, he hated to hear there were more unhappy folks.

With the sunset, the spring night had cooled. John noticed that the breeze raised goose bumps on Lacey's arms as they sat on the front porch watching the night. "You want to go in?"

"Huh un."

The rest of the family had gone to bed early after a hard day of moving in. John had watched as Lacey continued to tidy up for another hour after everyone else had quit. She rubbed down the pine paneling with a cloth, dusted the mantel and finally sat cross-legged on the hardwood floor in the living room where they still did not have furniture and polished the boards. Now she sat next to him, hands intertwined hugging her knees, and sighed deeply.

"Tired?"

"It's a good tired."

"You didn't have to do everything today."

She smiled at him like he couldn't possibly understand. "I know. It was nice of Cora and Norma to fix our room up so pretty. I always loved that double-wedding ring quilt. Course I was going to save it."

"Cora said you wouldn't never use it unless she got it out."

He could see her smile in the dark.

"That Cora is a case. And Jack and Norma are good friends to do all they done. This is going to be a fine place to live and raise a family, ain't it John?"

Despite the damper Jack had put on the day with his talk, John had to agree the Cumberland Homesteads was a fine place to live. "The finest place on earth."

"Oh, John, I am so happy," Lacey said.

Suddenly she giggled like a little girl. The sound of it made his heart jump. He thought he could easily die a satisfied man at that moment to hear her say she was happy. He couldn't imagine a man having more in life than he had at that moment. He looked at her fingers intertwined and thought again about how he had never bought her a wedding ring. Impulsively he said. "You know I always felt bad I never got you a wedding ring."

"Why John I never give it a thought. Look at all you've give me."

"Still, it bears on my mind," he said truthfully.

She waved her hand like brushing away a moth. "It don't make no never mind to me. I have all I need. More than I ever had a right to expect. You are such a good man, John."

She said it sincerely but he would rather she had said, "I love you John." He would take what he could get. She seemed content in the life they had made with each other. All and all it had been a fine day. He yawned and suddenly felt the full weight of the day on his shoulders. "What do you say we go in and try out that new quilt?"

She slipped easily into the crook of his arm without a word and it was a good feeling going into their new home on a warm spring night with everything good to look forward to.

He felt the weight of her tiny hand on his shoulder, no heavier than a feather, as he floated up from a deep sleep. It took a minute for him to realize they were in their bedroom in their new home. "Lacey, what's the matter?" he asked knowing instinctively that something was wrong.

"It's the baby," she moaned.

He jumped up and fumbled to light the lamp. They had been promised electricity but it had not come through yet and he cursed his shaking hands. In the sudden flare of the kerosene lamp, Lacey was as pale as the pillow her head rested on. He tried not to show his shock. He watched as she lifted the covers. The sheets were red with blood. Lacey clutched the covers and writhed in pain. He almost dropped the lamp as he turned and dashed up the steps to Cora's room. He shook her awake and she came without question. "It's Lacey," he said simply.

She took one look and whispered for him to get the doctor. He hated to leave Lacey and hesitated.

"Cora I've ruined your pretty quilt," Lacey said tears streaming down the sides of her face.

"Nonsense, honey, we'll fix it up good as new," Cora said gently stroking Lacey's cheek.

She motioned for John to go and he backed out slowly breaking into a run as he hit the porch. There was a nurse who lived near number one, he would stop and tell her first. Maybe she could help out until the doctor came. He was still pounding on the door as it opened. He almost fell through into the arms of the nurse. "It's my wife," he said breathlessly.

"My husband will drive us back and then get the doctor. Let me get dressed and we'll go," the nurse said with calm efficiency.

John gladly gave in to her efficient nature allowing him to be pushed into and out of the car.

When they got to the bedroom Cora warned him back with her eyes. The nurse went about her work quickly and quietly taking charge. John sat down helplessly at the kitchen table. He was aware of night passing and of the doctor's coming and going but it seemed like a dream, a nightmare he wanted to wake up from. It had been so horrible seeing all that blood and knowing it belonged to Lacey, knowing that she could die. He had thought it possible to lose her many times but never like this and not when she had just told him that very night that she was happy. His head pounded as his thoughts fought with each other. He cursed himself for letting her work so hard that day moving in. And the way she worked in the garden, he never should have allowed her to do that. And why hadn't he bought the truck he had thought about getting. They were willing to pay him to drive the men around to the job sites. He could have fetched the doctor in half the time if he had had a truck. Finally, the bedroom door opened and Cora came out. "Mama," he called.

Cora came up to him and put her hand on his shoulder. "The baby is gone son." He looked at her blankly. And then he was ashamed of himself. He had been so worried about Lacey he had forgotten about the baby. "Lacey," he croaked.

"She'll be fine son."

"It was my doing. I shouldn't have let her work so hard. She tried to do too much."

"Don't go talking foolish, now. This kind of thing happens. She's a strong girl. It will just take her a while to get her strength back. I lost two babies before I had you and two babies after. Why do you think I never had no more children than you? Lord, I always wanted me a house full."

John stared up at his mother blankly. He had never known this about her, had never really thought about her as a young woman bearing the same sorrow that Lacey now bore.

"The nurse is going to stay with her a day or two and make sure she's all right," Cora said shaking John's shoulder to make sure he heard.

"I want to see her."

"She's sleeping. It won't hurt to look in on her though. Just don't go waking her up. And then I want you to go on to work. It won't do her no good you moping around here all day acting like she's a dying."

He opened the door gently. The nurse looked up and nodded. As she passed him on her way out, she patted his shoulder. He felt like he was in a strange world of secrets that only women shared. Lacey looked like a child, small and pale, lost in the covers. He knelt by the bedside and watched the covers rise and fall with her breathing. He felt something on his head and reached up to touch her tiny hand. He looked up to see her looking at him. "Lacey," was all he could say.

"I'm sorry about the baby," she cried tears filling her eyes.

He couldn't form the words to tell her how he felt. "Lacey, I couldn't go on living if I lost you," he whispered. He watched the tears stream from the corners of her eyes. He felt overwhelmed by the pain he had caused her and the sadness in her eyes when only hours before she had been so happy. He vowed that if God would let her live, he would always see to it that she had whatever she wanted for the rest of her life. It was all he had to offer her. If he couldn't give her the farm, he was sure she'd have no reason to stay with him. Tomorrow, he'd get back to work. Tomorrow he would try harder to hold everything together. He stayed with her until she was asleep again and then he pressed the inside of her hand to his face and cried.

14

Susan came out of the bathroom and twirled around awkwardly letting him admire her dress. He whistled softly, "Gorgeous." She blushed like a schoolgirl. She came over to the bed where Coy lay smoking a cigarette, fiddling nervously with a matchbook cover and kissed him on the forehead.

"You always say that."

"It's always true," he said stroking her soft blond hair. She washed it everyday and it always smelled of lavender or jasmine or some smell he had never known until he met her. The compliments he gave her were sincere but she always seemed surprised and delighted like no one had ever told her that before. He guessed that was what he liked most about saying nice things to her. She seemed to hunger so for the words. He had never known anyone who had grown up rich and somehow he had always thought the rich had it figured out. It surprised him to discover that Susan could match his miserable childhood story for story.

"Coy, you should be getting dressed. We don't want to be late."

"They can't start without us. Your father is throwing this shindig in our honor."

"I know and I can't wait to show you off. All those girls who snubbed me in school, who made fun of me behind my back, who thought I would have to settle for some short, pockmarked toad, are invited to the party tonight. I never get tired of seeing their faces when they get one look at you. Even the old biddies pant when they see how handsome you are."

"I'm real proud you've made me such an important part of your revenge but I can't believe there could be anybody left that ain't seen me."

"Hasn't seen you," she gently corrected.

To hide a flash of anger, Coy looked the other way. They had been married for seven months. During that time, Susan had busied herself with stuffing him into suits, teaching him manners, correcting his speech and trying to get her father to accept him. Within a week after they married, Susan had moved them into a house in a nice neighborhood, hung drapes on the windows and invited guests for dinner.

For the bastard son of a moonshiner, he had come a long way. He was, at last, living the respectable life. Coy thought back to the night it had all been handed to him like a straight flush on the first deal and marveled at how simple it had been. They had been together late that night, as they had on many nights drinking and playing cards but mostly talking. Chick had long since gone to bed. Susan was talking about her father's business. She thought he was making a big mistake with some of his recent deals. She had a good head for that kind of thing and Coy had been impressed more than once by the advice she had given him. It frustrated her that her father would not listen to her. Suddenly, she started to cry. Coy put his arms around her to comfort her. "Do you know what it's like," she said, "knowing that nothing you do will ever be enough to make someone you love, love you back."

Her words had opened a wound deep within him that he thought had healed. He knew only too well what it was like to grow up with a parent who on a good day could only tolerate your presence. He was surprised that such a thin layer still there covered all the old hurt; it was a miracle he had held it in. The only difference between him and Susan was that he had stopped trying to please early on. It tore at his heart to watch her still struggling. They had ended up in bed and sometime during the night with her arms clinging to him and the tears fresh on her cheeks he had asked her to marry him. He had been afraid that with the light of day Susan might change her mind, but they had gone that morning and done it quickly. He had felt some guilt over using Susan but then she had gone off to her father brandishing the wedding certificate like a sword and he knew that she was using him too.

Susan's father had a fit, of course, having long ago checked Coy out and declared him worthless. He said a lot of ugly things to Susan and she had come back crying. She kept her hurts like lint in her pocket, pulling it out time and again to examine but never throwing it away. In time, Susan had convinced her father that, even if Coy had married her for her money, as he believed, they would just have to make the best of it. They had to do what proper social etiquette demanded. Coy pretended it was for Susan's sake that he allowed himself to be cleaned up, polished up and paraded about. He enjoyed pouring on the charm to Susan's old girl friends and watching them melt under his unyielding gaze. It was amazing, Coy thought, how Susan's money and fashion sense had changed him into someone he hardly recognized when he passed a mirror. He had had to swallow a lot of pride in the last seven months, pride he had not even been aware he possessed.

"Coy."

He looked up to see Susan staring at him. He felt like he had been away a long time. She sat down on the side of the bed. "Couldn't we skip it tonight?" he asked suddenly weary. "I really should be at the store. You know I do work and most of that work is at night."

"The party will be over early. There will be time after it's over to go to the store. Besides you know you don't have to do that any more."

"I know your father has a place picked out for me. It must have taken some persuading to get him to agree to that. But then he does have to keep up a good front. Has he given you a clue as to what it might be?"

He and Sam Holt were still feeling each other out. They were both as sharp-eyed as two hawks looking for the same rabbit. Coy sensed he could learn a lot from Sam if he played his cards right. And he intended to play his cards right. This was the most important game he had ever played and it would have to be played very carefully. He did not want to appear too eager.

"Actually, it's a very good position. It's managing a construction job he's about to start over next to the quarry. It's a factory to make radios. Of course you wouldn't really be managing right away. You would be under someone else for a while. But it's a place to start and you would be good at it."

"No, I would be lousy at it. You would be good at it. Only he won't give it to you so you want me to take it. For Christ sake Susan!"

"I could help you."

"Why do I feel like I'm being used?"

"And I thought I was hiding it so well," she said jokingly.

"It's not my way, Susan," he said seriously and hoped he sounded convincing. "You don't know what you are asking. Do I need to tell you what I have given up already letting you dress me, buying me handkerchiefs with initials on them?"

"Poor dear," she said with a pout.

"I'm serious, Susan," Coy said. "Taking from your father would change things. Change me. When you take a favor from somebody it always makes you beholden. I never liked that feeling," Coy said surprising himself by the honesty in his statement.

"I give you permission to take from my father without guilt. Do this for me. If you find after a while you can't do it, then we'll get out. We will get out whenever you say. All you have to do is say you want out," she said snapping her fingers, "and just like that we'll get out." She looked into his eyes, smiling her pleading smile. "Please, just promise me you'll talk to Father about it."

"And if I don't like it, I can walk away. Whenever I say?"

Susan nodded.

"No arguments. No crying, no questions."

"No arguments. No crying, I promise."

"No questions."

"I promise."

"All right then."

"Then you'll do it."

"I'll talk to your father."

She put her arms around him and kissed him on the lips. "Most men would welcome an opportunity like this."

"I'm not like most men, Susan. I thought you might have guessed that by now," he snapped. She pulled away from him. The expression on her face revealed nothing of what was happening inside her but he knew. She was scrambling to protect herself against the hurt his words had caused. He hated being that much like her that he could feel what she was feeling. He hated that he had snapped at her. It surprised him sometimes, this anger that flashed in him like a storm. It seemed that the more compliant, the more giving Susan was the more he wanted to lash out at her. He felt no better than her father. He pulled her back to him, kissing her softly on the lips.

He reached behind her to work the zipper on her dress. She did not try to stop him. She did not complain that they would be late. Instead, she buried her face in his neck and he could feel her warm breath. He never told her he loved her and she never asked.

For twenty minutes every morning, Coy stood before the men and went over the day's duties. He would later check on them two or three times a day to make sure they were doing their work but he tended mostly to let the men do their jobs. It was the deal he had struck with them early on and it had worked out so far. In the eight months he had been on the job, he had, as far as he could tell, shown a reasonable talent for the construction business. He liked being outside and he liked seeing something come together. No one had been more surprised than he that things had gone as well as they had.

He thought back on his meeting with Sam Holt to discuss the offer. He had been led into Sam's wood-paneled office in the Holt family residence. Sam had been cordial, even friendly, both of them pretending they had Susan's best interest at heart. Coy had known from the start that the job picked out for him would be one of the worst that Susan's father could find for him. Sam had not minced words. "I know what you are and why you married my daughter but I have a reputation in this community," he had snarled chomping unmercifully on his cigar. "I am giving you this job for one reason only. As far as this town is concerned I'm happy to have you in the family. As my son-in-law it would be expected of me to offer you an opportunity. In truth, I expect you to fall flat on your ass." With that Coy had been ushered out of the office.

The men he was given to supervise were the most unskilled, the most disgruntled, and the roughest of common laborers that Sam Holt could round up. The first day on the job when he faced them, he figured on lasting a week. He did the only thing he knew how, he played his hand. He told the men, "Sam Holt tells me y'all are a worthless bunch of sons-of-bitches." With that Coy had seen the fight come in their eyes and he knew he had them. "Now, don't let that upset you. I'm married to his daughter and he thinks a sight less of me." When the laughter died he said, "It would be worth a lot to me to prove him wrong." From that time on he had their loyalty and the job had come together like a charm.

He left his cigar store in Chick's hands and the auction house to Will's care. He had held on to them to hedge his bets against everything going wrong. So far, eight months later, everything had gone right. The project was going well. Susan's father left him alone, although Coy knew he watched his every move. He just couldn't figure out why the need came across him at least once a day to get in his truck and drive away. Not just across town but maybe across the country. He wasn't sure where he hoped to go. It was just a feeling. After all, he had just what he wanted. Susan was, of course, thrilled he had done so well. She had told him last night that she was pushing her father to put him in charge of the next project. The thought of her sitting with her father planning his future had sent an angry jolt through him and he had to set his jaw to keep from speaking his mind. He had to remind himself of one thing. Susan was simply handing him what he had hoped for and with a lot more ease than he had ever imagined. Still, he had left right after supper and gone to the cigar store to drink and play cards. He hadn't made it home all night but had left for work straight from the store. Now, he was feeling guilty, which was not a feeling he relished. Maybe he would run by the house and tell her it was late when he closed up and he had fallen asleep on a cot in the back. He got in his truck and started for home but found himself driving toward the auction house instead. He was already late. It wouldn't hurt to take a minute to check up on how things were doing before he went home.

Will was unloading a truckload of chairs as Coy drove up. He blew his horn and Will looked up and nodded. He sat the chair down and came up grinning to shake Coy's hand. "Well, howdy, Coy. We don't get to see much of you around here since you got so important."

"Yeah, I'm thinking about running for president I've got so important." Coy jumped up into the truck bed and started handing the chairs down to Will.

"I got some money for you. Things is going real good. I'll get it for you before you go."

"I ain't worried about it."

"You know I appreciate you letting me have a free hand here, Coy. Not many folks would of trusted me that way."

"And you done a good job with it, Will. Who's to say with my reputation you was the one shouldn't of trusted me," Coy said, laughing easily, slipping back into his old way. It felt good. He felt like a soldier just coming off an all night watch. The muscles in his neck suddenly let go their grip, and he reached up to rub the ache out. He noticed an old man sitting in a rocker by the door wrapped in a blanket. He seemed to be at home there like it was his regular spot. "Who's the old man?" he asked.

"That's Pa." Will said surprised that Coy didn't know him.

"That's Frank Conners?"

"Has he gone down that much? Being around him you get used to it. He had a stroke last spring and he ain't done no good at all. They's times he don't know nobody."

Coy couldn't believe that the man in the rocking chair was the same man who had once run him off of his place calling him a thief. It should have given him more satisfaction seeing him like this now but all he could think about was how Lacey would feel if she knew. The man looked at Coy but showed no signs of recognizing him. A little girl came out of the door and climbed into his lap. He grinned and patted her on the head. Ruby came out behind her and waved at Coy. She had gained a lot of weight and Coy watched fascinated as she waddled over carrying a baby in her arms. Coy jumped down from the truck to greet her. "Howdy Ruby."

"Howdy Coy. I seen you looking at me. I know I'm a sight but Will likes me this way. Don't you Will?" Ruby threw back her head and laughed.

Will grinned.

"This here's Franklin Coy Conners. He's 'bout near one year old. We appreciate the money you give Will when he was born."

"Yeah, I told Ruby we'd have us another one and name him Lynn. See if we couldn't get some more money," Will said, slapping his leg and laughing. Ruby shoved him hard throwing him off balance. "Lord, Will. What's Coy to think of us, you saying a thing like that?"

Coy laughed harder than he had laughed in months. When he looked down the little girl was holding her arms up for him. He bent down and lifted her up. "And is this Rachel?" he asked brushing a curl back from her face. She nodded, suddenly shy.

She was fair-skinned like Ruby but with Will's wiry build. He had always had tenderness in him for children, wanting to scoop them up and protect them from the harshness of the world. They always responded to him openly, free from any grown up fears. He remembered a bag of peppermint he had in the glove compartment of his truck. "Would you like to know a secret?" he whispered. The little girl nodded, shyly tucking her head into her shoulder. "In that truck over there is a whole bag of candy. Enough for a little girl to eat all she wants. Would you like that?"

"Enough for my Poppa to have a piece?"

"Your Poppa?" Coy asked.

Rachel pointed to the man in the rocker.

"There's plenty enough for your Poppa to have a piece." Coy carried her to the truck and got the candy. He handed her the bag and sat her down. She ran to the rocker and climbed onto the man's lap. She pulled the first piece from the bag and handed it to him. The next piece she put in her own mouth and they sat sucking on their candy and rocking contentedly. It struck him that this might have been Lacey as a baby.

"Pitiful to see him like that ain't it?" Ruby spoke up.

"Lacey must be worried sick," Coy wondered out loud, unable to catch himself. He was thinking that surely she might come north to visit him.

"Lacey don't know how bad he is," Ruby went on. "I just told her he'd been sick. It would kill her to see him like that. She and John are working so hard to make a go of it down in Tennessee. I don't have the heart to tell her about her pa."

Coy's ears picked up at the mention of Lacey's name. "Having a rough time of it are they?"

"Not that you'd ever hear it from Lacey. All I ever hear from her is about that farm of theirs. You'd think there had never been a place like it. She sounds as happy as can be. You know Lacey always did like growing stuff."

"I reckon, you're right," Coy said thinking how true Ruby's words were.

"I can't see no fun in hoeing taters," Will spoke up. "Can you, Coy?" he joked, poking Coy in the ribs.

"I'll just tell you Will, that trying to make an honest living can kill a man."

Will cracked up laughing and slapped Coy on the back. "Coy, you are a sight. One more sight," he said still chuckling.

"Well, I better be going. I just stopped by to see how things was going."

"You need to bring that wife of your'n and come to supper some time," Will spoke up.

"Thank you Will. We'll do that."

"It won't be nothing fancy."

"No, it won't be nothing fancy," Ruby chimed in blushing a deep strawberry. "I hear she's real fine," she said shyly. "She might be too good to eat country grub but she's sure enough welcome."

"I'll tell her you said so," Coy said trying to imagine Susan and Ruby together. Suddenly, he realized how much his life had changed in the last few months.

"I clean forgot," Will shouted. "Let me get you that money."

"Just hang on to it, Will. You never know when I might be needing it and if I take it now I'm likely to spend it."

"Well, whatever you say."

Coy drove off waving his arm out the window until he was out of sight.

Coy stood out on the back porch drinking a beer and watching a spider spin its web. Susan was still not home and it was almost twilight. She was likely upset with him for not coming home the night before. He had come home to explain. Of course he had gotten sidetracked when he went by the auction house. He went inside and got another beer and flipped on the porch light on his way out. He sat down in a wicker chair and put his feet up on the porch rail. He leaned back and tried to relax. He watched a moth buzz around the spider's web circling closer with each daredevil move. Suddenly, the moth came one wing tip too close. Coy wondered how long it would take him to realize he was caught. The moth flapped helplessly with all his might. The spider rushed down from the other end of the web, stung the moth senseless, wrapped a few quick strands around him and went on about his business. "It's over buddy. It was over from the first time you come within a foot of this porch. You knew it and I knew it. I could of reached up and pulled you loose, but, you'da just done it again. What a fool." Coy laughed because he knew that he had gone from talking about the moth to talking about himself. He felt trapped. He was wrapped up in a web of his own making. Life was going along just fine for him. He was making money and living a life the likes of which any man would envy. Wasn't he supposed to be enjoying it, he wondered? Instead, he felt like a moth that had buzzed the web one too many times. He had not realized how trapped he felt until Ruby's talk of Lacey had caused the panic to rise in his throat. All of a sudden, he had this picture of her there on the farm with John, laughing and happy. Maybe she had not even heard about how successful he had become. Maybe she didn't care. Knowing Lacey, she would just be happy for him that he had done so well for himself. He glanced up suddenly to find Susan standing in the doorway staring at him.

"Home at last?" she asked simply.

Her face was a mask Coy had worn many times himself. Whatever he had come to mean to her, whatever her feelings about their life together over the last few months, she was keeping carefully hidden behind that mask. He knew she was keeping her emotions wrapped tight inside her like every unloved child learns to do. Better that she should scream at him, call him the names she must be going over in her mind, he thought. Her control made him hold back his own emotions. The silence hung between them like fog in a valley. It was a standoff.

Susan surprised him by pulling up a chair and sitting down beside him. "Things are just going too well to suit you, aren't they, Coy?"

He looked at her out of the corner of his eye but she was staring straight ahead, not looking at him. He didn't want to ask her what she meant so he eased himself back into a more relaxed position and lit a cigarette. He flicked the match off the porch and watched as a tiny spiral of smoke rose from the grass.

"The men on the job think a lot of you," she said at last. "They like the way you trust them to do their jobs. I've heard them talk about you myself. Even Father has begun to grudgingly change his mind about you."

He raised his eyebrow to show that he had his doubts about just how much her father had gone toward changing his mind. "Not without a few words from you, I'm sure."

"That's not the point. The point is that like it or not you are a better person than you give yourself credit. Chick worships you as the first and only true friend he's ever had. You own two businesses of your own. Will and Ruby owe you their livelihood."

He dismissed her praise with a shrug of his shoulder. He had started out acting like he resented all her help and her father's and he had ended up convincing himself. When had he stopped playing them for fools and become one, he wondered?

"You just can't handle it, can you? The possibility that things might actually go right is scaring you to death. Don't think I don't see it in your eyes everyday. You can barely control the urge to run, to bolt before you have to face up to the fact that you're not as bad as you think. How long do you plan to go on running? How much harder could it be to stay and see if things fall apart?"

It stunned him that Susan had been reading his thoughts so clearly. He usually did a better job of hiding his feelings. How could he explain to Susan what he was at a loss to understand? All of his life he had been like a man whose table was full but could find no appetite for any of it. Even as he looked about the table with distaste, he knew that as soon as the food was taken away he would be famished. He wanted just once to partake with relish and be satisfied. And even as he sat there wanting to tell Susan that she was right, something stopped him. "I said I would give working for your father a try," he said. "If it didn't work out, you said I could walk away and there would be no arguments, no crying, and no questions." He could feel her eyes on him. He was surprised by the anger he felt toward her because she insisted on believing in him. Any day now, she would be expecting more from him than he could give. She would be expecting him to always be there for her. That was always the way with people if you let them get close, he thought.

"It has worked out." Susan went on. "You just won't admit it. You have a talent for making money, Coy. Use it and you could be one of the richest men in Anderson."

He couldn't believe she was begging him to do what he had planned on doing all along. He certainly wasn't ready to abandon his plan just yet. He couldn't even if he wanted to because it would prove Lacey had been right about him. This time he was determined to stick it out. He was just feeling a little crowded. It was the same old feeling that had haunted him all of his life. Still he couldn't resist the urge to say, "And you could be married to the richest, most powerful man."

"I don't need your money," she said indignantly. "My mother had a great deal of money when she married my father. When she died she set aside a sizable amount for me. Maybe she knew my father better than I thought," Susan said, more to herself than Coy.

Coy couldn't hide his surprise. So old Sam Holt had married for money too, he thought. That explained a lot about why he was so suspicious of Coy. They were too much alike for old Sam's taste. "Then why do you bother with him?" Coy asked honestly.

"My father?" she asked as though surprised by the question. She looked at him like she didn't have a choice. "We all have our weaknesses." she sighed. He could detect a slight quiver in her voice as she said the words, but her eyes were dry and cold.

"You hate him that much?" he asked, suddenly amazed that he had overlooked something so obvious. The question hung in the air between them almost like a living thing. Time stretched out until it ceased to be measured and still she did not reply.

"I was thinking it was time we took a honeymoon," Susan finally said matter-of-factly.

Coy raised one eyebrow and surveyed her out of the corner of his eye. She was a puzzle for sure, as soft as doe skin and as hard as a flint rock. He couldn't help but think he was underestimating her. Maybe she thought a trip would settle him down, get rid of whatever was ailing him. Could be she was right, he thought. "We never had a proper honeymoon, it's true. What must your friends be thinking," he said sarcastically.

"I'll make sure by the time Ann Mayfair Taylor reports our little trip in her society column they will all be green with envy," Susan said playing along with him.

He could tell by her look that she was already making plans. He could only shake his head and marvel at the force that churned inside her. The twilight settled into darkness as the evening wore on. Together, they sat each lost in thought, as they watched the spider suck the last bit of life from the moth.

15

Susan wasn't sure when she first realized the mistake she had made. She had somehow allowed herself to fall deeply in love. She had told herself in the beginning that it didn't matter that Coy loved her only for her money. The rational part of her told her they were both out to get what they could out of the marriage. If that did not include love, then she could bear it. At least that was what she had told herself in the beginning. Now, as she sat across from Coy, dining on pheasant at the Starlight Room in New York City, her hand trembled as she reached for her wineglass. They had come to New York for their honeymoon. It had been a glorious three weeks for her. She had loved having Coy to herself and occasionally showing him off to some of Sam Holt's most influential friends. They had attended the theater and added their own rave reviews to those given by the critics for "Life with Father." They had spent their nights dining, dancing and seeing the town.

Coy watched the dance floor, absently drinking his wine. He turned to her slowly and smiled. She could tell his mind had been a million miles away as it had been so many times on this trip. He reached his hand across the table and caught Susan off guard by declaring, "You're not having a good time."

His words stung her because she knew he was telling her his feelings. She looked out the window trying to collect her thoughts. She felt like she was walking a tightrope ten stories up. Coy sat across from her ready to cut the rope if she said one wrong word. "We appear to be," she said meeting his direct gaze with her own.

"For once forget appearances," Coy said taking her hesitation to mean she agreed with him. "What would you really like to do?"

"I would like to meet your parents," she said surprising herself. She had no idea where that had come from. It was just a desperate gamble for time but, suddenly, the thought appealed to her. Maybe meeting Coy's parents would give her a clue to his darker side. She could tell her request had shocked him.

"I don't think you would find that nearly as entertaining as the theater."

"Let's say, I would like to see the cloth you were cut from," Susan said hoping she wasn't being too honest.

"If that doesn't change your mind about me, nothing will," he said with a bitter chuckle. "When would you like to leave?"

She was surprised he had given in so quickly. She hoped she had not made a terrible mistake. But then what choice did she have? Every time she closed her eyes she could see Coy handsome beyond reason, smiling his dazzling smile as he cut the rope that held her aloft. "Can we dance one last dance?" she asked. She had never danced until her honeymoon. On their first night out, Coy had asked her to dance. She had blushed crimson with embarrassment and then confessed how awkward she would feel limping about the dance floor. He had taken her back to their room and taught her to dance by putting her feet on top of his like a child just leaning to dance with her father. She had twirled about the room with grace. And as long as she wore a long dress no one could tell.

Coy took her hand and led her to the dance floor. She pressed her face against his chest and felt his warmth. She thought of their lovemaking and felt the warmth spread through her. His hand on her back was like a firebrand burning her body. He was an ever-gentle lover, tender and patient. It was only when she looked into his eyes that she knew he was not making love to her.

Susan found Coy's mother to be the most superficial, cloying human being she had ever met. It was all she could do to be polite, but she was determined to get along. She had allowed Ellen to take her all around the town showing off her rich and refined daughter-in-law. Susan pretended to be delighted by it all. She had to laugh when Ellen made Coy's father, Seth, start coming to the table in a suit starched as stiff as a church pew.

Coy seemed to keep his distance from it all. He spent his time alone or with his father. He seemed nervous and could not put his mind to anything. He would spring up from his chair immediately and go out not telling anyone where he was going. Susan felt more isolated and alone than she had felt before.

Seth had finally said one night at the supper table, "Coy, you're as nervous as a man with his pants full of yeller jackets."

They had all laughed, but the truth of it hung in the air making the rest of the night stretch out in silence.

Finally, Susan started to make noises about needing to get back to Indiana. There seemed to be no need to stay longer. Maybe she had believed that by coming to Kentucky, Coy would make peace with his parents or she would learn some secret that would help her understand him. None of that had happened. Coy had withdrawn even more, ignoring her hints at going home.

It was a warm day, the sun bright but gentle, when Susan walked to the mailbox to post a letter to her brother. She missed him terribly and worried despite his plea that everything was going well for him back home. She worried about what her father might be thinking of their long absence. She had worked so hard to convince him that Coy was reliable, hard-working and stable. She was so lost in her thoughts she almost bumped into Coy as he walked to meet her. He surprised her by taking her in his arms and kissing her warmly on the lips. His eyes were dark and pleading as he looked up at her.

"I need you to do something for me," he whispered hoarsely.

"Anything," she said without hesitation, her voice catching in her throat. Her heart pounded and she felt sick because she knew more than he could know. She knew she meant exactly what she said.

_16_

The sun danced in the tree tops overhead. Occasionally a ray of light pierced the mass of leaves and struck the water below. A frog jumped from the creek bank splashing water into Daniel Lee's face in its haste to get away. Daniel Lee sputtered and wiped his face with the back of his tiny hand. Lacey lifted her dress tail and dried his face. He fussed and pulled his face away eager to get on with his playing. In his tiny hand he clutched a stick. He sat contentedly tossing twigs and pebbles into the creek while Lacey collected fresh cresses. They had discovered the creek at the back of the farm on one of their many walks together and it was a delight to both of them. They didn't get to come often because there was always so much work to be done. Even now, she felt guilty. That morning at the breakfast table she had announced that she and Daniel Lee might go down to the creek later to pick cresses. They had all given her that look she had come to know in the last few months. She supposed she had earned it from the strange way she had been behaving. Then Cora made a big fuss about her doing just that and John admitted that cresses would taste mighty good for supper. John was always on her to slow down, especially since they had lost the baby. In another week, it would be a year. Sometimes it seemed like a long time ago and sometimes it was as fresh as a new cut. For a long time after, she had wandered through her days like there was something she had forgotten to do. And then it would come to her that there was no need to do anything. There would be no need to knit sweaters or sew up baby gowns or make diddies. Each time in her mind she would have to fold up her thoughts like secret notes and tuck them away deep within herself. And into each crease was folded the guilt, the knowledge that it was all her fault the baby had died. She still blamed herself and always would, she guessed. She had worked too much in the garden just as John had said. She had been too eager to get her new house fixed up and had thought only of herself. The nurse had said, "You'll get over this, honey. Don't you worry, you'll have other babies." The nurse had meant well but she had been wrong about her getting over it. Looking back over her life, she couldn't remember a single thing that had ever happened to her that she had truly gotten over. She had never gotten over being hungry and afraid in Wilder. She had never gotten over her folks not loving her as much as they loved each other. She had never gotten over Ben being sick and nearly dying with pneumonia. She had never gotten over loving Coy even if she had taken off the locket he had given her and hidden it away after she got the letter from Ruby about his getting married. She didn't see how it could be that people got over things. She just simply added them to her life and carried them with her wherever she went, trying always to weave hope out of strands of despair. She wondered if that was why old people were sometimes bent and stooped. It wasn't from their bodies getting older; it was from the burden of a lifetime of memories, each added on to the other.

Daniel Lee's squeals brought Lacey's attention back. A hard shell bug clung fiercely to his shirtsleeve as he flung his arm around wildly trying to get it off. "Here baby, let mama help you." Lacey grabbed the bug and tossed it onto the bank and took her son in her arms. "It's time we was getting back anyway." Daniel Lee seemed content to be leaving the bug behind. He jabbered and pointed to the bank where Lacey had thrown the bug. She kissed him on the forehead and feathered back his dark hair with her fingers. He smelled like warm biscuits from the oven. He had grown so much in the last months losing his baby look and turning into a little boy. She had thought when she lost the baby that it might be God's punishment as a way of evening the score for all the happiness and good things that had been given her lately. Silently, she had given thanks that it had not been Daniel Lee who had been taken from her. She couldn't keep the thought from her mind once again, even if it did cause a feeling of shame to wash over her. She stooped to pick up the dishpan full of the greens she had picked and they headed back toward the house. Once out of the woods, Daniel Lee squirmed to be let down to walk. "I swear Daniel Lee you are getting heavier than a sack of flour and twice as hard to hold." Daniel Lee looked up grinning, proud of himself as though he had done a great trick. Her heart flip-flopped at the joy of him. "You are a clever thing, for sure Daniel Lee." He took off as fast as his tiny legs could carry him, eager to be at his next adventure. In her mind, she was always drawing imaginary circles around him to protect him from harm.

As they neared the barn, a hog snorted at being disturbed. Stretched out on the ground surrounded by a litter of hungry piglets was Gertrude. Lacey still laughed at the sight of her so long and thin and strange looking. She was unlike any pig Lacey had ever known. They had been encouraged by the Project to take her and three others as an experiment. They had come all the way from England and they were supposed to be an improvement over the kind of hogs folks around there had always raised. Lacey had tried to fatten them up but they had refused to cooperate and had only grown taller and thinner with each passing month. It was hard to see where they could be an improvement if there was no way to fatten them up for slaughter.

It seemed they were being asked to do something different everyday now and a lot of it didn't make sense to her. One thing she was finding out was the government could change directions faster than a grass fire. Lately there had been a lot more talk of farming. John said it was because they still had not been able to get a factory to locate there so people could have jobs. An Agricultural Experiment Station had been set up to see what would grow best around there. John had come home not more than a week ago with a whole sack of rutabaga seeds. He told her she was to plant them and there would be a woman come around to show her how to cook them up. She had been ashamed to admit she had never seen a rutabaga and didn't know if she could eat one if she did know how to cook it. It was hard to figure sometimes what was going on and where it was all headed. When she asked John what was going on, he had cut her off short and she had not questioned him again on it. She could tell he was upset a lot nowadays. He put such stock in everything always going right that it just seemed like he couldn't tolerate any disappointments. Not wanting to be one to him, she didn't know anything to do but stick the seeds in the ground and hope for the best.

Just last week, they had all been given study books to help them better understand what was meant by a cooperative community. Eleanor Roosevelt's words still rang in the back of her head and she did so want to make her proud. She studied it every chance she got hoping it would help her understand what was going on. She knew there was an increasing unhappiness among some of the people. Lacey felt it was fear more than anything else. Folks were just naturally afraid of things they did not understand.

She had grown to love their farm and relished each new day and each change of seasons. The winter on the plateau was the coldest in years and at times she thought the barn had been warmer than the new house with its one fireplace, but still she loved it. The only thing that marred her happiness in their new home was John's increasing moodiness.

She sat the dishpan down on the back steps and walked to the clothesline. The wash she had hung out earlier was dry. She pressed her face to it and took in the fresh, sunshiny smell.

"Ooo hoo," a voice called from behind her.

Lacey turned to see Norma coming up the road waving her arm. She waved back and took the wash inside. On the way back out she picked up Daniel Lee, handing him a cold biscuit and walked to meet her. "Where's your younguns?"

"I left them with my ma. I can't stay long. I just come from meeting with them Home Economics women."

"What was it about?" Lacey asked. They were always being encouraged to "improve" themselves. Lacey went to as many meetings as she could but she knew Norma had a hard time of it with so many folks to look after.

"Lordie Lacey, honey. I'm not right sure but we was there a right smart long time so it must of been important."

Lacey had to laugh. She loved the way Norma had taking everything in stride. "Come on in and I'll put Daniel Lee down and make us some coffee."

As they sat at the kitchen table drinking coffee and eating cold biscuits with new-made strawberry preserves, Norma tried to explain what the meeting had been about. "They want to pay me fifty cents an hour to feed the younguns soybeans."

"Soybeans? What kind of bean is that?"

"You got me there but they say they're real good for you. Better for you to eat than pinto beans. They say folks around here eat too much flour and lard."

She took a giant bite of the biscuit and preserves smiling at Lacey with full cheeks and lips tightly closed. "Goodness, honey, these strawberry preserves is a little bit of heaven."

"Thank you. Norma," Lacey said distractedly. She was still taken aback by what Norma had said before. "Eat too much flour and lard," she said puzzlement in her voice.

"I know what you're thinking. They's many a time we'd of starved to death if it weren't for flour and lard."

"I think of the times I would've give anything for a little flour and lard and now they're saying we eat too much of it."

"They don't mean it that way. They mean we're supposed to eat more different kinds of things like vegetables."

"Is a soybean a vegetable?"

"I reckon," Norma shrugged. "I was ashamed to ask too many questions at the meeting. I mostly was wanting to know if it could harm my younguns. To tell you the truth, I thought it was something you feed to the cows."

"Is that why they're paying you to eat them?" Lacey said laughing.

"Well, we don't just have to eat them. We have to count them too."

They both broke up laughing. "Count them." Lacey managed to gasp. "Do you get paid by the bean?"

"No, thank goodness. The way they smell when you cook'em, I think I can make more by the hour. They put some of them things in the oven to show us how we could roast them. Suppose to taste just like peanuts when you cook'em that way. I'm telling you them things stunk to high heaven."

They laughed until their sides hurt and tears rolled down their cheeks.

"What on earth have we got ourselves into?" Lacey asked when she caught her breath.

"Law me, if I know honey. Looks like they can't just let folks live here in peace. They got to keep fiddlin' with us. As long as they's money in it, I reckon I can put up with it. All I know is I better get home and get to it. It looks like I'll be busy most of the day."

"Oh, what are you up to?"

"Nothing special. It's just that, after I feed my younguns their soybeans, I got to measure them all to see if they growed any."

Lacey shook her head, grinning. "You reckon, it's worth fifty cents an hour?"

"I've done worse for less," Norma snickered.

Lacey nodded, still grinning.

"Where's Cora today?"

"She walked up to the Guest house to leave off her gourds."

"She going to try to sell them in the gift shop?"

"She was hoping to with all the folks passing through to take a look at this place. A man come through from New York last week and bought every quilt Louise Menter had made up."

"Cora needs to paint her up a bunch of them gourds for the craft sale in November."

"Yeah, I heard about that. It's to be an all day sale out in front of the Trading Post."

"It'll just be stuff that folks from the Homestead has made. I'm taking a whole bunch of my tatted pillowcases and doilies. I don't have time to do big pieces. Why don't you take something?"

"I don't have a talent for handicrafts, Norma."

"Pshaw. You can quilt and sew and can with the best of 'em. What about them rugs you been making at the Weave House? You know the women at the clubs just raves over them."

It was true, Lacey thought. She evidently had become quite a hand at weaving since folks often complimented her on the rugs she made, but somehow each one was special to her and she wasn't sure she wanted to sell any of them. "I'll think about it, Norma."

"Or why don't you take some of your homemade preserves. They's plenty of folks would love a jar of that."

"Oh, Norma, you say that about everything I cook. Besides you know you're welcome to a jar anytime you want one."

"I tell you what. I'll take a jar right now but I want to leave it here with you."

"Why on earth would you want to do that?"

"Cause it's more fun to come here to eat it," she said patting Lacey on the shoulder. "Now, you give some thought to what I said."

"Well, like I said, I'll think on it," Lacey said not convinced that Norma was right but pleased that she would think it.

"What you planting in that patch you got plowed up out there?" Norma asked pointing out toward the field.

Lacey looked at her sheepishly. "Rutabagas."

"Rugawhats?"

"Rutabagas."

"What's that?"

"I don't know. John says it's something like a turnip. I reckon we'll know for sure when it comes up."

Norma snorted a laugh through her nose and patted Lacey on the back. "What will they come up with next?"

"I don't know but whatever it is John will for sure have us in the middle of it." Lacey could still hear Norma laughing as she walked down the road toward home.

She needed to hurry. John would be there to pick her up any minute. They had been in town all morning to shop. They usually bought whatever they needed at the Trading Post but she loved it when something came up that could only be done in town. John had bought a truck a year ago and they paid him now and again to carry the men to job sites. It was still new to her having a way to get around. There was something wonderful about being able to go some place just because you wanted to. Secretly she longed to learn to drive but she dared not mention it to John for fear of looking foolish. Sometimes John would let Ben drive the truck in the yard or bring it around to the barn to load it. It was wonderfully appealing thing, the thought of being behind the steering wheel, guiding it wherever you wanted to go.

The only thing left to do was pick up her shoes at the shop where she had left them to be resoled. Lacey eased Daniel Lee off her hip inside the shoe store and watched as he scampered to the window that looked out at the railroad station. She put her packages down by the counter and searched her purse for her ticket stub.

"Good morning, Mrs. Trotter," the clerk said coming up to greet her. It always surprised her when someone called her Mrs. Trotter. It made her sound so grown up. Most of the time on the farm, she felt like a child playing at her favorite game.

"Good morning, Mr. Morgan. I just need to pick up a pair of shoes," Lacey said handing him the stub.

"Every youngun loves that window," he said motioning to Daniel Lee. "There'll be a train come through here any minute now. Stops right out there."

"He'd have a fit over that for sure, Mr. Morgan."

"I'll be right back with your shoes."

Lacey nodded, smiling. She looked down at the packages by her feet and thought of the lace curtains she had bought for the living room windows. Never in her life had she ever dreamed of having lace curtains on her windows. So many good things had happened to them since they had come to the Cumberland Homesteads. Even now, she could walk around her house rubbing her hand along the pine paneling or across the stone mantel over the fireplace and marvel at her good fortune. It was beyond her understanding that she had been singled out to have these things

"Here you go, Mrs. Trotter. Good as new," the clerk said handing her the package wrapped in brown paper and tied with twine.

"Thank you, Mr. Morgan," Lacey said just as the blast of the train whistle drowned out her voice. The railroad tracks cut across the main street of town and passed within a hundred feet of the store. When the train pulled into the station Daniel Lee let out a squeal of delight. Lacey went over to him and knelt down. He pointed out the window his hand quivering with excitement. "It's a train Daniel Lee. A train," she explained. She had grown up around the coming and going of the trains in the coal camp and it took her a minute to realize that Daniel Lee had never seen one. She was explaining about the engine that pulled it along and the red caboose on the end and all the cars in between when a man stepped down from one of the passenger cars. He stood looking around, tall and lean in his blue-black suit, hat in hand. The bright May sun shone on his coal black hair. Something in Lacey knew it was Coy long before her mind could comprehend the fact. It hit her with such a jolt she thought the floor had moved beneath her. She put her hand on a nearby shelf to steady herself. Her stomach was a pot of molten lead spilling out into her veins. All those months of dreading that Coy might come back and now, he had suddenly, quietly, unexpectedly appeared. Why had she felt that somehow she would know that he was coming? She felt betrayed by her own senses that she had not been warned somehow.

A woman stepped out behind Coy and he took her hand to help her down. She was blond and beautiful in a powder blue suit. The jacket was cut stylishly slim at her waist and flared at her hips. She had a flat purse tucked under one arm and she wore a navy blue hat tipped low over one eye. Still, Lacey recognized her from the picture she had seen in the paper. It was Coy's wife. The conductor walked by and Coy began to talk to him. He pointed down the street to the hotel and then he turned and pointed up the street past the shoe store. At that moment, Coy looked up and she could tell by the expression on his face that he had seen her. Instinctively, she grabbed her packages, picked up Daniel Lee, protesting at being pulled away from the window, and fled toward the door. As she opened the door to leave, Mr. Morgan called out to her.

"Young lady, you forgot your shoes."

She had left them on the floor near the window. "Thank you, Mr. Morgan. Just too much to carry," she stammered apologetically.

"Well, here now. Let me get you a bigger poke to put these in and you can put them other things right in here with your shoes."

She tried to protest but he had already left with her shoes. He came back, stuffed her other packages into the sack and put her shoes on top. She thanked him hurriedly and rushed out the door only to collide with someone coming up the street. Her packages spilled from the bag and scattered onto the sidewalk. Daniel Lee let out a howl of protest and she hurriedly soothed him before she bent down to pick up her packages. As she reached out to pick them up, a hand, dark and familiar met hers.

"Here, let me help you," he said, his voice a deep whisper.

She let him collect her things and help her up, unable to stop him, unable to look into his eyes. It seemed like hours passed. Finally, she raised her head and looked into his eyes.

His eyes searched her face for what seemed an eternity, asking a thousand unspoken questions. His hand was still on her arm, burning through her sleeve. He was more handsome than she remembered, in his fine suit and felt hat tipped low over his face. His eyes were fierce and dark, drawing her in. Then he looked away slowly to Daniel Lee and her heart stood still. For a moment he almost looked startled and then he flashed her a smile as though he had just then recognized her. Slowly he took off his hat.

"Why Lacey. Lacey Conners is it really you?" He smiled down at her, his eyes searching her face. "How good it is to see you again. Or is that Lacey Trotter now?"

Lacey nodded unable to speak. Only Coy could act so casual as though it could all be an accident their running in to each other like this. He stood boldly before her as though they were just old friends. She was uncomfortably aware of the person in blue standing next to Coy.

"Susan, this is Lacey Trotter from Wilder. I'm sure I've mentioned her to you."

"No, Coy, I don't believe you've ever mentioned Lacey, but it is very nice to meet you," Susan said her voice steady and self-assured. She smiled at Lacey, looking her over with unwavering eyes. "I'm Coy's wife."

"Nice to meet you too," Lacey said her voice raspy.

"Lacey and I have known each other since we were children, haven't we Lacey? What have you been doing with yourself?"

"John," she hesitated. "We have a farm now, me and John, on the Cumberland Homesteads."

"Yes, I do believe Will mentioned that to me. You are working on some kind of government project. And how is John?"

The tone of his voice turned it from something special to a handout in one sentence. Lacey bristled and sought the words to defend what they were doing. "John is doing real good. He works a lot of the time."

"That's John all right. He always was a hard worker. You'll tell him I asked after him, won't you?"

"I'll tell him."

"You know your brother Will and I are business partners now. I don't know if he ever wrote you about that. Quite a coincidence us running into each other like that, wasn't it?"

"Yes," was all that she could say. She noticed his expensive suit was perfectly tailored to fit his frame and wondered if he had come back to flaunt his good fortune.

"Who would have ever believed Will could have turned out to be such a fine businessman? Just goes to show you people can change, can't they Lacey?"

She felt the color drain from her face and her knees turn soft beneath her. His words stung her. If he was trying to give her a message, it had hit its target like an arrow. He wanted her to know that she had made a mistake when she had turned him away that day on the mountain. She could hear the woman speaking but her words were a jumble of sounds.

"Are you all right?" Susan asked.

Lacey nodded.

"We were just going up the street to have lunch before we check into our hotel. Would you care to join us?" Susan asked cordially.

"I couldn't," Lacey stammered. "I mean no thank you. You don't have to go up the street, though. There's a real nice restaurant in the hotel." She couldn't imagine why she had offered the information, except the woman had been nice enough to ask after her.

"Is that right," Susan said looking at Coy. "Coy you must have misunderstood the conductor."

Coy shrugged, undisturbed by her questioning.

"I have to be going," Lacey said not looking at either of them. "It was nice meeting you."

"It was nice meeting you Lacey," Susan said. "I hope we will have a chance to see you again while we are here."

"Oh, my word, of course," Lacey said embarrassed by her rudeness. "We'll have you out for Sunday dinner first chance you get. John will want to see Coy. And to meet you too."

"That sounds lovely," Susan said, smiling.

Lacey did not know anyone else who talked like Susan. Her voice was like warm and cold water swirling together so it was hard to know how she meant her words to be taken. "I best be going," she mumbled. She broke away and headed blindly down the street. Much to her dismay, Coy turned and followed her. His hand on her arm stopped her and she turned to face him, her heart beating in her throat.

"You forgot your packages," he said.

She took the bag from him and turned to go.

"Lacey," he whispered.

She stopped in mid-turn and looked at him.

"You look beautiful. You've cut your hair."

"You're looking good too, Coy. You have a beautiful wife. Ruby wrote me you was doing good in Indiana."

"So Ruby did write about me. I hoped she would. That was one reason I bought the auction house and let Will run it."

Lacey sucked in her breath.

Coy smiled at her surprise. "You're surprised to see me again. Aren't you, Lacey?"

She wanted to look away but couldn't, helpless as always in the wake of Coy's boldness. Her heart beat like the wings of a hummingbird caught in her chest. "What are you doing here Coy?" she whispered.

He stroked Daniel Lee's hair and smiled. "Fine looking boy you have Lacey. He must have been born soon after you and John married."

Lacey could feel her breath catch in her throat. She stood silent before him like a sacrifice. He held the power to destroy her in his hands and he used it to gently stroke the boy's hair. Coy's smile faded as he continued to stroke the boy's hair. "I told you someday I'd be back. You didn't believe me then did you, Lacey. But I've come back, just like I promised. I've come back."

17

John sat back in his chair and watched as the schoolhouse filled to overflowing with co-op members, far more than the fifty it took to make a quorum. He was not the most important member of the board of the Cumberland Homesteads Cooperative Association and for once he was glad. They were meeting tonight because some of the members had accused the Board of Directors of mismanagement. The Cumberland Homesteads, Inc. had originally been formed to operate the Trading Post. It had been a successful operation and had paid dividends from the beginning. Then in the summer of 1935 the government had encouraged the Board to expand the operation. They applied for a charter from the state and became the Cumberland Homesteads Cooperative Association. Looking back, John could see, it was at that point that they began to lose money. The government had loaned the Association eight thousand dollars so they could start selling tools and fertilizer to the farmers. The plan was to then sell their produce through the cooperative. The plan and the amount of money borrowed had not been an idea of their own making. Eight thousand dollars had turned out to be far more than they had needed for the project but they had had to pay interest on the entire amount. To make matters worse they had failed to make a profit on any of the produce. The profits from the successful operation of the Trading Post had been eaten up by the failure of this project. They were here to try to explain that to the members tonight.

John listened while Douglas Harris, president of the board called the meeting to order. Douglas wore a starched white shirt and dark blue tie. A barber had recently cut his hair. He appeared confident despite the crowd's unrest. Although the board was to be composed of only Homesteaders, the government had not seen fit to trust them to manage their own affairs and had included the project manager.

"Gentlemen, I'd like to call the meeting to order. We have several important matters to attend to tonight," Douglas said loudly over the drone of the crowd.

"The most important thing we have to discuss tonight is what happened to our money," a man yelled from the back of the room.

It was Rusty Ligon. He was a man known for his outspoken manner. John knew he had been one of the first men to be against the credit-hour system. He had come from the textile mills in Harriman and had a highly developed disrespect for authority.

"Well, Rusty. I take it that is what you'd like to discuss first," Douglas answered, appearing to take Rusty's anger in stride, but red splotches surfaced on his neck above his collar.

"You take it right," Rusty shouted. Rusty was a big man with meaty shoulders and a barrel chest that tapered to a narrow backside that was lost somewhere in his overalls. He had a shock of dark hair that stuck up on his head like a rooster's comb. He looked about the room as he spoke. The crowd grumbled their agreement. Clyde Reid sat next to him craning his neck to take in every last detail. His buddy Lon had paid his dues, but like many of the Homesteaders, he never attended the meetings.

John was amazed at how angry the men had become over the loss of a few dollars when only months before many of them had been on the verge of starving, unable to feed their families. He could only figure there had to be more to it than a few dollars. The construction jobs that had given them all a living wage for over two years were coming to completion with no sign of any other way to make a living. It was fear that was making the men so edgy. Ever since the government had stopped using the credit-hour system, the men had been receiving their full wages. They were earning more money than most of the folks in the county. Most likely they had not been as saving with it as they should have been but had been living the good life. The thought of losing wages of upward to a hundred dollars a month was scary to them all.

"The truth is," Douglas said over the crowds grumbling, "the Association failed to make a profit this time. And if we don't make a profit, we can't pay dividends."

John could only figure that since Douglas was a businessman at heart that alone explained it as far as he was concerned. There were ups and downs in business and that was the way it was but he could tell that Douglas had had more ups then downs. These men had seen mostly downs in their lives and could only see this as a familiar sign.

"What we're here to find out," Rusty interjected, "is why there weren't no profit made."

"As I was starting to explain," Douglas said looking at Rusty impatiently. "The Association failed to make a profit because the government encouraged us to experiment with a new program."

"We're tired of being a dang experiment for the government," a man yelled. "I didn't come here to be no experiment."

"They done told me what I could grow in my garden," another shouted.

"Ain't nobody got a right to tell a man what he can grow in his own garden," Rusty chimed in.

Although they had been promised no changes would be made in the project when it had been moved to the Resettlement Administration from the Subsistence Homesteads, John had soon learned different. In the beginning, under the Subsistence Homesteads, the project managers had had almost total freedom to create the kind of community they envisioned. Very few rules had been laid out for them. The country was in a terrible crisis. People were without food and work. The President of the United States was encouraging the managers not just to give the people a place to live but to build a new way of life with better housing, jobs, education and health care. It had not taken long for things to get out of hand. The cost quickly mounted with expensive construction. Mrs. Roosevelt had demanded that the homes been of the highest quality with the finest materials, inside plumbing and electric wiring. Costly mistakes had been made, creating a lot of negative publicity. The community projects were being called the "problem children" of the New Deal. Finally, the President had given control to the Resettlement Department. They had been instructed to reign in the projects and get control of the cost. They had done so by taking back most of the control and heavily supervising the project. They had sent in farm management experts to work out complete farm and home plans for each farm and each crop year. Families were required to keep itemized records. Despite Rusty's feelings that nobody had a right to tell a man what he could grow in his garden, John was sure the government felt they did have a right since they had loaned the money. Still he understood the resentment the controls had brought. John had continued to go along with each new change, trying to encourage the others to cooperate, hoping the government would soon have its fill.

"Gentlemen, let's stick to the matter at hand," Douglas said trying to calm them.

A tall, rangy man in overalls stood up, holding his sweat stained hat in his hand. The men all slowly turned their attention to him and the room grew quiet. John knew that Jimmy Carlton was a man of few words and if he was willing to stand up before the whole room he must have something important he wanted to say.

"Jimmy," Douglas asked. "You have something to say."

Jimmy shifted his weight and rolled his hat in his hand. "You know I'm a man of few words," he began, clearing his throat. They all waited expectantly. "I'll put it to you straight. I never joined nothing before. I've been a farmer all my life. You fellers talked me into joining this here Association and I done it on your word."

Jimmy looked them over as he spoke. John grew uncomfortable under his honest scrutiny. He had been the one to talk Jimmy into joining and it had not been easy. Jimmy had lived in the mountains all of his life and he was suspicious of most things outside his own family and especially if it involved the government. John had discovered that most of the men fell into two groups, union men who had worked in factories and coal mines and had come to distrust anyone in charge, and farmers who had never worked for anyone else in their lives. They had one thing in common: they disliked being told what to do without having some say in the matter. But there had been a time when John had spoken confidently to many of the men about joining the Association. He had taken great pride in its efficient operation and the fact that it had been a financial success. He felt a tremendous responsibility to these men but he also felt helpless in the face of the government's attempts to control everything.

Douglas started to speak but Jimmy merely nodded and stopped him before he could begin. "Hear me out," he said flatly. "I paid my dues because I was told I'd be paid cash money for my joining."

"And that's true," Douglas spoke up. "When we make money, we divide it among the members in the form of dividends."

"Well, the point I'm trying to make is, if they ain't no dividends, they ain't no co-operation. Now, that's just plain out my feelings on the matter."

The men in the room roared in agreement. John's head throbbed from the noise. He wanted to speak up and reassure them that just because they had not made a profit this quarter did not mean they would never make money again. But the truth was they had not made a profit since the summer of '35 and there didn't appear to be one on the horizon. To make matters worse, the government had just loaned the Association $550,000 dollars. That was more money than John could even picture. The Association was supposed to use the money to build other cooperative businesses that would provide employment to the men now that the construction was completed and still no industry had been found which wanted to locate there. They couldn't even agree on the kind of businesses they should be building. He didn't know if it was even safe to bring it up at the meeting tonight with the way the men were already feeling.

Jimmy sat down. Some of the men behind him patted him on the back. He nodded shyly and looked down at his hat uncomfortable with his new fame. Next to Jimmy sat Ben Stiles, calmly whittling on a chunk of wood, his lap covered with shavings. He stood up and the shavings fell to the floor like leaves from a tree. He continued to whittle as he spoke. "The thing is most of us has been buying our goods at the Trading Post because we was members of the co-op. They was times we might of felt them goods was a might high." He paused letting his words sink in. "Higher than we could a bought'em for elsewhere. Or sometimes they was things that might of looked better to us in them big stores in Crossville, but we was in favor of doing our trading here because it come back to us in the end."

John didn't believe that the prices were any better in
Crossville or that the merchandise was of any higher quality
but it was what the men believed that was important. All of this
discontent was weighing on him like a stone. He felt like
someone had a steel fist clenching the back of his neck.

"We appreciate that kind of cooperation Ben. That's what
makes a cooperative work," Douglas said trying to make a
point.

"The way it is though," Ben went on shaking his head. "We
didn't do ourselves no good cause it didn't come back to us in
the end."

"That isn't entirely true, Ben. The Association has paid
dividends in the past."

"Well, that appears to be in the 'past'," Ben said, hanging
on the word. "Now that that's changed maybe there will be
other things changing around here."

He never raised his head from the chunk of wood in his
hands but John could see him looking out from under his
lashes.

"What are you saying, Ben?" Douglas asked.

"I'm just speaking for myself," Ben said looking briefly at
the men. "But I may not be trading so much here on the
Homesteads as I once did. I may take my business elsewhere."

Most of the members agreed it was what they were
planning. John's stomach turned over and the bile rose to the
top of his throat. It was what he had feared would happen. If
the families went elsewhere to shop it could mean the end to
the only profitable business they had.

"I'm sorry to hear that men," Douglas spoke solemnly. "It
can only make matters worse for the Association. I'd
appreciate it if you'd think it over before you make up your
minds for good. You know you can't always know that
something's going to work out until you try it. We tried loaning
money for farm tools and seed and fertilizer. Many of you took
that opportunity to buy some fine equipment for your farms. It
turned out we didn't make any money off of it but that doesn't
mean it was a bad investment. I suggest we put this behind us,
and get on with the future."

Douglas had said two things John wished he had not. He
thought it better not to dwell on the fact they had tried and
failed and that they had lost money doing it. He knew the men

needed to be reassured that the Board knew what they were doing in running the Association. They needed to know that the men they had entrusted with their dues did not just go about trying things on a whim without any real idea as to whether they would work. Of course it had been the government that had forced them to expand but they could not safely bring that up either. And the idea that the money lost was not all that important could not set well with the men. Maybe it was impossible for Douglas to understand the importance of a few dollars but John had caught on quickly to how the men felt.

"We'll be happy to put this behind us," Rusty Ligon said, "If you can guarantee us a dividend next time out."

"The important thing here is not dividends." Douglas retorted.

"Excuse me Douglas," John interrupted knowing he was about to make the men very angry by trying to argue that dividends were not the issue here. "I don't mean to step in ahead of you but I think the men just want our assurance that we'll do the best we know how to run things right and that we'll have their best interest in mind with everything we do."

"Well, of course, John," Douglas said as though surprised they could think otherwise.

"And we understand that you men want a say in what happens here on the Homesteads. You know I've got as much at stake here as any of you. I've got a farm I'm hoping to keep and me and my family has made a home here. What Douglas means by dividends not being the important issue here is that we need to be looking to the future to finding a way to make a living wage now that the construction is near complete on the houses. We know that most of you have been giving some thought to what might happen when the construction jobs run out." He looked out over the room and he could tell by the uneasy expression on the men's faces that he had struck a cord with them. He glanced at Douglas, who indicated it was all right to go on with what he was saying. "I'll admit it looks bad," John said. It was his feeling that being honest with them was the best approach. Let them in on just where things stood. He didn't know how the rest of the board felt so he didn't look to see but plowed on with what he had to say. "We've tried hard to get some industry to move in here and so far we've had sorrier luck than an old maid getting to the altar."

The men laughed and poked each other in agreement. John could take being the butt of his own joke if it would get the men working together. "Now, we have a chance to start our own industry." John carefully avoided saying the government had loaned them the money. "What we need to discuss here tonight is what kind of business is best suited to the folks on the Cumberland Homesteads. You have a say so in what's to happen here so let's hear what you have to say on the subject. This here's your chance to speak up about it." John, having said his piece, sat back to show the men that it was up to them to decide what they wanted. He knew they did not have that kind of freedom when it came down to it, but it was important for the men to think so.

"There must be a dozen men here has worked in a textile plant," Rusty said.

"Takes plenty of money to start something like that," Ben Stiles said without taking his eye off the piece of wood he was turning into a horse. "What if we can't make a go of it? What then?"

"Why don't we try something smaller?" Dan Troy interjected.

"What you got in mind, Dan?" Rusty asked.

"Well, we got a little place already making furniture. Maybe we could look to making that bigger."

"I can't see myself making furniture," Jimmy Carlton said softly. "I been a farmer all my life. I think I'd best stick to what I know. That's what I come here to do."

"Jimmy's got a point," a man from the back said. Several people agreed.

"Well, we could make sorghum molasses. That way some folks could grow the cane and some could make the molasses," Mack Brown said like he had reached the perfect solution.

"You know anything about making molasses?" Rusty asked.

"No, but I seen it done."

They all laughed leaving Mack to fidget in his discomfort. "Well, you have to admit it wouldn't cost nothing the likes of building a factory," he retorted.

"John there was a coal miner," Ben pointed out. "Maybe we could start us a mine."

John tried to hide a grimace. The last thing he wanted to get involved in again was coal mining. The memories of Wilder were still too fresh. "We could check in to that, Ben. See what the chances are of locating a good seam around here."

"They ain't no way you're getting me underground," Clayton Wright argued. "Not until I'm dead and they're burying me."

The men laughed but John could only rub his forehead and frown at the men's inability to come to any kind of agreement about what they wanted to do. If they couldn't agree on what they needed to do, how could they ever get around to doing it or make a go of it if they did?

"I bet ole John don't care one way or the other what kinda work it is," Rusty spoke up.

He looked John straight in the eye. John knew he was up to trouble and he braced himself and waited, not taking his eye off Rusty.

"Ole John there will have a job no matter what 'cause he's in tight with the big boys. Ain't that right John?" Rusty baited.

The crowd grew silent, half turned to face John, half with their eyes on Rusty. The tension spread through the room like the heat from a grass fire. John was not a man given to violence but he thought how easy it would be to pick up a chair and smash it over Rusty's fat face.

"I just got one thing to say," Jack Percy yelled out into the silence. "I'd vote for the Association to build a sidewalk clear around this whole project, if they was willing to pay me to do it."

The men roared in agreement for the first time in the whole long discussion. John nodded a thank you to Jack for his words. But the men were soon back to debating and as the meeting wore on John realized that nothing would be decided that night. He was relieved when he could at last step out into the cool night air. He dropped Jack off at his house and drove home with the truck window down, taking in great gulps of the wind as it passed his face. The steel fist that had gripped the back of his neck seemed to be squeezing his brain up through the top of his head. Headaches were getting to be an everyday occurrence. It wasn't just that hairline cracks were showing up in the project, with the government trying to control everything from up in Washington D. C. and the men beginning to rebel against all the fiddling and lack of say about matters. No, there was more to it than that. Saturday, he had seen Coy Lynn Wilson on the streets of Crossville and it had hit him like a belt to the gut. He had been heading to pick up Lacey when he had seen him on the street. The shock of it had made him fuzzy headed and he had turned off on a side street to collect himself but not before he had seen Lacey not twenty feet away headed in the other direction from Coy. She had to have seen him, maybe even talked to him and yet she had said not a word about it. That had scared him almost more than the sight of Coy, lean and dark and handsome in his three-piece suit. He looked like he had done well for himself since they had last seen each other although it was hard to tell with men like Coy. He had always acted like the cock of the walk even when he didn't have a dime to his name. He guessed men like Coy always did well for themselves.

When he had come to himself he had been parked outside a furniture store. He thought of the page in the Sears and Roebuck Catalog that Lacey had thumbed nearly ragged. He had gone in right then and there and bought a sofa just like the one pictured in the catalog. Lacey had not asked him for it but he felt some satisfaction with himself when the deed was done. And now it was to have been delivered today.

He pulled around to the back of the house, his truck lights reflecting off the back door. A light glowed in the kitchen. He turned off his lights and sat in the dark trying to picture what Lacey was doing at that very moment. Would she be sitting on the sofa when he walked in? Would she run to meet him and throw her arms around him saying how he shouldn't have done it? He had thought about it over and over again during the day until he had built it up so in his mind he was half-afraid to go in. He went up the back steps slowly and opened the door. Cora was washing up the supper dishes. He peeked through to the living room and the sofa was there but Lacey wasn't sitting on it.

"She's upstairs, "Cora said without turning. "Ben's got a bellyache and its got her all tore up like it was smallpox. I told her it weren't nothing but he'd been eating too many of them wild strawberries."

He slumped into a chair at the kitchen table, disappointment tugging at his insides.

"Guess you think you're something," Cora commented, jerking her head toward the living room.

"Might be," he answered matter-of-factly.

"Lacey 'bout had a conniption fit when that truck come up the driveway with that thing on it. She said, 'You men must have the wrong house.' They said they reckon not if this was the John Trotter place. Said he'd ordered it out for his wife. Lacey still didn't hardly believe it."

John wanted to hear all of this from Lacey but didn't dare stop his mother when she was so full of the telling of it. Still her words pleased him and he couldn't hide a grin that tugged at the corners of his mouth. "Did she like it?"

"Like it! She had them men set it down like it was a china cup. She sat on the floor stroking it half the night. Wouldn't set down on it less it was some kind of mistake and it had to go back tomorrow. She's waiting to hear it from you."

He looked up to see Lacey standing in the doorway. She smiled and tilted her head to one side like he had seen her do sometimes when Daniel Lee had done something she thought was extra clever. He suddenly felt as awkward as a schoolboy and wondered if it was as obvious as that why he had done it.

"It's beautiful John, but you shouldn't of done it. It must have cost a fortune." She turned and went into the living room and stood admiring it, her hands folded in front of her. He came up behind her as she stood shaking her head. "How did you know? How did you know this was the one?"

He told her he'd found her marker in the Sears and Roebuck Catalog and then blushed crimson as though she had caught him spying on her. He thought maybe she would be upset that he had looked through her things but instead she smiled a soft and gentle smile. She squeezed his hand and kissed him sweetly on the cheek.

"John, you are the sweetest man," she whispered almost to herself.

He wanted to tell her he would buy her the moon to see that look on her face again. He started to sit down but she screamed and shouted, "No, John." He jumped up like a man on a hot stove. Lacey blushed and then laughed at her own foolishness. She pulled them both down on to the sofa to sit awkwardly like two strangers on a church pew. She stroked the nap lovingly and his heart ached at the sight of her. Then he was surprised to see tears well up in her eyes.

"You know you shouldn't have," she whispered, the words catching in her throat.

"And why not?" They had gotten most of their furniture from the factory on the Homesteads. It was sturdy but plain. He thought, she might mean that it was wrong of them to buy furniture outside the co-op.

She was silent for a while. He waited surprised by her sudden sadness.

"Pa used to buy things; you know when Ma would have her spells. Then sometimes, especially after the mines started to go down, he had a hard time paying for 'em."

John knew that Lacey's mother had been sick a lot and her Pa had spoiled her something awful, giving in to her every demand. And there had been quite a few demands from what John could gather. It had put a terrible burden on the whole family. "What are you saying, Lacey?"

"I'm just saying I don't want to burden you with my wants. There's things we need a heap more than I need a sofa."

"Lacey, you never asked for nothing," he said flatly. He wanted to say how he wished more than anything that she would ask just once.

She must have read something in his face because the tears spilled over on to her cheeks. "Asking is hard for me. I never learned it. I learned to make do."

It tore at his heart to see how hard it was for her to take something for herself. He'd see to it that as long as he lived she would never have to ask for anything. He wanted to throw his arms around her and tell her that very thing. He wanted to tell her that if she would just stay with him, give him time, he would try to make it up to her for every hurt she had ever endured. Instead he asked, "Is it the right color?"

She seemed not to realize what he meant. She was so lost in her own thoughts.

"The sofa? I didn't know about the color. The man at the store said any woman ort to like it." He regretted saying the words as soon as they left his lips. It didn't sound right like he was telling her she had to like it. But then, hadn't he expected her to run to him, throwing her arms around him, squealing in delight?

"Its perfect John," she said gently. "I reckon I just can't take it in yet."

They sat in silence until Cora came in to announce she was going to bed.

"How's Ben?" she asked.

"Asleep," Lacey answered.

"I'll look in on him on my way."

"Thanks, Cora. Goodnight."

"Goodnight, Ma."

"Goodnight, John. You two don't wear that thing out sitting on it tonight." she said winking at them.

They smiled at each other and listened to her footsteps as she climbed the stairs. "Cora said Ben had a bellyache," John said.

"She thinks he ate too many strawberries but I think he got too hot. A friend of his on Sawmill Road got a bicycle. I think they must of took turns riding it most of the day. I never seen Ben so excited. It was all he could talk about even if he was groaning and holding his belly while he done it. I wish you could have seen his face when he was talking. I don't know how he ever learned to ride it. He was skint up something awful."

She chuckled to herself over the thought and he marveled that she could take such pleasure in someone else's enjoyment. But then, wasn't that what he had done over the sofa? "Don't see many bicycles around here. It must of been a rough ride on these roads."

"I don't think it stopped'em none."

"Any of that cobbler left from supper?"

"Oh my, what was I thinking? You must be starved down after the meeting."

They went into the kitchen and John sat at the table while Lacey spooned cobbler into a bowl. She sat down to watch him eat it. It was one of those sweet things she did that John liked so much, the way she kept him company at the kitchen table. Usually, they were alone, the family long since gone to bed. Most often they talked about familiar things, like the garden or something Daniel Lee had done that day. John wondered if some night Lacey would bring up Coy.

"How did the meeting go?" she asked tentatively.

He thought of lying, not wanting to spoil the evening with the truth, but Lacey knew the reason for the meeting and had begged him to let her go. He had held out against it for fear things would turn ugly. "Folks were mighty upset. Seems like there's just a group of folks don't plan on being pleased about nothing."

"They're just afraid. They don't understand what's going on with the government and it makes them nervous about what's to happen."

"If any of us knew what was going on, we'd probably be more nervous. Sometimes I regret ever bringing us here to this place."

A look crossed her face, just a sudden widening of the eyes, and then it was gone. It was enough to make him regret his sudden honesty. Maybe he was wrong in not telling her the problems with the Association. It might give him some ease to share it with her. But when he looked across the table and met her blue eyes, brow crinkled with concern, lips pressed tight, he lost his courage. No need to burden her with something that might work itself out in the long run.

"Why, John, this is our home now. You love it as much as I do. We've got fine neighbors. If we need anything, they're right there ready to help out. Ben's in school. I'm taking a class at night. I never dreamed I'd ever get a chance to get more schooling." Lacey stopped suddenly breathless.

"You do love this place, don't you?" he said surprised by the sadness in his voice. He wondered how she would feel about him if she knew he might not be able to give her the farm.

Lacey did not answer but jumped suddenly from the table and came back with Daniel Lee. John had not even heard him. If he had been crying, he had not a tear in sight to prove it. He watched as Lacey forked her fingers through his hair, soothing him with her voice. She was the best mother John had ever seen. Her patience with Daniel Lee seemed to know no bounds and she delighted in finding ways to keep him entertained. It was hard not to envy the way she hugged him to her breast and cooed loving words into his ear. He sat back and watched and listened to the soft, sweet sounds of home, wanting to believe with all his being that nothing would ever change.

_18_

In the end there had been no other way. He had to tell her. Coy watched Susan sleeping peacefully, her breathing even and rhythmical. It was a mystery to him how she slept so soundly. He stood looking out of the hotel window watching the morning traffic move up and down Crossville's Main Street. Of course, he had not told her the whole truth.

He had explained to her that he needed to go to Tennessee. There were folks there who had never expected him to amount to much and he needed to show them they had been wrong. She had not questioned him but had packed her bags and they had left on the morning train, leaving Seth and Ellen as surprised by their departure as they had been by their arrival. On the train ride she had simply looked at him and said, "I'm real proud you've made me such an important part of your revenge." They were the very words he had used with her. In some ways she knew him so well, but the things she did not know made her seem so innocent and so trusting of him.

Now he was here in Crossville and he had seen Lacey by accident on their first day in town. She was more beautiful than he remembered, her skin browned by the sun, freckles racing across her nose and cheeks. When he had brushed close to her she had smelled like warm sunshine. It had been all he could do not to take her in is arms right there on the street. He had not come back with the real intention of hurting her. He had just wanted her to feel the rejection he had felt since she had sent him away. He wanted her to know that she had made a mistake. Then he had seen the baby and he had known in an instant that the boy belonged to him. It had thrown him for a minute, discovering that it was his child. A rage had come over him when he had looked into the boy's face and seen the obvious truth. Why had Lacey not tried to get word to him about the baby, he wondered? Surely she knew that he would have come.

Lacey had been wrong not to let him know. He had a right to claim his son. Surely John knew. It was written on the child's face. It made Coy laugh to think of him. He was a fine looking little fellow. A boy a man would be proud to claim. He intended to do just that. The boy deserved to grow up knowing his real father. He deserved the chance Coy had missed. Maybe he had come back just to flaunt his wealth, but now he intended to stay until he had the boy. He was not leaving without the boy, he thought as he pounded his fist one against the other.

It had shocked Lacey, he knew, to see him roll into town like that without a word of warning. His heart had leapt into his throat at the sight of her. She still had that power over him. He knew that if she had reached for him he would have walked away with her right then leaving behind everything. But she had not, and then he had seen the boy and her betrayal had cut him like a knife. Not only had she not loved him, he had not been good enough to claim his own son. His body almost twitched with the need to have it all out in the open.

He slipped from the room, easing the door shut behind him. With luck he would be back before Susan awoke. Her face was always so lovely in sleep, pale and soft against the pillow. He really didn't mean to hurt her. He had tried to spare her what was coming but in the end she would have to know. Maybe she would grow tired and bored of living out of a suitcase in a town that boasted of very little to keep her occupied and find her way back to Indiana long before he had to face her with the truth. He didn't know how she would accept the boy, but it didn't matter. It was the boy who mattered the most.

The early morning sun was already warming the sidewalks as he walked out onto the streets from the steps of the hotel. It was a weekday and the streets were fairly well deserted. He knew that if Crossville was like most small towns, it was never abuzz except on Saturdays. Even so, the town had a prosperous look about it for a small Southern town in the middle of the Great Depression. He strolled up Main Street casually smiling and tipping his hat to those he passed. His plan was to buy an automobile. He would need one if he was to make the four mile trip out to the Cumberland Homesteads. According to the hotel clerk there was an automobile dealer just four blocks from there. He planned to stop along the way and send a telegram to Will to let him know where he was just in case there was a problem with the auction house. Will would be surprised for sure to learn that Coy was in Crossville, Tennessee. He stepped into the corner drugstore that had a sign out front for Western Union.

"I'd like to send a telegram to Will Conners in Anderson, Indiana, please ma'am." he politely told the woman behind the counter.

"You wouldn't by chance happen to be Coy Lynn Wilson."

"Why, yes, I am," he said surprised.

"I'm holding a telegram for you right now from a Mr. Seth Ramsey. I was just about to have someone bring it to you. It concerns a Will Conners. That's how I recognized it must be you."

"Well, thank you. I'll just read it first then if you don't mind."

"Certainly." she said handing him the paper. "Sorry, if there has been a death in the family. You know I don't mean to pry. I'm not nosy," she reassured him with a smile while cleaning the lipstick off her teeth with her tongue. "It's just you have to read it when it comes in over the wire." she said as further apology.

"Yes. Thank you," he said not understanding what she could mean by a death in the family. He took the telegram eager to find out. He scanned it quickly. It was brief and simple in Seth's straightforward style. "Frank Conners dead. Will Conners trying to reach you. Lacey wants him brought home to Tennessee. Seth." He couldn't believe the once proud man who had stood between him and Lacey was now dead. And Lacey knew. He could imagine her hurt, knowing how close they had always been. He looked up to see the clerk staring at him, a look of concern creasing her brow. "Yes," he said. "I'll send that telegram, now."

"Go ahead when you are ready, sir." she said gently. "I'll write it down and have it right off for you."

"Sorry for your loss. Please see to it that Lacey gets her wish. Take the money I left in your charge and use it as you need. If you need more, see Chick at the store. If I can help call me at the Hotel Taylor, Crossville, Tennessee."

"Is that all Mr. Wilson?" She treated him like he was the most important person in the world. He thought of the suit that he was wearing and almost laughed. Susan had it made for him and he was sure it had cost her plenty. He thought of the

freshly starched shirt he put on every morning. He could tell
that she was impressed, convinced by the suit and perhaps the
telegram that he was rich. He nodded, giving her his most
charming smile. "That's all I can do for now." He would
telephone Will later from the hotel to make sure he had enough
money and he planned to do as Lacey wanted.

"Well, then that will be $1.75."

He handed her the money, smiled his most winning smile
and walked out into the sunlight. When he glanced back at the
window, he could see her standing looking out at him. He
watched as she darted out of sight. He laughed out loud at the
stir he had caused.

It suddenly struck him as odd to be walking up the street
knowing that Frank Conners was dead. He had always been
such a powerful force that even when Coy had seen him sick
and feeble, he still felt it. It wasn't just that Frank had been
against Lacey seeing him, or that he had thought Coy unworthy
of his daughter. Frank was just one of those people whose life
was such that his very existence caused him to be a judgment
on other people's lives. He never wavered from his principles,
never gave an inch even if it brought the very people he loved
to their knees. Of course, he had asked more of some than of
others. He knew it had cost Lacey plenty to try to live up to
Frank's standards and that in her trying, it had cost him Lacey.
It was too late to be glad Frank was dead. The harm had been
done long ago. Coy wouldn't wish him back even for Lacey's
sake. Anger still simmered too close to the surface. Still and
all, he knew Lacey and he could feel her pain as she grieved for
her father now, her heart broken.

As he walked down the street toward Hamilton Motor
Company, he was only scarcely aware of the warm sun
reflecting off the sidewalk. His thoughts were on Lacey and
how he could manage to get to her.

When he came to himself he was standing at the motor lot.
The salesman was coming at him with his hand extended.
"Good morning, sir. You're out bright and early this morning.
Let me introduce myself, I'm Carl Macgill."

"Coy Lynn Wilson," Coy said shaking the man's hand.

"And how may I help you, this morning?"

"I'm new in town and I'm just looking for a way to get
around."

"Well, of course. It's hard to get around without an automobile nowadays. I have a nice used 1934 Terraplane. Mint condition."

"No," Coy said flatly, not meaning to be rude, just trying to think it out. He looked around the lot. "I'll take that Chrysler over there. Is that the latest model you have?"

The man looked surprised. "Yes, sir 1937 model, Custom Imperial. Got a long wheelbase, ultra-wide seats, forward mounted engine, do 95 mph in the straightaway. Its brand new. Just got it in. That's a nice car for sure. Real expensive. Of course not for a man such as yourself."

Coy could see the man instantly regretted his words. He stood watching the man fidget in discomfort. It amused him to realize that once again he had fooled someone into thinking he was rich and important. He really did not like the design of the automobile. He much preferred the '32 convertible sedan sitting next to it, but he was going for show. "How much?"

"Three hundred and twenty five dollars."

He opened his wallet and counted out the money. He handed it to the stunned salesman.

"Wouldn't you like to drive it first?"

"No need. I know where to find you. I'll just need the keys."

"Yes sir. I'll be right back with your receipt and the keys."

Coy was waiting in the automobile when the man returned. He drove off the lot with the man still trailing after him, trying to thank him for his business. He laughed to himself at the impression he made on the man and knew he would be talking about it to everybody he saw that day.

He stopped long enough to fill his tank with gas and get directions to the Cumberland Homesteads. By the time he left the city and drove the four miles to the project, he was astonished at how isolated and raw it all seemed. Anderson was by no means a big city, not like Chicago or Los Angeles where he had spent time, but he was surprised by how accustomed he had become to traffic and buildings and people milling about him. He had driven the stretch between Crossville and the Cumberland Homesteads without meeting a single automobile. Now as he passed a built-up area, busy with people coming and going, trucks and automobiles parked here and there, he knew he would have to stop and ask directions if he was to ever find

Lacey's farm. A fat man in overalls stood alternately waving the trucks in and wiping his brow with a dirty handkerchief. A thin, toothless man was loading lumber onto the truck behind them. Coy pulled up beside the truck and yelled out the window. "You men know how I could get to the Trotter place from here?"

The fat man ambled over and started to bend down and rest his arms on the doorframe when Coy opened the door and stepped out. Coy watched as the man took in first him and then the automobile. He looked back nervously at his partner a couple of times before he stuck out his hand.

"Howdy now, I'm Clyde Reid and this here's Lon Carver."

Coy shook hands and tipped his hat to Lon who nodded without taking his eyes off his work.

"You're not from around here?"

"No. Just in for a visit," Coy said amused by the man's bluntness.

"You got relatives in these parts?"

"Old friends."

"Them be the Trotter's?"

Coy nodded.

"Fine folks. How is it you come to know'em?"

"We grew up together."

"They's from Wilder, best I remember. Is that where you grew up?"

"Look, I need to be getting on here," Coy said amazed by the man's endless stream of questions and that he had actually answered them. "If you could just give me some directions."

"Happy to," Clyde said not at all offended that Coy had interrupted his questioning. "Fine looking automobile you got there. Don't see too many new automobiles around here. That one don't hardly look like it's got a scratch on it. You just buy it, did you?"

"Yes, I did," Coy retorted, beginning to regret he had ever stopped. Perhaps it would have been better to find his way on his own but then he thought to use the moment to his own advantage. He threw open the automobile door to expose the plush interior. "A man has to have a way to get around," he said modestly.

"Lon," Clyde called. "Lookie here at this fine automobile."

Lon came over nervously holding his sweat-stained hat in his hand and walked around the automobile, his tongue working feverishly over his gums.

"Long wheelbase, ultra-wide seats, forward mounted engine, do 95 mph in the straightaway," Coy said repeating the words the salesman had used.

Clyde whistled.

Lon nodded.

Coy smiled that they were suitably impressed. "Now, those directions."

Clyde pointed down the road, said it was about five miles on the right. Lon stood in the background nodding, his tongue working alive, barely contained by his cheeks. They stood staring until Coy lost sight of them in the rear view mirror. He laughed at the sight of them and wondered at what they could be thinking and what stories they would tell.

He passed several houses along the way, all similar in design and built with the same stone exterior. They looked new but cozy and homelike. All of the farms had an unfinished but well-cared for look. The look of hope and possibilities was almost visible in the new sown fields. How like Lacey, he thought, and then quickly, banished the idea that she might somehow be happy here.

He was past the house before he spotted Ben walking up the long drive. He had grown some taller but was still thin as a willow reed. He still had the loose-limbed gait of a young boy. The house was neat and tidy, surrounded by new green lawn. A garden spot out back was alive with new growth. The windows were open to the summer breeze and a gentle wind stirred the curtains. Then he saw Lacey come out of the house and stand on the porch, her hand to her eyes as a shield against the noon sun. He drove on for a hundred yards and turned the automobile around. It was too far to see her clearly but he pulled over, afraid to risk being seen. She came down the steps and walked toward Ben. They put their arms around each other's waist and he could see Ben roughly wiping his eyes. She ran her fingers through Ben's hair and pulled him near to her as she spoke to him. He did not mean to be spying on them but the sight of Lacey, tender even in her grief, overwhelmed him. He could not help but wonder how it changed a person's life to have someone like that to run their fingers through your hair as a child and speak kind words of comfort, to praise the good things about you and forgive the bad. It had to make for a different kind of life than he had known. The urge was strong in him to go to her right then and there, even with Ben there, but so private was their embrace that it seemed to shut him out. He wondered where the boy was, his son. He was probably inside taking a nap. He would leave it be for the moment. It was enough for now that Lacey knew he was back.

He drove straight back to the hotel with the sudden thought that he had forgotten all about Susan. He had only just realized he had meant to go back to check on her after buying the automobile. Somehow word about Frank Conner's death had made his need to see Lacey, or at least where she lived, more urgent. He had been gone for over four hours. It was after one o'clock. Perhaps she had taken it upon herself to have breakfast in the hotel and he would be back in plenty of time to take her out to lunch.

He took the hotel steps two at a time. He opened the door to their room expecting to see Susan seated at the window expectantly. Instead the room was empty, silent in its reproach. Only a note welcomed him. He looked around to see that Susan's luggage was gone. He felt a sudden twinge in his stomach like a person who realizes they are falling and can't catch themselves. The note glared at him from the dresser. Slowly he opened the note and read:

Coy,

I have rented a house for us at 813 Riley Street.

My luggage has been taken on ahead. If your business doesn't keep you, perhaps you will join me there for dinner.

Susan

He was so stunned he could only laugh. And to think, he had actually believed she had left him to go back to Indiana. If only he could figure the woman out, he thought. Sitting down on the bed, note in hand, he could only stare at the pattern in the rug. It had never been his intention to settle down in Crossville even with Lacey. He could not figure what Susan could be thinking to rent a house. Did she really think they would be staying that long? There was no way of knowing what the woman had gotten into her head. She was a constant surprise to him. There seemed nothing left to do but grab his luggage and go in search of Riley Street.

19

Will put his arm around his mother and helped her up the steps to the house. A crowd of neighbors had already gathered from the funeral. The women had been by earlier with bowls of green beans, potato salad, and fried chicken. The tiny kitchen could barely contain the pies, cakes and fresh baked loaves of bread that were still being brought in. Lacey greeted each person, thanking them for coming and offering them something to eat. The men took plates piled high with food into the yard and ate with them balanced on their knees. The women sat about the living room where Annie sat fanning herself. The neighbor women listened attentively, and occasionally patted her on the hand to express their deep sympathy at her toss.

Lacey worked about the kitchen, scraping plates and washing them quickly so others could eat. Cora dried them and stacked them on the kitchen table. Norma offered to take the job from her but Lacey found it a comfort to stay busy. She stopped only long enough to take the coffee pot into the living room to see if some of the women wanted another cup. Her mother's voice followed after her as she returned to the kitchen.

"You know with my heart, I just never thought I would outlive my Frank. He was always the strong one. And now he's left me all alone, not a soul in the world to look after me."

Ruby and Lacey shot each other a glance. Ruby's plump face crinkled in such a look of hurt that Lacey went to her and took her hand squeezing it softly. "You mustn't pay her no mind. You and Will was wonderful to take them in these last few years." She glanced in to see her ma fanning herself vigorously. She had made quite a show at the funeral, crying out to her dead husband, having to be held up by Will and John. Lacey stood back, her arm around Ben, silent and tight-lipped in their grief.

Tears spilled from Ruby's already swollen eyes. "I thought Annie had been right happy living with us," Ruby choked out.

"I know you wrote me how she seemed as happy as she could be, never sick a day."

"It was your pa that never liked it. I don't believe he was happy a day from the time he got there, but he never complained. Kept it to hisself. You know I loved your pa."

"Of course, you did," Lacey said hugging her.

"It's Rachel that's going to miss him the most. She sure did love her Poppa. You know I told you how she liked to sit on his knee in their favorite chair. They could sit for hours like that. No telling what it was they talked about. Ooh, Lacey, I didn't mean to say you wouldn't miss him," Ruby moaned, her giant body shaking with sobs.

Lacey hugged Ruby's soft folds of flesh. How she had missed her. Her heart was ever tender as a new blade of grass and Lacey loved her for it. Lacey patted her on the back and whispered, "We'll all miss him."

"You know my own daughter left me," she heard her mother whining from the other room. "Up and got married when Frank and me needed her the most. I was about sick to death with my heart and Frank was out of work. But I told her to go on if it would make her happy."

Lacey looked at Ruby and they neither one knew whether to laugh or cry. They held on, giggling into each other's necks to hide the sound. For one brief second, Lacey hated her pa for loving this woman. Lacey thought of the times her ma and pa had sat at the kitchen table talking and drinking their coffee while she had moved about them doing the chores, invisible to them. He had listened to Annie's whining and endless prattle as though it was a kind of music to him that shut out everything and everyone else. Just once she would have liked for them to notice her. If he was aware of the pain his obsession brought to others, he never acknowledged it. Whatever it took to keep Annie happy, they had all been expected to give and give it without complaint.

Cora came up and tapped her on the shoulder. "Honey, folks is starting to leave."

"Thank you, Cora," she said. She went about the rooms thanking her friends for coming as they politely filed out. It touched her genuinely that the people that she and John had come to know as friends would come to console them even though they had never known her pa. When they had at last all gone and she had checked on the children who were piled up peacefully asleep on her bed, she sat down at the kitchen table to rest. She had not seen Ben around but she suspected he had gone off somewhere to be by himself.

"You need to eat something yourself, Lacey," Cora urged. "You've not eat since last night."

"I'll just have some coffee. I don't have much appetite for food."

Cora poured her a cup of coffee and set it down before her, her left hand resting for just a second on Lacey's shoulder.

Lacey looked up and smiled her thanks.

"It was a real nice funeral, honey," Cora said.

Lacey nodded, staring into her coffee cup. Now that everyone was gone and it was just family left she found it harder to hold herself together. She heard voices drifting from the living room and realized her mother was still holding someone captive there. She rose wearily from her chair and went to rescue the person. It was Norma, who looked up as wide-eyed as a frightened rabbit. Lacey could only wonder at what her ma had been telling her.

"Honey," she said to Lacey, jumping up from her chair. "I reckon me and Jack had better be getting on. The younguns will be having a fit. It's past time to feed the baby. You take care now, Mrs. Conners."

Annie looked up startled, to be losing the last of her audience. "I'll do the best I can. What choice does a poor widder-woman in bad health have?" she said, whimpering.

Norma looked at Lacey helplessly. "If there's anything I can do, sweetheart, you just let me know. I'll come running."

Lacey put her arm around Norma and eased her from the room. Jack sat on the porch with John and Will. John looked up, concern creasing his brow when he saw her. She smiled a reassuring smile.

"Jack, we better be getting on home," Norma said.

Jack stood up and shook hands with John and Will. He nodded to Lacey.

"I'll run you home in the truck," John spoke up.

"No, you stay here. We can just as well walk it."

Lacey stood watching after them for a while, not eager to go back inside.

"Folks was sure nice to turn out like they done," John said.

"They's good folks living here on the Homesteads. Real good neighbors," she said fighting back the tears. Kindness always did that to her. John put his arm around her waist and it sent a quiver through her. She thought she might break down at last. Her mother's voice brought her back like a sharp slap.

"Lord amercy," she whined. "I'm smothering down in here. Don't nobody care whether I live or die around here."

Lacey turned to go and was surprised when John held on to her for just a fleeting second. She patted the hand that held her waist. He let her go reluctantly. Ruby was already standing over Annie fanning her with a church fan.

"I'll get you some sassafras tea, Ma. It's probably been a while since you had a cup of sassafras tea."

"I think I need a doctor. It'll take more than tea to fix what's wrong with me."

"Well, maybe we will just try the tea first before we go calling a doctor," Lacey said gently.

"That girl don't care if I do die," she heard her mother say to Ruby as she disappeared from the room. She could hear Ruby soothing her mother like a baby. She busied herself with boiling the water and peeling off the sassafras root. She took the strong, hot tea and set it on the table next to her mother's chair. Her mother looked at it like it was poison. "I never could stand the taste of that stuff. Don't you have any coffee?"

Lacey thought of all the times her mother had sent her running to the woods to look for sassafras bark, saying that it was the only thing that helped her in the spring of the year. She took the cup back without a word and brought back a cup of coffee.

"I don't reckon there was any of that chess pie left," Annie asked taking the coffee.

"I'll get it," Ruby volunteered.

Annie slurped her coffee.

"Ma," Lacey ventured squatting down by her mother. "John and me want you to know that you are welcome to live here with us now."

Her mother's gasp stopped her. "Good heavens," she cried. "Live here in this wilderness-place! Why, I'd be scared to death to think about it."

"Well, Ma you lived in Wilder for nearly twenty years."

"That was different. They was people everywhere."

"There's plenty of people here on the Homesteads. They just don't live as close together as people did in Wilder."

"I reckon, you'd be expecting me to help out on the farm."

Lacey almost laughed at the thought of her mother helping her to plow the fields and put out a garden. "No, Ma. You wouldn't have to turn your hand to a thing."

"When I seen this place, I thought to myself, Frank should of let you gone with Coy when you was a mind to. He done made something of hisself."

Lacey looked up in horror to see John in the doorway. Her eyes tried to hold him but he slipped out without a word. Had he overheard her mother's remark, she wondered. She didn't worry whether anyone else had heard. She looked at her mother and felt the closest thing to hatred she had ever felt. She knew in an instant what she had refused to see all of her life that her mother was a mean and selfish woman who had only grown worse with the years.

"No," Annie stated flatly like she had known all along that Lacey would ask her to stay and had thought it out long ago. "I've thought it over and I've made up my mind. I'm going back with Will and Ruby. Ruby needs me to help her out with the younguns. You've got Cora here to help you. It wouldn't be fair for you to have us both."

Ruby walked up behind Lacey and handed the pie to Annie who dug into it with relish. She wondered if Ruby had expected any of this. She and John had discussed what was to be done with her mother long before the train had arrived bringing her pa's body home but she had had no chance to talk it over with Will and Ruby.

"It's not what I want so much as what's right, you understand," Annie said between bites.

Lacey stared at her mother, speechless.

Her mother shook her head. "Lacey you are going to have to learn not to be so selfish about these things. You always was one for getting your way."

She had obviously taken Lacey's silence as disappointment. "I know, Ma," was all she could say. She left her mother to enjoy her pie and went into the kitchen. The dishes had all been washed and stacked and the food covered with tea towels. Cora stood at the sink wringing out the dishtowels. "Cora, you didn't have to do all this. I meant to help out."

"Hush, now. It's done. Go on out and talk to your brother Will. Spend some time with him while you can. Visit with Ruby. I know you've missed her."

Ruby appeared in the doorway. "Come on, Ruby. Let's go feed the chickens," Lacey said.

A whining voice came from the living room. "Go on," Cora demanded.

"I should check on her," Lacey said without feeling.

"Don't worry. I'm just the one that can handle a poor widder-woman," Cora said, winking over her shoulder.

Ruby and Lacey slipped out the back door with a plateful of day old cornbread for the chickens. As soon as they were out of earshot of the house, Ruby said, "I should of told you beforehand that there weren't no way your ma was planning on staying here in Tennessee. I don't care what she says, she's been happy since the day we got to Anderson."

"It's not Ma I'm worried about. It's you."

"Don't you worry about me. Your ma never did expect from me like she done you. She always expected a heap of a lot more from you than she did from anybody else. She's got her friends and things to do up there that keep her busy. I hate to say it but here she'd just be a pure tolerable burden to you Lacey. Now it may be ugly of me to say but I have to say it. Your ma has got it in her to be a mean woman and she's always took that meanness out on you."

She looked to Lacey to see if her words had upset her. Lacey was surprised to hear Ruby say such a thing. Ruby had never acted as though she was aware of her ma's nature. In fact, Lacey had not thought of her as mean until today, just childish and selfish. Somehow the realization had lifted a burden from her shoulders. She knew now that no matter how hard she tried she could never please her mother and that it was not her fault. She smiled at Ruby to reassure her. "Ruby, you are too good to me. Will's lucky to have you as a wife and I'm lucky to have you as a friend."

Ruby blushed her face a pretty strawberry color. "I was afraid you would be mad at me."

"Over what you said about Ma?" she asked honestly.

"That and other things."

"What other things, Ruby?"

Ruby squirmed uncomfortably. Lacey could tell she had something on her mind. To give her time, she tossed the crumbled bread to the chickens. They squawked and climbed over each other fighting for more than their fair share. Fern and Fannie Mae, the two Bantam hens that were Lacey's pets, came out of the chicken house at the sound of the ruckus and started immediately to the center of the fray, loudly protesting being left out. Even though they were smaller than the other chickens, they were feisty and had soon gobbled up a large portion of the crumbs. Lacey opened the gate and sat down on the ground away from where the chickens were eating. The two Bantams left the crowd and came to her climbing all over her lap, pecking at the plate she still held.

"Lacey," Ruby cried in amazement. "You've done turned them hens into pets."

Lacey enjoyed Ruby's surprised look. "I named them Fern and Fannie Mae but the way they go on sometimes, I think I should've called them Fret and Fuss."

Ruby giggled behind her hand.

"Now, don't you go telling folks," Lacey teased. "I wouldn't let just anybody see me making a fool of myself over two hens but you've been my friend a long time."

"Then you're really not mad at me. We're still friends."

"I'm not mad," Lacey said exasperated by Ruby's meekness. "You want to tell me why I should be."

"Cause I didn't write to tell you how bad off your pa was."

So that was it, Lacey thought. In truth she had been hurt that she had not known until it was too late that he was so sick. She was sure Ruby had kept it from her out of love but still she would never forgive herself for not being there when her pa needed her. "I'm not mad Ruby. You done what you thought was right. There probably wasn't a thing I could have done anyway," she said sadly. She thought about her pa's frequent nosebleeds and the way his breath rattled in his lungs like a strong wind in a pine thicket. She stood up, sending the hens squawking in different directions. She slowly opened and closed the fence, taking her time, not looking at Ruby until she felt that none of her true feelings would show. Ruby stood before as helpless as a naughty child looking for forgiveness.

"I know how much you thought of your pa, Lacey."

Ruby looked right into Lacey's face and she thought she might not be able to contain the tears. "Let's walk. I need to stretch my legs." They took off towards the garden, arm in arm.

"I just want you to know that I thought the world of your pa too and I took the best care of him I knowed how," Ruby said earnestly.

Lacey patted the arm that was entwined with hers. "I'm telling you now, not to worry about it. You've done more than was your place to have to do."

"That's why I'm telling you all this," Ruby said her voice coming out in sighs. "Maybe you think it was your place to do what I done and you're feeling bad about it. It was your ma's choice to go to Indiana and your pa's choice to go along with her."

Lacey knew what Ruby was saying was the truth. Her ma had been dead set on going almost before Will and Ruby had had time to settle in and find a place to live. Her pa had held out as long as he could but eventually he had given in as always. She had not left them. They had left her, she realized suddenly with relief.

"There weren't nothing you could have done to change things if you had of been there," Ruby went on. "I knowed that you and John was working hard to make a go of it here. Me and Will talked it over and we decided not to worry you."

Lacey thought of her brother Will, who had always been the family hot-head and troublemaker. He had never gotten along with their pa from the time he was a little boy. It seemed strange to her that he would be the one to take him in at the end. Will had finally won the place in her father's heart she had so longed for. Part of her was jealous that it had worked out that way. Part of her was touched that the brother who had teased and tormented her as a child would want to save her any more worry. "You are sweet to tell me all of this, Ruby. It means a lot to me. You don't know how much I've missed having you close by."

"There ain't nothing in this world I wouldn't do for you," Ruby said honestly.

Lacey squeezed Ruby's arm, unable to speak for fear she would cry. They walked on in silence. Lacey wondered if her pa had seen the farm that she and John had built would he have been proud of her. She imagined him saying, "Gal, you've got a fine place here." He would call her gal again, as he had only in those moments when she suspected; he was especially pleased with her. She shook her head to clear away the thought. When they came to the garden plot, Lacey, without thinking, bent down and began pulling weeds from between the rows as she talked. "You and Will done enough by bringing Pa back here to Tennessee. That means a lot to me having him here. I want you to know that John will make it right with Will about the expenses for the funeral and all."

"Oh, that's took care of," Ruby said simply.

"What do you mean?" Lacey asked frowning up at Ruby.

"Coy give us the money."

The shock of the news made Lacey splay her hand out on the ground to catch herself. "Why ... what," Lacey stammered.

"Actually, it was money he'd left with us for safekeeping," Ruby went on, seeming not to notice Lacey's consternation. "When Will sent him a telegram saying we was bringing your pa home for burying, he wired back, for us to take the money and use whatever we needed. What he said was to make sure Lacey got whatever she wanted. Ain't that the nicest thing you ever heard?"

Lacey was stunned, too overwhelmed by the news to take it all in. She was touched and angry and frightened all at the same time. It was incredibly generous of Coy to pay for the burying of a man who had never shown him a moment's kindness. At the same time it was so like Coy to do such an unheard of thing that it shook her to the core to think of it. The thought that ran through her mind was that it was not his place to do this thing. He had stepped way over the line of what was proper. But when had Coy ever given thought to such matters? Hadn't he shown up at the funeral like he was family? Will had gone up to him first, warmly shaking his hand. And was there any wonder after what she had just learned? It was surprising to her that neither Will nor Ruby found anything unusual in what Coy had done.

John had not gone to shake Coy's hand, but had waited until he came to him, even then being barely civil. He must have been surprised to see him there; although word must have gotten out that he was in town. He had the whole town talking. She had avoided going into town for fear of running into him. Suddenly, thinking of Coy, she realized that her pa would not have been proud of her at all. He might have pointed out to her that he had been right all along. Hadn't he told her that loving Coy would be like holding fire in her hands? Who could know what Coy meant to do next? Her thoughts crowded in on her and she had to brush them aside like an insect buzzing around her face. "John will give Will the money and he can pay Coy back. It's our place to take care of our own," she said as matter-of-factly as possible.

"Will already offered and Coy wouldn't hear of it."

Lacey let it go to keep from revealing her true feelings to Ruby. She nodded as though the matter was settled. "Tell me what it's like living in Anderson," she said to change the subject. They walked on around the yard looking at the flowers Lacey had planted. They laughed and talked as they had as young girls in Wilder before the strike. It was just like old times. Only Lacey could know how much had changed since those days.

20

It was the kind of cold, gray November day that spoke of worse things to come. John had to admit he had become more aware of the changes in the weather since moving to the Cumberland Homesteads. It had not meant as much when he had worked in the mines, but even so the day struck him as unusually dismal. A mist hung in the cold, lead-colored air. The sky looked like dead ashes from a campfire. The damp seeped through John's clothes and quickly chilled him to the bone as he stood looking at the site the men had staked out. The Association had voted, at the urging of the government, to spend fifty-five thousand dollars to build a modern, well-equipped cannery. The plan was for some of the Homesteaders to grow the produce and others to work in the cannery getting it ready for market. John was to be in charge of the project.

A new manager for the Cumberland Homesteads had replaced Macy Stanton, and the Farm Security Administration had assumed control from the Resettlement Administration. It was the third change in as many years. They were being tossed from one agency to another like a hot coal from the fire. The rural farm projects had become a thorn in the side of the New Deal. They were all suffering from the same problems of high costs and no industry to support the communities now that they had been built. In many ways the people were as stranded as they had been before the projects were built.

The new manager was Major Oliver. He had been a major in the First World War and it showed in his rigid style. He was a man who believed in obedience to authority and strict discipline. It was his job, and the Farm Security Administration's desire, to bring the project under tighter control.

The idea was to build a cannery in an attempt to combine agriculture with the industry they so desperately needed. The idea did not have the full support of the Association but so far no project had. The sorghum mill they had started seemed already doomed to failure. There had not been enough rain to produce a good cane crop and then much of that had been lost due to the inexperience of the men at making syrup. More men had been hired to do the job than were really necessary and the extra overhead had quickly eaten up their profits. Once again, profits from the Trading Post had been siphoned off to cover the loss.

John could only shake his head at the money wasted. He could still remember, as clearly as though it was yesterday, the first payday he had drawn after being out of work so long. The look of the money in his hand and the feel of it in his pocket were an ever-present memory. It was interesting to him how quickly that payday could become the measure of a man's worth. How quickly the loss of it could take from a man everything he held dear, including his dignity.

He knew he had been brooding far too much lately. It was enough to make a man sick to see the way things were going. It was getting harder and harder for some folks to agree on anything. Even when they did more times than not it did not work out. Maybe he was the fool for expecting folks to get along. He shook his head to clear his thoughts, which were surely as gray as the morning mist that surrounded him.

The Association had asked him to try to open a coal mine in a valley not far from the Homesteads. The engineers had located what they thought was a fair-sized seam of coal. He had the experience to bring it out if he wanted the job, but his heart wasn't in it. As time went by, the idea of going underground again became less and less appealing. Of course he would do it if he had to, but he had been relieved when Major Oliver had come to him about building the cannery.

He didn't know a thing about building a cannery. That was why he was there now studying the situation. He had to admit he had learned a lot since he had been working on the Homesteads. He had picked up the carpentry skills just as Stanton had said he would and in many ways he had come to like the work. There was a challenge to starting with nothing but the raw materials and seeing it all come together piece by piece.

He had ordered the boiler from a company in Kentucky and it had just been delivered. It stood before him like a fat, angry man demanding attention. The problem was the boiler had a sixty-foot smokestack that had to be set atop it. Not a man on the place had any experience with a thing like that. So it had been up to him to figure out how to get it up there. He had gone to Crossville and bought a seventy-foot pole from the Tennessee Electric Company and he had set it in the ground next to the boiler. In his mind he was picturing how he would tie off the ropes and pulleys to pull the smokestack up where it could be eased onto the boiler.

Clyde Reid came up beside him and stood looking at the pole his arms resting on his belly. "Devil of a thing, ain't it."

John nodded, not willing to break up his concentration.

"Can you do it?"

"I got no choice."

"I mean, do you know how?"

John didn't look at Clyde. He didn't like the tone in his voice but he didn't let on. "I got a plan, if that's what you're asking. I'm pretty sure I can make it work."

"I don't doubt you, John. It's just that some of the men are saying you got this job because you and Major Oliver is buddies. They think you done went over to the other side."

John felt his back go rigid. "What other side Clyde?" he snapped irritably without turning to face Clyde. "They's just one side that I can see and that's whatever side can make this thing work so we can all go on living here." John could feel Clyde looking at him and he knew that he had passed over a certain line. He was not himself and it was beginning to show. For the first time in his life, he seemed unable to control his anger. He felt justified at his anger over what Clyde was saying but it was unlike him to lash out like that. He could tell that Clyde had made a note of it.

"Well, it ain't going to help nothing if they think you're on the side of the government. That's all I'm saying. Folks is beginning to feel like they don't have no say in what goes on around here anyway. They used to think with you on the board; they at least had someone looking out for their side. Now, that's just what I've been hearing."

Wearily John pulled himself together. Lately, he had felt like he was walking a rope bridge across a high gulch. His neck muscles tightened around his throat but he resisted reaching up to rub them. "They still have somebody looking out for them.

After all, I live here. Whatever happens to them happens to me too. They ought to be able to see that."

"They see you with a good job. They see you in the truck with Major Oliver driving through the Homesteads. They see that rich feller from up North driving his fancy automobile out towards your place."

The words hit John like a punch in the gut. He knew the rich fellow Clyde was speaking of was Coy. He could only imagine that he had been to visit Lacey when he was at work because he had not been there when John was home. Lacey had never mentioned it. Pain shot up the back of his neck and made his head pound. "I went with Major Oliver to look at a site to open a coal mine if it's anybody's business. I don't have to explain to folks what I do."

"I'm just telling you this for your own good, John. Major Oliver has a way of rubbing folks wrong. He's a military man all the way. If the folks in power say jump, he jumps and then he tells us to jump. And the folks in power is the United States government. It sure ain't the folks here on the Homesteads."

"I appreciate the advice," John lied. "Now, don't you have work to do?"

"Well, you study on it," Clyde said, ignoring the remark about work.

"I'll do that when I get time. I got a job to do."

Jack walked up behind them and John was relieved to see him. "For now Clyde, me and Jack is going to get in this truck and go load it up with fertilizer."

"What for?"

"So the wheels won't spin when we go to pull up that smokestack," John said as he got in the truck.

They drove the short distance to the Trading Post. Jack acted like he wanted to say something but if he did he kept it to himself. They worked in silence loading the truck. John was glad to have something to keep his hands busy. Soon he was sweating under his denim jacket but still he refused to slacken his pace. He needed to burn off the bad feeling that had a hold on him all morning. His anger slowly slipped away as he worked. He tried not to blame the folks on the Homestead for doubting his intentions. He tried to see their side of it. He was privy to a lot more information than they were and he was confused about what was going on. Each time the manager and the agency changed, the rules changed. Every time they made a change in Washington, they took more control away from the people. It was like they couldn't be trusted to run their own lives. After three years, they still didn't know if they would ever own their farms outright. It was hard to love something and care for it and live in fear of losing it. It was enough to make a person nervous about the future. He knew it was taking a toll on him. "That should just about do it, Jack," John said, throwing on one last bag.

"We got her pretty loaded," Jack commented as they drove back to the cannery site.

"I'm planning on climbing that pole and rigging up some ropes to a pulley. We'll tie the ropes to the truck and to the smokestack. You take off down that field with the truck and with any luck we can hoist that thing right up there. I'll have a couple of men climb up on the boiler and as you raise it up, they can set it in place."

"Ain't you afraid of high places?"

"I'm more afraid of not getting this thing to work."

Jack grinned and slapped him on the arm.

They climbed out of the truck and John gave his orders to the men. He could feel the men watching as he climbed the pegs of the pole to the top. The ropes were heavy on his shoulders but they hid the view below. It was just as well. John was terrified of heights. He could remember how as a youngun all his friends used to make a game of crossing the big Highland Trestle. It must have been a hundred feet to the rocks below. They made a dare out of running it. John could never do it as a dare even if it had left him feeling humiliated. He had once come back later and tried it alone. He had done it but it hadn't made him feel better. It had somehow made him more afraid, like challenging the danger had used up his luck on a foolish whim. Now, he really needed the courage he had used that day so recklessly. Of course he was a man now and there were worse things than fear. There was failure. He worked with that thought ever present in his mind and he soon had the ropes and pulley in place. The men tied them off. John gave Jack the signal to take off in the truck. With every foot the truck moved the smokestack eased up. John held his breath as it reached the top of the pole. He yelled for Jack to stop the truck and gave the sign for the men on the boiler to ease it into place. When it snapped perfectly into place the men cheered and John breathed a sigh of relief. He had not failed. They couldn't say he had gotten the job because he was a friend with the boss. He climbed down slowly; glad when his feet were again on solid ground. He sent two men to tie off the guide wires that were attached to the smokestack and would serve to steady it.

He allowed himself a moment of pride as he stood looking at the huge boiler with its tall smokestack. Someone tapped him on the shoulder and he turned to face Rusty Ligon. It set John's teeth on edge just seeing him. Rusty's meaty shoulders were packed into his shirt like stuffing in a sausage. He had black hair that covered not only his face but also a lot of his body. He had a face that reminded John of a wild boar. What worried John was that he had a personality to match. "What can I do for you Rusty?" he asked as friendly as possible.

"This cannery is coming right along here, I see."

"I'd say you better be thinking about what you're planning on planting in the spring."

"You got the wrong man, John. I ain't no farmer."

John wondered how many of the other men felt that way. They had all come there, he thought, with the dream of owning their own farms. Now, more and more of the men were finding that farming was not to their liking. "Just what were you planning on doing then Rusty."

"I plan on having me one of them cannery jobs."

John didn't say anything. He shifted his weight slightly and hunched one shoulder. The cold was getting to him again now that he wasn't working.

"We intend to bring in the union," Rusty announced.

Somehow John had known this was what Rusty was leading up to. There had been talk of unionizing almost from the beginning of the Homesteads. "Jack," he called out. "Take a couple of the men and go unload that truck. The rest of you men start digging on that foundation." He turned back to Rusty without comment.

"Just how do you feel about that?" Rusty prodded.

"I've always been a union man all my life. I got nothing against unions."

"How do you think the boss man is going to take to the idea?"

"That's not my place to say."

"Well, I never knowed a boss man yet that took to no union."

"This ain't no regular boss. This is the government."

"It's the same thing."

John shrugged.

"I thought maybe you hanging around them managers all the time, you might of changed your way of thinking."

John could feel his temper rise. This was the second time in one morning he had been asked to defend himself. What did folks want from him? "I always could think for myself, Rusty. What's got you so all fired up about the union?"

"For one thing, this here is a factory. They get you in a factory; they can make you do what they want unless you got a union standing up for you. I know, I worked in the textile mills over in Harriman."

"They've been pretty fair about things so far. They've paid a better than fair wage."

"That was when they needed us to clear the land and build the houses. Now, work's scarce. They could pay us what they want."

John stopped himself short of pointing out to Rusty that they hadn't been needed to clear the land. The land had been cleared as a way of giving men jobs. "Well, so far they've paid better than most folks around here make."

"That's another thing. That's another reason why we want a closed shop. They's plenty of folks around here looking for a job. We don't want nobody who ain't a Cumberland Homesteader and a union member being allowed to work in this cannery."

"Why would they go to all the trouble to build this cannery so folks could have a place to work and then bring in outsiders? That don't make sense."

"Don't have to make sense. They could do it. They'd do it just to show they don't have to pay us a good wage. Ain't that what they done in the mines?"

"They brought in scabs after we went on strike."

"See what I mean. And they paid them less than you'd been making. Ain't that right?"

"That's right."

"Then how come it sounds to me like you're arguing against the union."

"I don't care what it sounds like to you, Rusty," John snapped angrily, tired of Rusty's badgering.

"You know we voted you onto the board of the Association and we can vote you off. You don't see this union thing our way; we got enough votes to get you off of that board. We'll put us a man in there that can do us right."

John ground his teeth until his jaws bulged with the effort. He was not going to give Rusty the satisfaction of seeing his threat hit home. "Suit yourself, Rusty" he said as calmly as he could. "Now, I got to get back to work." He walked off, leaving Rusty standing.

Jack brought the truck around. "Bout dinner time," he said as he got out.

"I'm going home for dinner. You want a ride?"

"I brought something with me. You know how it is at my house with all the little ones running around. A man can get more peace and quiet here."

"Reckon, I'll see you in an hour then."

Jack came up to the truck and put his foot on the running board and one hand on the door. "What was Rusty talking about?"

"Union. A bunch of the men are wanting to bring the union into the cannery."

"What did you say?"

"Not my place to say, but I told him to suit hisself."

Jack nodded and dropped his foot from the running board and backed off. John drove off glad to be by himself for a while. He drove slowly trying to push the events of the morning out of his mind. He was glad he had told Lacey he would be coming home for dinner. It made him feel better to think of her there working about the place with that easy way of hers. In fact she had hardly been off the place in months. It was all he could do to get her into town anymore. There had been a time when she had loved going to Crossville on a busy Saturday to shop. Maybe her pa's death still had a hold on her. Maybe she didn't think it was proper just yet to be out. Whatever the reason, it was just as well. The last time he had been in Crossville he had run into Coy Lynn Wilson and his wife. He had given back the money Coy had loaned Will for the funeral. It had taken quite a chunk from what he had managed to put by, but it had to be done. Coy never said why he had come to Crossville. He had heard talk, of course. Talk was he had made friends with some real important people. That he had the bank president and his wife to supper twice. It was hard for a man like Coy to come into any town without causing a stir, but it was usually a different kind than he was creating in Crossville. It bothered John knowing how well things were going for Coy. Folks said he planned to buy a business in Crossville. That meant he planned on staying. It didn't even sound like Coy to him. He had always been such a loner. John knew from Will, Coy had money coming in from Indiana from his businesses up there. A man like Coy could always get by without having to hold down a job. That was what rubbed him so he guessed; just knowing that Coy would always get by seemingly with such ease, when he was working so hard to make it. And still things didn't seem to be working out.

When Coy had introduced him to Susan, she had been as warm and pretty as a winter fire. It had sparked a hope in him that maybe Coy had not come back for the reason he believed. Maybe Coy was happily married now and just looking for a place to settle down. There was still hope he had judged him wrong. He had ended up by apologizing to Susan for not having them out. He had explained that he knew Lacey would want to, but with her pa dying and all, and he had let it go at that. He had told them to plan on coming to Sunday dinner for sure. They had both smiled and thanked him. Said they looked forward to it. It made him sick knowing what he really wanted was to see Lacey and Coy together. He wanted to watch their eyes, search the expressions on their faces, and catch their furtive glances, like he had those months in Wilder. He had to know if Lacey still loved Coy and if that was why Coy was back.

Lacey was putting his plate on the table when he walked in the door. She smiled at him and went back to the stove to take the cornbread from the oven. He washed up at the kitchen sink. On the drain board sat jars of strawberry preserves Lacey had made back in the summer. She had washed off the jars, cleaning them up for the craft sale to be held at the Trading Post the next week. Cora had a time talking her into it. It had been hard convincing Lacey she had anything worth selling. He smiled at the shiny jars; glad she had decided to go through with it. Daniel Lee sat in the floor stacking empty spools of thread. John squatted down and ruffled his thick hair. Daniel Lee looked up still intent on his work and handed John a spool. "Here, Daddy," he said. It tugged at John's heart to hear the word daddy. No sooner had John thanked him than he reached and took the spool back and stacked it with the others. He handed John another spool and then quickly took it back. John stood up. "You keep up the good work there, son. I think I'm going to have me some dinner. I like to see a man who enjoys his work." Daniel Lee looked up and smiled his winning smile. The thought flashed through John's mind that here was another thing to lose. It was so unlike him to have such thoughts. It wasn't normal for him to be this way, but he couldn't stop himself. It was like everything was pressing in on him. He put the palm of his hand to his forehead and pressed against his suddenly aching temple.

"Are you all right, John?" Lacey asked. "Did you stand up too fast?"

He looked up to see Lacey looking at him her brow creased with worry. "I reckon I must have." He sat down at the kitchen table and stared at the food in front of him. He should have been hungry but he had no appetite. Lacey sat across from him. "You're not going to eat?" he asked when he saw she had not set a place for herself.

"I nibbled when I fed Daniel Lee. I don't seem to be much hungry."

"I see you're getting ready for the sale." He picked at his food.

"Foolishness, I guess. I'll probably just be toting them up there and toting them back. But if there's a chance of making some money, I thought I ought to take it."

"You ought to think more of yourself. You make the best strawberry preserves anybody ever ate." He had said it simply and truthfully. He was surprised to see her blush. She was unsure of herself over a jar of jam. She probably didn't even know that she was a wonderful mother and the best wife a man could have. She probably didn't even know that she held his life in her hands like a baby bird that had fallen from the nest. Life was as complicated to get through as a laurel thicket in springtime, he thought. He caught a sigh before it escaped his lips. He pushed his plate back, unable to pretend any longer that he was hungry. Lacey watched but did not say anything, for which he was grateful. She brought him his pipe already packed and refilled his coffee cup. As he sat sucking in the warm smoke as though he might draw strength from it, he looked up to see Cora standing in the doorway.

"I need to talk to you two and I reckon this is as good a time as any," she said, skittish as a colt.

"What's the matter, Mama?" John asked.

"Ain't nothing the matter, son," she answered twisting her mouth around and biting nervously on her lower lip.

John was unaccustomed to seeming his mother at a loss for words. He noticed that Lacey too was somewhat taken aback by Cora's behavior. They waited patiently for her to speak.

"Well, the thing is I ain't getting any younger. I don't look bad for my age, don't get me wrong," she said grinning weakly. "I just don't see my looks improving with age, that's all. Anyway, you know me and Mitch has been sorta spending time together. Lately, we've been talking about maybe..."

"Mama, are you and Mitch thinking about getting married?" John asked, surprise in his voice.

"You needn't sound so surprised. You didn't think I could go on living off you younguns forever, did you?"

Actually, John had thought Cora would go on living with them forever. He had never pictured it any other way. He remembered now that Lacey had hinted at what might be coming, but he hadn't taken her seriously.

"Mitch has a little house in Crossville. He's been fixing it up for us."

"You're moving to Crossville!" John almost yelled.

Cora and Lacey looked at him like he was the one who had lost his mind.

"I thought you'd be happy for me, son. I'm getting too old for stringing leather britches and putting food by and making quilts. From now on, I'm planning on buying all my goods at the grocery store and the only thing I'm planning on growing is peonies in my yard," she said with a chuckle.

Lacey jumped up and hugged Cora. "I'm real happy for you, Cora."

"It ain't like I mean to leave you here to do it all. I was just teasing about the work and all. I just waited this long because

I wanted to see you two settled in. They was so much to be done around here in the beginning. I couldn't see taking off then. It's not like I'll be far away. I'll be around when you need me. It's just the two of you need to have a home of your own without an old woman hanging around."

"Now, Cora, you know we love you," Lacey said, wiping a tear from her cheek.

"Hush Lacey. I know that," she said patting her shoulder gently.

"Mama, do you love Mitch?" John asked, still stunned by the news.

"Don't you go talking foolishness. He is as good a man as I'm likely to find at my age. He's got a house and a good job," she said, like the logic of it more than settled the matter.

"Mama, I just want you to be happy. I don't want you to do something because you feel like you have to. You're not a burden to us."

"You're a good son, John. Maybe I don't tell you that often enough. It's not my way. And Lacey, I couldn't have asked for a better daughter if you'd been born to me. I'm proud of you both. The truth is it's time I made a life for myself. I can't go on mourning your pa forever. You can just cry so much before you realize it won't bring him back."

His pa had been dead for almost five years, killed in a mining accident. This was the first sign from his mother that she had grieved for his father. It shocked him to know that in fact, she still grieved for him. She was a remarkable woman, but he had come to take her strength for granted, seeing only his mother and not the real person below the surface. He looked up to find her staring at him.

"I loved your daddy better then anything in this world. Me getting married again don't change that one bit. Can you understand that son?"

John nodded. "I didn't mean to suggest nothing like that. I just wanted to make sure you was doing this because you love Mitch and not because you think you ort to."

"Don't never go looking for love with your hand out, son. If I've learned anything in all my years, it's the world can't stand a beggar. If you go in with nothing, you'll most likely come out with nothing. So I always take with me what I'll be needing."

She looked at him like it was a lesson he needed to learn sooner or later and maybe telling him could spare him the in-between. It gave him a peculiar feeling that she should find him in need of such a talking to. Was it so obvious to her that he stood before Lacey waiting for a handout, he wondered? Was it so obvious to her that Lacey did not love him? He had always believed that only he could know. The thought made the shame rise up in him that his own mother might be feeling pity for him. "Well, I hope you know what you're doing," he snapped with more anger than he meant to show.

"Mercy son" she said shaking her head in frustration with her son's thick headedness. "Menfolk think a woman can't know her own mind. I'll admit sometimes a woman has a hard time making a choice and it comes off looking like she can't think for herself. The truth is most of them choices a woman has to make is between a rock and a hard place. That ain't the case here. I'm doing this because it's what I want to do. You remember that now and don't be fretting over it."

"All right Mama."

"Then I'd like your blessing."

"Of course Mama."

She came and put her hand under his chin and kissed his forehead. "Thank you son. I guess, I can tell Mitch to get his suit cleaned," she said smiling down at him.

"Cora," Lacey spoke up. "You have to let us have the wedding here. We'll have all the neighbors in."

"Lordie no," Cora gasped. "And me an old woman. What would folks think? It ain't that I don't appreciate it honey, but we are just a planning on having it done quick like at the court house."

It was the only time John had ever seen his mother truly embarrassed. It hurt him to think what this might be costing her but she was a stubborn woman and there would be no talking her out of it. He watched as she went over by the back door and picked up a bucket.

"Now, I better take this slop bucket out and slop them hogs," Cora said once again her practical self. "I heard them hogs out there fussing. They don't know the more they eat the faster they'll be bacon." She threw back her head and laughed big as she went out the door.

Lacey came and stood behind John and put her arm around his shoulder. The tenderness of it made him almost break down. He really was happy for his mother. Her talk of getting married had just stirred up a lot of emotions in him at a time when he seemed to be at his limit to handle anything more. He thought of his father, long dead. His mother must have loved him much as he loved Lacey. Now he was gone and there was no way to bring him back. He knew how the fear of losing Lacey left him almost short of breath. He wanted to turn and bury his face into Lacey's warm body and cry for all his worth. Cry for his father dead a young man, cry for his mother who might be marrying a man she didn't love, cry for the fears that gnawed at him and the tiny hope that kept him going. The tiny hope that Lacey would never forsake him. He thought of the little gold locket that he had found in the back of the dresser drawer when he had been looking for his lost pocketknife. It had been wrapped in a woman's hanky and he had not meant to pry. He just couldn't stop himself from unwrapping it and looking inside. When he had seen the strands of hair, one brown and the other black, he had at first thought they belonged to Lacey and Daniel Lee. Then it had hit him like a jolt. The dark strand belonged to Coy. With a sudden realization came the knowledge that so did Daniel Lee. He laughed in a bitter way to think that he hadn't known it all along. He guessed that somewhere deep inside, he had known but had shut it out. It made sense now, why she had married him when she had not really loved him. It made sense now why Coy was in Crossville. That was the first day of many days since that it had come to him that he would rather be dead than face losing Lacey and Daniel Lee. He wanted to tell Lacey that now. He wanted to turn to her now and tell her that he didn't want to go on living, couldn't go on living without her and without Daniel Lee. But in the end, he did not turn to her. He could not let her know how weak he was. Instead meanness rose up in him and he said, "I've invited Coy Lynn Wilson and his wife to Sunday dinner." He wanted to look at her to see the expression on her face but he could not bring himself to do it. He rose quickly and took his hat from the back of the chair where it hung and went out the back door. He held his breath until he was almost at the truck and then it exploded out of him. He leaned against the truck, weak and sick at his stomach.

Beads of sweat formed on his brow even in the chill air. It seemed a peculiar thing. When he looked up, Lacey was standing in the doorway staring at him. He couldn't remember why he had fled the house so quickly or how long he had been standing there. He couldn't bear the thought of her coming to check on him so he did the only thing that he knew how to keep things bound together. He got in his truck and went back to work.

21

Lacey loved the root cellar even in winter. It was cool and dark with just the light from the door falling across the shelves of canned goods and bags of potatoes. The house had been built without a basement and they had no place the first year to store their food for the winter. In the spring, John and Ben had dug a place under the house about eight by ten feet. They had built shelves along the walls to store the food Lacey canned and packed the dirt floor hard to hold the cabbages, potatoes and turnips through the winter. Every time Lacey walked down the three steps to enter the root cellar, she had to brush away the spider webs when she opened the door. She always felt apologetic to the spider whose web she had to destroy. She understood the hard work that had gone into its construction and marveled that the spider would start over that very night, never seeming to tire of its job. She guessed only people had the capacity to become tired and discouraged.

Lacey sat Daniel Lee on the top step and left him to play with the jumping jack Ben had made for him. Ben had hinged all the arms and legs and painted a face on the jumping jack. Daniel Lee had named the toy Boo because that was what Ben had said in play the first time he had taught him to pull on the string and make the thing dance. Daniel Lee had come to love Boo and carried him everywhere, talking to him like he was a real person.

Lacey pulled up her apron; squatted down and hurried to fill the pocket she had formed with potatoes. It was cold and she did not want to leave Daniel Lee sitting on the steps too long. John had not been eating well lately no matter what she fixed, but she thought that maybe a good stew might be just the thing for supper on such a cold day.

She looked around the root cellar scanning the shelves. John had said he had invited Coy and his wife for Sunday dinner. After all the months of avoiding Coy, she would have to face him in her own house. The thought made her ill. She had stayed away from Crossville but she had heard talk of him from plenty of folks. When he had first come back, she had hoped it was only for a visit, a few weeks at most, but the weeks had grown into months. He had somehow set himself up in town as an important person and the whole town was talking about him.

She could hear Daniel Lee jabbering and smiled to herself. He was probably telling Boo a story. A shadow crossed the doorway darkening the room. It caught Lacey by surprise because there had been no sun, only a dull gray haze. She looked up, her eyes adjusting to the new darkness. Coy stood in the doorway holding Daniel Lee in his arms. Lacey stumbled backward, spilling the potatoes on the ground. They rolled around the floor like marbles. She did not attempt to pick them up but pulled herself up on her knees.

"Hello, Lacey," Coy said his voice echoing through the cellar. "I hope I didn't scare you."

She jumped to her feet and took the boy from his arms pushing Coy back from the top step with the force of her body. Her hand brushed against the wool of his dark gray herringbone topcoat and she felt the warmth from his body. She took a step backwards and encircled Daniel Lee with her arms. "Coy," she said trying out her voice. It was raspy and weak, made worse by the fluttering of her heart. "I just wasn't expecting you." She was lying, of course. She had seen him drive by before and she had expected that any day she might have to face him.

"Aren't you going to invite me in for coffee?"

She hesitated not wanting to be in the house alone with him but Daniel Lee's hands felt cold. She wiped his runny nose with the corner of her apron. "Come on in. I've got coffee on the stove."

He followed her up the back steps and into the kitchen. She could feel him watching her as she took off her son's jacket, gave him a cracker and placed him on the floor next to his blocks. He gave Boo a bite of his cracker. Lacey kissed him on his head and he held Boo up for her to kiss. She kissed her finger and placed it on Boo's face, which satisfied Daniel Lee. She could feel Coy's eyes on her but she did not look at him.

Instead she went to the stove and poured two cups of coffee. When she carried them to the table, Coy was still standing with his coat buttoned and his hat in his hand. "Let me take your coat," she said trying to appear calm while easing the cups to the table. He slowly unbuttoned his coat, slipping it easily from his shoulders. He handed it to her and she carried it to the living room and laid it across the back of a chair. She felt the rich nap with her hand but resisted the urge to hold the coat close to her face.

When she returned to the kitchen, Coy sat drinking his coffee. She took her cup and stood by the sink sipping the warm coffee. There was an awkward silence between them. She did not know what to expect from him. He looked about the room taking in everything. His eyes came to rest on Daniel Lee and he smiled at the boy playing. Then the smile faded. "Why didn't you let me know, Lacey?"

She did not have to ask him what he meant. "It was too late. You were already gone."

"And you had already married John. You married him before you knew about the baby."

"Yes," she whispered, her voice cracking, "I didn't know about the baby when I married John."

"But you knew right away didn't you" he said accusingly.

"I had already sent you away. I was already married to John," she said helplessly.

"I would have come back."

"It's done now. We have both gotten on with our lives."

"Maybe we have gotten on with our lives. I wasn't given much choice in the matter, but it doesn't change the fact that the boy is my son. You might like me to conveniently forget that and let you get on with your life but I can't. How could you have done this to me, Lacey?"

He looked at her his eyes sad but unwavering. They bore into her, their dark, murkiness spilling over her until she had to look away.

"Of all the people on this earth, I thought you would be the one who would understand," he said his voice full of disappointment. "You were the only person I ever shared my feelings with about what it was like for me growing up. I found out when I was fifteen who my real father was but by then the damage had been done. Nobody had a right to do to me what my mother did. She denied me my real father because she couldn't face the truth."

Lacey knew everything Coy said was true. She felt that everything she had ever done in her whole life had been a mistake. "If you want to hear me say I was a coward, I'll say it. But you know I would never hurt Daniel Lee the way your mother hurt you." she said in weak defense.

"You have hurt me, Lacey. In a thousand ways, she never dreamed about."

Tears pooled in Lacey's eyes and she fought to hold them in. "I'm sorry, Coy. It does seem like in trying to do the right thing; I've done everything wrong. Now, I don't know how to make it right. Whatever I do will hurt someone, either you or John, or Daniel Lee. It's Daniel Lee I have to think of now."

"It's not your choice to make, Lacey. The boy is mine."

"Coy, if I hurt you so much," Lacey said with suddenly realization, "why did you come back? You didn't know about Daniel Lee until that day in Crossville. I saw it in your face."

"You're right. Thanks to you, I didn't know. It was a shock seeing him that day."

Coy stood up and went to the window. He touched the leaves of a violet that sat on the windowsill. A smile tugged at his lips as he took in the velvety softness. It caused an ache to catch in Lacey's throat. It was so like the gentle, tender Coy she had fallen in love with. He looked up to catch her staring. The old shadow came over his eyes that she had seen so often when he was trying to hide his feelings.

"I came back to see if you had had any regrets."

A sigh escaped her lips but she gave him no answer.

"You see I've done quite well for myself," he said matter-of-factly. "I guess I came back to make you regret what you had done."

"If it's only regrets you want from me Coy," she said sadly, "I won't deny you that. If I thought it would satisfy you I would lay them out before you like a sacrifice." She watched his face for signs that he was glad she had moments to regret her decision but he turned his face from her and stared out the window. "From that day in Wilder, when I sent you away, I've lived in fear that you would come back."

He turned and looked at her. "Well, I always imagined you thinking about me," he said a bemused smile on his lips. "But I had hoped for a little more than that."

She looked at him pleadingly. "That spring day when you come back to Wilder, you was so full of yourself. Life had gone real good for you in those months you'd been away."

"Lacey, I'd been working for Seth in his dry goods store. I thought that was what you wanted. I was excited, wanting to tell you all about it."

She held up her hand to stop him from saying any more. "You never asked how it had been for me, there in Wilder that winter. We nearly starved, you know. There was nothing to eat and no coal to heat the house. Then Ben got sick."

"Lacey, you can't blame me for Ben getting sick."

"No, I don't blame you. He followed me to your place. There was snow on the ground and he didn't have no coat nor shoes. He saw us together. You see I'd lied to him. Told him it was over and that it was best if we both forgot all about you. Only time I ever lied to him."

"Lacey, I did what I could. I gave John all the money I won gambling to buy food. Ben couldn't hold it against me for loving you."

"I tried to explain it to him about you spying on the company. Ben don't trust easy. He gets hurt real deep. Some folks are just that way," she said, suddenly angry.

"Why are you so angry with me?"

She looked at him like he should know the answer. "I thought you would know. I'm afraid. That's why I'm trying to explain."

"You mean explain why you married John."

"I couldn't explain to you that day on the mountain. You wouldn't let me and anyway I wouldn't of had the courage. Maybe if you understand why I married John you'll go back to Indiana and let things be." He started to speak but she shook her head to stop him. "Just listen to me, Coy."

The heat of the kitchen suddenly crowded in on her and she tugged at the neck of her dress. She was glad when Coy walked to the back door and opened it just a little. She watched as he lit a cigarette and stood blowing the smoke into the cold November air. He leaned back against the door facing and waited for her to continue.

"There had been so much fighting that year union against company, miners against gun thugs and finally family against family when some of the men went back to work. So much shooting and killing. Union men shooting at scabs, mine guards shooting at union men. Folks sleeping on the floor so they wouldn't be shot in their sleep when the gun thugs fired into the houses at night."

She was silent for a moment, her eyes closed remembering. "And the hunger, I'll never forget the hunger and the cold." Her body shook involuntarily at the memory.

"I was there Lacey. Remember?"

"Yes," she said looking at him at last. "When Ben got sick," she went on picking up the thread of her thoughts again. "I just couldn't take anymore. I could see where it wasn't meant for me to be happy. I felt like I was being punished for all the lies and deceiving I done to be with you. When it came to losing Ben, I couldn't do it. I just said all right, I give up. Maybe I was a coward, but the price was too high and I was too weak. I know you think this is foolishness and I don't hope to convince you otherwise."

"Lacey, you don't need God to punish you. You can think of enough ways yourself. You're not responsible for everything bad that happens in this world."

"But I was responsible for what happened to Ben."

"It might have happened anyway. Lots of folks were getting sick with no food and no heat."

She nodded realizing the truth in what he said, but it made no difference. "I made a promise. I can't take it back now. I don't blame you for being angry with me for what I done. I don't blame you for trying to get back at me. I'm just begging you not to do it."

"We were both fools. I should have made you go with me that day."

She smiled a sad smile thinking how impossible it all seemed now, the time that they had shared. "But you didn't, Coy. Don't you see?"

She watched as he put his hand to his temple rubbing his forehead. He seemed lost in the frustration of it all.

"Those times when we was together that I forgot all about the strike and the fear and the hunger." She gave him a whimsical smile and bit the corner of her lip.

Suddenly, he tossed his cigarette out the door. He came to her and took her in his arms. A tremor coursed through her body. He took her face in his hands and kissed her gently on the lips. "You still love me," he whispered hoarsely.

She leaned against him for just a moment catching the beat of his heart on her cheek. Then, she put her hand on his shoulder softly to push him away. The warmth of his body was still on her face and his smell filled her senses. "It's not my pride I'm trying to save here Coy," she whispered. "It's our son."

"Our son," he echoed, the words hanging in the air.

"Don't hurt him. Please, Coy," she begged. "I promise you I'll make a good life for him here."

"I have a right to see him."

"I know," she sighed.

"And someday he has to know."

She shook her head and tears flew from the corners of her eyes.

"Lacey, it's written all over his face. John has to know."

She looked at him horrified.

"John's a good man, but he can't be that big a fool," Coy said angrily.

Suddenly, she knew what he meant to do. "Oh Coy, please don't. Please don't tell him."

"He's bound to find out someday."

"Then let me be the one to tell him."

Coy looked at her until his dark, unrelenting gaze softened. "I won't wait long, Lacey."

She nodded.

"I'll see you Sunday, you know. John must have told you he's invited us for Sunday dinner."

"I can't tell him by Sunday. It's too soon," she pleaded. It had been her lack of courage that had caused all of this and now once again she felt ashamed of her weakness.

"I'd better be going."

"I'll get your coat."

When she came back holding his coat in her arms, he was bent down playing with the boy. It struck her how very much they looked alike and she knew he was right. Someday John would have to know and she prayed for the courage to be the one to tell him.

"Is he much like me?" Coy asked.

"He has your laugh."

Coy smiled, pleased by her words. "We could have had a good life."

"It's too late for us Coy. It's time for us to think of our son. He shouldn't have to suffer for our sins. No matter what we have done in the past, we can still make him proud of us by what we do from this point on."

"You still think your biggest sin was loving me," Coy lashed out. "What about the way you have lied to me? What about the way you are deceiving John even now? Are you sure it's Daniel Lee you are trying to protect or is it still that precious respectability you are trying to hold on to? You always did worry too much about what other people thought. Think about it, Lacey. I can give him everything."

"Coy," Lacey whispered, putting her arm over her face to stop the blow of his words. Tears spilled over her cheeks and she wiped them away with her hand. She knew her weakness was like a poison spreading out to touch everyone she loved.

Coy came to her and put his hands on her shoulders. He looked at her with a sudden tenderness. "Have you been happy here?" he asked unexpectedly.

"Yes," she replied honestly.

"And have you been happy?" she asked. "Your wife is beautiful."

"Susan. Her name is Susan."

Lacey nodded.

"See you Sunday," he said slipping the coat from her arms.

She noticed he had not said if he had been happy. She walked with him to the door and stood watching as he got into his automobile. She closed the door and pressed her forehead to the wood. She knew that night the dream would come.

22

"I'll drive," Susan said cheerfully as she jumped into the driver's side of the automobile.

"Are you sure?" Coy asked, irritated by her enthusiasm. "It's a long drive out to the Cumberland Homesteads and you haven't driven that much." At her request, he had been teaching her to drive around town.

"Oh, Coy," she said giving him a good-humored pat on the knee. "You're as nervous as a cat in a room full of rocking chairs." She laughed at her own cleverness.

"And where did you pick that up?" he asked.

"At the construction site in Anderson. That's what one of the brick masons said about you."

He shot her a look.

"Can I help it if the saying fits?" she chuckled. She was still a source of amazement to him. He thought by now she would have grown tired of the small-town life and begged to be taken back to Indiana. Instead she had set up housekeeping, acting for the world like she intended to stay in Crossville for the next thirty years. He had left the hotel that day after finding her note, and gone in search of her. The place she had rented was a large frame house surrounded by a picket fence and flower gardens. An elderly lady whose husband had died had owned it and she had gone to live with her children. Susan had told him all of this like it was the most fascinating story. Not once did she mention why she had rented a house. In fact, not once in all the months they had been there had they discussed their plans. They had simply come to this place and life had set up around them like a nomad camp.

From that first day when he had bought the automobile, he had realized that people were treating him differently, like he was somebody. He knew Susan was responsible, at least in part, for the way things had gone for him since they had arrived in Crossville. He figured he owed her for the way she had

polished him up since they had been married. To him it was
laughable that folks saw him as a man of means, when he knew
he was the same old Coy inside. Seth had always called himself
"fifth generation worthless." Coy figured he made it sixth
generation. But Susan had not grown up that way, and she
thought nothing of inviting the bank president and his wife to
the house for supper. He had on occasion seen her be snobbish
and cruel to her own friends when she wanted to be, but here
in Crossville she had been warm and endearing to everyone.
The house was always full of friends she had made, talking and
drinking coffee. She chummed with banker's wives as easily as
farmer's wives. It was almost like she was the one who had
come home and he was the outsider, a fact he took with bitter
amusement.

Before long, important businessmen in town started to ask
him his plans and he had been forced to come up with one. He
said he was looking to buy a business, and he enjoyed the stir
he was causing, chuckling at his own respectability.

He sat back in his seat and tried to content himself with
looking out the window. After refusing Susan's offer to go
with her to church, the morning had stretched out endlessly. It
surprised him to be this nervous about going to dinner at
Lacey's home. After all, this was why he had come back. His
plan had unfolded like a blueprint from that first day he had
run into Lacey on the street. She only had to look at him to see
how well he had done. What he had not been prepared for was
the sight of her. It had caught him off guard, the look of her.
He had forgotten how the sun brought the freckles out across
her nose and how her hair curled up around her cheeks. But it
had been the boy that had sent him reeling. He had only wanted
to show Lacey. He had not counted on having a son. He had
not counted on still loving Lacey so much.

Next to him, Susan hummed a maddeningly cheerful tune.
"Did you have to wear that dress?" he snapped, her good mood
wearing on his nerves.

Susan smiled, but kept her eyes on the road. "You like this
dress."

Coy let it drop. It was his favorite dress and he had often
told her so. Still he wished she had worn something less
expensive.

"This is really beautiful," Susan said looking around at the passing countryside.

Coy lit a cigarette.

"I can't believe you've never brought me out here," Susan said with a smile.

He shrugged.

"What's this?" she asked as they passed a built-up area of buildings.

"The office for the project. You do know about the Cumberland Homesteads project, don't you?"

"Of course, I keep up with it in the paper every week," she said pleasantly. "Besides, there are a lot of important businessmen in town involved with this project. Did you know that?"

He rolled down the window and flipped his cigarette out. "And I suppose you've met them all."

She gave him a smug look that told him he was right. Despite himself, he laughed out loud. "You know, I'm beginning to think your daddy's a fool for not letting you take over his business."

"Why, thank you, Coy. That's the nicest thing you've ever said to me," Susan said, genuinely pleased.

"Turn off at this next drive. That's the Trotter place."

As they pulled up to the house, John was just walking back from the barn. He came up to welcome them. He shook Coy's hand and gave Susan a polite nod.

"I better take y'all through the front way. Lacey would have my hide if I brought you in through the kitchen."

They followed John up the flagstone walk and up the front steps. Coy thought he saw a shadow at the window and wondered if Lacey had been watching them. But when they came into the house, Lacey was just coming through from the kitchen. Her face was flushed from the heat of the cookstove and she was brushing a small strand of hair back into place. She smiled at them shyly. She wore a blue dress the color of her eyes with tiny rosebuds. It was probably her Sunday best, Coy thought, and the thought made his heart jump.

"Lacey," Susan said, putting out her hand. "So good to see you again. Remember we met the first day Coy and I arrived. We were just getting off the train when we ran into you. It was kind of you to direct us to the hotel."

"Good to see you," Lacey stammered, shooting John a quick look from under her lashes. She put out her hand hesitantly, unaccustomed to shaking hands.

Coy could see the color rise in Lacey's cheeks. Obviously, she had not mentioned that meeting to John. Suddenly, he almost regretted coming; realizing how uncomfortable Lacey must be having him there with Susan.

"Won't you sit down? Dinner's almost ready," Lacey said softly.

Susan and Coy sat down on the sofa. John sat across from them in a chair by the fireplace. Coy thought it must be "his" chair. The place the man of the house always sits in the evenings after supper. Lacey perched nervously on the arm of a chair nearby.

"Did you have any trouble finding the place?" John asked.

"No," Susan interjected. "Coy knew right where it was."

"I just followed your directions, John," Coy quickly added. John nodded.

"It was a lovely drive," Susan commented.

"The road is a little rough yet," John said.

"Oh, I don't mind. I enjoy driving," Susan said as though she'd been driving all of her life.

"I guess I'd better check on the dinner," Lacey said.

"Let me help you," Susan said jumping up.

"No need," Lacey replied, surprised by Susan's offer.

"I want to," Susan said cheerfully. "It'll give us a chance to get to know each other."

Coy watched the two women leave the room. He noticed Susan walked that tight little walk she always used when she was trying to control her limp. It was the first sign from her that she was nervous. "So tell me, John," he asked to get his mind off the women, "how do you like being a farmer?"

"Well, I can't say I'm doing much farming. I've mostly been working on construction. You know there weren't nothing here but woods when we first come. All this land had to be cleared before a single house was built. They's near ten thousand acres here, and two hundred and fifty homes. I don't know if you noticed that big building up near the office."

"I believe I did. Big smokestack?"

"That's the one. That's to be the cannery. It's part of our latest plan to give folks on the Homestead a job. Some folks will grow the crops and some folks will work in the cannery."

Coy had picked up on the "our" when John mentioned the latest plan to put people there to work. "Looks to me like, things are going well for you here. Sounds to me like you're a real important man."

"Nothing like that, I'm just proud to have the chance."

Coy realized John was actually embarrassed to be caught bragging. If it had been anybody else that said it Coy would have thought he was putting on the humble act, but knowing it was John he could believe he was sincere. Still it got under his skin, the way John was always the decent sort. He had told Lacey that John surely knew about what had gone on between them in Wilder, but now he doubted the truth of that. Knowing the kind of man John was, and seemingly always would be, he would never suspect anybody of being any less decent than he had always been. "I reckon, you had your fill of coal mining after Wilder," he said holding up bad times to him like a specter.

He saw John's jaw tighten at the mention of Wilder but he simply nodded. A silence hung in the room.

"This life suits Lacey," John commented finally, looking Coy over with a steady gaze. There was something strange in the look that was unlike John but Coy couldn't place it.

"This is a nice house you have here," Coy said honestly.

John seemed pleased by the compliment. "The walls are eighteen inches thick. The stone was dug out of the quarries around here."

John talked on about the architect who had designed the houses and laid out the plans for the whole community. Coy's mind wandered to the kitchen where he could hear Susan's deep laughter and Lacey's softer voice, mingle. He wondered what they could possibly be talking about. Suddenly, Susan appeared in the doorway summoning them to the table with a sunny smile.

"I don't know about you, Coy, but I'm starved. Lacey makes me sing in church and that always gives me a powerful appetite."

Lacey gave John a tolerant look and Coy could tell that he had said this same thing to her many times before. Their familiarity with each other surprised him. He had not until that moment pictured them as really married. For three years now they had shared moments like this, little sayings, and familiar jokes. The realization sent a jolt of pain through him and he suddenly found himself hating John for having what he so desperately wanted.

Susan led them into the kitchen and Coy guessed there was no dining room in the house. When they sat around the small kitchen table, Susan beamed as though she personally had prepared the meal. "Isn't this lovely, Coy? Lacey grew practically this entire meal in her garden and canned it herself."

"Lacey always was a good hand at getting by," he said truthfully thinking of the times that they had scoured the fields and hills around Wilder for berries and wild plants to feed her family. He smiled across the table at her and he could tell by the look that passed between them that she was thinking the same thing.

Coy realized that John was looking at him. Solemnly John said, "Let us pray." As he listened to John's words whirling about him, he thought about how strange it was to be sitting in Lacey's home as a guest. It was something he could never have done when Frank Conners was alive. He looked around the crowded kitchen at all the things Lacey touched each day as she worked there. The flour-sack curtains on the kitchen windows were stiff and shiny from starch and a hot iron. He looked down at the table. It was set with thick, sturdy dishes. He thought how quickly he had become accustomed to eating on Susan's fine china handed down from her grandmother. He looked up at Susan who sat head bowed and folded hands as pious as a saint. Surely, he thought, she must find all of this very dull.

"Coy," John said.

He looked over to find John with a bowl in hand passing him the green beans. "Why, thank you, John. This looks delicious, Lacey."

"It's just plain cooking," she said looking down at her plate, embarrassed by his words.

"Lacey, you are too modest. You must tell me how you make this delicious fried chicken," Susan said cheerfully.

Lacey blushed and looked down at her plate. "I'd be happy to but there's not much to it," she said softly.

Something in Susan's manner made Coy want to kick her under the table. He couldn't believe Susan had the slightest interest in learning to cook fried chicken and he couldn't bear the thought of her making fun of Lacey.

"And Coy," Susan beamed, "you should see the beautiful things Lacey has made for the craft fair. All the women on the Homesteads are getting together to sell their homemade things for Christmas. Doesn't that sound like fun? It's going to be at those buildings we passed on the way."

"The Trading Post," John added.

"Well, I know I'm looking forward to it. If the other women are as talented as Lacey, it should be quite an event."

Coy wished Susan would quit gushing. "Where's Ben today?" Coy asked to change the subject.

Lacey squirmed uncomfortably in her chair. "He went to a friend's house after church. You know boys," she said as though to excuse him.

Coy wondered if Ben had known he was coming and didn't want to see him. Lacey jumped up suddenly and retrieved the coffeepot from the stove. She automatically refilled John's cup, a familiar gesture that Coy was certain she had done many times. Coy resented the way John took it as his due, this gentle loving thing that Lacey did for him. When she came to refill his cup, he wanted to reach out and touch her, but instead he just thanked her. She smiled a nervous smile and he saw her hand tremble. She returned the pot to the stove and came back with slices of fresh apple pie. It was hot and delicious and they ate with relish.

"Lacey, that was a wonderful meal," Coy said. It came out soft and loving like a caress. Lacey jumped up suddenly and left the room and he thought he had somehow said something wrong. When she came back she was carrying Daniel Lee. He was rubbing the sleep from his eyes. Only she had heard, he thought. Lacey was cooing to him. The sight of them together stirred an overpowering need in him.

"Hello there, little buddy," Coy said.

The boy was suddenly shy and put his face into Lacey's neck.

"Daniel Lee," Lacey gently chided, "say hello to Mr. and Mrs. Wilson."

Daniel Lee mumbled his greeting into Lacey's neck.

"He's still sleepy," Lacey said by way of apology.

"He's just adorable, isn't he, Coy?" Susan commented. "We hope to have children someday soon, don't we, dear?" she said smiling. Coy looked at her astonished, since she had never mentioned children to him before. He smiled back at her, but he had had just about enough of her cleverness. This was not the Susan he knew and he planned on telling her so in no uncertain terms when he got her alone again.

Lacey put Daniel Lee down and he went quickly to John's side. John reached down for the boy and slipped him gently onto his lap. The child eased back against John's chest and watched the visitors. Coy looked on fascinated and horrified to see his son up close, clinging to another man as his father. This, he thought angrily, was what he had agreed to, to stand by and watch but not to say anything. He wondered if this was how Seth felt years ago watching him grow up in another man's house. It was a sickening feeling and he wanted to snatch the boy from John's arms. Lacey went about fixing the boy a small plate of food. She put the plate on a tiny table nearby and took the boy from John. Coy could not take his eyes off Daniel Lee as he sat engrossed in his dinner. Lacey knelt next to the table talking to him gently and smoothing his thick, black hair.

"Let's go out on the front porch and have a smoke," John said, sliding back his chair.

Coy barely heard John's words and he knew he had been staring. "Why John, I don't remember you being a smoker," Coy said trying to keep his voice casual.

"I took up a pipe a few years back. Can't say why I done it but it's right enjoyable."

Lacey came up to him and handed him his pipe already packed with tobacco. John accepted it from her with a nod and smile.

Reluctantly, Coy left Lacey and Daniel Lee behind to join John on the front porch. There was a chill in the air that felt good after the warmth of the tight kitchen. They smoked and passed the time with idle talk. John asked him about his life in Indiana. As he talked, he had to laugh to himself to think how good it all sounded. If John thought him a fool for leaving, he didn't say, but then that wasn't his way. John was not one to let his true feelings show about anything. As Coy sat with his feelings coiled up inside himself like a spring, he wondered how John managed it.

Coy was ready to leave. The visit hadn't turned out quite like he had pictured it. Seeing Lacey here with John in their home had stuck in his throat like a bone. He had not imagined they would weave their lives into a pattern of comfort and routine like any other married couple. It set off a panic in him that was hard to control as he sat calmly listening to John ramble on about the project he was working on. After seeing, Lacey and Daniel Lee today he had to fight the urge to tell the truth and have it out, to claim what was rightfully his before it was too late. Only his promise to Lacey held him in check. "From what I hear this place has a lot of rules. I'm afraid to me it would be just like a mining camp without the dirt and soot," Coy found himself saying spitefully.

He could see John's eyes darken and his jaws tighten. He knew he had deliberately baited him but he could not help himself.

"You know I owe you, Coy. You saved my life once. And you saved Lacey's."

Coy waited, wondering what John was getting at, wondering how far he would go.

"That's a lot to owe one man," John said and the sound came out of him like the low, mean growl of a trapped animal. "That debt has been a burden to me at times."

"Consider the debt paid," Coy said rising from his chair.

"Then we understand each other," John said, rising to meet him. "Lacey's happy here."

"I think you mentioned that before. And I reckon you ought to know."

They stood looking at each other. Coy could tell by the look in John's eyes that he had underestimated him, that he knew everything. A sound at the screen door surprised them both and they turned to see Lacey staring out at them.

"I appreciate the hospitality," Coy said cordially. "I guess I'd better round up Susan and be getting back to Crossville. We'll be expecting you and Lacey to our house for dinner now real soon."

"Good to have you here," John said reaching out his hand to shake.

Coy shook his hand but he could see that John's eyes were still narrow with hate.

"I'll just go in and get Susan."

"Here, I'll go in with you."

"No, you stay and enjoy your pipe. I'll just say thanks to Lacey and be right back." He opened the screen door and Lacey backed up. "Lacey, that was a fine meal," he said as he followed her into the house.

John slowly eased himself back into the chair. Coy could still feel his eyes on him as he closed the door. The house was silent except for the ticking of the mantel clock. He started down hallway when suddenly Lacey turned to him.

"You didn't tell him, did you?" she said her voice a quiver.

"I don't have to. He knows."

"No, I know John. He doesn't know. He can't."

"Lacey, you asked me to let you be the one to tell him. I've agreed to that."

"Coy, think about what you're saying. Think about all the hurt that would cause. We don't have the right to do that." Her eyes darted from door to door to see if they were being observed. "We have to think of Daniel Lee. He's the most important thing in the world. He's more important than we are. We owe him a happy life."

"I am thinking of Daniel Lee, Lacey. I'm a rich man. And I do have the right. I am his father. If you can't find the courage to do it, I will," Coy threatened.

"Oh Coy, please don't," she pleaded, tears welling up in her eyes. He could see her heart beating under the fabric of her dress. "Give me until after Christmas."

Suddenly, the door flew open and Ben shot up the stairs, taking them two at a time.

Lacey jerked away from Coy liked she had been shot. "Ben," Lacey called to the boy. "Come back here."

Ben came back down the stairs slowly.

"Say hello to Coy," Lacey instructed.

"Hey Coy," Ben mumbled already starting to back up the steps.

"Ben, you've grown a foot since I saw you last," Coy said smiling his winning smile.

Ben nodded. "Yes sir."

Susan appeared in the hall, holding Daniel Lee in her arms. Coy and Susan's eyes met and locked.

"Why Coy, I was just coming to get you," she said without a hint of what she might be thinking. "Hadn't we better be going? We have guests coming tonight."

He knew they weren't expecting anyone that night, but he did not want to argue. "I was just thanking Lacey for the meal."

"Yes, Lacey. Thank you again for a very nice time. I can't tell you how much I have enjoyed this day," Susan said with a charming smile.

"Susan, this is Lacey's brother, Ben," Coy said.

"Hello, Ben. I'm Coy's wife," Susan said, hanging on the last word.

Ben smiled shyly. "Good to meet ya ma'am," he said, quickly slipping up the stairs before Lacey could call him back.

Daniel Lee reached for Lacey and Susan reluctantly slipped him into her arms with a sad smile. They all went out onto the porch and said their good-byes once again. Coy looked at Lacey and nodded. He would give her until after Christmas. He slid into the driver's seat without asking Susan. As they waved good-bye from the drive, Coy could see John slip his arm around Lacey's waist as they stood waving from the porch. He stomped on the gas pedal and sped away, causing Susan to catch her breath.

They rode in silence for several miles. Susan kept her eyes on the passing scenery. Finally, when he could stand it no longer he said. "Well, you certainly made a fool of yourself today."

"Oh," she said her voice deep with control. "I wasn't aware that I was the one making a fool of myself."

"You acted like you were having the time of your life. Praising the food like it was put together by some Paris chef. Like you'd give anything to be able to make biscuits and fry chicken."

She sat in silence staring at him. "I thought that was what you wanted in a wife, Coy," she said icily, "Someone to pour your coffee and pack your pipe."

"What gave you that idea?" he asked without looking at her.

"It's becoming quite obvious, you don't want me," she said without a hint of pity.

It was the first sign from her that she knew something was wrong between them. It shocked him that all of her good cheer and patience with him had been an act. She had known all along that he did not love her. He wondered how much else she knew. "So why do you stay?" he asked. It came out sounding cold and callous. He had not really meant it that way. He was just curious. He really did not want to hurt her but she would have no one to blame but her own stubborn self, especially, if it was true that she had known all along that he did not love her.

"You asked me along on this trip, or had you forgotten?"

He wheeled into their driveway and stopped the automobile. Susan got out without another word and went into the house without looking back. He couldn't say why her words had made him so angry. He just could not stand her self-righteous attitude, like she understood him better than he understood himself. He put the automobile in reverse and gunned it. He pulled out into the street eager to put some distance between Susan and her words and the memories of the day that haunted him.

23

"Just show me how to start the thing, Ben," Lacey begged.

"I don't know why you have to do this. John's not going to like you driving the truck," Ben said, irritated with his sister's determination.

It was a crisp, cool Saturday afternoon. John had taken Daniel Lee and walked to the Percy's house to talk over some things with Jack. He had no sooner been out of the house than Lacey had been after Ben to teach her to drive the truck. She knew John always left the keys in it.

"Go ahead, Ben. What do I do first?"

"You put your left foot on that there pedal," Ben said reluctantly giving in to Lacey's coaxing. "That's the clutch. Keep your right foot on this'un. That's the brake."

Lacey stretched her legs to reach the pedals. The seat was pulled up as far as it would go, but she could barely keep the clutch pushed in as Ben instructed. The idea of learning to drive had taken hold of her the moment she had seen Susan drive into her driveway behind the wheel of an automobile. It was something she had wanted from the first day John had driven the truck home, but she would never have had the nerve to try until the idea struck her that she might someday need to know. A day might come very soon, she realized, when she would need to drive the truck. Of course seeing Susan step out from behind the wheel so self-assured in all her finery had helped goad her into it. She had been nervous to the point of illness at having Coy and Susan there for Sunday dinner, but Susan had been very kind. Much to Lacey's dismay, she had liked Susan. She had sensed, to her surprise, that Susan was nervous too. She was so eager to please and Coy seemed not to notice. The way she walked trying to hide her limp, she seemed like such a strange mixture of self assurance and doubt, like she couldn't make up her mind what she was supposed to be.

She seemed almost like she was trying hard to be something she wasn't. It struck her that Coy and Susan had a lot in common.

Sunday had been a very difficult day for her. She had worried the whole time about what Coy might do or say. She cursed herself for her weakness whenever she was around him. She had spent the time on pins and needles watching every facial expression, every gesture for signs of impending disaster.

She had thought she was doing the right thing in marrying John. Before Coy had come back she had been sure of it, but he had a way of confusing her thinking. She had done so many things wrong, trying to do one thing right. Now she was no longer sure what was right and what was wrong. Like a leak in a dam, in trying to stop it one place, she had caused it in another. It seemed that the hurt that people did to one another just kept getting passed down from generation to generation, spreading out wider and wider like the ripples in a pond as families grew. The most important thing to her now was that the hurts never touch her son. Maybe she had been wrong to deny him his son. It was just that Daniel Lee belonged to her. She alone had given birth to him and loved him and cared for him as no one else could and in her heart that made him hers. But she knew that was just in her heart. The truth was she was terrified. The sins of the parents are visited upon the children, she thought with a chill.

"You scared?" Ben asked noticing the goose bumps on her arms.

"No," she lied. The truth was she was nearly sick with fear. She was beginning to think that she had somehow taken leave of her senses to try such a trick. Before Susan she had never known a woman to drive an automobile. It was because of Susan that she had decided to learn. It had come to be a test of courage in her and part of a plan she had to save her son. If she had to take off in the middle of the night, she could at least get to the train station.

"You ain't doing this 'cause of that woman are you?" Ben asked as though reading her thoughts.

"What woman?" she stammered thinking he had read her thoughts.

"Coy's wife. I seen her driving."

"When?"

"When they come to dinner. I hid out in the barn," he said sheepishly,

"Why did you do that? Why didn't you come in and eat dinner with us?"

He shrugged and looked away. "I didn't want to see Coy," he said boldly.

Lacey could feel herself grow warm. "He's a neighbor now, Ben. We'd be expected to have him and his wife to dinner. He's knowed John a long time. John asked them to dinner, hisself," she answered as honestly as she could.

It was clear now that Ben still did not trust them. And why should he, she thought, when nothing had really changed. They were still being dishonest with him.

"I don't like him being back like this," Ben said.

They both stared ahead unable to meet one another's gaze.

"Coy's a grown man. He can do what he likes."

Ben hit the dashboard with his fist.

She looked at him, taken aback by his anger. "Ben, what's wrong?"

"You're happy here, ain't you Lacey? Happy living here with John on the Homesteads?"

"Yes, Ben. I'm happy," she said weakly.

"Me too I like it here. I never want to leave."

"What's that got to do with Coy?" she asked knowing all along he meant.

"Coy always changes things. He stays just long enough to make folks think he's something special and then he takes off."

Lacey gripped the steering wheel until her knuckles turned white. She knew what Ben was saying was true. She also knew now that if she had to leave, Ben would not go with her. The realization that she was to lose Ben too made her ill.

"Are you all right?" Ben asked looking as her hands.

"I guess I am a little scared," she said truthfully. Ben obviously took it to mean she was scared about driving and he smiled back sympathetically.

"It's easy once you get the hang of it," he said earnestly. "Now, this here stick is the gearshift. I got it in first gear. You just ease your foot off the clutch and give it a little gas."

Lacey lifted her foot from the clutch and the truck jerked crazily up the drive until it choked to a stop.

Ben's fingers gripped the dash and he looked at Lacey wide-eyed.

"What did I do wrong?" she whispered hoarsely.

"You let out on the clutch too fast and you need to give it a little more gas."

Lacey squinted in concentration and tried again. Again the truck jerked to a stop. She looked to Ben for help.

"Try again, a little slower this time."

"Maybe, I'm just no good at this. You think I'm crazy to be doing this?"

"I think you're real brave to try," he said proudly.

"Why thank you, Ben," she said surprised that he would see it that way. At fourteen he was taller and heavier than she was, but still wiry. He had grown up so much since they had been on the farm. She had to keep reminding herself that just because she had raised him didn't mean she owned him. It was a hard lesson to be learned in one day and she knew she would have to learn it all over again with Daniel Lee.

"Lacey, try again," Ben said, calling her back from her thoughts.

She eased the clutch out and gently pressed on the gas. The truck eased forward. They were moving down the drive.

"Turn into the yard so we don't go out into the road," he instructed. Lacey turned the wheel amazed that the truck went in the direction she wanted to go. She smiled to herself and gave Ben a quick look.

He smiled back. "You're doing real good, Lacey."

She drove through the front yard and around the house again and again. As she came around the house for the third time she saw John coming up the driveway. "Oh my word Ben how do I stop this thing?" she cried.

"Push the clutch in and step on the brake."

She felt around helplessly with her feet. "I can't find the pedals, Ben."

"Turn, turn," Ben screamed as John jumped out of the way pushing Daniel Lee ahead of him.

They headed around the house as Lacey searched frantically for the pedals. She bent down to see if she could locate them. Suddenly, Ben screamed. When she looked up they were headed toward the henhouse. Lacey turned the wheel with all her might but it was too late and they hit the fencepost with a thud, knocking it down and taking the wire with it before the truck finally came to a stop within inches of the henhouse. The chickens flapped around squawking their alarm.

"Ben are you all right?" Lacey said grabbing him by the shoulders.

He looked at her wide-eyed. "I'm not hurt."

Lacey held on to him, feeling of his arms and shoulders and touching his face.

"Ah, Lacey, I said I ain't hurt." A grin spread at the corners of his mouth. "I'm a sight better than them chickens, I suspect."

"Oh, Ben," she laughed nervously giving him a hug. "I reckon, I'll just never learn."

"You can do it Lacey. You always do what ever you set your mind to."

She tried to smile her thanks for his praise. Suddenly his eyes widened.

"That is, if John ever let's you drive again," Ben stammered.

"John," she mouthed wordlessly. She looked to see him standing at the truck window holding Daniel Lee. He slowly opened the door. He had a peculiar look on his face like he couldn't believe what he had just witnessed.

"Are you two all right?" he asked.

"John. I could have killed you. And Daniel Lee too," Lacey said aghast.

"Not likely. We're too fast for that. Ain't we Daniel Lee?" John said teasingly.

Lacey hugged them both, covering Daniel Lee's face with kissing. "I'm sorry, John. I should have asked you about driving the truck, but I was afraid you'd make fun," she said her voice trailing off.

"Ben, you take Daniel Lee," John said solemnly.

Ben slid out of the truck and took the boy without a word. He stood back away from Lacey and John.

"I can fix the fence, John," Ben quietly offered. "Weren't none of the chickens hurt. It just shook'em up a might."

"Take the boy in the house, Ben. Where it's safe," John said without a smile.

Ben looked at him unsure about leaving.

"I'm going to teach your sister here to drive and it may not be safe out here," he said, a grin tugging at the corners of his mouth.

Ben started to laugh first. It took Lacey a moment to realize that John was teasing her. "John," she cried, hugging him around the waist. "You are the dearest thing."

He kissed her gently on the top of the head and lifted her into the truck. They spent the afternoon driving around and around the yard. Finally, they drove out on to the road and they stayed gone for a long time. When they came back Lacey went in to cook supper while John fixed the fence around the henhouse.

John drove Lacey to the Trading Post to set up her goods for the craft sale. He had tried to get her to drive the truck, but she had not learned her new skills to show off in front of all her neighbors. The place was already crowded with women bustling about setting up tables, covering them with starched white clothes and laying out their handmade goods. It had been their idea to have the sale before Christmas to encourage folks to buy their things for presents. Lacey hoped to make some money so she could buy Christmas presents for her family. She had never had a real Christmas with lots of presents under a tree and candy for the children. One really special Christmas when work had been good at the mines, they had all gotten an orange and a stick of peppermint candy. She wanted to give Ben and Daniel Lee a Christmas that would be a special memory for them forever. Somehow memories made in childhood stayed with a person longer and were more real. Maybe, she thought, if Daniel Lee's childhood memories were extra special they could somehow protect him from any hurt the future might hold. She needed this Christmas to be special to guard against what was to come.

It was fortunate for them that the weather had turned off warm because so many women had shown up that there had not been room inside the Trading Post. Extra tables had been set up in the yard. Ben with Daniel Lee in tow took off to where the other children had gathered to play. Lacey called after them to be careful.

Lacey picked a spot near a tree. John helped her set up her table. It was just a few planks of wood on sawhorses. She looked around at all the pretty quilts; doilies and hand embroidered tablecloths that adorned the tables. It made her proud to think of all the hard work these women had put into making such beautiful things even with all they had to do to care for their families and homes. "I'll be right back, John," she said giving him a pat on the arm. She went around to each table chatting with the women and honestly praising each quilt and baby blanket, each jar of jam and fruitcake, watching the women blush and blossom at her words. When she came back, John was leaning against the truck, whittling on a stick of wood and watching her from under his lashes as she approached. She was flushed and warm with excitement. "Oh John, there's just so many pretty things," she gushed.

"None as pretty as you, Lacey," he said taking her face in his hands and kissing her gently on the forehead. "That was a good thing you done going around like that. A lot of women couldn't of done that. They'd a maybe been jealous."

"John," she said taken aback by his action and his words. "You see goodness in me even when there is none." Suddenly, the truth of what she had said rang in her ears and she blushed. It was true; he seemed blind to the wickedness that haunted her. Always he saw only the best in her. She turned away, unable to meet his eyes.

Thomas Jefferson Morgan came from around the back of the truck; hat in hand, to greet them. "Howdy Lacey. John."

"Thomas," Lacey said in greeting. "We haven't been seeing much of you lately."

"Well, that's why I come by. I'm leaving the project."

"I hate to hear that, Thomas," John said.

"Millicent and me is getting married."

"John," Lacey exclaimed. "Isn't that good news?

"Well, ma'am," Thomas said sadly. "It's all in how you look at it. Millicent's folks is making her go home because they found out she was still seeing me. They won't have none of that on account of me being poor and all. We're running off to get married."

"I'm sorry to hear that," Lacey said kindly. "You're a fine young man and I'm just sorry they can't see that."

"I don't blame them none. Even I have to ask myself if I could be ruining Millicent's life. If I let her go back home she's likely to marry some rich man and live in luxury the rest of her life. What do I have to offer her?"

"Why, your love, Thomas," Lacey said taking his hand in hers.

"Let's hope she don't come to regret the trade," Thomas said with a wry smile. He gave Lacey a quick kiss on the cheek. "You and John sure have been good to me. I'll miss you both."

"Write and let us know how you're doing," John said, shaking Thomas' hand.

Thomas walked away. John and Lacey watched until he was out of sight.

"That is so sad," Lacey said.

"Who's to say he ain't right. She could be better off without him," John said coldly.

"John!" Lacey exclaimed, shocked that he could say such a thing.

"I'd better go," John said shuffling nervously behind her. "I've got work to do."

"Will you be back later?"

"I may not be back before this afternoon. Looks like you'll be busy enough though," he said nodding toward her table where several people were milling about.

"Cora's coming to sit with me sometime later in the morning."

"I reckon newlyweds don't get out as early as old married folks like us."

"Now, John, don't you tease your mama," she said shaking her finger at him. Cora and Mitch had married over a week ago quietly at the courthouse without a word to anyone. Cora had not even let them have a party with just the family but they had come to Thanksgiving dinner on Thursday. Lacey had made a cake and given Cora a pair of embroidered pillowcases. She thought it had pleased her. Lacey was really going to miss having Cora in the house with her, but she wished more than anything for her to be happy. "Go on to work now and I'll see you back here before dark."

John hesitated, hat in hand. He got into the truck slowly and sat behind the wheel for a minute before he cranked the motor. He rolled down the window.

Lacey walked up to the truck. "Is something the matter?" she asked. John opened his mouth like he wanted to say something but then he closed it and shook his head. He drove off with a wave of the hand. She waved back. She watched as he drove out of sight, worried by his behavior. So many times lately he seemed on the verge of telling her something but he always stopped himself short. She was sure it had something to do with his work on the cannery. There were problems and she knew that he brooded about them. Quiet by nature, he often spent the evening now without a word. Sometimes at night he went out to check on the livestock, she thought as an excuse to get out. He would be gone a long time, often not coming back until she was in bed. And he did not sleep well, but would get up in the middle of the night slipping out so as not to disturb her. She could have asked him at anytime. She could have gone to him and demanded to know what was bothering him, but she did not. She knew it was selfishness in her that she did not. She felt she couldn't bear anymore than she was bearing.

Lacey busied herself straightening her goods and putting out some more jams and jellies. Business was brisk with folks from Crossville and the Homesteads searching the tables for just the right thing. Money was still scarce for everyone and when Lacey finally sold a jar of her strawberry jam, she held the precious pennies in the palm of her hand staring at them with amazement. It was a strange feeling and she almost felt guilty taking cash for something she had done, something she would have given away if they had asked for it. She tucked the money into her sweater pocket.

When Lacey looked up Susan was just driving up. She stopped the automobile and searched the crowd before getting out. When she spotted Lacey, she waved a hesitant wave almost like a salute. Lacey smiled back, her heart beating rapidly in her chest, nervous at seeing Susan again but relieved she was alone. She had been afraid that Coy would choose the sale as a chance to see her again. At the sight of Susan, she felt guilty for the times she had thought of Coy in the past weeks.

Lacey noticed that Susan's navy suit fit her perfectly. The jacket was tight at her slim waist and the skirt flared at the bottom. Lacey winced at the plainness of her cotton dress and hand-knit wool sweater.

"Hello, Lacey," Susan said as she approached the table. "I just couldn't stay away after I saw all of the beautiful things you were gong to bring to the sale."

Lacey blushed, unaccustomed to such praise. "Well, I'm afraid my work is not much to talk about what with some of the women here can do. If you look around I'm sure you'll see."

"I'm sure there are some lovely things here and I will look around, thank you. I think what I'm interested in is right here at this table," Susan said, not taking her eyes off Lacey.

Lacey looked down unable to meet her steady gaze. She watched as Susan fingered the merchandise spread out on the table. Her hands were soft and pale with long slender fingers. Her hand stopped on a jar of jam. "I don't think I ever properly thanked you for having us over to dinner, Lacey. Coy enjoyed it very much. And I did too. We would love to return the favor sometime."

"That would be real nice," Lacey said softly. She looked at Susan surprised to see that she was nervously biting her lip. Her eyes were ringed with dark circles and Lacey could tell for the first time that she had been recently crying. "Well, we enjoyed having you both," she stammered.

"The meal was delicious."

"Nothing fancy, I'm sure..." she said letting her voice trail off. She had started to say she was sure Susan was used to better fare but stopped herself in time.

"You must teach me to cook like that. Coy does seem to so admire the way you do things."

Susan smiled when she said it but there was such a soft sweet sadness to her voice that made Lacey want to sink through the ground at the words. Something in her tone told Lacey more than she wanted to know. Beneath the smile and the cheerfulness that was Susan's shield was a woman deeply in love with a man who did not love her back. She knew it and was trying hard to be whatever it was Coy wanted her to be, whatever it was that would turn him around and make him love her. Lacey felt ashamed for having ever envied her. "I'm sure you're a good cook," she said weakly.

"No, I'm afraid I don't have much talent for whatever it is that wins a man's heart."

Lacey was saddened by the acceptance in Susan's voice as though she had long ago come to that conclusion but had suddenly been reminded of it. Lacey was struck dumb by the simple power of Susan's pain. "I've been cooking since I was seven years old. I never seen it as nothing special," Lacey said almost as an apology. Susan cocked her head to one side and looked at Lacey. "Oh, but it is," she said.

"I'd be happy to show you how, if you're really a mind to." "You're very kind. I may not be..." she hesitated. "That is I'm going to be very busy in the coming weeks." Lacey nodded unsure of what to say.

"I think I'll take this," Susan said holding up the jar of jam. She put the money on the table in front of Lacey.

"No, take it. A gift," Lacey said horrified by the sight of the coins. "I want you to have it. I would have given you a jar on Sunday if I had known you wanted one."

"Thank you, Lacey, but I always pay the price." She gave Lacey a knowing look. "Besides I'm glad I had a chance to see you today."

With that she turned and walked away the jar clutched to her chest. Lacey watched her drive away unable to take her eyes off the automobile until it had disappeared from sight. She had always thought that she had paid a price in giving up Coy but she could see now that there was a price for having him. Why had she really thought that the price of loving Coy would be less for any other woman than it had been for her? She scooped the coins from the table and threw them to the ground, grinding them into the dirt with her shoe until they had completely disappeared.

24

"She's just going to have to stop naming the livestock," John said shaking his head. He had his .22 caliber rifle in the crook of his arm. He and Ben were headed to the hog lot to shoot one of their Pollard China hogs. It was a chilly November day and the temperature was just right for slaughtering hogs. John had two other men on their way to help out with what was an all-day process of cleaning, cutting up and salting down the meat to cure.

"She just said she hoped it weren't Gertrude," Ben said embarrassed by the message he carried.

"Did she ask you to tell me that?"

"No, sir. She'd have my hide for sure, if she knowed I told. She was just fretting out loud."

"It won't be the brood sow. She knows that. Not this time anyhow but someday when we're done breeding her. Besides when we first got that sow, it was Lacey fussed the most about how she couldn't fatten the thing up. That's why it don't do for her to be naming the animals. Next thing you know Lacy will have me bringing the livestock in the house for the winter."

"You know, I think I heard her mention something like that," Ben said grinning.

John chuckled. "I swear I had to look you in the eye to tell if you was joshing. I wouldn't put it past Lacey that's for sure."

"She never could stand to see nothing suffer."

"I reckon you can't fault her for it," John said shaking his head and smiling. He turned suddenly serious, thinking that the whole thing of killing the hogs might be worrying the boy too. "It has to be done, son. We done spent too much fattening these hogs up on corn not to get a ham or two out of it. Got to be done, that's all," John said not looking at Ben. He wished Ben had not told him that Lacey was upset about the hog killing. She had not said a word to him about it the whole time he was building the smoke house and had been out to admire it half-a-dozen times. She had to know that the first cold day they would be slaughtering hogs.

He looked at Ben's face. He was wide-eyed and tight-lipped. John suspected he was torn between sympathy for Lacey and pride in being included with the men folk on such an important day. "Take these here matches, Ben and start a fire under that cast-iron pot. We need to get that water to boiling." John had earlier dug a pit to set the cast-iron pot into so that the hog would not have to be hoisted so high to be scalded.

"Yes, sir," he said seriously.

As soon as he was gone, John walked up to the pen where he had separated a barrow from the other hogs the night before and quickly slipped a .22 caliber bullet into the back of its head. The hog dropped without a sound. "Had to be done," John whispered. He jumped easily over the fence, took out a knife and cut the jugular vein on the left side of the throat about three inches back from the jawbone.

He turned at the sound of someone behind him and was surprised to see Lacey coming toward the pen carrying two dishpans. He quickly jumped the fence and came to take the pans.

"You'll need these pans. One's for sausage trimmings and the other is for lard. Put plenty of lean in the sausage pan," Lacey instructed, glancing over his shoulder.

He took the pans from her. "Cora said she'd be out before noon to help out."

Lacey nodded. "Send Ben in with the liver to soak as soon as you can."

John knew that keeping busy was Lacey's way of coping with what ever was troubling her. "The other men are due here any minute to help me string her up," he said stepping out of her way so she could get a clear view. He could see her relax when she saw that it was not Gertrude on the ground behind him.

"Well, I better get back to the house."

"Lacey," he called after her. "I thought you didn't like that old sow?"

She smiled back at him. "She's as contrary as anybody I ever met." she said her hands cocked on her hips. "And she's like me; there ain't no way to fatten us up. I think we're both turned funny." She gave him a wink and turned to go but stopped short and looked back at him. "It had to be done, John," she said simply as though she had read his mind. "We'll be proud to have the meat this winter. We're farmers now."

He gave her a wry smile. Just as he turned to get on with what was to be a long day, Jimmy Carlton drove up the drive in his rickety 1920 Model-T truck. He unfolded his rangy body from the cab and called out a greeting to John. Jack Percy got out from the passenger side, stamping his feet to knock the chill from the early morning air. When they saw that John had already killed the hog, they went to work without a sound. They dragged the carcass to the pot of boiling water that Ben had readied.

"I don't believe we can get this feller in that there pot, John," Jimmy concluded. "He is dang near longer than he is wide."

"Let's see if we can heft it up or we'll be all day scraping her down."

They strained to lift the gangly creature into the boiling water and rolled the body about to loosen the hair. They hauled it out and set about scraping with a newly sharpened knife until most of the hair was off the hide.

John hoisted a rope over a low hanging tree limb and together the men puffed the hog up by its hind legs. Jimmy stepped in and quickly gutted the creature with one long cut down the entire length of the underside from crotch to chin. The guts poured out and John caught them in a pail. He cut loose the liver and handed it to Ben. "Take this in to Lacey. She's waiting on it."

Ben took off running without a word, the liver warm and bloody in his hands.

"You ain't going to save those entrails, John?" Jimmy asked.

"Lacey done said she don't want nothing but the liver, Jimmy."

"You don't mind then, I'll take'em."

"You're welcome to them, but you'll be wanting more than that for your help."

"Don't owe me nothing for that, but I am partial to heart and kidneys. They make a man's blood rich."

"I've heard that," Jack said. "But I never felt poorly enough to make myself eat such as that."

"I've eat everything on a hog 'cepting its eyes," Jimmy said cutting the head off with one swift movement of his butcher knife. "You take this here head and grind up the snout, the jowls, brains and ears and make the best souse ever was. Leave out the ears if you don't like gristle. I never did mind it."

Jimmy worked on without looking up, his pipe dangling from his lips. Jack and John eyed each other doubtfully. "Jimmy, I had more in mind one of them fine hams cured up just in time for Christmas," John said.

"You men ain't getting above your raising, are you? Don't pay for a man to get above his raising or the good Lord will see to it he's took down a notch," Jimmy said, without looking at either of the men. "Hogs head stew now that's something I looked forward to when I was a youngun," Jimmy went on not missing a beat. "My mama made the best in the world mixed up with a little venison."

They worked on steadily for three hours with Ben running back and forth to carry parts of the hog in for Lacey to begin cutting up. When he announced to them all that Lacey had dinner ready, John was surprised to find he was hungry. They washed up in the crowded kitchen. Every available space was covered with hog parts. Cora stood at the cabinet grinding meat to make sausage. She looked up and spoke but went on with her work. The men sat down at the kitchen table. Lacey brought steaming hot biscuits from the stove. She had fried the tenderloin, fresh cut that day, until it was crisp and golden. Topped off with canned green beans from the garden and fried apples, John felt proud to offer such a meal to his friends. It amazed him that Lacey could put together such a meal with the clutter and work of preparing the hog meat for winter.

The women worked on while the men ate. They would eat later after the men had gone back to work and some of the dishes had been cleared.

"This is good tenderloin, John. You done a good job of fattening that hog up," Jack said.

"You can tell a hog fattened on corn," Jimmy commented. "Now chestnuts, that's the thing for a real sweet meat. Ain't nothing sweeter than a hog fattened on chestnuts."

"If it's tolerable at all, I owe it to Lacey. She's the one took care of the hogs. She liked to fed them things till they was foundered and they never did fatten up like no regular hog. Did they Lacey?" John asked.

"I know them hogs eat as well as we did 'cause I carried the scraps to them myself right off the table," she laughed.

"If this tenderloin is any sign, it surely was worth the trouble," Jimmy said.

"Thank you Jimmy I'm pleased you're enjoying it." Lacey said.

"We better be getting back out there if we are going to get that meat salted down by dark. Ben, are you 'bout ready?" John asked.

Ben nodded, cramming the last of a biscuit into his mouth.

"That was a good meal," Jack said patting his stomach with satisfaction.

She nodded her thanks. "I'll bring ya'll some more coffee out later."

They went out slowly into the crisp November air lighting their pipes as they went. The smoke hung in the air around their heads.

"Say, John," Jimmy said blowing smoke up toward the sky.

John looked at him waiting for him to say more.

"I didn't want to bring this up when we was all enjoying such a fine meal, but did you get your papers from the government?"

"You mean the purchase agreement on the farm?"

"Them's the ones."

"Yeah I got'em."

"What did you think about what they's asking us to do?"

"I can't say. I ain't studied it through yet," John answered. He had developed a grain of caution over the past months and was slower to give his opinion of late since more and more the people were squaring off against the government. The Homesteaders had been asking the government for some kind of agreement as to what their farms were to cost and how they were to go about paying them off for some time, but until now they had not received an answer. They had been paying rent on their places ever since the credit-hour system had been outlawed. John had to admit he had been disappointed when he had read the agreement they had waited so long to receive.

"But do you mean to sign it?"

Ben stood kicking the ground with the toe of his shoe and John thought about sending him on but then thought better of it. He did not want to embarrass the boy on his big day by treating him like a child. "I said I hadn't thought it through, but I reckon if I don't have no quarrels with it I will. What about you?"

"I don't believe I can see my way clear to sign it the way it is. It says the farm is to be paid off over forty years. Look at me, John. Do I look like a young man to you? I'm fifty years old. I'll be dead and in my grave before my place is paid for."

"We done lived here four years already and ain't got nothing to show for it," Jack interjected.

"They said they'd put part of the rent we paid toward the cost of the farm but they done set the price of the farms on what they is worth now. They are going to make us pay for all the stuff we done with our own hands to fix the places up like that chicken house of your'n and that smokehouse. Does that seem right to you, John?" Jimmy asked.

John just took a draw on his pipe and shook his head. Jimmy was right. The price they had been offered was a lot more than most of them had expected. The more a person had done to improve their own farm the more it was going to cost them.

"And what's more," Jimmy went on as though John had answered him, "it says right there that if they want to evict a man for any reason during those forty years they can. Throw him out and keep the farm. Now, I ain't too bright but I ain't a fool. You'll not catch me signing nothing like that."

"Won't they be making you move if you don't sign it?" Jack asked. "Ain't that what it says in them papers, to sign or leave?"

"They can't make us all move," Jimmy said matter-of-factly.

"What do you mean," John asked.

"Over half the people I talked to has done said they won't sign it. They say it's unfair. They're going to organize a big rent strike until they get somebody to listen to their terms."

"A rent strike!" John shouted unable to hide his surprise.

"That's what I said, weren't it," Jimmy retorted. "They don't plan on paying a penny of rent until they get that agreement rewrote to suit theirselves. Folks think it would mean a heap, if you'd go out with them on this. You've got some say with the bosses."

"I don't know about that, Jimmy. I'll be happy to speak up about getting their concerns heard, but I don't know about going on a rent strike."

Jimmy shrugged. "It might be to your favor to side with the common folks."

"What do you mean by that?"

"Well, they's a election coming up for the board. Not that I wouldn't vote for you, you understand. But a body hears talk they might vote against you if you don't sign."

"I reckon I just have to take my chances."

"Suit yourself, but folks is already set to go on strike. They're disgusted with the government spying around on them and making 'em do first one thing and then another."

John nodded wearily. "All right Jimmy, I'll see what I can do." The thought of yet another problem with the project made John want to throw up his hands. He sighed heavily, his breath visible in the cold air. "Now, let's get this hog put up before it ain't fit for nothing."

"That's what I'm here for," Jimmy said lifting a giant ham over his shoulder and carrying it to the smokehouse.

John joined him carrying the other half. John had spent weeks constructing the sturdy smokehouse. He had sealed it to keep the insects out and to keep the meat cool in summer. He had built shelving around the walls to hold the meat so it would get the right amount of air. He stood shoulder to shoulder with Jimmy salting down the hams, covering each one until it was white. When Jimmy went back to get more of the meat, taking Ben with him, John asked Jack, "How bad is it?" referring to the growing discontent among the Homesteaders.

Jack looked at him his eyes unwavering. He knew what John meant, "Bad enough. Most folks was real disappointed about this agreement."

"I admit the government thinks all this makes perfect sense. They think we ought to be grateful and just go along but I swear this agreement rubs like a cocklebur. They've put a lot of money into this project and I suspect they want it back."

"Think about what we have all put into John, our sweat and hard work. I'm telling you John. It would go better for you if you was to side with your neighbors on this one."

"I wish there didn't have to be taking sides on everything. Why can't we just work this out without it having to be a matter of taking sides?"

"That ain't the way with folks. You can't ask folks to go along with something ain't for their benefit."

John thought it was to their benefit to come to some kind of agreement before they decided to try a strike but he did not feel like arguing the point with Jack. He was just as glad that Jimmy picked that time to arrive with a pork shoulder with Ben right behind him, struggling to carry the other one. They worked on for the rest of the afternoon talking and laughing to pass the time, stopping only when Lacey brought them coffee. John tried to keep his mind on his work and off the new trouble that both men had promised him was brewing.

It was almost dark by the time Jimmy and Jack pulled away with the Model-T loaded down with fresh sausage, spareribs and a hog's head between them on the front seat of the truck. John waved good-bye calling his thanks once again for all of their help. He put his arm around Ben and together they took one last look at the meat that filled the shelves of the smokehouse. "You done a fine job today Ben, I appreciate the hard work." He could see Ben's teeth flash in the dark. They had grown closer of late especially since the boy's father had died.

"It's a good feeling knowing you got food to eat anytime you want it. Ain't it John?"

"The best in the world, son," John said. He was surprised by Ben's words because he had been thinking the same thing. "The best feeling in the world," he said again as much to himself as to Ben. "Now, let's get to the house and see if Lacey has any of that pie left over from dinner."

"Yeah, that'd be the second best feeling in the world."

They laughed at Ben's joke and together, arms around each other's necks; they wearily made their way to the house.

25

Coy sat at the kitchen table drinking another cup of coffee and leisurely reading the newspaper. It was Sunday morning. He had gotten up early and left Susan asleep upstairs. Now, he could hear her footsteps above him treading softly back and forth across the room. It stirred his curiosity but he did not make a move to check on her. They had spent Saturday evening at home. Susan had said simply that she was tired and did not want to be with other people as was their custom. She had been strangely quiet the night before and he had caught her looking at him at odd moments during the evening. She came into the room wearing the same blue traveling suit she had worn the day they had arrived in Crossville. In each hand she carried a suitcase. She sat them on the floor and stood looking at him. He hid his surprise and did not ask her intentions.

"I'm leaving you," she stated simply.

Coy narrowed his eyes but said nothing.

"I'm going back to Indiana."

"When did you decide this?" he asked. It was a question that meant nothing really. What did it matter at what point or for what reason even she had decided to go? It was after all what he had expected all along. Somehow, after so long a time having her there, her decision had caught him off guard.

"Oh, several weeks ago," she said wistfully, "after we had Sunday dinner at Lacey's. After I saw the two of you together and watched the way your eyes followed her around the room."

He leaned back in his seat, his expression guarded. "So you know," he said not trying to deny it but shocked that it had been so obvious.

"I know you are in love with her. I've known that for a long time."

"How long have you known?" he asked, surprised but doubtful.

"I've known since the day I gave Chick the money for you to buy the auction house."

Coy jumped up unable to hide his shock. "I don't believe you."

"Chick told me everything. I made him tell me before I gave him the money."

He felt dazed by Susan's words and he knew it showed on his face but there was nothing he could do. He looked back over their time together for any sign that what she was saying was true. If she had given any he had missed them. He had always prided himself on his ability to read people. It was what had kept him one step ahead of most folks; it was what had always protected him. Now, he felt shaken and confused. "Why did you marry me if you knew I was in love with Lacey?" he asked incredulous.

"You asked me. Or have you forgotten?" she said accusingly.

He started to answer but Susan stopped him with a wave of her hand. "I am sure you meant it at the time. Perhaps even until the next day, when you realized what you had done. Am I right?"

He met her gaze and kept his stance rigid. He felt like he had just awakened to find himself in an elaborate trap. He had to move cautiously or he would set it off. "Give me some credit," he quipped.

"I'm giving you more than you ever gave me. I took a gamble when I married you. I risked it all. You of all people should understand that. Now, let me ask the same question of you. Why did you marry me, knowing you were in love with another woman? No, don't answer. I might not care for what you have to say."

"I didn't marry you for your money, if that's what you were thinking."

Susan looked out the window. "Oh, that. I always thought that but, I also thought pity perhaps."

"It was never that. You're a beautiful woman, Susan."

"No, don't say anything more. I really couldn't bear it. I suppose whatever the reason; I am partly to blame. I remember crying that night, revealing a lot of things that were probably better left unsaid. So, just answer me this. Why do you think I married you?"

"To make your father mad," he said trying hard to cover himself.

"Nice to know you think so highly of me, Coy," she said smiling an icy smile. "The truth is I married you for one reason." She arched one eyebrow and waited.

Coy backed away from her and stood with his arms crossed defensively across his chest waiting for the blow. Silently he waited for her answer.

"I love you," she stated flatly.

He flinched at her words.

"Yes, I thought you wouldn't like that. So much easier to think that I am hard and cold, that I married you to show you off to my friends or to make my father angry. Well, I wanted that too, I suppose." She shrugged wearily. She went to the stove and poured herself a cup of coffee and sat down at the table. She sipped at it distractedly. She looked up at him suddenly and smiled a sad smile. "I loved you from that first day I saw you in the store. Remember, the first time I came to see Chick. When I brushed past you on the way out, it took my breath away." She laughed a bitter laugh. "Like a schoolgirl I came back hoping to run into you. All those nights we played cards you thought I was coming to check on my brother. I just left it at that." She waved her hand in front of her face brushing away the memory like a cobweb.

"It seems you have developed quite a face for poker after all," he said with obvious admiration. "I would never have guessed you were holding a loaded hand." Coy watched her still unable to believe that Susan had known from the very beginning about Lacey. He had never underestimated anyone to such a degree.

"I had the best teacher," she said her voice as sharp-edged as a sword.

Coy suddenly relaxed his stance and sat down across from Susan at the table. "Lucky you, huh," he laughed at the irony of it all. Suddenly, he had a glimpse of the old Susan. The one he had laughed and played cards with and schemed with in Indiana. He realized with a jolt how she had worked to change herself since they had been in Crossville. He saw her struggle to please him, to do the one right thing, to do whatever it took to win him over. It was the same struggle she had gone through all of her life for her father. It was the same struggle he had gone through for Lacey. He realized that if ever he had loved her it was now at this moment when he stood to lose her. It sent a shiver through him that came out more like a shrug.

"You think I don't have feelings, Coy," Susan said taking his shrug as a dismissal of her and all that she had said. "You think that no one can love another person the way you love Lacey."

It was the truth, he knew. He had not tried to look beneath the surface of her behavior. It was easier to think that she was using him to get revenge. It was harder to think that she might actually love him. "I just never imagined."

"Do imagine. Just imagine that I do love you that much. And then imagine that I am walking away knowing that I will love you forever and that it will never matter. You will never love me back. You once said that we were alike you and I. You said we both wanted something so badly that we were willing to sell our souls to the devil to get it and that the joke was on us because the devil wasn't buying. Do you remember that?"

Coy nodded, thinking back on that night.

"Only you thought what I wanted was my father's money and power."

"And now you are trying to tell me you don't?"

"Is it so hard for you to understand that I feel the same way about you that you feel about Lacey? I am not asking for your pity. You know I always found that a disgusting emotion. I am asking if it is possible for you to feel another person's pain. Or can you only feel your own?"

"You had to know it couldn't work out us being married."

"Oh, yes, you would like that wouldn't you, if I took the blame for my own broken heart. Let you off the hook as one last gesture of my love. You think because I followed you here that I am somehow responsible for my own suffering. I should have wised up sooner. Isn't that what you are thinking Coy?"

She had him dead to right and his instinct was to walk out of the room and leave her there but that was what she expected. That was why she kept pushing him. He would not give her the satisfaction of being right. He leaned back in the tall kitchen chair and lit a cigarette. He took his time holding in the smoke and blowing it out in long slow breaths.

When he did not answer she said, "No such luck, Coy. I'm calling your hand."

With that he could not help himself, he laughed out loud. He had to admit to a certain admiration for her determination. Like him, she was determined to get what she wanted and she was prepared to go to any length to get it. But unlike her, he was not going to let his feelings be known. "You think you've got me pretty well figured out, don't you?"

"I know this much about you. I know that in your whole life you've never looked back. You plow through people's lives like a runaway train. You go on down the line and leave it to other people to clean up the wreckage."

"Why Susan, that's almost poetic. The way you describe it, I can almost picture it. You forgot one thing though. You bought a ticket for this ride."

"And I paid for it in full. Lacey would understand what I mean. I am sure these months of having you here have been very difficult for her."

Almost as a reflex, Coy pulled back when she said it. "What do you mean? What do you know about Lacey?"

"I know this much. She has to know how much John loves her. She has to know how it would hurt him to know that she loves another man and that that man is the father of her baby."

"My god, Susan, you are a cold character."

"Why does knowing that make me cold?"

"Because you stayed."

"And what does that make you Coy that you meant to use the baby to get Lacey back?"

He was across the table with his hands around her arms shaking her before he realized what he was doing. He pushed her away from him and turned his back to her. He stood staring out of the window, holding himself up with an outstretched hand. "Why did you have to follow me here?"

"Follow you here! You make me sound like a stray puppy you've been feeding and now can't get rid of. I followed you here because I am your wife." She waved her hand as though that was not really an explanation. "No, I came because part of me really believed you just wanted a little revenge. I didn't mind rubbing in your success if that was what it was going to take to cure you of Lacey. After all, you had been such an exquisite part of my revenge. You have to admit I have worked hard at my part of the deal. I've come to see that was not enough for you. I wasn't prepared for the look you gave Lacey that day we arrived." She looked out the window lost in thought. Then her eyes met his, a sad look of resignation on her face. "I wasn't prepared for you to still be so in love with her."

"Susan," he said, but she stopped him short. He was reeling from her words. All those months she had known about Lacey. All those months, she had wined and dined the most important businessmen in town and cultivated their wives it had all been for his benefit.

"You seem to be very good at knowing what you expect other people to do for you to prove their love," she said her voice a low whisper. "I would wager a bet, and remember I'm a pretty good gambler, that you know exactly what you expect from Lacey."

"Don't you have a train to catch?" he snapped, suddenly angry that she knew him so well.

"Yes, I thought I was right. You want her to walk away from everything she holds dear, her family, her friends, and her home. I would venture to guess that you prefer she never mention the sacrifices she has made to be with you."

"Look Susan," Coy sighed unable to take any more of her accusations. "I'm sorry I got you involved in this. There was a time when I thought I would get over Lacey. Maybe I even imagined that the two of us would somehow make a go of it. But it didn't happen."

"I'm not stupid Coy. You never for a moment gave it a chance. It didn't happen because you prefer to chase after a dream you can't have. Do you really think that a woman like Lacey would run off with a married man leaving her family even to save her son?" Her last words came out a contemptuous snarl.

"I have a right to the boy. He's my son."

"You have a right to give your son the best life he can have. Can you offer him more than he already has?"

"He deserves to know who his real father is. I don't want him living the kind of life I lived."

"Lacey would never let that happen. He's happy where he is. And if you would admit it, so is Lacey. Lacey is a decent person. A person who is kind and caring with a gentleness and compassion you missed as a child. You and I grew up without those things and now we can only pretend to understand those feelings. We can admire them in others but we can't go back and remake our childhoods. Don't take from Lacey the very things you love about her. You would not like her without them. And in the end she will discover what I already know. That there aren't enough sacrifices she can make to prove her love to you. If you really love them both let them be."

"And come back to Indiana with you."

"Truthfully?" she asked standing up one hand on her hip.

He gave her a wry smile.

"Truthfully, you are not invited," she said.

The laugh burst from him without warning as her words took hold of him. He went to her and put his arms around her. "You are quite a woman Susan."

"I know and if there is any justice in the world you are going to miss the devil out of me."

He kissed her softly on the lips. "I'm sure I will," he said, shaking his head.

"Would you drive me to the train?" she asked.

"Susan," he whispered, caressing her cheek with his hand.

"You are such a charming scoundrel Coy." She pressed her cheek into his palm. "I'm going to miss that."

"You are amazing."

"Yes."

"What are you going to do with yourself in Indiana?"

"Oh I was thinking of beating my father at his own game. Start a business of my own."

Coy laughed at her daring. "Sorry, I'm going to miss that. Sounds like my kind of sport."

Susan shook her head and took a deep breath. "Oh Coy, what ever am I going to do about you," Susan said wistfully. "I want to hate you so much."

"Then you are part of a long and distinguished list."

"If you are ever back in Anderson, look me up."

Coy nodded almost imperceptibly.

"Oh, and by the way I won't wait forever."

26

Clyde Reid's eyes bounced like balls around the room trying to take in all that was happening. John knew Clyde was there because he expected an entertaining show. Small groups of people huddled together, their voices growing louder. Occasionally, someone pointed toward the table where the Cumberland Homesteads Association Board sat. John watched the crowd from under his eyelashes. He pretended to read the paper in front of him. He was tired beyond reason and his eyes would not focus.

The Cumberland Homestead Association was meeting to elect one member to the board. John's seat on the board was up for reelection. It was a meeting John had dreaded for months now. He had gone against many of his friends and neighbors by signing the purchase agreement the government had sent down from Washington D. C. He had even gone against his own commonsense. The contract was unfair. It represented the enormous power the government had over them. Not only did it seem the government was saying, sign or get out, but also the threat would last a lifetime. Any time a tenant displeased the government, they reserved the right to kick them out.

It was as though the government had tired of them all and would as soon be rid of them as not. They had brought them to this place with high hopes and great plans only to tire of them before the game was finished. Like a child, they wanted to take their toys and go home, but they could not because they still held real people's lives in their hands. If John could see one great wrong in all the government had done, it was in giving people such high expectations and hopes, even if much of it had been in the minds of the people and not written down in a contract.

Despite all of this, John still wanted the farm. The farm was all he had left to bargain with. He knew Coy would be coming soon and he could not stand before Lacey empty handed. So he had signed the agreement. Tonight he knew he would pay the price.

He still had many friends among the Homesteaders. He could pick out a friendly face now and again in the crowd. They had campaigned heavily for his reelection to the board and canvassed the other Homesteaders for votes.

He caught Jack's eye and nodded to him. They had often disagreed, but they had remained steadfast friends. He thought about how good and decent people most of the Homesteaders were. Some of them were not at the meeting tonight because they had long ago washed their hands of the project and the association. They simply went about their lives and hoped for the best. John wondered if he could feel any more powerless if he had chosen to do the same instead of entangling himself the way he had with the Board.

John missed Thomas Jefferson Morgan. A bit of his philosophy could come in handy at a time like this. Thomas and Millicent had married and taken off for California. Millicent's parents had tried to get the marriage annulled until she told them she was pregnant. They had finally given in and accepted Thomas. The last John had heard, the couple had gone to live in Washington with Millicent's parents and Thomas had gone to work in a bank. He hoped it was what the boy wanted. Maybe it was better if he was not here to see what was going to happen tonight.

The room was growing hot and stuffy even as an icy rain beat on the windowpanes. Douglas Harris stood up and called the meeting to order. A thick, heavy silence fell over the room. Only Rusty Ligon continued to stand leaning heavily against the wall with his arms crossed on his chest like swords. He looked at John with such hatred that he had to wonder what he had come to symbolize to this malcontent. John realized suddenly what he had been blind to in all the months he had struggled against the forces that sought to tear the project apart. It was impossible to separate all the chaff from the wheat. As hard as the government had tried to find people who could work hard and bind together to make a community, they had been unable to sift out all of the complainers and grumblers. The fact that the government had earned much of the distrust and discontent was beside the point. There had been a group of people like Rusty Ligon who from the very beginning had not liked anything that had gone on with the project. When Major Oliver took over as the third manager of the project, Rusty had developed an ever growing following of dissidents. The Major's military style and unwavering allegiance to Washington had made him an easy enemy.

In the past months, it seemed to John that a line had been drawn in the dirt dividing those opposed to, and those who supported management. As the election drew nearer, politics had become the issue of every meeting and all work activities, with each side trying to garner votes.

"We are here tonight to elect a board member for the coming year," Douglas Harris announced to the crowd, setting off a cacophony of sound that filled the room to bursting. Douglas hammered his gavel on the table demanding order. Reluctantly, the sound died down, the quiet moving across the room inch by inch as each person begrudgingly gave in.

John knew it was not Douglas's authority that made them yield, but their own desire to get on with the election.

"Before I open the floor to nominations," Douglas spoke firmly. "Let me warn all of you that I won't tolerate any unruliness. There have been a lot of hard feelings spreading through this project in these past months; some say even threats have been made against some of the members. Now, all I can say is that you'll get your chance to vote fair and square. In light of the fact we are all neighbors regardless of how this election turns out, I recommend the voting be done by secret ballot."

"I don't care what you think," Rusty Ligon burst out. "I want to know where I stand with my neighbors."

"We already know where you stand, Rusty. You done told anybody that would listen," Amos Macalby shouted from the back of the room. The room once again exploded.

It was ten minutes before Douglas could restore calm. "There will be one person speak at a time from here on or we will call this meeting to a halt right now," he said his eyes squinted in anger. "If you have a nomination, raise your hand and I'll call on you."

Leon Hubert raised his hand and Douglas pointed to him. "I nominate Rusty Ligon."

"Seconds?" Douglas asked.

"I second it," Jimmy Carlton growled.

"Any more nominations?" Douglas asked.

Jack stood up. Douglas nodded in his direction. "I nominate John Trotter."

John was pleased and somewhat amazed that his friend had come forward to nominate him despite their differences on many things. He hoped it wouldn't go hard with him among his other friends.

"I second it," Lon Carver spoke up, causing the whole crowd to turn in his direction. Not only had Lon rarely shown at a meeting, he had never spoken his opinion about anything to do with the project. John smiled his thanks.

"I open the floor to discussion, but mind you I mean discussion, not arguing," Douglas said emphatically.

"We all know that John here ain't no friend to the folks here on the project," Leon Hubert spoke up. "We've seen what he's done and we don't like it. It's time to get somebody on the board cares what happens to the folks here."

"That's a dang lie," Jack yelled. "If it weren't for John, you'da been outta work two years before this. Who do you think built the cannery and tried to get folks to farm around here like they was meant to do?"

"Who went against us and signed the contract sent down here from Washington meant to rob us of our farms," Jimmy Carlton shouted.

The crowd was heating up. Rusty Ligon looked at John, a smirk spreading across his face.

"Enough of this," Douglas said. "We've heard all of this before. It's time for a vote. We'll have a simple show of hands then. Clyde, you count on this side," Douglas said pointing to the left side of the room. "Amos, you count on this side. Now, all in favor of Rusty Ligon hold up your right hand."

The crowd looked around to see who was voting for Rusty and to make their own count. John tried not to look at the members who were voting against him but it was obvious there were quite a few.

"Gentleman, give your counts to Burt here at the end of the table," Douglas directed. The men walked over to Burt and whispered their numbers. "Now, all those in favor of John Trotter hold up your right hand."

John looked around the room. It would be a close vote. Douglas took the vote from Burt who had scribbled the totals on a piece of paper. "The vote is sixty-one in favor of Rusty Ligon and fifty-nine in favor of John Trotter. Rusty Ligon is our new board member."

The crowd erupted in cheers, many of the members patting Rusty on the back or shaking his hand. John tried not to react. The floor seemed to be falling out from under him. In all the weeks he had dreaded this, he never really believed he would be defeated. He had believed that in the end people could see how much he cared about the project and how hard he had worked to make it succeed. But in the end, they had only seen him as a traitor. He was just someone who had sided with the management against them. He got up slowly and walked over to congratulate Rusty on his win. When John put out his hand to Rusty, he only sneered and refused to offer his hand. "I told you if you didn't listen, we would run you off this board," Rusty said with a hiss.

John turned and walked away without a word. The shame of his failure hung on him like an oversized cloak. He had let everybody down. He took one last look at the crowd and walked out into the bone-chilling December rain long before he could hear Douglas Harris thank him for all his hard work.

27

Ben came in shaking the snow from his cap. A grin split his face and made his frozen cheeks stand out like polished apples. Lacey stopped herself from saying anything about the snow that was puddling up on the kitchen floor. She stirred the hot cocoa and smiled back waiting for him to tell the news.

"We got it and it's a beauty. Taller than me," Ben exclaimed holding his hand up above his head.

Lacey laughed and clapped her hands together. It was Christmas eve and she had sent John and Ben to fetch a tree. She had been planning for Christmas for over a month and she had a picture in her mind of just how it was to be. She knew there was a danger in laying things out beforehand because there was always the possibility of disappointment if life couldn't live up to your dreams. It had come to her so often since Daniel Lee had been born that she had never really had a childhood. By the time she was seven or eight she had taken on most of the household chores. More than that she had taken on the worries her mother had refused to shoulder. Not that there had not been special times. She had memories that would always be dear to her. There had been times when she had run to meet her pa after work, when he would reach into his dinner pail and pull out a cold biscuit he had saved for her. It didn't take much to please a child and the memories stayed with a person forever. That was what she wanted to give to Daniel Lee, memories that could stay with him for the rest of his life and keep him safe and whole. "Where's John?" she asked.

"He's right outside nailing a brace on the bottom of the tree so it'll stand up. I got to go help him," Ben said excitedly. "I just come to tell you we got the tree."

Just then, John came struggling through the door with the tree in tow.

"I was coming to help you," Ben said.

"Then grab hold," John sputtered trying to hold the branches out of his face. "Where do you want this thing Lacey?"

"In the living room in the corner by the front window."

Daniel Lee, who had been playing in the floor by the cookstove, jumped up and grabbed hold of one of the branches. "I help you Daddy."

"Why thank you son," John said proudly. "You're getting to be a big help around here." He flashed Lacey a smile and a wink.

She smiled back hoping her smile conveyed some of the gratitude she felt to John for his gentleness with Daniel Lee. Sometimes lately, his temper flared unexpectedly, leaving them all stunned and John silent with remorse.

"Look Mama, I helping." Daniel Lee said holding gingerly to one tiny twig.

"That's mama's big boy."

"Yeah, Daniel Lee, good thing you was here or we might never of got this thing in the house. Right, John?" Ben said grinning.

They all laughed all but Daniel Lee who was full of his own importance at the moment. They eased the tree into the corner and everyone stood back to look at it. The top of the tree just touched the ceiling.

"It's perfect," Lacey whispered clasping her hands to her chest.

"Let's get the decorations on it." Ben shouted eagerly.

They had been stringing popcorn and making paper decorations for a week. Lacey brought out the box that held the decorations, carrying it like a prize. Ben grabbed for the box. "Wait, Ben. I was hoping Cora and Mitch would get here to help us."

"You know they said to start without them. They had folks to visit with before they come out," John said.

"All right," Lacey said hesitantly. "First we put on the strings of popcorn."

Ben groaned and looked at John.

John shrugged. "Lacey knows how she wants things to be."

"I'll get'em," Ben shouted. He came back carrying the popcorn strings. He handed them to Lacey. "How come you're so dead set on having a Christmas tree, Lacey? We never had one before. And how come we have to have popcorn on it? Why can't we have those strings of shiny stuff like they put on at the schoolhouse?"

Lacey blushed. Her pa had thought it was foolishness to have a Christmas tree when she was a little girl. She didn't hold it against him. He had a hard life and maybe it did seem a waste to him but this was her home now and she intended to have the things she had missed as a child. "In a way it's your doing," she teased. "I read about this family that had the most wonderful Christmas in one of the books you brought home from the bookmobile. It was called "Five Little Peppers and How they Grew." She looked at him shyly hoping he would not laugh at her for being so caught up in a child's book. "It was about a family that didn't have much 'cause their pa was dead but still and all they had the finest Christmas. They thought if they couldn't have anything else, they could have a tree. They didn't have anything to decorate it with but popcorn and pretty paper. They laid it all out in the book the way they done it and what a good time they all had and I declared right then that that was the way it was going to be for us. I wouldn't settle for nothing less."

"Well, then tell us what you want and we'll do it," Ben said agreeably, caught up in Lacey's excitement.

Lacey hugged him sweetly. "First you wrap them popcorn strings around and around the tree. Then we hang these decorations from the tree limbs."

As soon as the tree was strung, Lacey stood back with her hands on her hips and admired their placement. "Oh, my," she sighed with pleasure. Daniel Lee who had been quietly watching, walked to the tree and pulled on a strand of popcorn trying to get it into his mouth. Everyone yelled "no" at the same time. Daniel Lee let go of the strand and stood looking at them wide-eyed. His bottom lip began to pucker.

"Oh baby, mama is sorry she yelled," Lacey said kneeling down to hug Daniel Lee. She looked up at Ben and John shamefaced. "I reckon I got caught up in making everything nice and forgot why we was doing it. Here, help mama put on the decorations." From behind the sofa, she pulled a small box. Gently, she lifted a paper snowflake from the box. As she held it up for the others to see, it spun on its string and caught the light from the fireplace. She heard Ben take in a breath and it pleased her.

"It's a snowflake, ain't it?" Ben said with amazement.

Lacey nodded.

"Where did you learn to make those, Lacey?" John asked with obvious admiration.

"A lady come to one of our club meetings and showed us how. It took my eye-teeth when I first saw her make one. I didn't think I'd be able to do it but I practiced aright smart," she said shyly.

"They turned out pretty as could be," John said lifting it from her hand and holding it up to the electric light.

Lacey watched overcome by the pleasure he was taking in it. It was a special pleasure to watch the night come since they had only recently gotten electricity.

Daniel Lee cried out for the goody he had missed out on. John looked down surprised and embarrassed that he had been so lost in the snowflake himself. He handed it back to Lacey who quickly put it into the boy's tiny hand and guided it to the tree. She had to coax him to let it go. John and Ben applauded his efforts bringing a triumphant smile to his face. "John, you next," Lacey said. "Ben, you too. I made plenty. And there's the things we made together to put on."

Ben smiled. "How 'bout some of that hot cocoa you was making when I come in?"

"That does sound good," John chimed in.

"I'll bring it in here so we can finish the tree," Lacey said pulling herself up from the floor. As she brushed her dress off, the door opened. Cora and Mitch burst in as though pushed by the cold night air. Cora balanced a cake in one hand and a pie in the other. Mitch followed close behind his arms loaded with packages. Everyone rushed to meet them and help them unload.

"There's something here for everyone," Mitch said handing over his bounty of neatly wrapped presents.

"There's more food to be brought in if you two are looking for something to do," Cora said to John and Ben.

"I'll get it," Ben yelled, heading out the door in his shirtsleeves.

"Here boy, I'll help you," Mitch called, grabbing Ben's coat on the way out.

Lacey took the cake and pie from Cora and took them into the kitchen. When she returned Cora stood admiring the tree. "That sure is a pretty thing. Where on earth did you get these pretty decorations?"

"We made them," Lacey said proudly.

"Well, I never seen nothing finer."

"Thank you, Cora."

"Son, are you doing all right?" Cora asked turning to John.

"Fine mama."

Cora patted him on the shoulder awkwardly in an uncharacteristic show of affection. John put his hand over hers and held it there briefly. Lacey watched her throat suddenly tight. She wondered if Cora had noticed the difference in John lately too.

"Honey, what smells so good?" Cora said lightheartedly turning to Lacey with a smile.

"I've got gingerbread in the oven. It should be about ready to come out."

Cora followed Lacey into the kitchen. "Hot cocoa," she asked peering down into the pot on the stove.

Lacey nodded. She opened the oven on the cookstove and took out a fresh hot pan of gingerbread made with sorghum molasses. She sliced the gingerbread into thick generous slabs, the smell of it making her mouth water. Cora began to fill cups with the warm cocoa. The women worked along side each other with ease. Cora hummed softly as she moved about the kitchen. "You seem mighty happy," Lacey remarked.

Cora leaned back against the kitchen sink and pondered Lacey's remark. "Why, I reckon I've been happy all of my life."

Lacey could not help but stare at Cora in amazement. It was obvious Cora meant every word of what she had said but it was a wonder to Lacey how she managed it. She had certainly not had an easy life but it seemed not to touch that part of her from which her happiness came. It seemed to Lacey that she could no sooner get her life laid out, than somehow it was always turned topsy-turvy. The past months had been a nightmare of pain and confusion to her, with Coy coming back to stir up feelings in her she did not welcome and threatening to take away everything she held dear.

"Lacey," Cora whispered giving her arm a shake.

"Oh," Lacey cried blushing deeply. "I must have been thinking about something."

"You must have been wondering how an old woman like me could talk such foolishness. Ain't I right?"

"I reckon that was it," Lacey admitted.

"Let me tell you a secret. Folks can have four good things happen to them and one bad thing and which do you think they'll dwell on?"

"The one bad thing," Lacey agreed knowing she was guilty of just that thing.

"You know it's true. They'll dwell on that one bad thing until the good just ups and leaves 'em. Pretty soon they can't hardly remember it at all."

Lacey busied herself at the stove unable to look at Cora. She could feel Cora's eyes hot on her back and wondered if she was saying all of this for her benefit or if it was just Lacey's own guilt that made her feel so.

"If you got something good in your life, you better study on it," Cora added matter-of-factly. "Don't never give yourself reason to look back in sadness and regret."

Cora's words made her spine prickle. "We had better get the food in there before it gets cold." she said picking up the platter of cake and heading off without turning to look at Cora. When she carried the food in Ben and John looked at her like eager children. It made her heart leap. Mitch sat on the floor with Daniel Lee and Ben spinning a wooden top.

"Mitch Jennings, did you let that youngun open his presents," Cora said disapprovingly.

"Well, it won't hurt nothing," Mitch said pleasantly. "We'll just wrap it back up after he goes to bed and it'll be all new to him tomorrow."

"You're probably right at that," Cora said laughing heartily.

Lacey admired the easy way they had with each other. She was glad for Cora that it had turned out that way. They sat around the tree admiring their handiwork and eating their goodies. Lacey could not put out of her mind the things that Cora had said in the kitchen.

"This sure is good gingerbread, Lacey," John commented between bites.

"Made it from the molasses made here on the Homesteads."

John nodded his mouth full.

Lacey fed Daniel Lee small bites of the gingerbread from her fingers. He smacked his lips and made noises of delight. They all laughed, for it expressed their own feelings of joy. Suddenly Ben jumped up and disappeared from the room. When he came back he was carrying a small package wrapped in brown paper and tied with twine. He handed it to Lacey.

"Why, Ben, what is it?"

"Open it and see."

"Should I open it now or wait for Christmas?

"No, you have to open it now."

Lacey carefully opened the package, treating the brown paper like beautiful Christmas wrap. Inside was a wooden star painted gold. "Oh Ben, it's beautiful."

"It goes on top of the tree. See it's got that little hook on the back so's it'll stay up there. I made it myself in the carpentry shop. Mrs. Norris give me the paint," he said proudly.

"Put it up for me, please, John," she cried.

John carefully hooked the star to the top of the tree. He smiled at her, his eyes asking for approval.

"Oh, I can't believe how perfect it looks, John."

He gave her a shy smile and she could tell he was pleased. It was gratifying to see him so happy. For the last several weeks he had been silent much of the time, speaking only when questioned and very little then. It broke her heart to think about what she would soon have to do.

Everyone stood back to have a look at the star topping the tree.

"It's just like in a storybook Ben," Lacey sighed.

"Is it the way you pictured it, Lacey?" Ben asked.

"Better. Better than I pictured it," she said hugging him tightly. She reached down and picked up Daniel Lee. They all stood looking at the tree; each lost in their own thoughts. All of their hopes and dreams seemed to be wrapped like strands around the tree, some hanging precariously from a limb by tiny threads.

"We had better finish putting on the decorations," Lacey said hating to break the silence. "Cora and Mitch, you help too."

"Well, let me see what we have here," Cora said digging into the box and coming up with a paper angel.

They worked until all the decorations were gone and they were full to bursting with gingerbread and cocoa. "Now, boys," Lacey said finally, hating to end the beautiful evening, "you two need to get to bed if Santa Claus is to come."

"Ah Lacey, I'm too old for Santa Claus"

"I see being too old didn't stop you from hanging your stocking on the fireplace mantel," Lacey said tousling his hair.

"I didn't say I was too old for presents," he said with a grin. Ben gave Lacey a hug and a kiss on the cheek and said goodnight. He had grown up so and become so independent, it surprised and pleased her that she had not had to ask him for it.

"Goodnight," Cora and Mitch said in unison.

"Goodnight, Ben," John said solemnly. "I love you, son."

Ben and Lacey looked at John, surprised by his show of affection. Ben gave John a smile and headed up the steps to bed.

When Lacey came out of the bedroom from putting Daniel Lee down, John and Cora had talked Mitch into taking out his fiddle. Softly, he played "Away in a Manger." Lacey slipped in and sat on the floor by John's knee. John stroked her hair and she reached up and took his hand and smiled up at him. It was a moment she wanted to hold in time. They listened silently, almost reverently, until Lacey was sure Mitch must have been growing tired of playing. As though he had read her thoughts he put down the fiddle and motioned to Cora with a nod.

"I reckon, we'll be getting on to bed," Cora said.

"Let me get you an extra quilt," Lacey said following them up the steps.

"See you in the morning," Cora called to John from the stairs.

John did not answer and Cora shrugged to Lacey and went on up after her. When Lacey returned to the living room, John was nowhere to be found. From the window she could see John standing in the moonlight smoking his pipe. She slipped into

Ben's denim jacket hanging by the door and went out to join him. She was nearly upon him before he jumped with a start.

"Lacey?" he asked.

"Did I scare you?"

"I suppose my mind had drifted off someplace. You shouldn't be out in the cold like this." He put his arm around her and drew her close.

She slipped her arms around his waist. "It sure was a pleasant evening, trimming the tree, drinking hot cocoa, Ben making me that pretty star. It was just like something off a picture postcard. We owe it all to you John. You are the one who made it so. I just wanted you to know that." She looked up at him and kissed him lightly on the lips. He pulled away and held her face in his hand. He looked at her for a long time and sadness spread across his face. "Why, John, what ever is the matter?"

He let go of her face and turned away gazing up at the moon. "I'm afraid you give me more credit than I deserve," he said simply, his voice flat.

"I don't think that's possible, John," Lacey said sincerely.

"I always wanted to make you happy, Lacey. Give you whatever you wanted. That's all I ever wanted out of life."

"And you have, John," Lacey said.

He gave her the same sad look.

"I love you Lacey. All my life I've loved you. Even when you was just a little girl growing up, I dreamed about us getting married."

"Oh, John," she whispered, her throat closing tight around the words. As always she wanted to say more but the words would not come. She could not understand his glum mood and his strange behavior after such a wonderful day.

"I best go check on the livestock," John said.

"You'll bring the sled in from the smokehouse, won't you?" They had ordered a sled for Ben from a mail-order catalog and had kept it at the Trading Post until John had brought it home a few nights before and stowed it away in the smokehouse.

John nodded.

"Don't be gone long," she said. They were feeble words to express the worry she felt. She watched him all the way to the barn before she turned and went back into the house.

She busied herself by covering the pies and cakes she had baked with clean dishtowels. She tidied up the kitchen and stood back to give it one last inspection. Tomorrow they would have a big Christmas dinner. Suddenly, she wished that Will and Ruby and her ma could be there with the younguns. They would laugh and tease each other. She smiled to herself, thinking how she had hated Will's teasing when she was a little girl.

Lacey walked to the window and searched the backyard for any sign of John. His lonely silhouette that she had so often seen against the night sky in the last few weeks was still not visible in the moonlight. She had awakened many nights of late to find her bed empty where John had slipped out sometime after she had fallen asleep. A few times she had gone in search of him only to see him through the window sitting on the front porch, smoking his pipe, or standing in the dark staring up at the sky. Most nights she would just lie awake for hours worrying about him. His customary silence had turned to brooding, and because it was not their habit to talk about their darkest thoughts, she was loath to make a start.

She shook off the chills that possessed her and tiptoed into the bedroom. Daniel Lee slept peacefully on a small bed in the corner of the room. It was time, she knew, that he was moved out and into the upstairs bedroom but it seemed so far away and she worried about him trying to come down the stairs at night. She worried about not hearing him if he cried out in the night with bad dreams. Ben had offered to sleep with him but a tiny selfish part of her could not relinquish him just yet. Of course, she suddenly realized, soon there would be no need.

Lacey took down the blankets from the top shelf of the closet. Reaching far back, she felt for the Christmas presents she had hidden away. She slowly collected the packages wrapped in pretty paper and sat them on the dressing table. She recognized their shapes. There were scarves and mittens for Daniel Lee, a pull toy and a whistle John had made him. For John there was a new pipe bought with the help of Ben. They had worried over their choices in the mail-order catalog until they had nearly worn the pages out. She hoped John would be proud of it for Ben's sake. John had sent all the way to New York for a book for Ben. He had written off to some bookstore and asked for a book on building bridges. It had come only last week and John had brought it in to her to wrap holding it like the prize it was. She couldn't wait to see Ben's face when he unwrapped it. It was going to be the most wonderful Christmas, just as she had pictured it.

She tiptoed out of the room and placed the presents gently under the tree as though they were all breakable. She was growing uneasy about John. She sat for a long time on the floor looking at the tree trying to get back the feeling of contentment she had had earlier. When she failed to conjure it up again, she rose stiffly from the floor and filled Ben and Daniel Lee's stockings with candy and oranges. Then she went back into the bedroom and getting down on all fours she reached far under the bed and pulled out John's Christmas present. It was a fiddle. She had asked Mitch to make it for John months ago. It was to be a gift from all of them. Proudly, she placed it under the tree. Before going to bed, she checked the window once more for John. Reluctantly she turned off all the lights but the one lone light on the back porch. She hoped it would be a beacon calling him in for the night.

Lacey's eyes opened suddenly in the middle of the night and she realized that she was fully awake. It amazed her that she had fallen asleep and she had no recollection of it. The room had the look of daybreak but she had the sense that she had not slept that long so she was sure it had to be the light from a three-quarter moon. Cautiously, she reached out across the bed. The place next to her was empty and cold. It came to her that she had been a fool going off to bed like that, leaving John to brood. Why hadn't she gone after him? How had they fallen into this strange ritual of pretending that everything was fine? They were both guilty, she suspected, of trying to make up for past suffering. She was guilty, she knew, of trying to hold off the future. Quickly, she threw on her thin robe and slipped into her work shoes. She was out the door running, stumbling in the slick snow, unsure of why she had to hurry so. She could hear her heart beating in her throat and the icy night air clawed at her lungs. She could not stop herself until she had flung open the barn door. She stood clinging to it, waiting to catch her breath and for her eyes to focus. A lantern hung on a nail in the middle of the room. In the far corner she could just make out a figure sitting on a bale of hay. She came closer slowly and the figure looked up but he seemed not to recognize her.

"John." she called softly.

He did not answer.

She came closer. That was when she saw it. He held the gun in his right hand and cradled the barrel in his left. She could not take it in, this sight of her husband sitting alone in the cold dark shadows, his green eyes now dark haunted caverns of despair. Fear held her in place and numbed her more than the cold. "It was you," she heard herself say. All this time she had feared losing Daniel Lee. She had thought that if something was coming to steal away her happiness it would first strike at the heart of her. It would strike her child. She had been making all her plans to protect him. It had never occurred to her that John would be the one. Or maybe he was just the first, she thought. "Oh. John," she cried falling to her knees in front of him. She placed her hands gently over the gun.

He looked at her as though he had just realized her presence.

"John, come with me." she coaxed. "Let's go inside."

"No, you go on. It's too cold for you out here," he said as though it was any ordinary day and not the middle of the night.

"John, come inside with me now," Lacey begged.

He looked down at her as though he had only then realized she was there. "I've failed you, Lacey," he whispered hoarsely.

"No, John, don't say that. It isn't true. What could make you think such a thing?"

"They voted me off the board," he confessed suddenly.

"Why, John! Who would do that to you after all you've done?"

"Union men," he said with a bitter laugh. "They say I ain't worked hard enough to get the union in to the cannery. They say I've sided with the government when I signed that purchase agreement. They got enough men together to vote me out."

"Nobody could care more about the men than you do John. They couldn't know much about you if they don't know that." She laid her head in his lap and put her arm around his waist. She felt his hand on her head.

"There just don't seem to be no way to win, Lacey. I've tried to prove myself to you, Lacey. I've tried to prove I was somebody that was worthy of you. But now..."

Lacey looked up as John's voice trailed off. Her heart was breaking at the sight of him in so much pain. What a fool she had been to think the burden he carried was less because he always carried it without complaint. "I've been a fool, John. I've let you carry it all on your shoulders. I couldn't help but know they was problems but I never asked. I never did anything to ease the burden for you. I was selfish in wanting to pretend everything was all right."

"I wanted it that way," he said tenderly. "I didn't want nothing in the world except for you to be happy and not to have to worry again for the rest of your life."

"I am happy, John."

"Lacey, I don't see how things can work out with the Homesteads. They's just too many problems. Too many folks on both sides is wanting too many things out of it. They're tearing it apart."

"John, these are decent folks. They may fight amongst themselves but it don't mean they're not good people. You can't always make things work out the way you dream it, but it don't mean that what you get is any less."

"We might lose the farm if things don't work out."

Hearing him say it took her breath away but she held herself steady. In all their time together they had never talked like this. It sickened her to think that she had almost come too late. Whatever had propelled her out into the night in search of John had brought her to him within a heartbeat of despair. She searched her mind for the right words. "This is the finest place on earth and I thank you for giving me the time we've had here, but if we have to walk away from here tomorrow, we'll make it. I have always known that. Life is what you share with other people and that is where we've been wrong, not to share our burdens with each other." She was trying to be honest with him, but she thought of all the things she had never told him and how could she possibly tell him now?

"I was thinking if I couldn't give you the farm, you might not want to stay."

"You think I stay because of the farm?" she said incredulously.

"I don't blame you."

"John, I'm your wife."

"I found the locket," he said simply.

His words went through her like an electric shock leaving her stunned and shaking. Her body trembled against her will. He was telling her more than just the words he had spoken. He was telling her he knew about Coy. In the face of her complete selfishness and lack of courage she marveled that he could still love her, could ever have loved her at all. Her treachery and betrayal seemed an act as unspeakable as the one he now contemplated. She could have told John about Coy herself but instead she had held the memories dear and thought in her heart she could love another man without hurting him. And now, despite the wrong she had done him, as his final act of love, he was offering her a way out. Her throat closed up around the words she needed to say, and useless tears streamed down her face, a pathetic offering in exchange for his suffering.

John moved suddenly and she jumped back, afraid that her silence had provoked him into carrying out his plans. She saw him look down at the gun with sudden recognition. A wave of sadness passed over his face. He took off his coat slowly, holding the gun first in his right hand and then in his left. He put the gun in his lap and slipped the coat around Lacey's shoulders. "You're chilling."

"John darling let's go in now. We'll both catch a cold out like this." She tried to keep her voice matter-of-fact but her words came out thick and raspy.

"I've always loved you, Lacey. I've come to see where that don't really change nothing though. I used to think if I loved you enough, you'd have to love me back, but that ain't the way it works. You can't force nobody to feel what don't come natural to 'em."

His voice was soft and pleasant. They could have been sitting out on the front porch watching the stars and talking about the day. "John," she cried her voice trembling.

"You go in now, Lacey. I'll be in directly."

"No, John. I won't go without you."

"I just have to check on the mules. I can't remember if I put hay in their stalls." He stared off in the distance as though pondering.

"I won't go without you, John. Tomorrow is Christmas. I want you there when the boys open their presents. I want you to see the look on Ben's face when he sees the book you bought him. I want you there to tell Daniel Lee he has to hush blowing that whistle you made him, before he drives his mama and daddy crazy." She tried to make her voice sound happy and lighthearted. She smiled at him and slowly a timorous smile touched the corners of his mouth. She reached cautiously and slipped the gun from his lap. With one arm around his waist she urged him to come with her. "Let's go in. Tomorrow is a new day." A new day in which she could atone for what she had done, she thought. Tomorrow was new day and she would be brave. John deserved that from her.

They walked side by side slowly through the night toward the house. Lacey chatted, fearful that if she stopped he might change his mind. Her left arm she held at her side, the gun through the crook of her arm for safety like John had taught her. "You know I was thinking that in the spring we might put a peach orchard over past the grape arbor." It was another lie, she knew. Long before spring she would be gone. By the time she told him the truth as she intended to do, John would feel it was good to have her gone. "It'd take a few years before those trees would bear fruit but some things are just worth the wait. Nothing better than a peach cobbler come summer. Don't you agree, John?"

John looked down at her and she could see his tears glistening in the moonlight.

At dawn, when Ben came down the stairs, Lacey and John were sitting at the kitchen table drinking coffee. Lacey watched Ben rub the sleep from his eyes and hoped that he could not guess she and John had never gone to bed.

"Merry Christmas, Ben," Lacey said.

"Why didn't you come and wake me up?" he asked.

Daniel Lee, awakened by their voices, came into the room and put his arms up to Lacey. She picked him up and gave him a kiss. "Ben, it's early enough. You haven't missed Christmas," Lacey reassured him. Ben looked at John's tired face and eyes ringed with dark circles. Lacey held her breath, hoping he would not say anything. "You can go see what Santa Claus left you under the tree but you're not to open anything until Cora and Mitch come down and we've had a big breakfast."

Ben took off like a shot. Daniel Lee squirmed to be let down to follow Ben. "You watch after him, Ben," Lacey called after Daniel Lee.

"They sure are excited," John said giving her a weak smile. She came to him and he put his arms around her waist and pressed his face into her. She stroked his head, running her fingers through his hair as she had often done for Daniel Lee. "It's a wonderful day, John. It's Christmas."

He looked up at her; tears threatened to spill over the corners of his eyes. "I'm sorry, Lacey. I almost spoiled it for you."

"Sssh," she whispered, her heart breaking that his only thought on barely escaping death was that it would spoil Christmas for her. After she coaxed him in from the barn and put away the gun, they had sat at the table too stunned to speak. Slowly, painfully John had begun to talk to her. He surprised her by going way back to when his pa had been killed in the mines. They had been very close. It had been that closeness that had driven him to work so hard for the union. It seemed a way of making it up to him, to show his pa that he was taking good care of his mother. And he had done it to show Lacey, that he could provide for her and give her the home she wanted. Always, it seemed there had been somebody counting on him. And more times than not, he had come through with his promise. Lacey realized that shouldering the load had quickly become his lot in life as it had for her in her own family. It was a new thing to him not being able to carry the burden, not being able to make it work no matter how hard he tried. Just before the first rays of sunlight lit up the morning sky, he had told her about the Homestead project and the endless stream of problems that had besieged them at every turn. She did not understand how he had kept it all inside, but she knew that she was much to blame for it. She had come to expect it from him just as other people had. It made her life easier that he bear the burden alone and she had selfishly allowed him to do it. All the while he talked, she had held herself in place like a shattered window pane, knowing the slightest movement would send her life crashing around her. It was new to her to have John stand before her a wounded man. She had always thought she wanted him to talk to her, to share his life with her, but now that he had, she found herself at a loss as to what to do. Finally, John sat in silence; his emotions spilled out before her like an overturned cup. There seemed nothing she could offer him that was worthy of what he had given her, nothing that could soothe his pain. He had brought up Coy only once and that had been to explain that he had tried to make it up to her for not being her first choice. Foolishly, she had sought to explain about Coy, as though there could be an explanation. He had stopped her in a flash at the mention of Coy's name. "Hush," he had said, "What's done is done." Her shame had caught in her throat. She could not blame him, if he couldn't bear to hear the story. Still, it had felt like being pushed off a cliff backwards. Even as she stood in her own kitchen at that moment, she could not stop the sensation.

"Lacey," John whispered.

"Yes, John," she said, holding her voice steady.

"I clean forgot Ben's sled. It's still out in the smokehouse."

"That's all right," she sighed breathlessly, relieved to be talking about something ordinary. "He's as well believe that Santa Claus could leave it there as under the tree. You can take him out and show him after we open the other gifts."

John nodded, pleased with Lacey's solution to the problem.

"Now, I had better get breakfast started. These youngun's won't wait much longer to see what they got." She kissed John softly on the head. He pulled her down on to his lap and felt her face like a blind man. She held on to his hand, kissing his fingers one by one like she had done many times to comfort Daniel Lee.

John looked up startled and Lacey followed his eyes to see Cora and the rest of the family standing in the doorway. Lacey jumped up feeling herself blush as they continued to stare.

"Lacey, Ben tells me you intend to make him wait until after breakfast to open his packages," Cora stated with righteous indignation. "That don't hardly seem fair."

Lacey laughed and went to give Cora an unexpected hug. "Well, I reckon, if you can wait to eat, I can."

Ben beamed. They all gathered around the tree. "John, would you give out the gifts?" Lacey asked handing him the first package. John took it and proudly handed it to Ben. The whole family waited as he opened it. It was the book on bridges that John had bought for him.

Ben held it like a treasure, staring at its cover. "Thank you, John," Ben said with wonder.

John smiled and nodded a look passing between the two of them. Then John turned to hand out the other gifts. They waited in turn; watching as each gift was opened, marveling at each one, happy at the other person's pleasure in what they had received.

Lacey at last pulled the fiddle from behind the tree and presented it to John. She watched as his eyes went wide in amazement. He cradled it in his arms like a newborn baby. The silence stretched out as he continued to stare at it. When he looked up, she said, "I thought it might give you pleasure to play it in the evenings after work." He said nothing but continued to stroke the fiddle.

"I'll be happy to show you how, son," Mitch offered congenially.

"That's right kind of you, Mitch," John said his voice catching in his throat. "I think I would like that."

Lacey slowly let out her breath, relieved that John liked his gift.

"We better be getting something on the table for these menfolk to eat," Cora said cheerfully. Lacey followed her into the kitchen and they set about making a huge breakfast, falling quickly back into their routines. Lacey could hear the children playing and the men talking in the other room. The terrible memories of the night before seemed like a bad dream and she struggled to believe they had actually happened. She had a terrible sense that at any moment she would fall back into the dream.

"Lacey," John called from the other room.

She wiped her hands and went to him expecting him to be practicing his fiddle. Instead he stood by the window holding a small box.

"I forgot to give you your Christmas present," John said, holding out the gift to her.

"John, I wasn't expecting anything." She held the box in her hand turning it over as though the box could be the gift.

"Open it," John said.

She lifted the lid and peered inside. John reached in and took out the snow dome and held it before her.

"See it's a winter scene with a tree and when you turn it upside down and back it looks like its snowing."

His voice held all the amazement of a child's and Lacey had to fight back the tears. "Oh, John, it's beautiful."

"It's so you can have Christmas anytime you want."

She kissed him on the cheek and she was helpless to stop the tears. They stood looking at the snow dome for a long time before Cora finally called them to breakfast.

28

It was getting late and John had not come home. No need to worry yet, she thought. He had probably carried some of the men home after work. It was a bad night to be out walking. Lacey pushed his supper to the back of the stove to keep it warm. She had fed Ben and Daniel Lee some time ago. Finally, when John had not come, she had sent Ben off upstairs to put Daniel Lee to bed. She had given in and allowed Daniel Lee's bed to be moved upstairs and he had taken to it, like a game, peeking through the rungs of the stairs, stopping at each step waving goodnight. The thought of him so sweet and loving made her heart turn over in her chest. Her head swam and she felt suddenly faint. She took in a deep breath and steadied herself on the kitchen sink. All the worries of the past weeks pricked at her neck and made her head throb. She rubbed her temples and felt the pressure pulsing like the heartbeat of an animal quick and fierce. Since the night she had found John in the barn, she had slept very little, waking several times in the night to make sure he was still there with her. Once awake, the shame she had felt that night would come back to her, filling her with dread and guilt. She had been over it a thousand times in her mind and she could find nothing redeemable in what she had done. There was no counterweight to balance out her shameful behavior. She had married a man she did not love and passed off another man's child as his. And in her heart she had continued to love the other man. In doing so she had driven the kindest man she had ever known to the brink of despair. Looking back she tried to piece together the path she had taken, the first misstep that had led her to be this despicable person. It had started as a longing, a feeling without words that had led her to meet Coy by the river that day. It had not been an act of courage but rather one of weakness. She had wanted to throw off all the burdens her family had placed on her and for that brief time Coy had made it seem possible. Coy made everything seem possible because he was not haunted by the aftermath. She had always wondered what her life would have been like if she had gone with him that day on the mountain. Maybe if she had gone, in the end fewer people would have been hurt. Only she would have paid the price. As it was the circle of fire had expanded to take in John and Susan and Daniel Lee. Had she not seen the pain of it in Susan's eyes that day at the craft sale? Only Daniel Lee was yet unscarred but the time was surely at hand. She would have only herself to blame because she had wanted him, loved him all the more because he was part of Coy.

She shook her head to clear her thoughts and tried to busy herself by cleaning up the dishes but she could find no peace. Even as she tried to unweave the web that she had so carelessly spun, she still found herself tangled in the strands. Since the night that John had tried to kill himself, she had made a vow to be honest with him. Each night with the fire banked and the younguns in bed asleep she had sat with him as he smoked his pipe and told him about Coy. At first, he would not listen, but finally seeing her need to tell it he had let her speak. She tempered her honesty not to spare herself but to save John the worst of what she had done. She told him about the times that she and Coy had met. The lies she had told her family, the way she had deceived him. She offered no explanation that could have saved her, simply letting the words tell the story. She left out only one thing, that Coy was Daniel Lee's real father. Each time she tried to say the words, her courage failed her, but she planned to try again that night. John had said nothing in all the nights she had spun out her sorry tale but had simply smoked his pipe and watched the embers of the fire glowing hottest just before they died. Sometimes he would announce, "That's enough now, Lacey." They would then go to bed without another word. She refused to go to bed without him and so some nights they sat up all night, the hours slowly ticking away until dawn. Lacey didn't mind because she knew that when the story was finally told that it would all be over. She had even begun to pack a few of her things, folding them carefully, smoothing them over and over with her hand. She didn't know where she planned to go but she hoped that Will would take her in for a while. There was no point asking John to forgive her. That in itself seemed a sin after all she had done. She planned to take the truck into town and catch the train. That had been in her plans when she had learned to drive. She would leave a note for John so he would know where she had left it. In the morning, she would explain it all to Ben and hope that he would see his way clear to go with her, but she had come to suspect that his heart was here with John. It seemed an appropriate punishment, that they might all in time come to despise her.

John had not talked to her again about that night. He had simply acted like nothing had happened. In fact, he had acted like he had never been happier. Instead of going out into the night after supper to wander the farm, he would take up his fiddle and gamely pluck out a tune, laughing at his own mistakes. Ben would sit nearby; pouring over the book John had given him. She felt like she was walking on a newly frozen pond constantly alert to the sounds of thin ice.

When she had awakened one morning and felt for John next to her, and he had not been there, the terror had all come back to her. She had flung herself from the bed and raced through the house calling his name. When he did not answer she had run out into the yard in only her gown to look for him. She had come upon him at the woodpile with an armload of wood for the fire. Breathless and embarrassed, she had collected a few sticks of kindling and walked back into the house feeling foolish with the tail of her gown soaked by the snow and her bare feet frozen.

She tried not to think about what it would do to him when she finally told him. She knew her time was running out and if she wanted to be the one to tell him it would have to be soon.

The dishes washed and the sink scrubbed, Lacey dried her hands and went upstairs to check on the boys. They were both in Ben's bed, on top of the covers sound asleep. She picked up Ben's pens and papers covered with drawings of bridges and stacked them neatly on his dresser. She took a quilt from the hall closet and covered them both; kissing their foreheads and smoothing back their hair. Silently she asked them to forgive her for what the night might bring.

At the top of the stairs, she was alert to the sound of a motor outside. She raced down the steps and to the front window. It was not John's truck but an automobile coming up the drive. She knew even in the black of night that it was Coy.

She had not seen him since that Sunday in November. As he bounded toward the door, she thought about turning off the light and waiting in the dark until he left but she had had enough of cowardliness in her life. She opened the door before he knocked to see him standing before her bold and handsome in the chill night air.

"Lacey," he said surprised.

"Come in, Coy, before you get cold," her voice as steady as she could make it. He wore an expensive double-breasted topcoat and black felt hat. He followed her into the living room but did not sit down when she asked.

"You don't seem surprised to see me," he said.

"I've been expecting you."

"Oh?"

"I heard Susan had left... had gone back to Indiana."

"You were right the first time. She left me."

"I was sorry to hear it."

He said nothing but stood looking at her.

"Let me take your hat and coat," she said.

He handed her his hat and slowly took off his coat and gave it to her. "I'm leaving town myself."

He stepped a little closer as he spoke. She backed up. He smiled and came to stand by the fire, his hand on the mantel. A framed silhouette of Daniel Lee hung above his hand. She watched the muscles in his back move through the clean pressed wool of his suit jacket. "You were wrong not to go with me that first time."

"I know," she said surprising him. The look showed on his face for just a second then it was gone and he was in control again.

"I've come to take you with me this time."

"No," she said finally. She put his coat over the back of a chair and stood smoothing it with her hand.

"But you said..."

"That don't mean it's right this time."

He turned and took her in his arms. He kissed her tenderly on the mouth. His lips were warm and moist and she found herself giving in to him. She lingered just a second before she pulled away.

"You're going to stay here with John," he whispered hoarsely.

She shook her head. "I can't do that neither. John knows about you but not about the baby. I am going to tell him tonight when he gets home. He won't forgive me that."

"He's not here?"

"I thought you knew coming in here so bold like you done."

"I was coming one way or the other. It had to be done. Would you stay if he'd let you?"

"It's Daniel Lee that's important."

"Did you really plan to tell him?"

"Yes, now I see I owe him that."

"If you think he won't forgive you, why won't you come with me?"

"No. There has to be an end to all of this."

"You have to punish yourself, don't you Lacey."

"No, its just time I did the right thing. It's time I acted with courage."

"It seems to me your whole life has been an act of courage."

Lacey smiled a crooked smile. "I wish I believed that. You are a better man than you allow Coy. The man I fell in love with in Wilder was a better man."

"Lacey," he said taking her by the arms and looking into her eyes. "You do love me."

She pulled away and went to stand by the window. There was a chill even through the curtain and frost was beginning to form on the inside of the panes. "Sometimes that isn't enough. Susan loves you."

He shrugged.

"You forget that she followed you here. Left her family and came with you to Tennessee not knowing what to expect. That was more than I was willing to do."

"Tell me you don't love me and I'll go."

She couldn't look at him but stared at the fire blinking back the tears that threatened to spill over. "I don't know if I am sure what real love means. I feel like a part of me will love you until the day I die. That's just a weakness in me. But I also feel like real love should make you a better person. I know that loving Daniel Lee has done that for me. I love Daniel Lee more than anyone on this earth. Now, I am asking you to love him more than you love me."

They looked at each other for a long time until a sound at the door made them both jump. "John," Lacey said as she saw the shadowy figure in the doorway.

As he came forward into the light Lacey let out a soft gasp. "You're hurt," she cried. Blood ran from his temple down over his eye. He staggered slightly as she led him to the sofa.

"Oh John," she whispered soothingly. Her heart turned over in her chest at sight of his wound. She kissed his face even as she whispered words of comfort.

"Truck turned over," he said.

She quickly examined the cut on his head and ran past Coy to the kitchen for a clean cloth and a pan of water. Expertly she cleaned and dressed the wound, oblivious to Coy's presence. "There now," she said as she finished up. "It don't appear to be too bad."

"No," he said. "I'm fine. Some of the men was hurt and I had to see after them."

"How'd you get home?"

"I walked."

"Why didn't you wait for some of the men to fetch a truck and carry you home?" she asked.

"I was afraid you'd be worried," he said, looking up at Coy.

They stared at one another for a long while. Lacey busied herself by cleaning up. When she left them alone to rinse out the pan and put away the antiseptic she felt soaked through to her fingertips with fear. She came back into the room not knowing what to expect. To her surprise Coy stood with his coat on, hat in hand.

"I was just telling John here that I dropped by to say good-bye. Reckon I'll be heading back up to Indiana for a while. Susan's waiting for me and I got some business to take care of up there."

Lacey stood holding her breath, unable to take in what Coy was saying. Suddenly he pointed to the picture of Daniel Lee that hung over the mantel. She could feel her heart leap to her throat. As his parting shot, he was going to take her son from her. He was going to claim him and take him away. Her knees began to buckle.

"That's a fine son you got there, John," he said.

John looked at Coy and his eyes narrowed for just a second. "We're right proud of him."

"You should be," he said looking at Lacey.

Lacey's lips parted and she tried to speak. Coy put his hand up ever so slightly to stop her. She wasn't sure what he meant for her to do.

"Well, I better be going," he said softly. "Susan will be expecting me."

"You be careful taking off on a night like this," Lacey stammered uncomprehending. "It's beginning to snow," she whispered.

He flashed a wry smile. "Don't worry about me; I got the devil in my hind pocket."

He was out the door without another word. Lacey ran after him oblivious to the cold air that whistled past her. "Coy," she called as she came up behind him. He turned and she stopped short.

"Why?" Lacey whispered.

He came and took her face in his hands. "Because you asked me to," Coy said. "And because real love should make you a better person. Someone very wise once told me that."

Tears ran down Lacey's cheeks. "You are a good man, Coy, whether you realize it or not."

Coy put on his hat and pulled the brim low over his eyes. "If Daniel Lee ever finds out about me, tell him I did it because I love him and because I love his Mama."

"I will, Coy," she whispered. "I promise, I'll tell him."

Gently Coy wiped away the hot tears that burned her cheeks. "Good-bye, Lacey," he whispered, and then he turned and walked away.

Slowly she walked back to the house, stunned by the wonderful thing that Coy had done. She closed the door and whispered a soft word of thanks. Then she turned and headed into the living room to tell John the truth herself. She hoped he would let them stay until dawn.

John stood at the mantel looking at the picture of Daniel Lee. When he turned to look at her, Lacey knew at that moment that John knew and that he had probably known for some time. He put out his arms and she came into them. "John, there's something I need to tell you about Daniel Lee."

"What's that little dickens been up to now?" John said, trying to sound lighthearted.

"It's not that, John. Daniel Lee is . . .." she hesitated.

John took her chin in his hand. "Daniel Lee is as fine a son as a man could want."

"John," she whispered.

He covered her lips with the tips of his fingers. "Sssh, that's all I need to know. I just let you tell me those other things because I thought it was something you needed to do."

Tears spilled down her cheeks. She took his fingers gently away from her lips. "I was just going to say I love you." It had come to her as she said it that it was true. She had come to love this sweet, gentle man who could see no wrong in her, who never judged her and found her wanting as others had, as she had so often done of herself. He had taught her patiently, day by day the real meaning of love. He had let it out to her little by little, like a rope down a well until she had finally caught hold of it.

"That's all I ever wanted to hear," he said, and he kissed her softly in the curve of her neck. They held each other for a long time while outside a new snow covered the ground.

29

L acey stood at the edge of the garden in the hot August sun watching the storm clouds gather on the horizon. The garden had been bountiful, and although she had put up most of it, it was still a pleasure to know it would go right on producing until frost. It was a good feeling to know she could walk out her own back door and gather enough food to cook a meal for her family.

Ben had not been around as much this summer to help her with the farm. He had worked all summer as water boy with the Civilian Conservation Corps building the Cumberland Homesteads State Park. It was going to be a recreation area for the Homesteaders. There was to be a lake and Ben had been so excited about the dam that was being constructed that she had not had the heart to keep him away. He was growing up and she wanted him to have his dream. Everybody needed something that made waking up in the mornings a pleasure, she thought.

John had told her that a gristmill had also been built at the site and was complete except for the wheel and the grinding machinery but it seemed unlikely that it would ever operate. The local mills were complaining that a mill run by the government would be unfair competition. Four years into the project and still there was no way to employ the men. It seemed at every turn; they were still met with problems. At least now, John shared them with her more and they seemed to bother him less.

She took the letter from her apron pocket and read again the words that Ruby had written. They seemed at the same time familiar and distant like memories. Will was doing well in his business and they had moved to a bigger house. Rachel was to start school soon and she was very excited about being so grown up. Little Franklin was a pistol and a lot like Will must have been as a boy, Ruby had said. If that were true, Lacey thought, Ruby would have her days cut out for her. It was hard for Lacey to think of Will as anything but the rowdy, hot-tempered boy of her childhood. Her ma's health, it seemed, was truly failing her, at last. Lacey thought of all the times her ma had cried wolf and sent the family in search of a doctor. It seemed a sad thing to always be dying when there was so much life to be had. Looking back over her life, she couldn't say she was grateful for the hardships, but they had taught her to take pleasure in the smallest things. Even now as she stood there, she could imagine the joy of a touch of shade on a hot August afternoon, or a cool drink from the well. She leaned back, hands on her hips and took in a breath of warm air with the smell of rain in it. She wondered if this was what Cora meant when she said she had been happy all of her life. It wasn't that there were not bad times. She had just learned to let them go and take pleasure in the good. Lacey realized that she had been keeping the bad times alive by giving them a place in her heart.

Daniel Lee came around the side of the smokehouse with Jasper in tow. Jasper was a long-legged hound the color of fresh churned butter that had wandered onto the place in the spring. Daniel Lee had come in begging for the table scraps Lacey usually fed the hogs. When she had asked him why he needed them, he had taken her outside to show her the hound, bones almost poking through the skin, weak with hunger. Daniel Lee's eyes had been ablaze with delight as he hugged the bony creature around the neck. She had gone back in to mix up some cornbread and milk to feed the dog. She really thought the dog was too far gone to save, but Daniel Lee had taken to the hound like lost kinfolk come home, so she had nursed it night and day. Daniel Lee had refused to leave the dog's side and cried to sleep in the barn with it. She had gotten sharp with the boy over the matter until John reminded her that if the boy had a tender heart toward creatures it was her own doing that had caused it. After that, she had let him have his way with the dog and they had become inseparable. The dog had long since fattened up and been brought into the house to sleep by Daniel Lee's bed at night.

"Mama, guess what." Daniel Lee said, as he and Jasper plopped down next to where Lacey stood.

"Well, I don't know. What have my boys been up to today?" Lacey asked. She looked down at the boy as brown as fresh baked gingerbread, black hair almost blue in the sunlight. He was so much the image of Coy; it always quickened a nerve in her when she looked at him. Sometimes, when they were in the house and she could hear him laughing in the other room, it startled her how much his laugh was like Coy's. But strangely, he had none of the wildness that was Coy. His nature was more quiet and inward like John's and he had her love of animals and all the things of the green earth.

"We've been working," Daniel Lee said seriously leaning back to rest his head on Jasper's side.

"Is that right?"

"Yep, we was hunting a squirrel for supper. Jasper seen a squirrel and he took out after it and I followed him."

"Did you catch it?"

"Well, we about near did," he said, sounding disappointed.

"That's pretty good, I reckon."

"Yeah, I reckon too," he said, suddenly proud.

"All that work makes a man hungry, I bet."

"That's what Jasper was just saying," Daniel Lee agreed.

"Oh, he was," Lacey said and thought of the times she had talked to her Bantam hens and felt she knew what they were thinking.

"Yeah."

"Well, I have some teacakes on the kitchen table. Do you think if you and Jasper had one a piece it would spoil your supper?"

"No, ma'am," Daniel Lee answered, jumping up and taking off toward the house in a run with Jasper right behind him.

"And wash your hands before you handle them teacakes, Daniel Lee," she called out doubting he heard her. She stood with her hands on her hips and stretched her back. Closing her eyes and craning her face to the sun, she savored the joy of a young child with a goody to share with a friend. The thought brought a smile to her lips. Warm familiar arms encircled her ever-growing waistline. "John," she gasped softly, opening her eyes.

"Did I scare you?"

She shook her head and put her arms over his the letter from Ruby still in hand. He patted her stomach softly. The baby was due in a month.

"How are my two girls today?" John asked.

"Now, John you don't know it's to be a girl."

"Mark my words, it's a girl," he teased. "With soft curls winding down her back and snapping blue eyes like her mama."

Lacey laughed at the thought of a little child the image of herself. She hugged herself tighter to John, grateful for the familiar feel of him. "You're home early."

"Mitch is coming over later to teach me a new fiddle tune. Besides, with you so near to having the baby, I just wanted to be here with you."

"Oh, I've got plenty of time yet."

"Well, then I just wanted to be with you," John said and kissed her on the neck.

Lacey smiled to herself. "How was work?"

"It looks like the cannery may not do so well. Not enough folks want to grow a crop and the ones that did can't produce enough to make it pay off. We don't have the kind of acreage it takes for truck farming."

"I hate to hear it, John. We'll just have to try something else, I reckon. We've come this far on hope."

"We'll make it." Lacey said, as a feeling of complete peace spread over her. It still amazed her the change in John in the last months. "We were meant to be here, and there will be a way for us to stay, somehow."

It seemed, looking back, how despite the hardships of Wilder and all the problems on the Homesteads; they had been carefully guided to that point. They had been led by a steady hand to this place on earth to build a better life for Daniel Lee and this new baby.

Lightning flashed to the west of them. "Storm's getting closer. Where's Daniel Lee?"

"He's inside eating a teacake and probably feeding half of it to Jasper."

"And Ben?"

"He'll be coming in from work directly."

"You're not worried about him being out in this storm," he inquired, turning her face to look into her eyes.

"I didn't say that. He's not so big that I've stopped worrying about him just yet," she said grinning up at John.

"No, and I don't reckon he ever will be," he said smiling and kissing her on the forehead. "What's that you got in your hand?"

"It's a letter from Ruby."

"They doing all right?"

"Mostly. Ma's ailing and I think it's serious this time."

"How can you tell?" he asked honestly.

"Oh, John," she rebuked him, and then she laughed. "I reckon you're right, it would be hard to tell, but I just have a feeling."

"If you're worried about her, after the baby comes, we can make us a trip up to Indiana and you can see for yourself."

"Oh, John, could we?" she said, turning to throw her arms around his neck. "I sure would like that. I miss seeing Ruby and Will and the younguns too."

"Then it's a promise. As soon as you're ready."

She kissed him warmly on the lips and laid her head on his chest. Unexpectedly, a sigh escaped her lips. John pulled her from his shoulder and looked at her.

"What else did Ruby have to say?" he questioned, his eyes probing her face.

"Coy's on his way back to Anderson."

"Where's he been all these months?"

"Canada mostly," Lacey said. She had soon discovered from Ruby that Coy had not gone back to Indiana that snowy January night, but had left their house and taken off to parts unknown. She wondered if he had known all along that he was not going back.

"What's he been doing up there?"

"Looking around, he said in his letter to Will."

"Do you think he will go back to Susan?"

"I wouldn't doubt it. He's given her just about enough time to give up on him."

John shook his head in wonderment. "Does it bother you hearing about him?"

She nodded not able to meet his eyes. "Not like it used to."

He took her under the chin and forced her to look at him. "Do you think about him much?"

"Don't you? But I don't worry about it. I know whatever happens, we will face it together."

John nodded.

"I guess he will just always be a part of our lives. But John, you are the one who showed me what it means to love somebody and care for them and always be there for them. You knew all along what it meant to go through things together and support each other, and you had the patience to wait till I learned it too. I was so blind to how I was hurting you and you forgave me everything. I vowed from then on to always be honest with you."

"Lacey," he whispered.

"You are God's grace raining down on me like a soft spring rain. I could never deserve you if I tried, but I will forever strive to do just that. And I will cherish you until I die."

"I reckon a man could grow to like that," he said smiling warmly down at her and caressing her face with his hand. The wind had picked up around them as the storm moved closer and the warm air spun around them.

"John, answer something for me. In those weeks, after..." Lacey said hesitantly. "After the night in the barn," she went on. "You seemed so happy. I didn't know what to make of it."

"I had a feeling Coy would be coming soon. I didn't want you to feel you had to stay out of pity. Besides, something happened to me that night. I thought it would free us both, if I just done away with myself, but I seen where it would bind us together forever in the worst way. It just come to me that night that I would have to accept whatever happened. I couldn't make everything turn out to suit my bidding. And it come to me that I was wasting what precious time I might have with you worrying about what might be coming. I meant to have some joy. The night Coy come by the house, I was sure you would go with him. Then when you didn't go, I couldn't believe it. That was all I ever wanted out of life. It was like when I finally let go and quit trying to hold on to you, was when you finally decided on your own to stay."

"John, my darling I will never leave you. You must understand that above all things."

"I understand that I love every minute I have with you and that's enough."

"When I said Coy would always be a part of our lives, I meant ... well, see that thundercloud," she said pointing off in the distance. "If Coy looked up to see a fierce, dark thundercloud, he's just as likely to run headlong into it. That's his way. There's part of me that would like to do that too. Part of me wonders what it would be like to live that way. Can you understand that?"

"Why, of course, Lacey. I've wondered that myself."

"Have you, John? Have you really?" she said amazed.

"Lacey, I've had my reasons to envy Coy, but I've had reason to admire him too. I don't think the man knows to be afraid of anything. The way he could take off on some adventure without a second thought or a nickel in his pocket."

"Why John I didn't know," she said, astounded by this side of her husband she had never imagined.

"Course, I've had reason to want to take a shotgun to his head," John said solemnly and then laughed.

"Oh, John," Lacey laughed, knowing that what he was saying was true, but relieved that he was only teasing her.

"But Lacey, can't you see we are on a big adventure. This Cumberland Homesteads is just that. Folks will look back on this and think we must have been a different sort of people to take on something like this. They are going to wonder if they have what it takes to do what we done."

Lacey thought about what Mrs. Roosevelt had said that day about them being the hope for the future, and how they had come to build a better place to raise their children. No matter what happened now, Lacey knew they had taken on the challenge the First Lady had laid out for them and they had done their best.

Lightning suddenly crackled and split the sky open. Rain came down in huge pelting drops. "We better make a run for it," Lacey shouted, as she took off toward the house. John grabbed her hand and pulled her back.

"No," he yelled, "just this once let's run headlong into it."

They took off, hand in hand, through the field with the rain drenching their clothes and hair. It ran down into their eyes and mouths as they laughed joyously. They stopped finally, exhausted. John took her under her arms, and lifted her up, and twirled her around. Slowly, he eased her down into his arms. And their laughter could be heard above the sounds of the rain and lightning and thunder.

POSTSCRIPT

Although the Cumberland Homesteads never fulfilled the dreams of the idealists, politicians, and social planners who conceived it, the community did in time provide a wonderful home and a new way of life for many of the people who came there looking not for a handout but for a "toehold in life."

The Subsistence Homestead project was born out of the desperation of the Great Depression. It was thrown together in haste because immediate relief was needed to help the thousands of hungry, destitute and stranded people. Many people, including Eleanor Roosevelt, saw this project as an opportunity to bring a new order to society. It was to be a community where people would have the finest in education, housing, and health care. It was to be a place where labor would never again be exploited by industry. As always these utopian ideals of creating a new order did not allow for the diversity and individuality of the people who were to populate this new planned community.

By 1938 the Dexdale Hosiery mill had been persuaded to locate on the Cumberland Homesteads, creating a small economic base. World War II brought an increased demand for skilled labor. Many of the men, using the skills of carpentry, bricklaying, and stonemasonry they had learned on the project, found work away from the project either by leaving their families behind to work in Detroit, Akron or Dayton, or by commuting to Watts Bar Dam, Douglas Dam or Oak Ridge.

The government finally left the project in 1947. Many of the stone homes built during this time still stand as a tribute to their unique design and fine construction. The Cumberland Mountain State Park, originally built as a recreation area for the Homesteaders by the boys of the Civilian Conservation Corps, now attracts tourists from all over the world.

My grandfather was an original Homesteader who moved there in 1934 and lived there until his death. My family moved to the Cumberland Homesteads when I was young. I attended elementary school in the beautiful buildings first dedicated in 1938. They are still being used today.

In 1984, the Cumberland Homesteads was declared a Historic District. The Homesteads Tower Museum is located at 96 Highway 68, Crossville, TN 38555. The Cumberland Homesteads Tower Association is dedicated to the preservation of this wonderful historic community. The Crabtree House on Pigeon Ridge Road has recently been opened as a Living Museum to help visitors gain insight into what life was like during those beginning years on the Homesteads.

The project brought together honest, hardworking, and willing people, who once given that toehold, were unstoppable. Eleanor Roosevelt challenged the people there to build a better life for their children than they had known. This was the hope and dream that united them despite their differences. In the end it was what they did best.